Cassethea of Mercia

By

Regina A. Hanel

ISBN 978-1-61929-454-7

Cover Design by AcornGraphics

Editors Staci Blevins and Nann Dunne

Publisher's Note:

Acknowledgments

Special thanks to Patty Schramm, Publisher/Owner of Flashpoint Publications, for taking Regal Crest Enterprises into the fold and for helping bring *Cassethea of Mercia* to light with Flashpoint. It's great to be working together again.

I'd like to thank my editor Staci Blevins for her keen eye, recommendations, and supportive words, as well as Nann Dunne who caught what I couldn't see. All books are better thanks to their editors. Also, kind thanks for Ann McMan's creative expertise on the cover design. I loved it at first sight. It was perfect. To everyone at Flashpoint who helped make this book a reality, thank you.

Boundless love and thanks to my partner, Veronica, for giving me the time, understanding, and quiet to fall into my own little world while writing.

And heartfelt thanks to you, the reader, for choosing this book and spending your time and imagination in that other world. Feel free to contact me on my website at www.rhanel.com. And if you enjoyed the book, please help spread the word so others can enjoy it as well.

Dedication

To my mom, who remains one
of the brightest stars in the sky.

Chapter One

Jessica Madison stood in front of the window of her second-floor office in Tudor Hall and gazed at the expansive courtyard below. Dressed in a designer, navy-blue skirt and matching blazer, white blouse and three-inch heels that accentuated well-defined calves, she cradled a softcover book in her hands. Head tilted slightly to the right, she feathered the pages with her thumb. The whispery accordion sound added to the trance-like state she'd lapsed into.

"I knew you'd still be here," a female voice said. Her tone was one of a mother scolding a child.

Jessica straightened with a jolt. The feathering halted. She faced her colleague and best friend, Ellie Compton. "And where else would I be? On second thought, don't answer that. Besides, you're still at work, too. What does that say about you?"

Ellie stood in the doorway, shoulder pressed against the doorjamb, arms crossed, one eyebrow raised. She wore a fashionable gray pantsuit, teal blouse, and black heels. "Point taken. However, in my defense, I was on my way out while you...I don't know. Where were you?"

"Nowhere."

"I don't believe you, professor. What if I give you a penny for your thoughts?"

"A penny won't get you far these days."

"True enough. Make it a dollar."

"You're quite the spender, El. How do I resist such an offer?" Jessica walked half a dozen steps to the bookshelf behind her desk and slid the inch-thick book into its resting place between two other research books. The slender fingers of her right hand skimmed slowly over the ancient binder before she broke contact with the book. She sensed El's glare didn't waver.

She turned and placed her hands on the back of her chair. "If you must know, I harbor no spendworthy thoughts. I was deciding what to take home and what to leave in the office during the break. And also, I can't believe another semester is over again."

"Bullshit, Jess. Fine, don't tell me, but eventually I'll drag it out of you. I always do."

Jess appreciated El's concession not to press the matter further. As good of a friend as El was to her, she wasn't comfortable sharing her most troublesome thoughts on this day. She didn't do internal sharing well with anyone for that matter, unless in dire need of help.

At this particular moment she should be exuberant. She should be a ball of excitement for having locked in her trip. She should be enjoying the positive end to months spent writing proposals and running through hoops with the less-than-pleasant Office of Grants and Contracts department head. Behind her lay weeks of endless waiting on decisions by the grants faculty board, director of finance, and board of trustees, as if their decision were over the construction of a new dormitory and not over funding for a six-person, ten-week archeological dig.

Yet, nerves over the flight overseas and the risk of an unsuccessful dig took dominance over happier thoughts. A change of topic was in order. "What really brings you by, El?"

"As if," El huffed. "Please don't feign ignorance with me. You know why I popped in. To make sure you left at a reasonable hour so you'd have adequate time to primp."

"Time to primp? For what? Wait. What are you talking about? I don't primp."

"Oh yes, you do."

"No. I don't. And even if I did, what exactly would I need to primp for? You make no sense right now." Jess stuffed several papers in a folder and added them to the attaché bag on her desk. At the last minute, she grabbed the book she'd cradled earlier and inserted it as well.

"Is that right?" El uncrossed her arms and entered the neat, ten-by-twelve-foot office until she stood two feet from her friend. She studied her closely. "You're serious, aren't you? You forgot about your date tonight, didn't you?"

"Date?"

"Yes, date. This woman is a friend of a close friend. She's someone with your intellect and interests, at least I'm pretty sure she has similar interests. You can't squirm out of this again."

"I don't know what you're talking about. I don't have a date," Jess said.

"When was last time you went on a date? Trust me when I say the lack thereof has made you cranky."

"I don't see the importance of answering that question, and I am not cranky." Jess smoothed her hands along the sides of her skirt, even though the skirt hugged her hips perfectly and remained without a wrinkle.

"No, clearly you're not." Ellie breathed deep. "I told you about Gayle over a month ago. I said that on the last day of the semester, when you had no more work-related excuses, I'd set up a dinner date for the two of you, didn't I?"

"I don't believe you did. None of this sounds familiar."

"I told you I reserved a table at Cattervan's at eight o'clock. I told you not to be late. And I told you to write it on your calendar. You agreed. With reluctance, I'll admit, but you said you'd go. Now here we are, and you act like we never had that conversation."

Realization of truth dawned on Jess. Her cheeks flushed as their conversation in April replayed in her mind. "Oh, my God." Jess ran her fingers through her curly, shoulder-length, brown hair. "I'm so sorry, El. You're right. I don't know how I forgot in less than two months. Wait. I do know how."

Jessica was not a fan of blind dates. Setups reeked of being forced and artificial to her. If she were meant to meet someone, then she believed fate would intervene at that time. Fine, she'd hit a dry spell and no one of interest crossed her path in months, but she retained clear memories of prior El setups gone terribly wrong. She glanced at her friend and straightened. "Look, El, I'm sorry, truly, but there's no way I can go on this date tonight. Please call her for me and explain."

"You want me to call her? And explain what? I absolutely will not. You're a grown-up. You can make your own phone call."

"Please?" Jessica tacked on a sad, pouty face for emphasis. She counted on the oft-used expression, that held a soft spot with El, to secure her way. But when she observed no signs of a softened demeanor on El, she continued. "I don't even know her. The thing is...I was going to call you later tonight and fill you in."

"Fill me in on what? This should be ripe."

"Remember the archeological dig grant I worked on for what seemed like forever?"

"Of course I do. It's all you talked about for months."

"The approval came through. I'll be off on the dig this summer—in England. And by 'this summer' I mean my flight leaves at seven o'clock tonight." Jess lowered her head, eyes focused on the tips of her shoes, her hands tight around the handle of her attaché bag.

"Jesus H.—"

"Watch your mouth if you please. Saint Albans is a Catholic establishment after all."

"Whatever. Fine." El softened her voice and leaned in toward Jess. "It's bad enough we have to hide our sexuality, and now I can't even swear when no one's around. What's next, a dress code?"

Jess raised an eyebrow but didn't answer.

El straightened and shook her head. "Never mind all that, but are you serious right now about your trip? No, scratch that. Of course you're serious. This is so you. Nice work, Jess. Real nice."

"What's that supposed to mean?"

"You know exactly what I mean."

"No, I don't. I've kept the news a secret until now. For one, because I didn't know the outcome until a couple of weeks ago myself, and as you recall, you've been busy the past two weeks also."

"Don't push this on me," El said.

"Second, I didn't want you to yell at me or try to convince me to change my mind." Jess held up her hand before El responded, adding, "And don't say you wouldn't, because we both know you would. Like everyone else, you think I'm chasing a ghost."

"You never quit, do you? Your statement is completely untrue. Yes, I may have tried to stop you, but only for your own good and because I love you. I went out of my way to set this date up. In fact, I now owe a friend a favor I'm not exactly keen on repaying. But that little tidbit of information means nothing to you, I'm sure. Heaven forbid you think about someone besides yourself for a change." El stomped toward the sofa-like chair in front of Jess's desk and descended with a plop, hands crossed in front of her chest.

Jess stared at her for a moment, angry at her diatribe, until she noticed the worry evident in El's eyes. The words settled and comfort spread through her chest. "I'm sorry. I honestly would have called you when I got home today...and I admit I should have talked to you earlier about the final approval and the date of the trip."

"You think?" Silence filled the room for an uncomfortable time before El spoke again. "I'm sorry I implied you're selfish. That's not fair and completely untrue. But you frustrate me to such an extent at times. And all you ever do is work. You're becoming the parents you complain about."

"That's not fair," Jess said, but part of her knew the words rang true. She'd told herself she didn't work all the time and she allowed prior relationships to form—she wasn't a nun after all. Granted, those relationships lasted perhaps a month or two, but work wasn't her only focus. She'd never be as centered on work as her parents were. Correction, as her parents are.

Jess released her grasp from the attaché bag and skirted around the desk. She rested her hand on El's arm. "You're right to be angry. I'm sorry. I shouldn't have forgotten about the date. And I do appreciate your effort, but you know how much I hate blind dates."

"I'm beginning to think you've begged off dating altogether."

Jess tilted her head and scrunched her face. The corner of her lip angled upward.

"Okay, probably not a true statement," El said.

"Definitely not true, I assure you, but I am sorry on both counts."

"No, you have no reason to apologize. I do. I shouldn't have rehashed old issues. I wish you wouldn't bury yourself in your work all the time, though. There is more to life. Why won't you let me help you find someone?"

The irony in El's last statement didn't pass Jess by, even though El bore no clue of what she'd said. Jess's goal was to find someone, someone long ago forgotten, but not a love interest. Her search centered on the proof of existence of someone whom she believed in her core to be a strong and heroic woman, a woman who lived through the turn of the first millennium, who received no accolades for her achievements as she would have were she a man. But with scant hard evidence to support Jess's belief this woman once existed, other than brief, anecdotal passages in ancient clergy literature, the prior references made to Jess about chasing a ghost would remain intact.

Jess leaned forward and held her friend's face between her palms. "I'm thankful for how much you care for me and for your effort to find someone for me. I am. But I think finding that special someone is a road I need to travel on my own and in my own time."

"Of course you do."

"It's not like I've never dated, as you well know, or that I never will again. I merely entertain different priorities now, okay. I love you. I always will. That fact won't change." Jess placed a peck on Ellie's forehead and stepped away.

A snicker from her friend followed, and Jess relaxed considerably. She said, "Thank you for understanding."

El stood. "Yeah, yeah. Whatever. You're lucky I have a soft spot for you. And don't think that pout earlier didn't rip me up inside. What I'm trying to say is, this better be one hell of a trip, because I'm telling you, from what I hear, you're making a big mistake skipping out on this date. Hell, I even contemplated keeping her for myself."

"Were you now? Keeping her? Are you some sort of cavewoman all of a sudden? I kid, but if this woman is such a hot catch, maybe you should meet her for dinner on my behalf. Then you can explain my crazy work preoccupation to her, and who knows? The sky might be the limit for the two of you."

Another raised eyebrow met Jess's stare. "You know what, Ms. Madison? A blind date is not an altogether bad idea, though I never said she was hot. I'm not saying she's not, but again, didn't say she was, either. Plus there's more to a person than beauty alone."

"Yes, of course. You're so right," Jess said.

"Don't patronize me. I may take you up on your suggestion."

"I think you should."

"I think I will."

"Great."

"Yes, it is great. Now tell me all about this trip."

Chapter Two

Jess didn't find the time to steal a nap after work as she'd originally planned, due to the unexpected conversation with her friend. At least now, with El filled in about the trip, her conscience was clear and her mood lightened. Enthusiasm surrounding the trip returned.

In the weeks leading up to this day, Jess worried often why her excitement hadn't grown, especially after she'd been told the board, that cast the final vote, accepted her proposal. At one point, she'd questioned the value of the trip altogether, but her emotion confirmed part of the problem was the guilt of not telling El that weighed her down. Now that she'd explained to El what she hoped to find, the flame of excitement rekindled. She still stressed about the flight, though. She'd traveled often enough that her jumbled mess of a stomach shouldn't have been jumbled at all, but it remained in shambles. As a result, she opted not to eat a full meal before the trip and munched on two celery sticks with peanut butter instead.

Jess placed her oversized duffle bag and backpack on the tile foyer floor, three feet from the front door. The remainder of her gear, and the gear of her students, was scheduled to be sent ahead and delivered to the site before she arrived. She double-checked the inner pocket of her purple cargo vest for her passport, tickets, and mints, and checked the side pants pocket for her wallet.

According to plan, she'd arrive at the dig two days early, before meeting up with her crew, which consisted of two graduate students working towards their master's and three undergrads, as well as a local hired handyman. Jess remained both anxious and excited. With half a dozen people less on this excavation than the prior ones she'd been on, due to funding constraints, she knew uncovering artifacts, cleaning them, and cataloging would take double the time. But she also believed she'd enjoy leading the smaller group. She couldn't think of a better way to spend her summer.

Anxious to move the trip along, she peeked out the third-story window of her apartment and spotted the limo driver as he pulled the black Lincoln alongside the curb. She glanced around the apartment one more time, breathed deep, gathered her bags, and strode out the door. Ghost or no ghost, she was going to England and she was going to have a good time.

****

The flight from Bradley International Airport to Heathrow, with its one-hour-forty-five-minute stopover in Newark, New Jersey, arrived in London on time, ten minutes past ten the following morning. Though Heathrow was farther from her final destination than the Birmingham or Bristol airports, she'd saved a considerable amount of money on airfare with the flight to Heathrow. And the way she figured, a thirty-pound bus ride to Gloucester, though it would add over two hours to her trip, would allow her to sit, unwind, and see the countryside without the worry of driving on the wrong side of the road and ending up in a ditch. Not that she was a bad driver.

But her plans didn't unfold precisely as she'd thought. Jess hadn't counted on an argument over ownership of her duffle bag with a male passenger who grabbed it from the carousel by mistake. Nor had she envisioned the bus, which was to take her to her final destination of Gloucester, would suffer a flat tire at the halfway point, or that the room she'd rented two months earlier, at a private residence in the outskirts of Devonsbury, would suddenly be unavailable. If she didn't know better, she'd think she'd landed the starring role in a bad movie. Okay, maybe not the starring role. She wasn't an actress or, in her mind, anywhere near movie-worthy material.

Regardless, the series of unfortunate events thrust upon her weren't scenes in an unnamed movie. She was in less than stellar spirits when the hired handyman, Joel Fisher, who met her in Gloucester and drove her to Devonsbury, dropped her off in front of a pub at the far end of town, while he searched for temporary living accommodations for her.

Joel drove off as she stood alone on the cobblestone street, computer slung over her shoulder. He claimed the establishment he'd left her at served the best food in town and promised to pick her up an hour or so later. Temporarily homeless and hungry, Jess didn't have the energy to argue with his choice. Yet part of her wondered, if the establishment served the best food in town, why didn't he stay and have dinner with her? They could have searched for a rental together after.

With all of her bad luck so far, Jess's thoughts backtracked to the question of whether this trip was such a good idea after all, or if she should have stayed home and gone on the date El suggested. The chance to share the company of another woman sounded nice at that moment. Nothing wrong with wanting to have another person desire her or maybe even value her for her accomplishments and knowledge, though at this point, desire alone would suffice. Two years had passed since she'd experienced the heat of another woman wrapped around her and known the comfort the closeness provided.

Before her thoughts wandered any further, fat, cold, raindrops tapped the top of her head and rolled along her scalp. Jess threw her hands in the air and laughed out loud. "Well, that takes the cake, doesn't it? Par for the course today, Jessica, par for the course," she said—and she didn't even play golf.

She pulled on the heavy, wooden door and entered the dim, yet quaint pub. The room buzzed with loud chatter among the mass of people already inside. A hint of vanilla and char from a well-used fireplace, mixed with the essence of barley and hops, wafted past. She could either remain angry the day hadn't gone to plan, or she could simply go with the flow. She decided anger wasn't an option, but to get to a Zen state of mind, she'd need a drink, or two, and fast.

As she scanned the room for a seat, no one paid her much notice; bodies streamed in and pushed past her. For the most part, a positive energy oozed throughout the crowd. Jess caught a glimpse of one table where the men were entrenched in heated debate, and she opted away from the opinionated group. As soon as she spotted an unoccupied two-person table across the room by a window, she strode toward it and hunkered down on the lacquered, teak-stained, wooden chair. The table provided her with a view of the bar and the entrance.

Jess hadn't caught the name of the pub when she stood outside, but the establishment was likely hundreds of years old, well maintained, with low ceilings and dark, wooden furniture, but it also benefited from the modern conveniences of two fifty-five-inch HD televisions hung on opposite walls.

Bronze light fixtures hung from the ceiling, and sconces on the walls emitted a soft, yellow hue. Old photos, taken of the town and what she guessed were surrounding neighborhoods, decorated the walls alongside photos of what she assumed were the local rugby teams. A dozen well-worn, chunky, wooden tables and chairs filled the space on the wood floor. Jess saw no food scraps or dirt on the floor, and her table shone clean as well, for which she was thankful.

On the far side of the room, to the right of the entrance, stood an expansive bar. A large, wooden carving of an eagle, wings spread, chest forward, hung over the rear wall. A swinging door from the kitchen flanked the bar on the right. Restrooms and a wooden stairway with an intricately carved, wooden banister, which led to a second story, flanked the bar on the left.

As she waited on service, a couple walked in and sidled up to the bar. Once served, they located a seat at a table. Behind the bar stood a five-foot-six-inch, broad-shouldered woman, whose age Jess estimated as perhaps in her early thirties. The woman's blonde hair was cut tight on the sides but several inches longer at the top. Next to her, a male likeness of the woman stood and dried a beer mug with a dishtowel. His face was rounded, hers more angular, though his shoulders were much broader and he wore a well-trimmed beard. The woman's eyes shifted in her direction. With a flip of the head, she indicated for Jess to come forward, or so Jess thought. Jess pointed at herself, and the woman signaled acknowledgment. Embarrassed after being caught in her observations of the woman, Jess made her way to the bar with trepidation.

"You're not from around here, are you?" the woman said. The smooth, raspy voice carried a tone too sarcastic for Jess's palate.

"No, I'm from Connecticut...the United States. What gave me away?" Jess's cheeks flushed.

"You appeared to be waiting for someone to bring you a menu, but it doesn't work that way here. You have to order at the bar. Then we bring the food to your table." As if she noticed Jess's discomfort, the woman added, "No worries, though. It happens all the time."

"Good to know. I appreciate you not letting me wait unattended at the table forever."

"Something told me you wouldn't have waited there much longer. I simply didn't want—what I'm guessing by then would have been an irate person—storming the bar and asking why she hadn't been served yet."

"Is that right? I see. So, self-interest prevails first and foremost with you," Jess said.

The woman didn't flinch or change her expression in any way. "What can I get you? Did you want something to eat, to drink, or both?"

Jess glanced into the bluest eyes she'd ever seen. She hadn't noticed them initially. But then, she hadn't made eye contact with the bartender until now. She'd focused on the menu on the board behind her, but once she did notice her, she found it difficult to pry her focus away. The woman was breathtakingly gorgeous. Mesmerizing eyes, a creamy complexion, fit, and by the grin on her face, she appeared cognizant Jess thought as much. Too bad she oozed sarcasm, Jess thought. "I'll have both, actually. I'm famished. And after the day I've had, I think I'll start with a glass of beer."

"A half then?"

Jess didn't answer at first, blushing even more than earlier. She cursed herself for not having researched details as simple as local etiquette when she'd booked the trip, though in her defense, she'd been given only two weeks notice and was more concerned with securing housing at that point and ensuring the on-time arrival of their equipment.

Normally, in countries she'd not previously visited, she made an extra effort to know all those minute, seemingly unimportant facts up front. Now she wished she had done the same for this trip, rather than come across as ill informed. "Uh..."

"A half of a pint?" the woman asked a second time, her tone snarky.

Jess wanted to ask, "Jeez, what crawled into your shorts and bit you, a crab?" but instead took a short breath. "A half will be fine. If you wouldn't mind selecting a local ale for me, I'd appreciate it."

"Done. Anything to eat? Menu's on the chalkboard behind me."

Jess narrowed her eyes. As if she hadn't seen the menu—of course she'd seen it. "I'll try the cheddar burger and chips." Jess waited for her drink, paid, and proceeded to her table, more than content to place distance between herself and the woman who made her feel inferior for the first time since middle school.

As the first sip of the cool ale ran down her throat, Jess relaxed. She extricated herself from her cargo vest and draped it over her chair. Soon she caught herself glancing at the female bartender again. Why, she didn't know. She watched the ease with which she talked with her patrons; the smile on her face lit the space around her. Not a favor provided to her, but one of support and encouragement to those around the woman, nonetheless. And at the same time, she was annoyed at herself for having given the woman any additional attention, considering the woman's rather cold demeanor as it pertained to Jess. If Jess placed herself in the woman's shoes, she was certain she'd be much friendlier and carry no hint of sarcasm when engaged with new customers.

When Jess cast a brief glimpse to the bar once more, she observed the woman taking orders and replacing drinks, but her male counterpart's eyes focused directly on Jess. Jess shifted in her seat and glanced away at one of the television screens. She certainly wasn't searching for male attention and didn't want to appear as if the attention was welcome.

Bored having to read the subscript on the television for several long minutes, not able to hear from where she sat, she pulled out her computer and went over the plan layout for the dig, ensuring she knew exactly where to stake out the perimeter and imprinting it in her mind for when she'd see the site in person.

As the beer found its mark, she relaxed to a point, but unease crept up her spine as she realized Joel, who still held her luggage, was basically a stranger to her. She didn't know Joel on a personal level, except for the tidbits of information she learned about him on her ride from Gloucester to Devonsbury, though he came recommended through the university. She hoped he was honest and trustworthy. She also hoped he'd the sense to stop at the side of the road and transfer her bags from the rear of his pickup into the truck's cab. It'd be her luck he'd pick her up and her bags would be soaked. Before she drifted off into worry land much further, the young man behind the bar interrupted her thoughts when he placed a plate of food on the table.

"Here you are, miss, one cheddar burger and chips," he said.

"Thank you."

"The name's Baron, by the way. I see you're from the States."

Jess followed the man's line of sight to the front of her polo shirt, which read "St. Albans University," and underneath, "Connecticut." She huffed and added, "Well, don't I feel stupid now?"

"Excuse me?" Baron said.

"Nothing. I'm sorry. My name's Jessica. Your coworker and I engaged in a discussion earlier when she surmised I wasn't from here. I asked her how she guessed, but she never stated the obvious. I feel a bit stupid now."

"Don't worry about her, she's a ball buster all right, but she means no harm. She's what I refer to as 'slow to warm.' Plus, she tends to get a bit snarky when it comes to educators. No offense, but I assume you're not a student, right?"

"Is that a clever way of calling me old?"

"No, no. I'm so sorry. That's not what I meant."

"It's fine. I'm thirty, not sixty. But yes, I teach history and archaeology at the university." Jess added ketchup to her burger and fries.

"There you have it then," Baron said.

What seemed all too clear to Baron, as if a mystery had been solved, was by no means clear to Jess, but she didn't much care. "If you say so," she said. She was starved and eyed her burger, itching to pick it up and take a mouthful, but not wanting to be rude to Baron.

As if he understood he'd lingered too long, Baron said, "Right. I'll let you get on with eating and hope to see you again soon. Will you be in the area for a while?"

"If all goes well, I should be here for the summer." Jess was glad at least someone in the pub was friendly.

"Excellent. I'm happy to hear it. I'll see you around."

Baron's mouth stretched from ear to ear before he spun on his heel and returned to the bar. Jess grabbed the burger with both hands and chomped down. A multitude of flavors exploded on her tongue, and she caught herself shy of allowing a moan to escape. Joel had been right. The food was excellent, and she regretted she'd initially not trusted him.

In absolute food heaven, Jess glanced past Baron and caught sight of the blonde woman behind the bar. Jess could have sworn the woman's line of sight suddenly shifted from her to another patron at the counter. Was the woman studying her? And if Jess saw correctly, why was she of interest to her? Did she appear a disheveled mess? She shrugged, too tired to care and too hungry to think about much of anything other than the juicy, and oh-so-fabulous, burger in her grip.

Chapter Three

As promised, Joel Fisher picked Jess up early in the morning from the local inn, which held one room open the prior night, but now she was out of luck as they were fully booked for the next three weeks. She had tossed and turned part of the night. She prayed the rest of her group would be taken in by the homeowners as previously arranged, and that no other glitches would throw off their plans. When she and Joel arrived at the dig site, an early morning fog lifted.

A narrow, white trailer, which would be the group's makeshift lab and storage area, sat perched on braces set on two slabs of stone. Next to the trailer lay numerous barriers, wheelbarrows, shovels, pickaxes, buckets, planks, sifters, hoses, and an array of other items.

Jess opened the truck door and stepped out. "So this is the site then?"

"It is," Joel said.

"Excellent."

The place was a flat, grassy field at the edge of town, less than a hundred yards from a wooded area off to the right, with a stream nearby. "If I knew we were this close to the pub, I'd have stopped here yesterday afternoon to take a look around," Jess said.

"With the rain and all, I figured the better option was we waited until today. I'm sorry I didn't think to ask you first." Joel stood with feet apart, hands clenched behind his back.

"No, it's fine not to have mentioned it. After I ate yesterday, I had trouble keeping my eyes open. One afternoon more or less didn't make a difference. I'm pleased to see our equipment arrived." Jess scanned over the inventory to see if anything was obviously missing, but all appeared in order.

"I brought the trailer over yesterday, after I dropped you at the inn, and the boxed and fragile equipment I locked inside the trailer, which by the way..." He paused and handed Jess the keys. "These keys belong to you now. It's the only set, so be careful with them."

Jess took the keys. "Don't worry. I've never lost a set of keys before."

"I'm not worried, but I am responsible. Hopefully she'll meet your needs. She's a decent trailer. Single wide 3.7 by 9.75 meters, complete with loo."

Jess recalculated the trailer size in her head to be about twelve by thirty-two feet. "Should be more than sufficient. A bathroom's a plus, too—no port-a-potty."

Joel laughed. "Not much better, I bet. That loo's tight on leg room for sure."

"She'll do. I think I'll spend an hour or two getting her in order then." Jess purposely used the gender he referred to the trailer in, not something she'd normally do, but she wanted to gauge his reaction. However, no recognition of her having teased him crossed his face. *Guess it's back to business then,* Jess said to herself. "Oh, I almost forgot. Will the backhoe operator be here tomorrow morning?"

"My plan is to drive over to Morey's to make sure the backhoe delivery remains on for tomorrow, but I'm sure there won't be any glitches. Morey owns a construction business in the next town over. I do some filler jobs for him when he needs an extra hand."

"I appreciate you double-checking. Thank you."

"After I touch base with Morey, I thought I'd search out availability again regarding a place for you to stay. Why don't I pick you up at lunchtime, and we can update each other on how the morning went? We can eat at the pub if you don't mind eating there two days in a row."

Jess grimaced at the thought of supporting the semi-unfriendly tavern with her business but, unfamiliar with where else to go, agreed. Plus, the food was delicious. At least the burger she had the night before was, and Baron came across nice enough. She made a mental note to take a walk through town later in the day to see what other food options existed. Starting Monday, lunch would be catered, but that left breakfasts and dinners to think about. "Sounds like a plan." Jess took multiple strides toward the trailer. "I'll meet you there, though. Say 12:15?"

"Sure, 12:15 works for me."

"Great. And, Joel, thanks again for all the help. I really do appreciate it."

Joel turned and marched toward his truck. "My pleasure. It's what you hired me for."

When Jess popped the key in the trailer door lock and turned the handle, the door remained shut, but after four jiggles of the handle, the door unstuck and allowed her entrance. The enclosure was dark and smelled of dust and stale air. Her first thought was to ask Joel at lunchtime to buy her an air freshener and also a broom. In the meantime, she opened the blinds on the window to her right and slid the lower panel open for fresh air, even if dampness remained to the outside air.

She continued around the inside of the trailer, past a sixteen-foot-long center table, and opened the rear windows. She passed the bathroom and peeked inside. Tight on legroom was an understatement, Jess was happy for once to be five-foot-three. At the rate Joel made progress regarding living accommodations, she thought it a real possibility the trailer might become her temporary home during the excavation. Not an ideal situation, to live in the trailer, but not terrible either.

She shut the bathroom door and rounded the corner toward the office. The office space measured about twelve feet long by eight feet wide. She could definitely make do sleeping in the office if she needed to, though she hoped she'd not have to. Next, she opened the last set of blinds and window, ambled toward a stack of boxes, and unpacked them.

****

Noon rolled around quickly. Jess enjoyed the stroll to the pub. The moderate temperature hovered at seventy-eight degrees, and the sun shone. Outside the entrance, she made note of the painted sign which read "Eagles Landing." The name sounded familiar, but she couldn't place where she'd seen or heard of it before. Once inside, she spotted Joel at a table, two tables removed from the one she occupied the prior afternoon. A glass of soda sat in front of him. "Did you order already?"

"I did. The lunch crowd rolls in quick, so you have to order when you can," Joel said.

"Yeah, I see that. I'll be right back. Any suggestions?"

"I ordered the aubergine hero. I've had it before. It's quite good."

Jess flashed Joel a puzzled look.

"I believe it's what you Americans call eggplant."

"Gotcha." Jess walked away and placed her order with Baron, whose face lit up when Jess approached. He delivered her food to the table ten minutes later and inclined his head in acknowledgment to Joel.

Jess took a hefty bite into the warm, peppered eggplant. In between mouthfuls, she talked awhile with Joel. She learned he married young at twenty and he and his wife were the proud parents of two young children: a son, Josh, age six, and a daughter, Maddie, age four. His wife stayed home to tend to the children. And before his employ as an assistant on Jess's project, he'd been laid off from his job due to a downturn in the economy.

"I've not experienced any luck locating you a place to stay, Jess, I'm sorry. The woman whose house you were supposed to stay in suffered a mild stroke and was admitted to hospital. I've checked everywhere I can think of, including with her granddaughter, but no luck. I'll keep my eyes open, but right now there's nothing."

"I appreciate your effort. I can understand people not wanting strangers in their home. I'm sure her granddaughter has her own life." Jess picked up a couple of fries.

Joel held her stare. "True, but it's not like she doesn't have the space. In fact, she rents out a room up—"

"And it's not her commitment to keep," Jess said. "It's not an insurmountable problem. I can make the trailer work. I've stayed in lesser accommodations on other digs. If you don't mind taking me shopping after lunch, I'll need a few essentials."

"Glad to help. Not a problem at all."

Jess ate the fries and took another bite of her eggplant sandwich, followed by a hefty sip of ginger ale, and listened as Joel continued their conversation. She was relieved that he didn't ask much about her home life. She wasn't comfortable revealing her lifestyle to strangers. Besides, other than work lately, she didn't have much else going on and wouldn't know what to tell him anyway.

Jess recalled her conversation with El at the university and thought the situation ironic. Okay, so her friend hit the mark with regard to her love life. What of it? Jess scanned the bar. Subconsciously she searched for the sarcastic blonde bartender with stunning blue eyes and a smile that could warm an entire room. Stunning blue eyes and a smile that could warm an entire room? Where the hell did that thought come from? More like ice-blue eyes and a sarcastic smirk cast out to make the recipient consider their presence unwelcome and insignificant. A moment later, she heard Joel speak.

"Are you okay?" he asked.

"What? I'm sorry. Yeah, I'm fine."

"You ready to go then?"

"Absolutely."

****

After she placed her purchases in the trailer, Jess sauntered into town to gain a sense of the area around where she'd reside for the next couple of months and to search for an alternate locale in which to eat. The inn where she'd stayed the first night included a restaurant, but the inn was on the outskirts of the other side of town, not within a comfortable walking distance. A half-hour trek was not optimal to venture at night alone when unfamiliar with the area. No guarantee the younger members of her team would be interested in going to dinner with her once they arrived, especially since they'd likely all be rationing their money. Plus, their accommodations in the homes in which they'd be roomed included breakfast and dinner as part of the monthly payment.

Devonsbury was a picture from a travel guide, a quaint town with cobbled sidewalks and interesting, medieval, Tudor-style architectural work, some of which dated back hundreds of years. The limestone bricks from which most of the buildings were constructed were typical of the local stone available in the Cotswolds area.

Round, trimmed, green shrubs, ferns, and other assorted-color plants graced the space between the buildings and sidewalks, and ivy climbed the sides of many buildings. Darker ivy was visible at the base of the structures and lighter ivy higher up where the younger sprouts grew. She passed several residences and buildings for commercial use, as well as another inn and pub. A couple greeted her as they passed hand in hand, and she greeted them in return.

At a cross street, Jess altered direction and detoured along a narrow aisle. She made her way around the hind side of more buildings, through a narrow alleyway, and spotted a church, another tavern, and what she estimated to be a convenience store. The cleanliness of not only the main streets but also the side streets, impressed her. She envisioned what life was like here hundreds of years ago. Whose feet touched the same cobblestones hers now stood on? In Devonsbury, the construction was such as if time stood still.

She wandered about until the sun made its way lower in the sky. She sensed she was being watched. She glanced to both sides and searched window openings but saw no one. Her hearing became heightened, and her heart rate elevated as she continued on, her imagination claiming more ground than logic. Certain she was being followed, she breathed deep. She pulled on her inner strength and pivoted to confront her follower.

Jess exhaled a sigh of relief as a lone, adorable mutt stared at her in return. "Now, here's a surprise. I can honestly say, I wasn't expecting the likes of you."

At shoulder height, the dog stood slightly above her knee, and he sported a multi-colored coat sprinkled with brown, grey, white, and black short hair. His deep, globe-like, chocolate eyes found hers, and her heart warmed. She took several steps toward him but didn't see a collar. Glancing around to see if his owner was nearby, she saw no one.

"Hey there, buddy. Are you a friendly fella?" Jess said,

in a soft tone. "You sure are cute, aren't you?"

The dog wagged his tail, which Jess took as a good sign. She held out her hand and bent slightly, careful not to scare him. He sniffed her hand, touched it with his damp nose, and pushed his head up against her hand as if wanting to be petted. Jess complied, and when she finished, he retreated and licked her hand.

Jess laughed. "Guess you're not a biter then." Relaxed, she continued to talk in a slow, mild manner while she petted him, his coat surprisingly soft.

"Where's your owner, huh?" She looked once more to see if anyone was around, but she saw no one. To this point, no one called out for him. Jess breathed deep. "Now what? I'm kind of out of my element here, buddy. Not sure what I can do for you. I'm kind of homeless myself right now."

The dog half barked and grunted as he wagged his tail and pranced off in the opposite direction. He sniffed the sidewalk and entrances to several establishments, seemingly interested in all the smells.

Jess decided to return to the trailer. "Since you're going in my direction anyway, I'll follow you for a spell and see if you lead me to your home, okay?" Jess felt guilty already, knowing she'd eventually have to abandon him if he didn't part from her first.

The dog didn't show signs of malnourishment, but he was on the slim side. The farther along the two of them walked, the more worried she became that he was, in fact, homeless. She couldn't follow him forever, but if she were honest with herself, she didn't think she could leave him alone either.

Options limited, Jess decided to stop by Eagles Landing and see if Baron knew who owned the dog. If he didn't, she thought he might offer the dog food and water and check with the police to see if anyone called in a missing dog with his description. The newly formed plan counted on the dog following her once she took the lead.

Plan intact, Jess sped up her steps. She estimated they were another five minutes from the pub, and each time she glanced around to see if her walking partner was still with her, he was. Jess obviously didn't know Baron well, but he appeared to be a nice enough person from their limited encounters. She couldn't imagine he'd not help them. Also, she didn't want to bother Joel at this hour; he'd likely be home with his family eating dinner. At the thought of food, her stomach growled.

Once they stood before the rear door of Eagles Landing, Jess debated whether or not to knock. Was her plan truly a good idea? What if Baron wasn't there? What if he was? He didn't know her from Jack. And what incentive did he have to help her? He'd probably get mad she brought a stray dog around the establishment. Strays couldn't be good for business, but who could resist his cute Labrador-like face, she thought, and those wide, sad, brown eyes. Before she firmly decided to suck it up and knock, a certain someone barked, and barked, and barked some more.

Jess bent at the waist and held both hands up at her newest acquaintance. "Shsh, shsh, what are you doing?" she whispered. "I need to think here. You need to let me do this on my time."

He barked again.

"Let me handle this, would you?" she scolded, as his tail wagged more fiercely with each reprimand. As if sensing someone watching her once more, Jess slowly followed the dog's line of sight as he glanced up and barked. Her heart sank into her stomach.

Behind the screen door stood not Baron, but the blue-eyed woman from behind the bar. Jess couldn't read her expression, but she guessed she wasn't happy.

"Is there something I can help you with?" the woman asked. Her tone bit, but it contrasted with the slight smirk she brandished as she peered through the screen door.

Jess's partner in crime continued to wag his tail ferociously, while Jess felt ridiculous. She clenched her hands. Darn this dog. "I, ugh, was looking for Baron, actually."

The woman raised an eyebrow. "Baron, huh? Interesting. He's busy."

Something about the woman's demeanor was unsettling, almost overpowering. She stood a few inches taller than Jess and appeared well muscled, but Jess wasn't normally intimidated by others. She could hold her own. Regardless, she shifted her weight from one foot to another. "You probably don't remember me but—"

"Oh, I remember you."

"Lucky me," Jess whispered, a hair too loud.

"Is that sarcasm I detect?"

"It might be. Seems it slipped out. Sorry. You weren't supposed to hear. Seeing as I'm not in the best position to be a smart-aleck, I'll get to the point. I was out for a walk, trying to get my bearings around here, when I came across this incredibly cute, but apparently stray, dog several blocks from here." Jess glanced at her scruffy partner. "I don't know anyone from around here and thought maybe Baron knew who owned him. And if he didn't, maybe he could've given him some food scraps while we called the police and waited to see if they could find his owner. I couldn't leave him out here by himself. He has no tags."

"You're friends with Baron already?"

"Out of everything I said, your question is if I'm friends with Baron?"

Jess received no response, merely raised eyebrows that indicated an answer to the original question was warranted, not a question of her own. "Okay, no. I'm not exactly friends with Baron, but he's been nice to me the couple of times I've been here to eat. I thought he might help." Unlike you, who probably won't lift a finger, she thought.

"I see. And are you sure this dog is a stray? He doesn't look undernourished to me. Maybe he found you and brought you here."

"Seriously? What is it with you? Do you find humor in this situation at my expense again? You know what? Forget it. Sorry I asked."

Unexpectedly, the woman smiled. "Hold on, hold on. Don't get your knickers in a twist."

"My knickers?"

"Like the phrase, do you? Here's the lot of it, okay? I'm sorry. It wasn't my intent to upset you, and yes, I was having a bit of fun at your expense. I didn't think you'd take it badly, though. You seem pretty tough...for a foreigner."

Undecided at first if the comment was a compliment or

another jab, by the woman's expression, Jess leaned toward compliment.

"And before you get mad again, the furball sitting at your side is named George. He was a stray, two years ago, but he found me one day, sort of how he found you, and adopted me. That's why I made the joke about him bringing you here. He's the boss, you should know."

Jess relaxed. Had she overreacted? Possibly. Heat rose in her cheeks. Now, what was she to say next? Okay? Thanks, and walk away? Instead, she said, "Good to know."

The woman opened the door, and as soon as she did, George bounded past them both. "Please, come in."

"I shouldn't."

"Please."

"All right, for a minute I suppose." Jess entered the kitchen. The chef stood in front of the stove and gave a quick glance in their direction.

"The handsome man to your left is Phillip, our incredible chef," the woman said loud enough for him to overhear.

His face beamed.

The woman returned eye contact with Jess and held it, making Jess feel exposed. Then she extended her hand. "And my name's Rayne," she added in a raspy voice. "Again, I'm sorry if I offended you. In no way was it my intent. And thank you for escorting George. He tends to wander at times."

Jess's first thought was that Rayne was a cool name. Her second thought, after taking Rayne's extended hand in hers, was that she had soft hands and sounded sincere, which, based on their past run-ins, she couldn't couple with the person staring back at her.

"It's nice to meet you, Rayne, and good to match a name to the face. I'm Jessica Madison, but please call me Jess," she said. Her third thought was to let go of the hand she'd been holding a hair too long. She let go of Rayne's hand and cleared her throat. "If George is your dog, why doesn't he wear a collar? Not making him easily identifiable seems highly irresponsible." Jess watched Rayne's eyes narrow.

"You don't mince words, do you?'

"I try not to."

"I respect directness to a degree. I don't believe in

marking my dog as a possession. A collar signifies I own him, and I don't. He's with me because he chooses to be. Besides, everyone in town knows him. And, he also has a chip implant with all his information on it. Don't you, boy?" Rayne reached for George and briskly rubbed him on the head and between his ears. Then she walked toward the refrigerator and pulled out a square, glass container.

"I see. Yet with all of the tourism around here, a collar probably wouldn't be a bad idea," Jess stated. She hoped she didn't come across like she'd just called Rayne irresponsible when clearly she had.

"The funny thing is, in the two years George's been with me, you're the first person to stop and try to find his owner. Apparently, no other tourists thought to do so." Rayne glanced at Jess before she opened the glass container and placed a bowl of meat with vegetable scraps on the floor for George. Straightening, and before Jess could respond, she added, "And before you say anything, I meant that as a compliment, not as criticism."

Jess felt her cheeks redden even deeper. Okay, she deserved the dig. She did walk in with both guns loaded. "Thanks for the compliment, I think."

"You're welcome. I also like your necklace. I have one very much like it."

Jess absentmindedly fingered the flattened-silver, fat, backward-looking-K-shape pendant with five inscribed rune symbols her mother had given her years ago. Knowing it had to have been handcrafted and unique, she mumbled, "I doubt it."

"I'm sorry, I couldn't hear what you said."

Jess's stomach grumbled as she stood. "I said I should go. I believe I've held you up long enough already."

George looked up at Jess, tilted his head, and made a whining noise.

Oh God, Jess hoped Rayne hadn't heard the rumble, too, but by the amused expression on her face, she must have.

"You don't take compliments well, do you? Have you eaten? Let me heat up a dinner for you."

Great, Jess thought. Not only had Rayne caught her smart comment, but probably even Phillip at the other end of the kitchen heard her stomach growl. When she glanced in his direction, she caught him looking back with an amused expression similar to Rayne's. "No, and no, I appreciate the offer, but I don't want to be a bother."

"You're not a bother. In fact, I recommend a pasta dish I think you'll love. I can reheat it in no time. And actually, I need to check the bar for a second or Baron will think someone abducted me, so you'd be doing me a huge favor if you stayed and kept an eye on George. I'm sure he'll enjoy the company, too."

"Will he stay with me? I don't think he'll listen to me."

"Oh, he'll listen. He's a good boy, aren't you, George?"

In response, George nudged Rayne in the leg with his nose. He lay on the floor next to Jess's feet, placed his head between his outstretched front paws, and closed his eyes.

Jess met Rayne's gaze, only to see a smirk widen before she placed Jess's dinner in the microwave, set a plate and cutlery in front of her, and exited the kitchen. Jess found the entire situation strange and confusing. Rayne presented herself as cold one minute and warm the next. Had Rayne been snarky and condescending the day before in the pub, or had Jess judged her too quickly? No, she was definitely snarky and condescending but also maybe more. Maybe she'd judged Rayne too quickly, and maybe Rayne came to realize she'd judged Jess too quickly as well.

Chapter Four

At the trailer, after she unpacked her purchases and pieced together her sleeping quarters, Jess lay in her sleeping bag and listened to the sounds of the countryside evening, the whish of the wind and chirping of insects, feeling somehow less alone. She replayed the moments of when she'd first met Rayne, from the afternoon at the pub after a grueling day of travel, to the next day when she thought she'd caught Rayne watching her at lunchtime, to meeting up with her and George that night.

When Rayne returned to the kitchen, after Jess finished her meal and George slept, they'd talked for over an hour. Rayne asked about Jess's trip and the excavation, and Jess briefly explained her interest in medieval history, especially before and around the year 1000. She explained how she managed to secure the funding for the project at her Catholic university and how St. Albans had arranged with UK Berkeley University of History and Archaeology for her to give a presentation of her findings.

She touched on the history of the Norsemen—Vikings—from Denmark, Norway, and Sweden, and how they raided towns and pillaged monasteries in northern England in the late 8th century, around 793 A.D., and how the raids continued into southern England in the late 9th and early 10th centuries.

Jess clarified that although history supported the fact that the majority of Viking settlements were located in the eastern part of England, she explained how, through new satellite imagery, she and her team discovered what they estimated to be a single family settlement in southwestern England. How the unusual location of the discovery, coupled with additional research of recently restored and translated ancient church documents, suggests Bishop Leon II of Mettlenbury may have died at the hands of Vikings in what is Devonsbury today. Jess explained she was able to convince the university to fund the overseas excavation based mainly on that suggestion.

She also mentioned, though not terribly religious herself, that she had another reason for having wanted to secure the funds, unrelated to the university's interest. Without providing detail, she explained she was simply following her gut and hoping to discover truth in what was otherwise currently myth. She also told Rayne that if she had disclosed to the university her true reasoning for requesting the excavation, she was certain her project would never have seen the light of day. And although Jess saw Rayne was interested in Jess's true reasons for having requested this project, she didn't press Jess for more, for which Jess was grateful.

Throughout their conversation, each time Jess noticed Rayne look at her with an intensity that was unsettling, she was unable to discern why her attention was unsettling or why she let Rayne unnerve her as she did. And if she were truthful with herself, after a couple of hours spent in the kitchen of Eagles Landing, she'd admit part of her was glad Rayne and not Baron answered the door due to George's barks. At least she glimpsed a different side to Rayne, a side less intimidating and warmer. Warmer? Warm, as in the opposite of ice cold? Yes, she hated to admit this revelation, but she saw a softer side to Rayne, which she found endearing. And with that thought, she drifted off into a deep, much-needed sleep.

****

Jess woke refreshed and excited to greet her graduate and undergraduate students. With the students on hand, they'd finally start the excavation. Jess's conversation the night before with Rayne about the excavation brought Jess renewed enthusiasm for the project. She hoped she'd not bored her with talk of satellite imaging, site layout, and carbon dating, since she knew she'd definitely put George to sleep. She unzipped her sleeping bag and sat up. The exercise mat underneath, which she'd also purchased on her shopping trip with Joel, didn't do much to relieve the stiffness in her hip. Apparently, the mat cushioned only part of the hardness of the trailer floor, but all things considered, at least the trailer provided a roof over her head. Without somewhere to stay, she'd have had a great deal more to complain about.

Jess stretched, grabbed socks, underwear, a T-shirt, and cargo pants, and ambled into the tight bathroom enclosure. She'd placed essential toiletries in the bathroom the night before. Though cumbersome to wash without a shower, Jess used a washcloth efficiently for the task. The faucet produced barely lukewarm water, which chilled on the washcloth almost as soon as she removed it from under the faucet and wrung it out. Goosebumps rose on her arms as she washed. She dried off and dressed in sections to keep warm. Once dressed, she washed her hair in the sink, which also proved difficult due to the low clearance between the tip of the faucet and the basin.

In the room she designated as the office and bedroom, she heated a kettle of water and poured a cup of coffee through a Melita filter. Besides the sleeping bag purchase yesterday afternoon, she'd purchased other essentials such as the tea kettle, a hot plate, the Melita ceramic coffee filter holder and filters, coffee, a box of pastries, two boxes of cereal, and soy milk. The cabinets along one side of the office contained a hotel-room-sized refrigerator built into the center bottom cabinet. Jess purchased items for breakfast and dinner, since lunch would be catered. After she consumed a bowl of a medley cereal mix, her stomach gurgled with nerves over the excitement of breaking ground.

Dressed in green cargo pants, work boots, a plain orange T-shirt under a black polo shirt, and grey sweat jacket over top the polo, Jess oversaw the truck that transported the backhoe as it pulled onto the site. She dressed in layers on the site. In that way, as the day heated, she could easily take off one layer at a time and properly control her temperature. Her students were scheduled to arrive at different times throughout the day, which worked fine, since they couldn't do much until the backhoe did its job.

The truck driver loosened the fastenings from the

backhoe to the trailer bed and drove it backward down the ramp. After an hour, he had removed the top meter of soil from the first quadrant and worked on the second quadrant. In the meantime, Joel delivered her graduate student Marco, who would eventually work on cataloging and computer site reconstruction, and left a second time to retrieve her undergrad student Susan.

After a morning spent listening to metallic banging and the constant humming of the machine, Jess welcomed the quiet that remained after the backhoe came to a pause during a lunch break. By this time, three-quarters of the site had been cleared of the top meter of soil. Jess was impressed. She thought the digging would have taken longer. Marco and Susan spent the morning in the trailer, where they set up the equipment, emptied boxes of supplies, and prepared the center table for cataloging.

As Jess perused the site, she heard a raspy, "Hey there," and didn't need to see the person to know who stood behind her. Goosebumps paraded up Jess's arms as Rayne's voice radiated through her in a not unpleasant, but unexpected, fashion.

"Rayne, hi. What brings you here?" Jess asked. But seconds after the words left her mouth, she already found her answer. The memory of where she'd first seen the words "Eagles Landing" returned to her. The university chose Eagles Landing as the caterer to deliver their lunches; she'd seen their name on a purchase order.

Rayne held up a sturdy, white, paper bag with handles. "I think it's obvious, don't you? Where would you like it?"

"I knew the name of the pub looked familiar, but until now I couldn't place why. You can set the food out on the folding table to your left if you don't mind. Thanks." Jess couldn't read Rayne this morning. She was uncertain if Rayne was being sarcastic with her question or simply stated the obvious. Either way, she was happy the food had arrived. Earlier, as she stood and watched the backhoe operator work, a wave of lightheadedness, bordering on nausea, temporarily swept over her and she thought she might pass out. But after about a minute, the nausea subsided. She thought at the time hunger caused her reaction and was glad to now be able to eat.

"No problem." Rayne pulled the contents from the bag. On the table, she set wrapped sandwiches, two bowls containing different salads, a bowl of potato chips, paper plates, napkins, plastic utensils, and drinks.

Jess started for the trailer in search of Marco and Susan. She reversed course when she spotted them making their way in her direction. When they stood only feet away, she said, "Dig in. There's more here than all of us can eat."

Jess appreciated the fact she'd have food left over for dinner. She gestured toward Rayne with her hand. "Susan, Marco, this is Rayne. She works at Eagles Landing, a pub up the street, and they're also our caterer."

"Rad," Marco said.

Rayne stretched out her hand. "Nice to meet you both," she said to Marco and Susan while her eyes focused on Jess. "Excuse us a moment," Rayne said after she shook their hands. She pulled Jess to the side and whispered in her ear, "Besides the Bishop of wherever—Mettlenbury if I recall properly—are you at some near point in the near future going to tell me what you want to find at the site? The not knowing is killing me."

The touch of Rayne's hand on her arm, and the flicker of air that brushed across Jess's ear caused an involuntary gulp. "You're right, he was from Mettlenbury, but the rest is kind of a long story."

Rayne inclined her head. "Maybe you'll tell me another time. I need to get back anyway. Baron has his hands full. Enjoy the food. One more question before I go, though."

Jess waited, but when no question came, she said, "Shoot."

"Last night, after I teased you about George, you asked if I found humor with your situation at your expense again. What did you mean by 'at your expense again'?"

Jess's eyes opened wider and the lines between her brows furrowed. "You remembered my exact words?"

"I did."

"Hmm. And you seriously don't know what I meant?"

Rayne's right eyebrow rose. "If I knew, I wouldn't have asked."

Jess noticed Marco and Susan walk away from the table, plates full and drinks in hand. "When I walked up to the bar Saturday night and you observed I wasn't one of the locals, I asked you how you knew. You said you knew because I was sitting there waiting for someone to bring me a menu and that it didn't work that way around here." Jess jammed her hands in her pockets.

"That is what I said, and what I said was true, but I don't see how my choice of words would have upset you."

"I was wearing my university polo shirt, with St. Albans University in Connecticut clearly emblazoned on it. Baron pointed that fact out to me later. You were clearly making fun."

"I can see now how you'd take what I said the wrong way, but in my defense, I couldn't see what was written on your shirt when you were sitting at the table. So, yeah, once you came closer the shirt confirmed my suspicion, but I answered your question honestly. It was only the fact that you were sitting there so long and seemed lost—and possibly a tad angry—that I knew you didn't live around here," Rayne said.

Now Jess felt like a jerk. Twice she'd made incorrect assumptions about Rayne. "If I thought I felt stupid yesterday with George, I feel even more so now. I may have misread you. I'd like to make it up to you."

"No need. I may have been a tad edgy when we met. Some say I'm not the easiest to get to know. Anyhow, I need to return to the pub."

"Fine, but first agree to have dinner with me? Tomorrow night?"

"I can't, I'm busy."

"What about the following night?"

"Also busy. I promised someone else a visit."

Jess wondered if her dinner invitation was a good idea after all, given that Rayne obviously had better things to do. "Okay, this is your last chance. How about on Saturday, if you haven't already made plans? You can choose the restaurant."

"I don't know. You don't need to buy me dinner. Besides, if anyone should be taking anyone out it should be me for what you did with George. I'm off. Enjoy lunch. I'll see you tomorrow."

Jess watched befuddled as Rayne walked away. She didn't understand her, but the woman exuded confidence with each step, which Jess found sexy. Sexy? Oh, no. No way. Don't go there, Jess. Baron said his sister had a bug up her butt about educators, and Jess was an educator. No good could come from such a scenario. And Rayne obviously was in no rush to accept her apology or get to know her better. The most she could hope for would be to gain a friend, but that likelihood was not speeding to fruition either. Jess filled her plate, found a spot next to Marco and Susan, and sat.

After she'd swallowed the last piece of the first half of her sandwich, Susan elbowed Jess. "So, Professor Madison—"

"Oh, no you don't. We're out of the classroom. Call me Jess while we're on site."

"Okay, Jess. The caterer seems pretty nice, doesn't she?" Susan asked.

"Mmm-hmm."

"Not bad to look at either," Susan continued.

"I'll say," Marco added.

Susan ignored Marco. "And she looks to be about your age."

Jess peeked at Susan. "Is that right? What exactly are you driving at?"

Susan feigned ignorance. She placed her hand on her chest. "Who, me? Nothing. I was merely being observant. Rayne watched you fill your plate. Just saying. Something we should know about?"

Jess swallowed the last forkful of potato salad and sipped on a bottle of tea. Had Rayne taken a second glance her way, when Jess thought she was well on her way? No, why would she? And if she did, what significance would such an action hold? "Maybe she's observant like you are. I don't know more than you do." She spoke the truth, didn't she? Or did she?

****

Jess polished off a leftover sandwich from lunch that served as her dinner. Later, in bed, thoughts from the day flooded in. Her student crew had arrived safely, first her graduate student Marco and undergrad Susan, then her other graduate student Shelly and the two remaining undergrads Justin and Mike. The last three had checked-in with their respective homeowners. The homeowners agreed to house the students for the summer at a reasonable cost, a tab the university paid for. Jess was surprised the group decided to go out for dinner and drinks the first night. They invited Jess along, but she was tired. She also thought they'd have more fun if they went out on their own, so she declined. She'd planned to read a few chapters in a romance novel she'd brought along before going to sleep, cognizant of the fact she'd be up early again the next morning.

Lying in her sleeping bag, Jess placed her book on the floor, several chapters in. Her eyes grew heavy, and her breathing slowed. On the cusp of sleep, the lightheaded, almost nauseous feeling she experienced earlier in the day returned. She was half in a trance it seemed. Heat rose within her, and her equilibrium shifted off center, and although she tried, she couldn't rise. Instead, she flattened her palms at her side to provide her body a hint of stability and support. Her eyelids grew heavy. She strained to keep them open, but could not, and then, it was as though her mind floated from her body and she became a voyeur into someone else's life. She heard a young girl yell...

Chapter Five

"See you later," Cassethea hollered as she flung open the heavy, wooden door to the house and ran three steps into the cool morning mist before her mother's bellowing voice landed in her ears.

"One moment, youngling," Arielwund shouted as she stood in the doorway. "How many times have I told you not to leave uneaten food on your plate?"

Cass pivoted. She stared into narrowed eyes as the silence grew, uncertain as to whether her mother wanted a response or not. When her mother's arm set on her hip and her eyebrows lifted, Cass answered, "Many."

"Yes, many. Now get in here and finish your morning meal. And next time, don't run from the house, walk."

Cass lowered her head, eyes glancing downward at her bare feet on the hard dirt floor as she reentered the house and passed by her mother. Her brothers and father stared at her as she sat on the bench at the table. The table was situated in the center of the room, four feet from the central hearth. As she sat, her eyes readjusted to the darker interior. Her younger sister, Emma, bread held between fingers over a bowl of mash, paid Cass no attention.

"You'd think you were running off to meet a fine young lad this morning, not taking the sheep to pasture," her father, William, said. "I don't know anyone who enjoys work as much as you do. Maybe I should herd the sheep and not you, and you spend more time in the fields."

Cass flashed her father a defiant scowl. She noticed her brothers' wicked grins as they clearly enjoyed her scolding. Only Gollyn, her brother of nine, sat quiet, eyes downcast. Her father always brought up the subject of men, as if marrying her off were his main goal in life. She was only fifteen summers of age, and the thought of having to cower under another man's will brought anger to the forefront, but she knew better than to speak. At this moment, all she wanted to do was exit the house and breathe in freedom. She wanted to see her best friend, Julianta. She wiped the last piece of bread around her bowl, sopped up the remainder of the mash, and stuffed the soaked bread into her mouth. "May I go now?" A sharp tone hung at the edge of her question.

"Yes, you may go now," her father said. "But when you return with the sheep tonight, make sure you've caught us a decent-sized fish or two for dinner as well. And do not be late."

"Yes, sir." Cass swung her legs from under the table and exited the house. She wore a tan, worn, woolen dress, similar to the dresses her mother and Emma wore, that scratched at her shoulders when she moved. Relieved to be out of the house, she welcomed the cool mist on her heated cheeks and set off toward the barn in a walk, not a run. She opened the barn door and greeted the sheep she considered her friends. Her family tended the sheep for the king in return for the farmland their house stood on, or rather, she tended them.

When Cass reached the top of the hill, she didn't see Julia. She sat under their favorite tree and chewed on the end of a blade of grass while the sheep grazed. By noon, with still no Julia in sight, Cass's enthusiasm from earlier in the morning of seeing her friend had waned. The day dragged on drudgingly with Cass eventually taking a nap. When she awoke, the sun was well past the middle of the sky and she'd not yet been fishing. But by later in the afternoon, she caught two gudgeon for dinner, and by doing so, hoped to avoid her father's wrath.

****

Cassethea traipsed down the hillside leading the herd of twenty sheep home. After having waded in the stream while fishing, her dress slapped wet with mud against her ankles. The sun sank lower behind the trees. Eventide set in. Soon, from the bottom of the hill, she saw the silhouettes of her brothers sparring with wooden swords in the yard and quickened her pace. She was the second eldest of five siblings at fifteen, with three brothers and her sister, Emma, the youngest, at only six.

After she dashed across the open field of grass, she rushed toward her brothers and stopped. The herd stopped with her. She set her basket of fish at her feet. "Hi, Sedwick! Hi, Alfred!"

"Hi, Cass," both brothers responded in unison. But otherwise, neither gave her heed nor faced in her direction.

"Hey, Alfred, can I play, too?"

Alfred, older than his sister by a year, didn't take his eyes off his brother Sedwick's stick and continued his strikes as sweat trickled along his temple. Alfred was competitive by nature. Losing was not an option with him.

"This isn't a game, Cass, it's training," he grunted. Alfred advanced as his brother stepped backward. "Soon I'll be a soldier in the king's army, protecting the people."

"I want to be a soldier, too. You know I do. Please teach me to spar, please," Cass pleaded.

"Stop talking foolishness. You couldn't lift a real sword let alone swing it, and besides, a woman belongs in the home, caring for her family. You are so strange, Cass. Don't let father hear you speak of your wants. Why can't you act like other girls? Humph, a woman soldier...that's crazy talk." Alfred slashed the stick from twelve-year-old Sedwick's hand.

Cass let her eyes trail to the muddied ground at her feet. "I am not strange...or crazy," she mumbled, wringing her hands.

Alfred tapped his brother on the shoulder. "Good job, Sedwick. You almost had me there for a minute."

"I did, didn't I?" Sedwick leaned over to pick up his fake sword.

Alfred faced Cass. "Look, I'm sorry, all right? I didn't mean what I said. But you have to face reality at some point." He paused, and quickly added, "You should guide the sheep into their pen. You're late and Father isn't happy about it. You best tread softly with him tonight."

Cass lifted her head in acknowledgment, but before she took a step, her father's voice bellowed over her.

"Cassethea! Get those sheep put away and get into this

house now! Same goes for you boys, too. Stop playing and get in here. I'm hungrier than an ox and tired of waiting."

Cassethea handed the bucket of fish to her eldest brother. "Here, you best take this in to Mum." After she escorted the sheep into the barn, she slogged toward the house and crossed the threshold. Her father and siblings sat around the rectangular table in their usual places. Alfred and Sedwick sat across from one another closest to her father who sat on one end of the table. Gollyn sat next to Sedwick, while the seat across from Gollyn remained empty, and Emma sat next to Cass's empty spot nearest her mother, whose place was at the other end of the table. Arielwund hefted the iron kettle from the hearth and placed it on the table, giving her daughter a quick, understanding glance before she served her family the fish stew.

When Cass took a step toward her seat, her father stood from the head of the table and kicked out the stool from beneath him. He took two strides toward his daughter and slapped her hard across the face with his left hand. "Not you! You will not eat tonight. You can go to bed now. When you learn to listen to me, you will be fed. This is the second night in a row you've come home late. I won't tolerate such disrespect. Now go!"

Arielwund held the wooden ladle frozen over Sedwick's bowl. "William, please," she pleaded.

"No, she's got to learn. She's always the troublemaker, this one. She's old enough to know better. She's so dammed headstrong and defiant. Something has to break her. She's old enough to marry, but at this rate, she'll never wed and we'll have another mouth to feed for another winter."

"Please don't speak in such a manner. I know you don't mean what you said," Arielwund said.

"I do mean what I said. Enough is enough. Now let's eat."

Cass lay quiet in her cot at the other end of the hut, unable to sleep. Her stomach grumbled, and her face burned hot where her father struck her. Anger toward her father raged inside, and not for the first time. She couldn't understand how her mother lived with such a man. The thought of marriage sickened her except for the fact that living with someone else would get her away from him.

After five minutes of silence, Cass heard her father's voice low, but clear, as he started the dinner conversation. He spoke about what he and the boys had accomplished in the field during the day, their dwindling stores of food leftover from the winter, and his concerns regarding King Ethelred II, from the north.

"I know I shouldn't speak badly about King Ethelred, but he is nothing like the kings before him. He is certainly nothing like Alfred the Great, God rest his soul. My father told me stories about Alfred that his father told him and his father before. They called him the shepherd of his people. He was a true military leader of the Anglo Saxons. He watched out for and fought for his flock. Ethelred's a shadow of such a man. He raises England's taxes but provides little in the way of protection against the Danes or Vikings, and I hear tell that now winter is over, Viking raiding ships are making their way south once again by way of the North Sea. I pray they leave England alone and wreak havoc on the Danes or Norse instead. I fear these are hard times to come upon us soon, hard times indeed," William said.

"When I'm made a soldier, Father, I'll fight all those who hope to harm us and I will do my name justice, of that I swear," Alfred said.

"I know you will, my son. I see greatness ahead of you. You will make our family proud, and people will honor your name."

As the stories continued, Cass's eyes grew heavy and she finally drifted to sleep. Later, she sprang up suddenly when she sensed fingers stroking through her hair.

"Shssh. Be quiet so your father doesn't hear. I brought you some stew," Arielwund whispered. Arielwund was careful not to wake the others, who slept as always, in a row to the left and right of Cass, arranged by age, like piglets in a pen.

"I don't want any dinner," Cass whispered.

"Don't be so stubborn. As much as you dislike your father, you certainly have his stubbornness. Now eat."

Cass turned her head away from Arielwund.

"Eat. Please."

Cass turned back and studied her mother. She capped her pride, took the wooden bowl, and scooped the fish and barley soup into her mouth. "It's cold."

"It's food. Now eat. You need your energy. Your father did what he did tonight because he was worried about you. When it gets late, danger lurks in the woods. I'm not saying he's justified in his actions, but I believe he did what he did because he cares."

Cass gulped down the food surprisingly quickly. She scooped up the last bits, with her fingers pressed against the bowl, to scrape off every last morsel. She looked up at her mother. "Then you remain alone in your belief."

The remainder of the night didn't bode much better for Cass, regardless of the fact she'd eaten. Guilt encroached on her for internalizing hatred toward her father, and sleep wouldn't claim her. The dank cold seeped through the stick-and-moss hut built to protect them from the worst of what lay outside, but even with the hearth still warm from dinner, Cass trembled. In part, she knew her father was right. She should listen more. But she didn't want to grow up if it meant living under the command of another. She'd seen enough of the effect of how one person controlled another, but she also understood there were no other options. She heard movement on her parents' side of the hut and sounds she did not want to hear, and now she wished she'd snuck out earlier and slept in the barn with the sheep, chilly April night or not.

"Stop, William. I don't think all the kids are asleep yet," Cass heard her mother whisper.

"That's impossible. I could have sheared a couple of sheep by now. For certain they must be asleep," William responded.

Cass heard the creak of their cot as she assumed her father rolled onto his side.

"Cassethea might still be up, and besides, my head hurts. I'm exhausted and would rather not tonight."

"Whether she's asleep or not is her problem, not mine, and what ails you at this moment is of little concern to me as well. I've had a tough day, too, and I'm certain you can find some energy for your husband when all is said and done. It's not like you need to do anything but lay there. The matter isn't up for discussion."

The cot creaked again, louder this time, and Cass covered her ears with her hands and held tight. She closed her eyes and pictured herself on top of the grassy hill with the sheep, the sun warming her ashen face, and her best friend Julia at her side.

Chapter Six

For the remainder of the week, Jessica planned to place as much focus on the excavation as she could, but the recollection of the dream she'd experienced Monday night left her shaken and confused on two fronts. One, because the dream felt so real, and two, because the girl in the dream, or whatever she'd experienced during sleep, owned the same name as the woman at the center of her archeological obsession—Cassethea of Mercia. With all the excitement surrounding the start of the dig, could Jess have invented this story subconsciously? Could she have intertwined her knowledge of history with her desire to prove Cassethea was real, to the point she invented a made-up glimpse into this girl's life in her sleep?

If that were true, where did all the other family members come from? And why would she invent an unhappy childhood situation for her heroine? Why would she envision her as a child in the first place, when what scant written word and art that existed of Cassethea depicted her as a warrior? Jess didn't have answers, but the lack of answers didn't stop her from obsessing over this unnervingly odd experience. Plus, she knew she hadn't invented the nauseous feeling she had before she fell asleep. Jess told herself not to obsess. She convinced herself that her seemingly voyeuristic trip was nothing more than the combination of stress and excitement.

Initially, her mixed-up state of mind throughout the week put a damper on her dinner plans with Rayne for Saturday. Two days after she'd first asked Rayne to dinner, she'd asked once more and Rayne finally relented. And although Jess's mind was confused about what happened to her Monday night in her sleep, the more she thought about Rayne, the more she realized she looked forward to seeing her, and that maybe the distraction of spending time with Rayne would overshadow her own problems.

Rayne was someone to take her mind off the dig and all the aspects that went with it, which now included strange dreams. Was a distraction all Rayne was to Jess, or were they becoming friends as well? Jess remembered the rush of adrenaline that coursed through her when she'd unexpectedly asked Rayne to dinner. The flush in her cheeks made her wonder why the woman caused her heartbeat to quicken and the temperature in her body to rise. Not that she minded, but her reaction was certainly not one she normally experienced when she thought about her friends.

****

Rayne selected the restaurant Saturday night, as Jess requested, and Jess was not disappointed with her choice. The mix of aromas she breathed in as they entered the establishment caused her stomach to rumble. Seared fish intertwined with the char of a well-grilled steak tickled her nostrils. The dimly lit restaurant was packed, the ambiance homey, and their table, which Rayne must have reserved in advance, was situated in the garden off the back of the restaurant. Round, wrought-iron tables covered in white tablecloths with matching, padded, wrought-iron chairs sat on a red paver patio. Ivy climbed up the eight-foot walls and over light poles. Ample potted plants sat stoically along the walls, all of which gave the garden a sanctuary-like feel. A built-in barbeque adorned one corner, and slender space heaters chased the chill from the night air.

"Oh my God, this place is beautiful," Jess said, as they were directed to a table, "and the food smells so good."

"Yeah, I was here once before, a few years ago and loved it. The food was fantastic. They use only fresh, local ingredients. I looked them up again the other night to make sure the place hadn't changed. The ratings are as high as they were the first time I came. Their prices are surprisingly reasonable, too, considering their popularity."

Jess picked up the menu. "I'm not worried about the price. I mean, not that I'm wealthy or anything on a professor's salary, but I do okay. My goal was to take you to a nice place, and it looks like we've accomplished that, so I'm happy." When Jess saw Rayne smile and pick up her menu, she opened and perused hers as well.

Jess wondered under what circumstances and with whom Rayne had visited the restaurant previously. Jess guessed she was probably there with a girlfriend, a sexy model, no doubt. She'd probably strutted in with the kind of person on her arm that attracts everyone's attention when they enter a room. Anyone as handsome and put together as Rayne could easily attract such a person. Jess didn't see herself as particularly beautiful or model-like. She saw herself as average, not bad to look at, but not gorgeous either.

Yet, when Rayne stopped by the trailer earlier in the evening and Jess opened the door, she thought she saw appreciation in Rayne's eyes, the knowledge of which made her feel special. That same knowledge sent a jolt of warmth throughout her body as well. She recalled in that moment, she'd caught herself staring at Rayne in her tight black slacks, simple dress shoes, and a snug fitting, white, short-sleeve shirt. A shirt that revealed not only ample breasts, but well-defined shoulders, biceps, and forearms, traits Jess was particularly fond of. Not that she'd noticed in any way other than in an observing fashion, and not that she was now glancing in appreciation over Rayne's torso once again. No, she was absolutely not doing that.

"Decided what you'd like to order yet?" Rayne asked in a light, amused tone as she folded her menu and placed it on the table.

Jess snapped her line of sight back to her menu, fearing she'd been caught staring, and trying her best to figure out how to sound nonchalant about that fact in a response she knew she needed to give, and quickly. Besides, she wasn't staring—she'd only glanced over at Rayne after all. "Hmm, I think so. What are you ordering?" Jess's tone was calm, which surprised her.

"I think I'll start with the mozzarella, plum tomato, and basil oil salad. For the main dish I'm eying the Aberdeen Angus burger."

"Sounds good, but why don't you try the Aberdeen Angus filet?" Jess sensed Rayne picked the less-expensive cut of meat to keep the price reasonable, which was sweet, but Jess didn't want price to be the deciding factor and wanted Rayne to have a memorable meal. "I thought I might try the filet as well. The steak comes with smoked garlic, tender broccoli stems, and a Madagascan green peppercorn sauce. I almost can't finish describing the meal without wanting to chomp right in."

The corner of Rayne's mouth turned upward. "I had considered that dish, too. All right then, sold on the filet."

"Excellent." After they ordered, they fell into easy conversation. "I hope I didn't get you in trouble the other day with the owner when I brought George by the pub."

"No, not at all. Baron loves dogs, especially George. He's guiltier of feeding him there than I am," Rayne said.

"Baron owns the pub? He's so young."

"Baron and I own it jointly, actually. Eagles Landing is a brother-and-sister establishment."

"I'm sorry. I had no idea. Why didn't you correct me when I introduced you to Marco and Susan as a worker there?"

"I didn't think the additional information was relevant, and you weren't totally wrong. I do work at Eagles Landing."

"Of course. Whether you own the pub or not makes no difference. When I first saw you and Baron behind the bar I thought the two of you resembled one another and could be brother and sister, or cousins."

"Thank you. Since Baron does well with the ladies, I'll take that as a compliment. I think he may have his eye on you."

Startled, Jess replied, "Who, me? No, that's silly. I don't think so. I mean, I'm not...I don't...never mind."

Rayne appeared to enjoy Jess's discomfort for a moment but soon let her off the hook. "As for the business, there'd be no way for you to know we owned it unless someone told you. Our dad left the place to us. It's been in the family for generations. As he grew older, standing on his feet twelve hours a day was no longer an option, and my mum didn't like that he was always at the pub. She wanted to travel more. Once Baron and I were old enough, and had amassed savings of our own, we gave my father what money we'd both saved, and the rest we pay to him as a percentage of earnings each month. The payments are part of our parents' retirement fund. The agreement works out for everyone. Even if we didn't own the business, we'd have supported them as best we could."

"That's nice. Not all kids are as thoughtful or responsible when it comes to looking after their parents."

"I guess, though running the pub isn't what I originally wanted to do."

Jess sensed more to the story but decided not to pry. "You both do a good job, though. The food is excellent. And I love the architecture there. I love the architecture of all these old buildings."

"I figured you might, in your line of work. Speaking of which, what did the satellite images reveal that made you think there might be a Viking settlement buried in that location in Devonsbury?"

"The image disclosed the outline of what could possibly be a longhouse, and therefore a settlement," Jess said. "And, as I mentioned the other night, the location is around the area documented to be the last sighting of where Bishop Leon II went missing."

"I didn't recall you mentioning he went missing before. So your Roman Catholic university sees interest in that type of situation from a historical standpoint?" Rayne asked.

"Exactly. This subject matter doesn't bore you?"

"No. On the contrary. I took a particular liking to medieval art and artifacts at university, which unfortunately landed me in trouble down the road with an ex."

Jess crinkled her eyes.

"Long story. Best kept for another day," Rayne said, "or forgotten altogether."

Jess nodded, but sensed a downward shift in Rayne's mood that stayed with her for the remainder of dinner and the quiet ride home. Jess couldn't say the ride was an uncomfortable quiet, but it was definitely quiet.

****

Jess couldn't fall asleep after Rayne dropped her off at

the trailer. She was surprised she'd enjoyed the evening as much as she had, not that she expected it to be horrible, but she thought for sure Rayne's sarcastic side would have shown through at some point, but it never did. Her quietness on the ride home was somewhat of a concern, but she shrugged the uneasiness off. Instead, she decided to talk with El about her experience from Monday night and catch up at the same time, but Jess got her voicemail after she rang her. She didn't leave a message. She decided she'd call her first thing the next morning instead.

Jess replayed the moment in her evening when Rayne placed her hand on the lower part of her back, directing her gently into the garden area where they had dinner, the gesture tender and warming. She'd had many pleasant thoughts that day, as she recalled, and all were related to Rayne. As her eyes grew heavy, heat once again rose within her and a slight sick feeling took hold, similar to what she'd experienced Monday night, but much less intense. She felt her mind begin to float in that nowhere state between where she was now and another place and time, but this time, she didn't fight it. She allowed her mind to float where it may, and it floated to Cassethea.

Chapter Seven

When Cass awoke, she knew her father and two eldest brothers would already be in the field working the soil for spring planting, with her youngest brother, Gollyn, doing his best to keep pace. She empathized with Gollyn's plight of not being smart enough in her father's eyes or strong enough, but at the same time, she was grateful her father was out in the fields with them instead of at home. She didn't want to face her father so soon after her scolding and the sounds she heard after—she shook the thoughts from her mind.

Cass didn't understand why her mother allowed her father to treat her not as a wife, but in Cass's eyes, as no better than a servant. She often attempted to talk to her mother about her concerns but received comments about her being too young to understand, about how the world worked and where their place was in society, and that Cass needed to accept the facts as they were. Cass valued her mother's knowledge and strength, but she did not understand, regardless of what her mother said, why she stayed with her father. Cass felt certain she'd not allow her life to become like the life her mother led. She wanted to talk to her best friend Julia and clear her mind. She hoped she'd see Julia this day, and those thoughts alone cheered her up.

She walked from the cot into the central living and cooking area and rushed over to her sister, Emma. She picked her up off the wooden bench by the table, swung her around, and kissed her cheek. "How's my little sister doing today?" Cass asked.

Emma's bright brown eyes shone like stones washed smooth in a creek as they focused on Cass. Laughter erupted from her doll-like figure.

"I'll take your wordless response to suggest 'I'm well this day,' sis," Cass said as she set Emma's feet upon the ground. She released her sister and directed her attention to her mother. She kissed her mother on the cheek as well. "Morning, Mum."

"Good morning, Cassethea. I'm pleased to see you in better spirits this morning," Arielwund said.

"The sun is up, it's a new day, and we're well, so aye, I suppose my spirits are fine."

"Excellent, then I foresee you won't mind if the sheep graze in the south field while you collect mushrooms today."

Cass struggled with her mother's request but hid her displeasure. She might not see Julia, the hunt for mushrooms often time-consuming. If she fussed, she'd find herself in the same position but with an angry mother to boot. Besides, with mushrooms more plentiful in the spring than in the height of the summer, the possibility existed she'd gather enough of them and still have time left over to see Julia.

"You foresaw correctly," Cass said. She sat in quiet and ate her morning meal. She decided quiet was her best option and would save her the most time. After she swallowed the last piece of bread, she took the basket from her mother and scampered out the door, glad to breathe in the fresh air and break free from the mental shackles that surrounded her. She also anticipated the mushrooms would add delicious flavor to the evening meal.

"Keep a watchful eye for wolves, Cassethea," Arielwund yelled from the doorway, hands on her hips. "Saewyn said she thought she saw one yesterday at the edge of the forest. And do not come home late. I don't need to remind you your father has no patience for disobedience, especially after yesterday."

"Yes, Mum. You need not worry." Cass smiled to herself as she glided along the worn foot path from the house, past the pigs' pen. She released the sheep, led them to the south field to forage, then proceeded into the woods. The day prior, she'd taken the sheep through the lower meadow to the grassy field at the top of the hill several miles from home. The top of the hill was where she often met with her best friend, Julianta, named after St. Julian Church in Middle Saxon, according to what King Herrwald, Julianta's father, had told Julia.

By the time midday passed, mushrooms lay piled above the rim of Cass's basket. Satisfied with her effort, she left the woods and strode toward the hill. She hoped she'd see Julia as she reached the top, but was uncertain Julia would wait for her if she didn't see Cass right away, since Cass was normally the first to arrive and wait, not the other way around. But as she crested the hill and looked across the grassy, flat surface, across the wide expanse to a grove of trees on the right, she spotted Julia and ran toward her, careful not to lose one mushroom from the basket.

"Cass!" Julia yelled as she rose and hugged her friend. "I wasn't sure I'd see you today, but I'm glad you came. Come, sit with me."

Cass placed her basket of mushrooms in the shade of the trees and sat on the blanket Julia brought with her during her visits. The blanket was as soft as Julia's dress, much unlike her own dress, which scratched her skin.

Julia opened her basket. "Are you hungry?"

"Starved as usual," Cass said. She enjoyed the food Julia brought from the castle. Although most items were leftovers, the bountiful amounts consisted of the types of food Cass's family could not afford. At times, she'd bring fruit or figs, which were special treats. Those days ultimately racked Cass with guilt. She couldn't bring home what they didn't eat, or her family would know she'd spent time with her friend rather than focus on the tasks they'd given her such as watching over the sheep, hunting for small game, or gathering berries or mushrooms, much like today.

On the other hand, Cass didn't understand why they'd be mad, since the sheep pretty much hung together and listened to her without any issues. No matter, she valued her free time, and the hours spent with Julia were the happiest hours in her day. They'd talk about silly or stupid actions their family members took, or rumors they heard, or a dozen other nonsensical things, but today wasn't going to be one of those days. Cass wanted to talk about last night, but she soon found out Julia held other ideas on how she wanted to spend their day.

Cass ate and savored the white bread, cheese, and figs Julia brought. Cass was likely the only member of her family who'd eaten white bread, since only the rich could afford to grow wheat, which required many more nutrients to thrive than barley. As she ate, she noticed Julia's vision fixated on her. Julia's green eyes sparkled in the sun, as did her golden hair, which hung to below shoulder length. It was tied into a braid, and loose strands of hair framed Julia's gentle face. The directed attention made Cass anxious, and at the same time, provided a sense she was special.

"What's going on?" she finally asked.

Julia glanced around their space on the hill and inched toward Cass. "Do you ever wonder who you'll end up marrying, and what it'll be like to be with that person? And by be with, I don't mean live with."

Cass wasn't entirely certain what Julia meant by her question, but a part of her liked the direction the conversation had veered. "I try not to think about marriage much. It's not a place I see as a positive in my life." Cass watched as Julia digested what she'd said, and yet noticed her friend appeared baffled by her words as well.

"I've thought about it a lot recently. Yesterday, I saw a moment pass between my parents that I don't think I was supposed to see. I climbed over a waist-high dividing wall, a stone's throw from my servant's quarters, and rounded a shed at the edge of my parents' private garden. I saw them sitting on a bench, thighs touching. My father gently stroked my mother's face. When he did, her expression changed. I can't explain how, but I knew the effect on her was special. Could I touch your face like that, Cass, and would you tell me what you feel?"

Cass swallowed hard. She'd never thought of being touched by her friend in the way she suggested. She knew such an act would be wrong. If anyone saw them, they'd be in grave trouble. But the curiosity and the strange tingly feeling in her stomach at the mention of the maneuver made her nod in agreement.

Cass trembled as Julia focused her attention on her and touched her face with the softest of hands. They glided like a whisper across her heated cheeks, torturously slow and deliberate, as green eyes bore into hers, seemingly in an effort to gather as much information as possible. When Julia glanced at Cass's lips, a jolt coursed through her body to her center. The surprise was immediate. The intake of her breath quickened, as did her heartbeat.

"Anything?" Julia asked.

Cass nodded but could not speak.

"What did it feel like?"

Cass shook her head. "I...I can't. Good."

"Should I continue?"

Cass signaled in the affirmative, but this time, Julia's heated fingers slid along her bare arm, a sensation which overwhelmed Cass. Her body reacted in ways she was certain were not pure.

"Tell me," Julia breathed.

Cass couldn't answer at first. She was stunned and excited and breathless and confused. Very, very much confused. "I...I don't think I can," she said, but when she saw the disappointment on Julia's face, her heart ached and she extended her hand toward Julia. "No, it's all right. I'll show you."

Cass gently touched the side of Julia's face. She wanted to give Julia the same intense gift she was given moments ago. A gift she knew she'd not soon forget. She stroked Julia's cheek gently with her thumb and stared into her eyes. She wanted to stay in that place an eternity and melt into Julia. As Cass's breathing became more ragged, Julia's eyes changed; they seemed to darken. Emboldened, Cass ran her other hand along the inside of Julia's arm and registered Julia's reaction. She scooted closer and let her eyes linger on Julia's lips. She caught the hitch in Julia's breath and the acceptance in Julia's expression seconds before their lips connected, and in that moment, she knew her life would never be the same again.

The kiss lasted only a second, and both girls backed away at the same time and placed distance between themselves. As they looked at each other, Julia smiled first, which lifted a heavy weight from Cass's shoulders. "Oh, my God, Cass. I knew it would be incredible. It was...I can't explain it. That kiss was better than wonderful."

"I know." Cass wanted to say much more, but the two words were the only ones she mustered.

"If the kiss was this good with you, imagine what kissing a boy would be like. Now I really can't wait to get married. We need to practice more."

For some reason, the kiss didn't make Cass want to get married any more now than she did before. If anything, the kiss caused the opposite effect. When the words about kissing a boy escaped from Julia's mouth, they upset Cass. At a deeper level, she understood she should have been happy for her friend's revelation, but she was anything but. Instead, a sharp pain stabbed at her chest, one she'd never felt before. Cass stood up and grabbed her basket. "Great. I'm happy for you. I've got to go. I can't be late today or my father will likely kill me."

Julia stood and placed her hand on Cass's arm. The heat radiated through her. "Are you feeling well? You don't look it. You're not angry with me, are you?"

Cass wished she understood what the jumble of feelings inside her meant, but anger wasn't one of them. "No, I'm not angry. I just...I don't know. I need to go, though." Cass hesitated. "Today was special. Thank you," she said before she ran off.

Chapter Eight

The next few days meeting Julia on the hill were strange for Cass as she struggled with her feelings, but as each day went by and they hadn't kissed, Cass's emotions settled. As much as she wanted to revel in the softness of Julia's lips, she sensed what they had done was wrong. If her father found out, she was certain he wouldn't approve and probably would beat her, or worse, forbid her to see Julia again. Plus, Cass recognized Julia merely used her to experiment on what kissing a boy would feel like. Somehow, Cass didn't believe the sensation of kissing a boy would be as wonderful or even equal to kissing Julia. How or why she felt that way she didn't know.

She watched the sheep as they munched on fresh grass sprigs. For the most part, the sheep huddled together. When one strayed toward the woods or lagged behind the others, Cass thought, "Oh no you don't, get back with the herd." And each time before she moved to retrieve them, they fell in line on their own. She wondered if the hill trapped magical powers, or if she was simply lucky the sheep appeared to somehow know her thoughts, but either way, it made her job much easier.

Arms stretched behind her, hands propped on the ground, Cass faced the sky and absorbed the warmth of the sun. A light breeze tickled her skin as she listened to the birds call to one another. Moments later, she felt a hand on her shoulder.

"Hey, girl," Julia said. "Shouldn't you be keeping an eye on the sheep?"

"They're pretty well-behaved. I'm not worried about them."

"No, you don't appear to be." Julia placed her blanket on the ground next to Cass and sat. She put her hands behind her billowy dress. "What about wolves? Shouldn't you be on the lookout for them?"

Cass sat up and brushed the dirt and pebbles from her hands. "Wolves never bothered with the herd before. I'm not worried. Although you're right and I probably should watch them more closely." Cass narrowed her eyes to shield the sun's glare. "How long have you been standing there?"

"A couple of minutes, maybe longer, I'm not sure. Come sit with me," Julia said. She patted the spot next to her.

Cass stood and moved onto the blanket next to Julia. Julia watched her every step with the same darkness and heated intensity in her eyes that she sensed the first time they kissed. The pull toward Julia was so strong, but Cass resisted. Instead, she thought of something to say to take her mind off Julia's lips. "I overheard my father talk to my mother last night about the Vikings moving farther south and the villages near us being pillaged."

Julia straightened her dress. "You don't need to worry about Vikings. My father will protect his people. His army is a thousand strong."

"That may be true, but unless he knows an attack is coming, he can't do anything to stop it. Often, the raids take place at night. Also, Father said in the Kingdom of Andron, north of the River Trent, women and young children are taken from their homes to work as slaves for the king."

"I've overhead Father talk about King Andron as well. He taxes his people harder than some. He allows them less freedom as well, which is true, but never have I heard of him taking people from their homes. That sounds like a story made up in a drinking hole somewhere that started as one story and ended as another. Unwelcome capture is slavery, and slaves are only taken by a lord or king if the person broke a law—had stolen or committed incest—and then only a man would be taken. A woman would never be taken. She'd go into the service of the bishop."

"You seem to know a lot about these matters of the rule of law."

"Like you, I listen too much. Neither of us should listen in to this kind of talk at all. These issues are best left for the men to work out." A half grin etched Julia's cheek.

"I suppose so."

"I know so. And besides, you're friends with the king's daughter. How much safer could you be?"

"The king doesn't know who I am, or that we're friends. If I caught a salmon from one of his rivers and didn't put it back for say a grayling instead, or if I killed a rabbit instead of a squirrel, he could have my hands cut off," Cass said in defiance, "and there wouldn't be anything you could do about it."

"There are laws for reasons, all of which I don't know the reasons for, but certainly I'd never let him cut off your hands. I would absolutely interfere. You are too precious to me." Julia stretched and touched the side of Cass's cheek. Her fingers stroked the soft skin beneath.

Regardless of the vigor in Cass about injustices in the kingdom, or at least injustices as she perceived them, Julia's touch melted her from inside. She hated her new-found weakness. She didn't want to desire Julia. She knew Julia's feelings toward her weren't equal to her own, yet the power wielded over her by Julia's glances and her touch was too intense to fight.

Cass dropped her line of sight and took Julia's lips onto her own. She held Julia's head between her hands and kissed her until she felt Julia's lips part and felt Julia's tongue seek entrance. Cass opened her mouth as the heat within her rose beyond comprehension. Her breath quickened. Her chest rose and fell as tongues intertwined, as if she'd run a marathon. She could spend her days happy like this forever, but she sensed this forever could not become reality.

****

The next day, excitement filled Cass due to her desire to see Julia again. She didn't care if their actions were wrong, or if Julia didn't feel the same way. She only needed to get lost in the warmth of the moment, even if the moment wasn't real or wouldn't last. She'd deal with reality when the time came.

Breathing heavily from the ascent up the hill and from her heated thoughts, Cass heard the clash of sword on sword vibrate through the air before she crested the top. She gathered the sheep and instructed them to stay together and hidden and not to move. Only if danger threatened, should they come to her. Not knowing why she understood this at a deeper level, she knew they would listen.

With only a knife-sharpened tip on the walking stick she held in her right hand, which she carried for protection when she tended sheep, Cass bent lower to the ground as she inched up the hill. Her heart raced in the hope Julia was nowhere near. She wished today was a hunting day so she'd have had her bow and arrows with her for protection. She hoped if she stayed out of sight she'd be safe, but at the same time, she had to know Julia wasn't in danger. She wanted to understand what the noise was all about in case she needed to warn her family of danger. Sweat trickled along the sides of her face and between her small breasts. Her nervousness intensified the closer she ventured.

And then she saw them. One man, a soldier, dressed in mesh armor over his clothes of white, yellow, and bright red, and a taller man, not a soldier, with a dull tunic of grey and wrapped leggings and leather wrappings over his feet and up the ankle. Both were off their horses and stood facing each other a sword's length apart.

Cass watched from behind a tree as each man cursed and swore and stepped forward and back in a swirling and jabbing of blades. The clang of each strike rang in her ears. Never had she stood this close to a real fight before. On days she was alone on the hilltop, and when hawks circled overhead, she'd watch soldiers in the distance, in the fields, spar in mock battle. She'd see the men as if through a hawk's eyes, the soldiers normally too far away to study with the naked eye. She never told anyone of this odd ability, as she was sure they'd think she was either mad or lying. Sometimes she wondered if she were mad or if she imagined she saw things she really couldn't see from her vantage point. Either way, up close, the men she now watched appeared much taller and broader than the soldiers in the fields.

Finally, after several minutes of battle, the soldier sliced his blade into the arm of his opponent. The bearded man in the dull tunic dropped his sword and clutched a bleeding right arm. "Lucky strike." He swore and staggered toward his horse.

"Not lucky. I would say merciful. If I wanted you dead, then dead you would be. Now leave here, thief, and don't let me see you in my travels again or you will suffer a different fate."

The injured man mounted his horse with difficulty and rode north, in a direction away from her. On the ground lay what appeared to be another sheathed sword with jewels reflecting the sunlight, but the soldier didn't move toward the sword. He stumbled backward toward his horse and sat on the ground clutching his left ribcage.

Not thinking, Cass dropped her walking stick and ran. "Are you okay? Are you a soldier in King Herrwald's army?" She realized as soon as she spoke his colors were slightly different than those of the soldiers she'd often seen from the hill.

Startled at first, but then seemingly relieved to see Cass was a girl, he responded. "I've been better and worse, so I think I'll live, and no, I'm not from around here. I come from Cumberland, in Northumbria and serve as knight to King Alfred III. Your king and our king are cousins, and their ancestors fought together once against a dark evil."

Cass stared as if spellbound. "I've not been on any travels, but my father and my brothers, who want to join King Herrwald's army, talk about other lands. Northumbria is north of the River Trent, is it not?"

"It is."

"You have no dealings with King Andron?"

"That horse's arse? Sorry, I meant to say horse's backside. No. I have nothing to do with one of such vacant moral character and lack of honor as he. If Alfred were able to carry out his wishes, Andron would be eliminated, but there are intricacies to peace that have to be considered and weighed, and cooler heads that often need to prevail...not to mention an old treaty..." As the man moved, he squirmed in pain.

"Stay still. I'm not a healer, but my mother taught me the healing properties of plants and I can help you," Cass said as she stood.

"You live in Mercia then?"

"I do. I take care of our sheep, among other chores." As

if on cue, the sheep topped the hill and meandered to the open grass to feed. Cass laughed. "I told you all to stay put, but go ahead and eat, it's safe now."

The man looked strangely at Cass.

"I'm going to hunt for those herbs. Stay mostly still while I'm gone, but also tear off a piece of cloth from your tunic. When I return, I'll use the material to hold on the herbs and stop the bleeding."

In less than ten minutes, Cass returned holding a flat rock, a small round rock, a bunch of yellow flowers, and a patch of moss cradled to her chest. She set the flat rock on the ground and pulled petals from the yellow-flowered plant. "I'm Cassethea, by the way. You can call me Cass."

"Very well, Cass. My name is William."

"William's my father's name also."

"I hope I do the name justice then. I appreciate you helping me."

Cass wanted to tell William how her father was most likely nothing like him—not honorable, not kind—but she kept quiet. "Of course I want to help you. You're hurt." Cass wondered what this knight's experiences were that he'd think she'd not help a person in need. There was much of the world outside her village she knew nothing about.

She ground the leaves with one rock against the other and wiped the moss into the mix. "The oils from this evening primrose will help the pain and help you heal. The moss will keep infection away. If you hold open the tear in your tunic, I'll place it on the wound for you and then we'll wrap it tight. Do you have a satchel or some other vessel I can place the remainder of the mixture in? You can take it with you and replace the dressing daily until it's gone."

From under his tunic he pulled out a black satchel and handed it to Cass. "Use this. There's only one coin left in it, which you can keep."

"No. I don't want payment for helping you. Please keep it." Cass handed the coin to William and filled the satchel with the mixture. When she completed her task, she stood and sauntered over to the sheathed sword on the ground.

"Oh, don't worry about the sword," William said as he moved his feet under him and rose. "I'll get it. You won't be able to lift it."

"I'm stronger than I look." Cass easily picked up the sword, amazed it felt almost feather-like. It was much lighter than it appeared. She'd lifted rocks before that felt much heavier than they looked but never experienced the opposite.

"Is this sword what the other man was trying to steal?" When Cass received no answer, she walked toward William and noticed a shocked expression on his face. Thinking his vision was locked on someone behind her, Cass spun around but saw no one. She turned back. "What is it? What's wrong?"

"You...the sword... It can't be."

"Can't be what? What are you trying to say?" Cass handed William the sword.

When she did, the blade sank to the ground momentarily before he lifted it up with both hands and with what appeared to be extreme effort. "How did you lift the sword? I can barely keep it up myself. This sword is not a typical sword. It's touched by magic. It's to be wielded only by a star born who will fight evil and free the oppressed—a warrior. Only the chosen one should be able to lift this." William stared a bit longer then glanced between the sheep and Cass. "I've been looking for its owner for two years now. I always assumed the warrior would be a man. But for some reason, the gods have brought me to you."

"I don't know anything about a star born. I'm a simple farmer's daughter. You must be mistaken."

"Take the sword from its sheath. Move it as if you were fighting with it," William said.

Cass pulled the shining sword from its leather covering. Her fingers barely stretched around the hilt, but the balance felt perfect. She swung it overhead and around to the left and right. The blade sung as it sliced through the air. "This is amazing!"

William gave her the sheath and bowed. "This, Lady of Mercia, is yours to keep. Show it to no one and tell no one about it. One day I believe it will serve you well. Until then, protect it. If ever you need anything from me, know that I'll be there for you. Having found you has truly been an honor." He unstrapped a matching dagger from around the bottom of his right leg. "Take this, too, as a personal gift from me. It has served me well, and I'd like you to have it."

Cass stood perplexed and at a loss for words. She took the dagger and held it next to the sheath as she slid the sword in its place. "I don't know what to say. You are much too kind. I still think you're mistaken about me, though."

"I assure you. I made no mistake. Many a man has tried to hold up this sword and failed, myself included. The sword has found its owner, of that I'm certain. Time will tell the rest of this story." William grabbed the reins of his sleek black horse, and with a painful grunt, swung onto the saddle. "Take care, Cassethea of Mercia, and may the gods always grace you," he said, and rode off.

Chapter Nine

The next three days, Jess's team made good progress on the dig. Indication of the walls and entrance posts from the longhouse came into view, identified by the slight variations in the soil coloring. But her excitement wasn't as evident as one might expect. First, Rayne had been unusually quiet and distant since their dinner and the mention of her prior ex. She only talked about the weather or nothing at all when she delivered their lunchtime meals.

Plus, Jess's mind continued recalling images of Cass's life at inopportune times, or what she believed were insights into Cass's life. The vision she saw of Cassethea kissing another female? Was she gay? It appeared so. The revelation was more than she'd hoped for. But were the images real? They certainly felt real to Jess. Either the dreams she experienced were actual images or visions from a prior time, or she sat at the precipice about to lose her mind. Both options were equally viable, but one was clearly preferable over the other. By the time Wednesday evening rolled around, Jess grasped the notion only one option remained open to her to maintain her sanity; she needed to call El.

The phone rang twice before a familiar voice answered.

"Hey, stranger," El said. "You have good timing. What's up?"

"Hey, El, it's so good to hear your voice. What are you doing?" Jess asked.

"I just finished lunch. I polished off leftover lasagna from my dinner out with Gayle last night."

"Gayle, as in the woman you tried to set me up with?"

"Yes, one and the same. You know I wouldn't set you up with a loser, and I did say I'd meet with her, which I did, and so far, she's been great. We hit it off the first night. We have another date Saturday night."

Jess ran her fingers through her hair. "That's fantastic, El. I'm so happy for you. I told you everything happened for a reason. Or, at least I used to believe a reason existed."

"What's that supposed to mean? What's going on, Jess? Is something wrong? Are you okay? And do not—in capital letters—bullshit me."

"You stated that as suavely as ever, my friend."

"Thank you. Now spill it."

"Okay, fine. You would consider me a generally sane person, wouldn't you?"

"I would."

"And I've never been one to fantasize or exaggerate the truth or spin tall tales, have I?"

"Not for as long as I've known you, no."

"Okay, then how is it, since I've been here, I've seen visions of the woman I've been searching to find and hoping is buried at this site?" Jess asked, exasperation evident in her voice.

"And by visions, you mean...?"

"Dreams mostly, I think. I see Cassethea as a young woman, in her house with her family: a mother, a father, three brothers, and a younger sister. I see her tending sheep and getting into trouble. I see her with her friend, Julianta, the king's daughter. She kisses her for God's sake! She...she...meets a knight from Northumbria...a man searching for the person destined to hold the magic sword Cassethea's later known to be connected with...she goes by the nickname Cass...and she's star born...whatever that means."

"Holy hell! Don't hold back now, by all means."

"Funny. You think I'm crazy, don't you? Hell, I think I'm crazy."

A moment of silence passed. "No. Not necessarily, though stress and working too hard have been known to cause mental breaks in people similar to what you've explained, but I don't see a mental breakdown in your cards. You've spent years successfully coping with stress. And yes, I think a modicum of humor is appropriate at this moment. Seriously though, Jess, when did the dreams start? And be specific."

Jess remained quiet as she tried to remember the day and

what had transpired before the dream. A few moments later, she said, "The first dream happened the night after we broke ground at the site. I felt odd, nauseous, almost. I felt it earlier in the day, too, around lunchtime. I figured I needed food. But that night it felt like I couldn't move and things got kind of fuzzy and suddenly I was thrust into this girl's world. It was as though I was reliving her life through her. I've never experienced anything like it. And I can't see how it can be real and yet at the same time, I don't know how or why I'd make this all up."

"I have to agree with you, Jess. I don't see how you'd have come to certain details on your own, either, or why you'd create them. And what strikes me particularly odd is you've always had a fascination for uncovering the past. For years, you've been drawn to finding out more about this one person. It's possible your obsession is no coincidence."

"Obsession is harsh," Jess said.

"Regardless, once you broke ground, you experienced these dreams, which honestly, I'd be more apt to call visions. The timing is too coincidental. Visions can be an extension of the soul. There's no concrete proof of one's continued existence, but in theory, existence beyond death is possible. I'm talking about reincarnation, transcendence, immortality of the soul, call it what you will, but in the end, the continuation of a person's existence or soul and/or mind through time and space, whether through divine intervention or by some other means, is real. The Egyptians, of whom you know I'm particularly fond, believed the spirit, the body's life force, its immortal soul or Ka, lived forever. Today, youth talk about living forever, achieved by downloading their brainwaves or some such nonsense into a cloud or other expansive storage device. Students in my classes have held in-depth discussions with me on this very matter, and they take it seriously. And who knows, in a thousand years from now, maybe immortality attained through downloading brainwaves won't be considered nonsense. What I think happened here, Jess, is something amazing but also something you need to be very, very careful of. Stay grounded, but don't shut out these visions. There's a reason you've been granted this insight, of that I'm certain."

Jess breathed a sigh of relief. Being told she wasn't crazy was an enormous weight lifted off her mind. And everything El said made perfect sense. She just couldn't believe this was happening to her. "Thank you, El. I knew I called the right person. I can't tell you how much your evaluation of my situation, and your insight, mean to me."

"You're always welcome, and yes, of course I was the right person. I know you can't see me wink right now, but I'm winking at you."

Jess let a chuckle escape. "Thanks for the visual. I'd hug you big time right now if I could. I'm so exhausted at this minute. I think I could fall asleep where I'm standing."

"Chill out, my friend. Have a beer. Go out and have some fun. Take your mind off your work for one night, at least, and feel honored that you were apparently chosen for something special here. I mean hell, who has a chance to go back in time and truly experience the world as it was, am I right?"

"You're right on both counts, El. I owe you. And good luck with Gayle. I look forward to meeting her." Jess clicked off the phone. She ignored her tiredness, threw on a light jacket, and marched out the door to Eagles Landing.

****

"What do I need to do around here to get served?" Jess said to Rayne, with a smirk. She'd surprised herself to learn, when El told her to relax and have fun, the first thought that popped into her mind was to see Rayne. Granted, she and Rayne had a nice dinner out, but that was days ago, and Rayne had been unusually quiet on the ride home and quiet since. Rayne was a difficult person to figure out, but that didn't deter Jess from trying. "And why have you been so quiet ever since our last outing?"

"You are direct, aren't you?" Rayne said.

"You already know I am. Now, I'm going to order, possibly something of your suggestion, and then I'm going to wait for you to bring the meal to my table and for you to take a fifteen-minute break to talk to me. How does that sound?"

"The first words that come to mind are commanding and not bloody likely. However, considering I've been a bit of a bugger of late, I'd say your request sounds fair."

"Yes, 'fair' is a better word." Jess spun on her heel and located an empty table.

Moments later, Rayne approached Jess with a plate holding a roasted half side of duck, mashed potatoes, and string beans, and she carried two half pints of ale. Jess smiled. "The food looks and smells fabulous."

"Hopefully it tastes equally good or better." Rayne set the plate in front of Jess and put the drinks on the table.

"Drinking on the job are we, or are both of these for me?"

"I can't speak for you, but my day's officially over," Rayne said as she sat next to Jess.

"Is it? Good to know, though interesting you didn't mention it before. Have you eaten?"

"I have." Rayne paused as Jess cut off a piece of duck, added a dollop of potato, and pierced a string bean. "And before you ask, which I know you will, I'm aware I have some explaining to do." A smile graced Rayne's face at the apparent look of approval from Jess.

Jess swallowed and took a sip of ale. She found she liked the beer at cellar temperature rather than ice cold. "You do, but I'm patient."

Rayne flashed a sideways glance in Jess's direction. "Right, I mean you did wait four whole days to confront me."

"To my credit, I did, so please continue."

Rayne shook her head. "You are something else. I give you kudos. Fine. When we discussed the excavation at dinner, and I mentioned my interest in medieval art and artifacts at university, the conversation brought with it unwanted memories of my ex, Zara. Zara taught a British Literature class that crossed over into the historical arts. I thought the class would be an interesting elective, and it turned out I was right, but not in the way I thought. Zara drove me arse-over-tit before I knew it."

"Wow, don't withhold details on my account," Jess said. "Although...your colorful language makes you sound a good deal like my best friend, Ellie. The two of you would undoubtedly get along well."

"My apologies if I spoke too frankly. Sometimes working

the pub rubs off on me in the wrong way."

"No need to apologize. I'm sorry I interrupted you. Go on." Jess leaned against the chair with her drink in hand.

"Right. At any rate, we spent a lot of time together, just the two of us in the beginning, but as time moved on, she wanted me involved more and more with her friends and colleagues. She convinced me to attend boring parties, which I interpreted as intellectual fencing matches, where the people who attended did so to see who could one-up the other. Needless to say, I didn't have much to add to the conversations and felt uncomfortable most of the time, but Zara didn't seem to mind or care. And in the presence of these gatherings of so-called friends, I saw her in a different light. Maybe it's the first time I actually saw her for who she was, and I didn't like what I saw. Our relationship fell apart after more and more of those gatherings. Our discussions became emotionally distant and pretentious. I swore I'd never bother with another teacher again."

"I'm sure you realize we're not all like your ex and her friends."

"Jury's still out on that one." Rayne finished her ale and noticed Jess's empty mug as well. "Would you like another?"

"Sure, thanks. I'll go up and get them."

"No, let me," Rayne insisted. "My pub...my rules. I wouldn't want you to get the wrong impression that I'm easy to command." Rayne gathered Jess's empty plate and their mugs and marched toward the bar before Jess was able to formulate a worthy response.

Jess tried not to watch Rayne's every step as she walked away from the table, but she couldn't help herself. She blamed the side effect of the strong ale as having interfered with her otherwise better judgment. She and Rayne lived on two separate continents, literally. No good could come from contemplating anything except a friendship with Rayne. When Rayne stepped behind the bar, Jess realized Baron's line of sight focused on her, and when he saw Jess notice him, he waved.

Seconds after his wave, Baron became the recipient of what appeared to be a playful shove from his sister, which he promptly returned. Jess sensed the two were probably very close. Likely they had to be if they worked together nearly every day. The patrons at the bar were vocal and interacted with the brother and sister pair as well, though Jess couldn't hear what they all said to one another. When Rayne returned, Jess forced herself to look elsewhere rather than be caught staring.

"Rowdy bunch up there tonight." Rayne placed the drinks on the table.

"Seems you started the commotion with the shove you gave your brother."

"He deserved it. He was unabashedly staring at you. Not that there's anything wrong with that, necessarily, but..." Rayne paused, appearing to search for her next words.

Jess eyed Rayne skeptically. "But...what?"

"But staring isn't polite, is what."

"Is that right? And why did everyone else at the bar get into the action?"

"The answer to that question I can't give you right now, nor may I ever," Rayne said.

"I'll grant you a pass for now. But you should know, I will drag the facts from you eventually. It's a skill taught to me by my best friend. By the way, did you know George visits me at the site almost every day?"

"Another one enthralled with you? This has to stop," Rayne joked.

Jess's puzzled stare returned her gaze.

"Seriously though, if George bothers you, I'll tell him to stop."

"You'll tell him to stop, and poof, just like that he will?"

"I told you. He's a very smart dog."

Jess didn't answer immediately but then added, "He must be. He likes me. I don't want you to tell him to stop his visits. I love the company. Granted, I don't have time to give him a lot of attention, but he makes his rounds, and he stays outside the dig site lines. He's a great dog. Everyone likes him. What breed is he anyway, or is he a mix?"

"Did you say 'a mix,' as in...is George a mutt?" Rayne asked. She pretended to be offended as she swallowed half her ale. "He is a mix, but not the way you'd think. He's a designer breed—an Alaskan Malador. At least, that's what the vet said."

"I've not heard of that breed before."

"They're not common in America. After I found out what breed he was, I looked him up on the Internet. An Alaskan Malador is a mix between an Alaskan Malamute and a Labrador Retriever. They're known for their loyalty. They're playful, friendly, super smart, and affectionate. But they're not great at being ignored, which you can apparently attest to."

"I've not seen an Alaskan Malamute before, but Labs are super popular in the States. As for affectionate, I noticed he does enjoy a good belly rub."

Rayne rolled her eyes. "On another note, how's the excavation going? From what my untrained eyes have seen, you appear to be making good progress."

"We are, but I'd probably need another half-dozen people if I wanted this wrapped up in six weeks. I'm not sure we'll finish by the end of the summer."

"Can you extend your time if you need to?"

"Only if I get additional funding and only up until the fall semester starts," Jess said. "Then I've got classes again. Looks like extra hours might be in order. Speaking of work, I should go. I want to finish cleaning and cataloging the items we dug up today, and I've taken up enough of your free evening."

"You found artifacts already?"

"We did. They're pottery fragments mostly, nothing overly exciting."

"If you're leaving now, I'll walk with you. My place is only a short distance around the corner from where the site is," Rayne said.

"Really?" Jess said.

"Really. This is a small town after all. How far away could I be?"

"True, I suppose."

As they exited, Rayne held the door open for Jess. "Have you had a chance to sightsee in our fabulous country yet?"

"I don't have time for self-indulgences really. As I said, there's still so much to do."

"Don't you get the weekends off?"

"Yes and no. We usually work Saturdays. Sundays we're technically off, though I planned to use that time to review the drawings and our records while it's quiet."

"Then you definitely wouldn't be interested in a trip to Gloucester Cathedral in Gloucestershire, where they shot some exterior scenes from the Harry Potter film and the Hogwarts corridors, I take it?"

The pause was demonstrable. "How do you know I'm a huge J.K. Rowling fan?"

"It's not like I Googled you or anything."

"Good to know."

"But seriously, who's not a fan? Let's call my insight women's intuition." As Rayne waited for an answer that didn't come quickly, she added, "And you could consider it a way for me to make up for my foul behavior of ignoring you the last four days."

"When you put it that way, I suppose I can't refuse."

"Brilliant. I'll see what time the cathedral's closed for services, so we can work around their schedule."

"Great. I look forward to it."

Chapter Ten

Cass sat across from Gollyn and ate the rye bread given to her for breakfast. Alfred spoke about joining the king's army and the training he'd heard new members went through, but she only half listened. In only weeks, her father would let him join. The calends of May was upon them. With repairs to the thatched roof completed, the fields ploughed, fertilized, and planted, and with Sedwick, Gollyn, and Cass left to help their father on the farm, plus the promise of one less mouth to feed, Cass was certain her father would now let Alfred go. She'd miss her brother terribly. In many ways, Alfred and Cass were similar, but he chose a life ahead of him that he wanted, whereas she worried her life would be dictated to her.

The events from the prior month kept her up many nights. She often wondered about what Knight William had revealed, thinking still he must have been mistaken about her. Keeping her secret weighed on her. She'd done as promised and told no one of her encounter, not even Julia, and hid the sword and dagger in the trunk of a hollowed-out tree on her favorite hilltop. When no one was around, she practiced throwing the dagger and wielding the sword at an imaginary opponent. She kept herself entertained outside of her current reality.

"Cassethea? Did you hear what I said?" her mother asked.

Cass glanced at her father whose narrowed eyes revealed he was not pleased. "Sorry, I didn't."

"While your father goes into town today to see the blacksmith, you will help your brothers weed the fields and keep the crows away. Work the farthest field with Gollyn. You can take the sheep with you to graze in the adjoining meadow," Arielwund said.

Before Cass moved to answer, her father bellowed,

"Let's get to work. We've another long day ahead of us."

****

Cass's back ached from hours spent bent over, pulling weeds. She wasn't used to working in the field. She worked hard though. She cleared four rows to every two Gollyn cleared so he didn't have to work as hard. Gollyn was different from his brothers in that he was thinner than both of them, got sick more often, and didn't have an interest in play fighting or seeing who could jump the farthest or hold their breath the longest. In terms of the way their father viewed the two of them, her and Gollyn, they were similar. Both were looked down upon, but for different reasons.

Not getting many chances to talk to Gollyn alone otherwise, Cass took their lunch break as an opportunity to learn his thoughts and possibly fears. "What do you think about Alfred leaving soon?" Cass asked, as she sat with her feet crossed at the edge of the field. She handed Gollyn a slice of bread and cheese.

"I'm happy for him, I suppose, but worried at the same time. What if there's a war? He could get killed." Gollyn ate the bread with little gusto.

"He's strong and smart. He'll be fine. It's what he wants to do...where his heart is."

"Yes, I know. Sedwick wants to be exactly like him. He idolizes him."

"Yes. And what about you, what do you want? You've never really said."

"I don't care much about fighting. I'd like to learn how to read and write. I think there's a lot to learn about the world, but we never get to see any of it. That won't change for me, either, I don't think. I've sometimes dreamed of joining the monastery. Maybe one day I'd become a priest. I'd like to help people."

On some level, Cass guessed he embraced such an interest. "Does Father know?"

"No, and please don't say anything to anyone, especially him. I'm sure Father wouldn't approve. He'd want me to join the army like Alfred and Sedwick. He probably thinks it manlier."

"Yes, no doubt he would. Be careful, though. I think that a monastery has the potential to be a different kind of prison." Cass swallowed the last piece of cheese.

****

The air sucked from Cassethea's lungs when she heard her father announce at dinner that Princess Julianta was betrothed to Prince Richard from Normandy and that they were to be wed midsummer. Cass fought to keep her expression neutral as her insides churned at the revelation. How could this be happening? Why hadn't Julia told her? Did Julia want to marry this Prince Richard? Had she ever even met him before?

Cass listened half-heartedly as her father reminded everyone that Princess Julianta was Cass's age. He talked about what he saw as the benefit of the marriage, that England might strengthen its military forces in fighting off the Vikings. But all Cass could think about was losing Julia from her life forever, which would happen if the marriage took place. Only Gollyn appeared to take note of Cass's distress, although she did catch her mother glance away at one point. Cass understood that she and Julia could not continue on as they had in recent weeks, that they'd eventually have to live their own lives. She didn't think she'd never see her best friend again. But there was nothing to do this eventide. Tomorrow she'd talk to Julia, or at least she hoped she would, and maybe none of what her father said would reveal true.

****

But Cass soon found out his words rang accurate. This day, when she rounded the top of the hill with the sheep, Julia waited for her. Cass stood frozen when she saw her. It was as though Julia already guessed Cass had heard the rumors. "Why? Why didn't you tell me? Is it true? Are you to marry this man from Normandy?"

Julia ran to Cass and hugged her. "Cass, I'm sorry."

Cass pushed her away. "Please, don't." Cass held back

the tears. "You should have told me."

Julia stepped away. "I'd only been told two days ago myself, Cass, and when I came to tell you yesterday, you weren't here. That's why I'm so early today. Please don't be cross."

Cass was unsure what to say. She possessed no right to act upset with Julia. This was how the world was supposed to be, yet she felt betrayed. The closeness they'd shared. Swimming in the stream together, telling each other secrets, holding hands...kissing. The kisses were Cass's downfall, and she'd realized it after their first time. She should have known better. She should have been stronger. Now she'd pay the price. "Do you want to marry him?"

"I've not thought much about what I want and don't want, Cass. Marrying a man my family chooses for me is the path my life was meant to take. I'm fine with my father's selection, if that's what you're asking."

"Have you met him before? How old is he?"

"I met him six months ago, when he visited his aunt with his father. He was pleasant enough and not bad to look at. I believe he's nine and twenty winters."

"Nine and twenty winters? He's almost twice your age!"

"What does age matter? As long as he loves me and cares for me?" Julia asked.

"Loves you? He doesn't even know you."

Julia shook her head. "I don't know why you're so upset, Cass. Why are you always trying to buck everything that is? Nothing is ever good enough for you. Can't you live your life like everyone else and accept life as it comes? Do you have to stand alone against the tide? In some ways, I admire you for your uniqueness and conviction, but in other ways, I feel sorry for you because of it."

"I don't need you to feel sorry for me. I have a mind of my own, and I plan to use it," Cass said, before she faced in the opposite direction.

Julia extended her hand. "Don't go, Cass. Let's not leave our friendship like this, please? Please let's just spend some time together. Let's talk and be together, all right? Let the dust settle. Tomorrow all of this will seem different to you. And in truth, none of what is happening should really be a surprise, only who and when were the unknowns."

Cass stood firm for several minutes until her resolve faltered. Of course Julia was right. Of course she knew what the outcome of their relationship would eventually be. But she didn't have to like it. Cass took Julia's hand and let her lead her to their blanket, the blanket Julia always brought with her to the hill. They talked for two hours, ate lunch, and talked more, and they'd kissed, over and over, regardless of how painful Cass knew the kisses would be. In the end, they'd fallen asleep together. But when Cass woke, the world had not changed. Julia would still be married within months. Worst of all, marriage was what Julia wanted.

****

The walk home that evening spanned the longest stretch of time Cass had ever taken. She couldn't get her feet to move. She lagged behind the sheep, as if walking slower would keep her near Julia longer or change the inevitable. Enveloped in a mind fog, her entire body felt sluggish and weak. She felt as though she could collapse where she stood and sleep forever. But her clouded state meant she wasn't thinking about protecting the animals. Her mind didn't subconsciously ward off predators as she normally did, and her lapse in judgment was about to change her life in an irreversible way.

Before she sensed danger, she heard her father yell. The sheep were only a hundred yards from the barn, with Cass another fifty yards behind. A massive wolf stood on the edge of the forest. Her father placed an arrow on the bowstring. Cass bolted toward the herd of sheep. She quickly caught up and then surpassed them. "No!" she yelled to her father as he strung the bow and aimed. By this time, Arielwund stood outside as well. Cass ran between her father and the wolf. "Leave the sheep! Back up now!" she yelled in the wolf's direction. Then she faced her father.

The wolf arched out of his pouncing stance and took several steps backward toward the woods.

"Don't shoot him, Father, please!"

"Get out of my way!" he yelled. "We can't afford to lose

one of the king's sheep. How will we repay him?"

"You won't lose one sheep, I swear. The wolf is retreating. Look." Cass's heart beat wildly. She watched the realization hit her father that the wolf was indeed backing off and no longer appeared to be a threat.

"What is this?" William yelled. "What are you, a damned witch?"

Arielwund and Cass's brothers and sister stood outside and watched the nightmare unfold as Cass stood facing her father with nothing to say.

"Get the hell out of my way, witch, while I make sure that killer thinks twice before coming here again to harm our animals." William strung the bow tight and let the arrow fly.

The arrow made a whizzing sound as it barely missed Cass's head and stunned her for a moment. But just as quickly, she recovered, turned, and yelled "No! Run!" But the arrow found its mark in the wolf's hind flank.

William's face colored red and contorted with anger. "You! Witch! I knew there was something not right with you. For years I knew it, but your mother always protected you. Not anymore!"

"William, no, please!" Arielwund stood next to her sons, while Emma held her hand and cried.

"Hold your tongue! I don't want to hear anymore. This witch needs to leave our home and never come back. There is an evil inside her," William bellowed.

Arielwund pleaded. "You're wrong, William. You don't mean what you say. You're angry right now, but you'll see in the morning that all of this is a misunderstanding. Cassethea protected the sheep the way she knew how. She did nothing wrong."

"You have a half an hour to pack her things and get her out of my sight. I should have tossed her out years ago. There is no further discussion in this matter." William flung the bow to the ground and marched off toward the fields.

Cass stood shaking in front of her family, holding back the tears. "I'm not a witch," she whispered. "I'm not."

Arielwund picked up Emma and ran to Cass and hugged her. "I know you're not. I know. Your father...he doesn't understand. He doesn't understand... many things. I've never been able to talk to him. He's more stubborn than anyone I know. But that knowledge doesn't help us now. It will grow dark soon. We have no time to waste. Get inside. I'll pack your shoulder bag. God knows you can't go off without food or decent clothes. And God forgive us when you do."

Cass stood still at first, her mind and body seemingly in shock. As she finally passed her brothers, they stared blankly, as if uncertain whether they should believe their father or their mother regarding Cass. Their apathy stung more than her father's words.

Inside, Arielwund grabbed clothes and food and any useful items from what little they owned and stuffed them into the spacious shoulder bag. She tied off the top with a thin strip of leather. Arielwund held her head close to her daughter's. Cass felt her mother tremble as she spoke.

"Listen to me. There are many things I should have told you many winters ago, but I didn't know if you'd be ready to hear them. You are special. Do you hear me? There is nothing wrong with you, and you are not a witch. But you are special. Remember that always, and remember that I love you more than I cherish my own life. Be strong. Hide when you need to. I packed a set of Sedwick's clothes. Wear those and get rid of that dress. Trust me on this. It will be better for you if you are mistaken for a boy. And most of all, remember who you are and where you came from through your dreams. Your dreams will be your pathway to understanding. All will become clear, I promise. I love you." Arielwund kissed the top of Cass's head. She handed her the bow and arrow. "Take these. Your brother can make another. Now go before your father comes home. In his state of mind, I don't know what he could do. And please be safe, and strong, and good. Always be good. Promise me."

Tears poured from Cass. "I will, Mum, I promise."

"Hurry now. Off you go. Use what God and the universe have given you. I think you already experienced some of what those gifts are. If you can, find a way to let me know you are well."

Cass barely managed to say, "I'll try. Good-bye." At that moment, though, she bore no idea what she was supposed to do, where to go, or how she'd survive. In her mind, her father doled out the equivalent of a death sentence for her, a slow death rather than a quick one. And by the look on her mother's face, Cass sensed she thought so, too. Unable to bear the sadness any longer, Cass ran from the house to the only other place she felt somewhat safe. She ran to the hilltop.

****

Cass sensed she was being followed soon after she left the house but didn't glance behind her until she hiked to the top of the hill. There, fifty feet below her, lagged the injured wolf. His mass was greater than any wolf she'd seen before, which may have added to the fright she'd seen in her father's eyes, or maybe the wolf appeared larger because of his proximity.

Cass approached him one slow step at a time, her hand extended. The wolf stood stoic, head held high, his stare fixed on Cass, but not in an intimidating way. He allowed her to step next to him and pushed his head against her hand as she did.

"There you go. You know I won't hurt you, don't you? I'm not like my father. I apologize for what he did to you. Sit if you can. I'd like to examine your hind flank." Cass stroked his head. When the wolf sat, Cass continued to glide her hands over him, from his head to his front leg, to his side, and ultimately the rear leg. He twitched at her touch, when her fingers slid over the arrow stuck there.

Cass didn't know if the wolf would understand her words, probably he did not, but she sensed he understood she would help, rather than hurt him. "Stay here. I'm going to gather plants that will help heal your wound, and then we are going to pull that arrow out, hopefully in one piece." The wolf lowered his paws and lay on his good side before she walked away.

When Cass returned, dusk engulfed the hill. Touch, rather than sight, became her main ally now. She mashed a healing poultice for the wolf's leg and set it to the side. She prayed the wolf wouldn't bite her. She grabbed the end of the arrow nearest his leg before she could change her mind and yanked the obstruction from him. He yelped as his body jerked from the pain. "That's it now, boy. The worst is over. You will survive," she said in a soothing tone.

Once she'd applied the poultice and wrapped the leg, exhaustion overtook her. She reached into her bag and pulled out a blanket her mum folded up for her. She laid it on the ground behind the wolf and snuggled against him. He pushed into her, and within moments, she slept.

****

The sun's warm rays caressed Cass's face after she awoke from a long night spent on the hard ground. For the briefest of moments, she thought she'd dreamt about the incident with her father and the wolf, but there he lay, by her side. She was sorry her father injured him, but at the same time, she was thankful for the wolf's presence.

Cass wondered if Julia would come to the hill today and whether she should tell her what happened. But she was embarrassed by her father's actions. She didn't want to repeat the false name he called her to anyone, especially not to Julia. She knew she wasn't a witch, but the word stung nonetheless. And how would she explain her injured partner to Julia?

Cass chewed on the end of a blade of grass as she contemplated what to do. Where would she go? How would she survive? She knew Julia wouldn't be around many more days. Being near her was becoming too painful anyway, and holding onto the growing secrets she carried felt deceitful.

Cass's stomach growled and tossed her from her inner thoughts. She squinted at her furry partner. "You're hungry, too, aren't you? You probably blame me for your empty stomach. I'd blame me, too, if I were you. I'll make it up to you, I promise. Stay here and I'll be back."

Cass grabbed her bag and her bow and arrow. When she reached the stream, she knelt and washed her face. Seeing her reflection, she remembered her mother's words. She glanced around her, and seeing no one, took off her woolen dress, washed, and changed into her brother's tunic. The tunic extended mid thigh. Next, she slid on his woolen trousers which, although they felt awkward at first, were more freeing than the dress.

Cass returned with breakfast, which consisted of a beaver for the wolf and a squirrel for herself. She'd recovered the dagger Sir William had gifted her from the hollowed base of the oak tree she'd hidden it in. With it, she skinned both animals. She threw the beaver carcass to the wolf and marveled how fast he ripped it apart and devoured it, bones and all. A shiver ran up her spine as the realization set in that he was a wild animal after all.

While the wolf licked his paws, Cass cleared an area of grass and brush and dug a hole for a fire. In it she placed twigs and other dry leaves as well as wood shavings from a dead branch she broke off a birch tree. She wished she'd taken a hot coal from the hearth at home, knowing that starting a fire from scratch would be an arduous task, and one not guaranteed to be successful. But since wishing for something was not enough to make it come true, she went to work.

With the dagger, she split the thickest part of the birch branch into three pieces, separating a flat part from the middle of the branch that she laid on the ground. In the flat piece, she carved a hole. From the next largest piece, she hacked one end almost round and stripped the bark from it. The third piece of the branch she kept for wood shavings. She placed the rounded end of the bare stick into the carved hole of the wood on the ground and held the flat part of the wood with her feet. With her palms, she started at the top of the stick, rubbed it between her hands, and slid her hands along the stick from top to bottom. She continued the motion over and over and over until her hands were reddened, hot, and sore, but produced a pebble-sized coal at the base of the stick. She lifted the flat piece of wood and gingerly dropped the coal into a nest of dried grass, held it between her hands, and blew on it until the smoke intensified and a flame ignited. Careful not to burn her hands, she placed the nest into the hole in the ground and watched it ignite the other grass, wood shavings, and twigs, as the flame took on its own life. She tucked the newly fashioned homemade fire starter and her dagger into her shoulder bag and waited while the squirrel cooked.

****

Stomach filled, Cass wondered how she'd explain her current situation to Julia. Would she ever see Julia again? Part of her wished she'd not see her, and part of her still craved her touch. Perhaps, in a way, Julia's marriage was a blessing. Her feelings for Julia had to be unnatural. She never heard of or saw other women kiss or touch as they had done. Those acts were reserved for between a man and a woman. Why then, had it felt so right? None of the past mattered now, though. Cass needed to put the thought of Julia as anything other than a friend behind her. Her one-sided feelings would do her no service. She needed to focus on the future, whatever that meant.

She thought about what her mother had said, about being safer if she dressed like her brother and looked like a boy. And while she was dressed like her brother now, she'd not been able to bring herself to cut short her long brown hair. While she remained on the hilltop, perhaps a day or two more days until the wolf's leg healed enough for him to walk without a limp, and while he chose to stay with her, she felt safe, long hair and all. Once she left the hilltop, she understood she'd need to cut her hair. And if she were to see Julia again before leaving, cutting her hair would require an explanation she wasn't prepared to give. For wearing her brother's clothes, she was certain she would find an excuse for Julia if she thought hard enough on it.

The rest of the day, Cass gathered dry, dead wood, scraped clean the skin from the squirrel and rubbed it smooth with a stone. She let it dry in the sun and later wrapped it around the jeweled end of her dagger. She'd need to wrap the sword hilt in animal hide as well before she left the hilltop, but the beaver pelt she fashioned into a makeshift water bladder to carry water to camp for the wolf.

****

Cass smelled smoke and sprang from the blanket, this the third night on the hill with Gray, whom she named the day before. The two had been left alone—no Julia, and no visits from her family, not that her family had any reason to think she'd be nearby. Gray stood as well, the swelling on his leg gone and wound near healed.

"Something's not right. I need to check on my mother and Emma." Cass collected her shoulder bag and other belongings. "This is likely good-bye, my friend. Thank you for your companionship these past days. I don't know how I would've survived mentally out here without you. You take care of yourself." She stroked Gray one last time on the head, sadness in her heart. "I'll miss you."

Cass turned, and before she could cry, ran off down the hill toward the dwelling she'd once called home. As her home came into view, or what remained of the home, Cass's steps slowed to a near stop. She stood before the burned-out and smoldering remains of the stick-and-mud structure once called home, stunned and dumbfounded by what her eyes took in. All around her, homes were burned. The sheep were gone, as were the pigs. She yelled, but no one answered, and yelled again. She glanced around the property and staggered toward the fields, yelling for her mother and brothers until her eyes locked on an object.

With legs of lead, she stumbled forward toward a body lying face down near the edge of the closest field, nearly hidden in the tall grass. Nausea crept up her throat as she fought it back. "No, no, no...please not one of us...please, not one of us," she repeated, her stare laser focused. Sweat dripped between her breasts the closer she got to the body until she recognized the figure and dropped to her knees. Gently, she rolled the body over. Young, innocent Gollyn, eyes frozen open, body sliced through the middle and blood soaked, stared back with lifeless eyes.

Cass grabbed him into her arms and wailed. His cold cheek sent chills through her already numb body. Who could commit such a violent act against another person? Embodied this person no soul?

The grief Cass thought she'd experienced the past week for what she knew to be the final chapter with Julia, being cast from her home, and leaving Gray, was nothing compared to her new reality. She rocked and rocked with Gollyn in her arms, for how many minutes or hours she didn't know. Finally, she released Gollyn and closed his eyes. Only then did she survey the area once more from where she knelt. She saw nothing but devastation throughout their village, but no bodies other than her brother's. What about her mother, father, Alfred, Sedwick, and Emma? What happened to them? Cass barely pulled her thoughts together, but she registered Gollyn deserved a burial.

Rummaging through the remains of their home, she found a spade whose handle was charred but not fully damaged. She located a metal pot and two wooden bowls that she placed in her shoulder bag for future use. She also located an ax.

Feet from where Gollyn lay, within the edge of the garden, she sliced the spade into the ground. She dug the remainder of the day as her back ached in protest. She rested only long enough to eat what was left of the dry, now hardened, bread her mother had given her days before. As she ate, tears rolled down her cheeks. When she finished her task and Gollyn was covered by mother earth, she sat and prayed.

As the sun sank lower in the sky, she heard her name called out. "Cassethea? Is that you?" a woman yelled.

Cass stood, brushed the soil from her trousers, and trudged toward the dirt road where a lone figure stood. Her neighbor, Saewyn, stood in the road, a russet sack in hand, about as dirty and disheveled as Cass. "Saewyn. What happened? Where is everyone?"

Saewyn placed her hand in the crux of Cass's back. "Let's talk while we walk as the sun will soon set." Saewyn told Cass of the Viking raid the night before, and how the men or boys who'd been killed were buried by the king's army who came looking for the Vikings. "Some of those who survived are living in the next village over. That's where our family is...with my sister. Many men were injured, but most of the women were taken. For some reason, our family was spared. Brethel, my husband, was injured, but he will live. Your brothers, Alfred and Sedwick, joined the army, as did other boys their age. A band of men took them to the castle, while the others moved on after the Vikings."

"What about my father? Were Emma and my mother

taken?" Cass asked, fear in her eyes.

"From what rumors I hear, your father and a few cowardly others have found solace in the tavern, seemingly unhurt and uncaring."

Cass seethed in anger. She wished he stood in front of her now so she could slap his face and yell at his heartless, yellow soul. "Sadly, I'm not surprised."

"There's also recent rumor that Princess Julianta was taken."

"What? No, that can't be true." As shaken and washed out as she no doubt already appeared, Cass felt the remaining color drain from her. Julia hadn't been to the hill. It wasn't because she chose not to go, but because she was taken. How could the day get any worse? She felt her knees weaken. "And what of my mother and Emma?" She barely managed to whisper.

"Taken."

Chapter Eleven

Sluggishness engulfed Jess as she woke to start her day after another round of haunted visions. Her body moved as though she'd not eaten in days. Although she still looked forward to the sightseeing tour with Rayne, which included a visit to the cathedral, her prior abnormal excitement over the excursion waned in the shadow of her visions.

Jess experienced difficulty clearing her mind of the knowledge of what Cass's father had done to Cass. What possessed the man to throw his own daughter from her home? The medieval era carried enough hardships and survival struggles for those with shelter and family support, but to discard a fifteen-year-old girl, with no heart or remorse, as a result of stupid superstitious beliefs, rose beyond the pale. In Jess's eyes, Cass's father's actions were unforgiveable.

Jess understood in those days the concept to oppose a husband wouldn't have been instilled in Arielwund. The notion of disobedience didn't exist. Independence of mind and spirit didn't exist. Women possessed no such free will or power, which made Cass all the more of an anomaly, a fact her friend Julia alluded to in their last discussion on the hill. Julia told Cass she acted more like a boy than a girl. She pointed out she knew no girl or woman who wanted to engage in swordplay, learn how to read and write, join the army, or be able to marry whom she wanted, when she wanted. Cass though, rejected Julia's words.

Jess couldn't imagine the fear that must have run through Cass's mind, and the betrayal she felt in her heart, when her father banned her from the family. And as if the separation wasn't enough to bear, piled on that came Gollyn's death and the uncertainty of not knowing what happened to the rest of her family and her best friend. The anguish must have been unbearable.

Jess clutched her chest as a sharp pain pierced her heart and caused her to skip a breath, her empathy for Cass all too real. "Relax and breathe, Jess," she told herself. "Relax and breathe."

After she washed, ate breakfast, and tackled two hours of work, Jess rebounded into some semblance of normal. She convinced herself not to take her dreams to heart, that the dreams belonged to the past and simply reflected those times. As a scholar and scientist, certainly she could compartmentalize facts without drawing in her own emotions. Other than a keen interest in medieval history and in the life story of Cassethea of Mercia, she held no ties to Cassethea. She needed to treat this excavation the same as any other. She told herself the excavation was no different. The fact she experienced visions she'd never experienced before was a unique twist, but the visions didn't prove El's speculation that Cass's soul was reaching out to her. The visions might still be dreams created by her imagination. And as much as Jess wanted the latter possibility to be true on some level, her gut told her the visions were more than dreams. Regardless of the truth, emotional indifference was the solution Jess settled on as a means to allow her to see the project through to the end.

****

After spending the afternoon with Rayne, emotional indifference was a goal Jess was certain she'd not been able to attain with Rayne. Immediately upon seeing her face, the saturated clouds that hung over Jess from earlier in the day simply vanished and the sun shone brightly through. Jess couldn't fathom how one woman so captured her attention and muddled her thoughts. She found Rayne to be intuitive on a higher level, and caring, even though she came off the opposite at times.

Today, Rayne had kept quiet when she likely sensed Jess was troubled. She interjected a timely joke or two to lighten Jess's mood, and simply listened when Jess talked. Rayne also possessed a decent understanding of medieval history and a love of all Harry Potter, which added to her likeability,

Jess thought as she glanced out the car's side window.

"What's so funny?" Rayne asked, eyes focused on the road.

"Hmm, what? Did I say something?"

"You laughed. I wondered what at."

"I did? I didn't realize. I thought it's kind of funny how we both like the Harry Potter books, considering they're basically children's books. When we walked through the cloister, we both acted as if we entered the actual Hogwarts corridors."

"Yeah, the experience was nifty. I'm sure other people fantasize the same way. There must be millions of adults who loved the Harry Potter stories as much as the children did. And aside from the fictional story, a walk through a building steeped in history does somehow transport you into the past, don't you think?"

Jess admired the rolling green hills as they sped along highway A38. "Honestly, experiencing England and the Cotswolds, no offense, is like being thrust into the past. The architecture is so different from what I'm used to, and any thoughts of what life in medieval times was like is much easier to imagine here. I mean, the architecture of the Gloucester Cathedral proved magnificent. The stonework and pointed towers, the arched corridors and stained glass windows. Yes, we preserve some interesting old buildings and architecture in the US as well, but the aura here is different somehow. I can't find the right words to explain it," Jess said, before her stomach growled.

With a grin etched on her face, Rayne said, "I understand. What you sense is what draws many tourists to the region, lucky for Baron and me. Sightseeing makes people hungry and thirsty, after all, which I glean is a truth you can attest to, no?"

"What gave me away?" Jess said. She enjoyed Rayne's playful banter.

****

After a quiet morning in which they'd uncovered zero artifacts, Susan yelled, "Jess, come quick. I think I found a body." The break in silence and content of the declaration brought not only Jess to Susan's dig area to inspect her discovery, but also Shelly, Justin, and Mike. Jess knelt next to Susan, who eyed her expectantly. Jess scraped around the area of exposed bone and dusted away more dirt particles, until she confirmed Susan's find. "As you can see, Susan uncovered the frontal section of a skull. Now we need to confirm it's human."

After another hour of careful removal of the surrounding soil, Jess, Susan, and the other students had in fact confirmed they'd uncovered a human skull. The excitement at the site sparked electric. Jess assigned Shelly, her other graduate student, to assist Susan with the body excavation. After the discovery, even Joel visited the site more frequently to check on their progress. Jess figured he probably visited to gain tidbits of information he then went home to tell his wife and kids about. With children ages four and six, she figured he thought they'd find the information interesting and maybe think what their father did for a living was pretty cool as well.

With the extra attention as well as distractions, Jess needed to insure the excavation of the remainder of the site didn't suffer or slow, since the reconstruction of the entire home site was paramount to properly reconstruct history. But Jess needn't have worried. With the added excitement came more and more unearthing of artifacts along with another body three feet from, and to the left side of, the first. The first body, per the size of the femur, they determined to be male.

Jess found herself entrenched in work since the day of the first body's discovery, so much so she hadn't deciphered a way to find time to see Rayne, except on the days when Rayne dropped off their lunch. More often than not, however, Baron delivered lunch, not Rayne. Jess liked Baron well enough. He was friendly and polite and usually told a Rayne story if coaxed, but hearing a story about Rayne wasn't the same as seeing the person. Missing Rayne during work was a new experience for Jess, and she wasn't certain how to handle it, other than to suppress it.

✶✶✶✶

By the following Friday, word spread throughout the town and beyond that one of the bodies Jess and her students had uncovered was likely that of a bishop who'd lived a thousand years ago. Once she and her students uncovered the corpse's hand, they found a gold ring with a ruby center, buried several inches from his fingers. They also unearthed a silver necklace with a cross at the end framed in rubies, which had hung around his neck. However, they also observed an unnatural amount of permineralization to the skeletal structure, leaving it far better intact than the other body. The unexampled discovery for remains this age pushed Jess to have their team collect additional soil samples surrounding the skeleton, which they sent with bone fragments to a top taphonomist at the Oxford University Museum of Natural History, some forty miles away.

Jess initially instructed her students to keep the facts about their discovery quiet, mainly the facts about the jewelry, to prevent unwanted outside attention, but in a small town, secrets were few, if any.

When Baron delivered their lunch yet another day, Jess's heart sank unexpectedly. She hated that she missed Rayne as much as she did, and that work no longer engulfed her every thought, especially after such exciting discoveries, but miss her she did. At the same time, she wondered why Rayne no longer delivered their lunchtime meal. Was Rayne ignoring her, and if so, why? Granted, the last time Rayne was at the site, she hadn't interacted much with her, but that was the day of Susan's huge breakthrough. Surely Rayne should understand the discovery required her attention more, no? Jess frowned when she answered her own question. Rather, when she heard El's imaginary voice answer it for her.

"Hello, Jessica," Baron yelled as he approached the lunch table.

"Hey, Baron. I think it's safe to call me Jess now, don't you? Only my mother calls me Jessica, and only when she's angry."

Baron laughed. "I apologize. I didn't know you preferred Jess over Jessica."

"No worries."

"I'm a little early today, but we're expecting a large lunch crowd, so I thought I'd take care of you all first before we get trounced. Are you hungry?"

The corner of Jess's mouth curled up. "Of course I'm hungry. I'm always hungry, and the food at your place is beyond wonderful."

"Glad to hear you say so." Baron moved from one foot to the other then placed the bag on the table and glanced around. "Um, before everyone rushes over, I wondered if you might... if...well if you're not too busy and all...if you might consider or maybe want to eat dinner with me tonight?"

Jess tried not to let her smile fade and express her surprise. She sensed Baron liked her, but she hadn't thought his interest extended into dating her and she wondered if she gave him the wrong impression somewhere along the line. She didn't think so, but clearly he misread her. Rayne mentioned he might like her, but she thought Rayne was teasing her. Did he think because she asked him to call her Jess that she wanted to be more than friends? Hadn't he known she and Rayne had been out twice? Didn't Rayne tell him? Granted, she and Rayne hadn't been on official dates, and they were only friends, but still. When Jess caught the shift in Baron's expression from one of hopefulness to something faded, she surmised she'd waited too long to answer.

Baron unpacked the lunch bag contents. "I...I'm sorry, Jess. I overstepped. I guess I thought—never mind. I'm stupid. I...I should have known. It's Rayne, isn't it? You like her, don't you?"

"Baron, I'm sorry. I like you, I do. And Rayne, I...I mean, we don't know each other well enough yet, but yes, maybe. Shoot. I don't know. This conversation is awkward. Why did you ask me about my feelings toward Rayne? Did she say anything to you? She's been distant lately."

A partial smile graced Baron's face. "Funny, she said the same thing about you. Not about being distant, but busy. And then she said it was probably better that way." Baron set out the remainder of the food. "I asked her what she meant by her statement, but of course, she didn't clarify. I asked her if she liked you. She sort of shrugged me off, but I should have known better. The regulars at the bar knew. I didn't believe them, though. I'm sorry, Jess. If I had truly known, I'd not have asked you to dinner."

"Please, don't be sorry. I'm flattered. I want us to be friends. You're the first person who looked out for me when I arrived in Devonsbury or bothered to give me the time of day. Unlike your sister, I might add." Jess pushed a loose strand of hair behind her ear.

"Yeah, well it goes without saying that I'm the far better catch," Baron joked. "But second best would be my sister. Speaking of which, I better get back before the boss grills me. Besides, your famished posse is on its way over."

Jess glanced to her left to see her students gathered together and marching in their direction. "Speaking of the boss, is she working tonight?"

"Yes, she's on all night, and as I said, Fridays are crazy busy. She's on tomorrow night, too. I happen to know she's only working until six on Sunday, though, so if you wanted to see her, I'd pop by Sunday night. That is, if I were you," he said and winked.

"Thanks, Baron." Jess leaned over and kissed him on the cheek. "You're the best."

"You know it."

As Baron walked away with reddened cheeks, Susan flashed Jess a sideways glance.

"What?" Jess said, her tone indignant. "Just eat, would you?"

"Yes, ma'am," Susan replied.

Chapter Twelve

Saewyn and her sister were gracious enough to share what scant food their families retained from the harsh winter months, and Cass thanked them numerous times. She also slept on the floor with a roof over her head that night. The next morning, however, she bade Saewyn and her family farewell. She was determined to find her mother, Emma, and Julia, and rescue them from the Vikings. How she thought she'd manage that feat, a young woman on her own, clueless about so much in life, she'd not yet planned out, but she could not, and would not, sit around like her father and do nothing.

The more she thought of her father, William, the more the hatred for him burned inside. She was well aware Gollyn was not his favorite of sons, but for him to not so much as search for him and to leave him to rot in the fields registered unimaginable to her. His inaction reeked as bad as the Vikings' actions. For his indifference, she'd never forgive him. In fact, it would take much of her willpower not to kill him.

Cass shook the horrible thoughts from her mind and prayed God forgive her for her terrible musings. As she traveled the road west, in the direction Saewyn indicated the army thought the Vikings traveled, she tucked a loose strand of hair from her face to behind her ear. The motion reminded her of what she yet needed to do—per her mother's instructions—cut her hair. She decided staying on the main road would be dangerous, so she meandered off the road and ambled toward the forest. She planned not to go too deep into the woods, just deep enough to stay hidden from other travelers. She found comfort in the fact that if Julia had indeed been taken as Saewyn indicated, then surely King Herrwald would have spared no expense to find her. Which meant the others who were taken, like her mother and Emma, would have a better chance of being rescued as well. Wouldn't they?

After a half an hour of brisk walking, Cass stumbled across the trunk of a fallen oak tree less than five feet from a pond, and sat. She hauled off the shoulder bag, rummaged inside, and pulled out her dagger. She gathered her hair from behind, and as she pictured Alfred in her mind, sliced the blade to and fro at the point she thought the length right. Immediately, with so much of her hair gone, she felt exposed and naked. Short hair, which was supposed to keep her feeling safe and hidden, seemed to have had the opposite effect. Cass wondered what she looked like. She crept toward the pond, knelt on the edge of the water, and looked in. The mud soaked her trousers at the knees, but she didn't move. The reflection that stared back was somewhat boy-like indeed. She shifted her face right and left. In an odd way, she didn't look as bad as she feared she might. She trimmed other parts of her hair to give a layered look that was, in the end, not half bad. In fact, she kind of liked it.

As she straightened off her knees, she heard the crack of broken twigs. Cass froze then spun on her heel to see a wolf's eyes glaring at her. The corners of her mouth turned upward, and she jumped. "Gray!" she yelled, before she ran. Within a couple of steps, she wrapped her arms around the befuddled wolf. "It's so good to see you. Did you follow me all this way after all? I can't believe you stayed by me."

Gray let out a rumble and pressed his head against Cass's chest. He sniffed her and then lay at her feet.

The presence of Gray lifted Cass's spirits beyond what she could voice. The fact Gray stayed with her was paramount. Why he stayed, she didn't know, but gratitude filled her emptiness. Her grief must have been so intense she'd not sensed him near her earlier, and his presence now rekindled a glimmer of life within her and pushed out the slivers of the anger gnawing at her from inside about the Vikings and her father.

Elated to have her companion back, Cass strapped the dagger to her leg, under her trousers, and she and Gray walked twelve more miles, nonstop, in the woods. Cass found renewed energy and hope thanks to Gray. They followed the road west for over an hour and then moved north toward the River Severn, per Saewyn's instructions. Viking ships were last seen along the river.

The rough undergrowth treacherous on her bare feet, Cass decided they'd rest for the day. They were far enough into the forest and away from the dirt road that a fire would be safe to light. She found an opening in the canopy, cleared the ground, and collected rocks to encircle the firepit. A creek trickled nearby for water; the spot was optimal for the night.

****

Cass experienced a fitful sleep. She couldn't remember falling asleep, but as her eyes closed, her heart raced and her limbs stiffened. Familiar stories flooded her mind. Stories she heard as clear as day in her mother, Arielwund's, voice. Stories she realized she'd heard, but not registered, before. Stories her mother told about King Alfred the Great, the overlord of Western Mercia, military leader of the Anglo Saxons. The first king who'd, for a time, rid the seas of Viking raiders. King Alfred begat five children, including Edward the Elder, who'd conquered Eastern Danelaw (Eastern and Northern England), and an eldest daughter, AEthelflaed, known as the Lady of Mercia after her husband AEthelred died around 911. Cass's mother had said AEthelflaed was Cass's great-great-grandmother and one of the first female rulers in England. Edward the Elder had a son, AEthelstan, who would become the first king of all England in 924 and rule through 940, ten years before Arielwund's birth, even though the other kings retained local power. He fought the Vikings with AEthelred. AEthelred and AEthelflaed begat a daughter, AElfwynn. AElfwynn was educated with her cousin AEthelflaed, but later pushed from power by her uncle, Edward. Not many records exist of AElfwynn as a result, but people thought she bore a daughter out of wedlock, and that her daughter bore a daughter who was the mother of Arielwund. Arielwund told Cass that although no records would prove her story true, Cass was in fact the offspring of royalty. And that she was star born.

Cass woke groggily, not knowing where she was and not able to move. As she opened her eyes, she gasped in horror. Not only had her fire gone out to the point no smoke rose from the pit, but her body below the neck was completely encased in white threads: a spider's web. Twenty feet from the end of her feet crept a spider, larger than Gray in size with a fat, hairy body and segmented legs with pointed talons at the ends. Its eyes, two large and two small, were massive pits of black. Cass swallowed hard. In her mind, she called for Gray. Where was he? Was he dead? Had the spider gotten him first, or had he been out hunting? She hoped for her sake he'd been hunting. She tried to connect in her mind with the spider but remained unable. The spider's smaller front legs, one on either side of its sharp mandibles, flicked constantly, as if excited by the food it captured and was about to gorge on.

Cass tried desperately to move and to reach for her sword, but the spider's threads bound her limbs to her body too tightly. She leaned slightly to her right, and as she did so, inched her fingers along her side and stretched for the dagger. Sweat beaded on her forehead as the anticipation of being sucked dry of her blood and lifeline played in her mind. Death wouldn't be so bad, but if she died, she'd not be able to rescue her mother, Emma, and Julia, and those defeatist thoughts both saddened and angered her. And what of the revelation of being star born? After much doubt, her dreams revealed Sir William was right all along. Her mother kept her ancestral history from her conscious self, likely to protect her, yet still found a way to let her know who she was in her dreams. What it meant to be star born, however, she'd yet to learn, if she survived her current predicament.

Never had she laid eyes on a spider the size of an ox. She'd heard stories about the forest and the dangerous creatures therein, and how some travelers entered and never returned. But she thought them exaggerated tales spun to keep children like her from wandering off.

A crow caught Cass's attention as it flew overhead. She cleared her thoughts and imagined herself high in the air, the wind in her face. Her mind connected with the bird, and she saw through his eyes her dire situation. She estimated mere minutes remained before the spider towered over her. Her journey to save her family and friend would end before it started if she didn't act quickly.

Cass continued with her struggle to reach the dagger but couldn't. From the crow's point of vision, she searched wider and spotted Gray. A sliver of hope ran through her. She spoke to Gray in her mind and told him not to attack the spider, but to run to her as fast as he was able and to drag his claws along the side of her body to free her. From the direction he ran, he'd reach her from her right side. The side she kept her dagger.

When Gray arrived, the spider stood up on its four hind legs in a threatening pose, but Gray sprung underneath and tore at Cass's side. The webbing released its constricting hold. Cass breathed deep. She sensed Gray's readiness to attack the spider. She asked him to wait, and he did. Satisfied, she let loose the mental connection with the crow. She grabbed the dagger from its sheath and held it upright, tight above her chest, with both hands. The spider dropped to its four front legs, jaws spread wide. The dagger hit a soft spot in the spider's underbelly. Cass thrust the blade away from her and split the spider open. Its four left legs bent first. It toppled to its left side, hairy legs twitching. At last the twitches stopped.

Cass breathed a sigh of relief and cut herself out of what remained of the spider's cocoon. Gray whimpered, likely in fear and relief to see Cass unharmed except for scratches on her right hand and arm from Gray's claws. "You did great, Gray. You did great. You saved my life," Cass said.

Gray ran off and returned seconds later holding a limp rabbit in his jaws, which Cass supposed he'd dropped earlier from his nightly hunt, before she'd mind-called to him. He plopped the rabbit in front of her feet. Cass petted him on the head. "Thank you, my friend, but you don't mind if we move away from here and eat this later, do you? I'm not so hungry at this moment."

****

Several days passed since the nightmarish spider

incident, the result of which kept Cass walking less in the woods and more on the roadways or in open fields, with Gray nearby but out of sight. She understood the road might draw other dangers, but at this time, when pitch-dark spider eyes and opening and closing mandibles filled the better part of her dreams, Cass ventured she'd take the risk. As it turned out, she made better time on the road, though she'd not located the Vikings or seen any of their ships. Nor had she seen any of the king's army who were supposedly hunting the Vikings.

The fact she'd not come across the army by now worried her. Perhaps Julia hadn't been taken in the first place or she was already safe in the kingdom. Safe and free to think about marriage. Either way, such an outcome might mean the army concluded its search. And as for Julia's marriage situation, Cass reminded herself the decision to marry Prince Richard remained Julia's, and since Julia wasn't upset about the marriage, she shouldn't be either. In fact, Julia conveyed happiness when she spoke of the marriage. Cass would need to accept the situation and suppress her own wants and needs. With Gollyn dead and part of her family missing, she had more important things to think about than Julia. And if she were ever to be intimate with another, she'd want it to be with someone who wanted her as much as she wanted them. Cass recognized Julia no longer wanted her in the same way, if she even ever had.

Caught deep in her thoughts, she didn't hear the band of Viking men sneak up behind her. Before their presence registered with Cass, they grabbed her and threw her to the ground. Quickly, Cass sent thoughts to Gray to stay hidden. She didn't want him hurt. She knew without a doubt the Vikings would kill him, and she wouldn't be able to stomach or accept that fate for him. She eyed the strapping strong men who surrounded her. She lifted her torso on her elbow and slowly stood. Her bow and arrow lay on the ground.

"Ha! What have we here but a scrap of a lad playing warrior?" the broad-shouldered man in the lead said, as he pushed Cass once more. She stumbled but didn't fall. "What do you have strapped to your back, a sword?"

Cass didn't respond. These were likely the men who

killed her brother. She seethed in anger, the expression riddled on her face.

"Taka the sword off and gefa it to me, or I'll taka it myself," he said.

Cass understood what the man said, as many of his words sounded similar to her own, even though his dialect was different. With reluctance, she slung the sword over her shoulder and set the sword, in the casing, tip down, onto the ground.

The man yanked the sword from Cass's hands, but managed only to drag it two feet before he let it drop. He laughed heartily. "No wonder you can't stand on your fetr! Where'd you geta this useless sword? It must be made of iron, it's so heavy." He laughed some more. "Sure, it makes a good-looking deterrent I suppose, but it's not worth the metal it's made of. Not used either from what I can see. Not a nick in this blade. Not a one." He winked at the other three men standing beside him. One of the men held a gutted deer around his shoulders, blood smeared on his neck and hands. If Cass or anyone in her village had killed a deer, they would be imprisoned or killed by the king. But these men obviously didn't care. They weren't concerned at all. "I suppose if you can carry that anchor around with you on the road, then you can't be that veikr. Perhaps I can use you to taka my place rowing the boat." He laughed some more.

Another man spoke up. "I think you will anger Tove if you do."

"Tove doesn't need to know."

"I don't see how you'd keep him from her, Koll," he said.

"Let me worry about Tove. You taka his bow and arrows and shoulder baggin. The sword he can either leave here or carry himself. It's worthless and not something he'd be able to lifta against us," Koll said.

By this time, Cass had easily assimilated their dialect into her own, hearing the Vikings as if they spoke the same as Cass. She also realized how lucky she was that her mother had the forethought to have her dress in Sedwick's clothes and cut her hair. She passed as a boy, for now at least, and thanked her mother silently. And although she'd not come upon the Vikings as she had hoped she would and follow them undetected, she wasn't dead yet. Maybe capture wasn't the worst that could have happened. Maybe they'd take her to their camp and to her mother and Emma. Worrying about how to save them, she'd do later. They'd not patted her down though, and therefore were unaware of her dagger, and of the value of her sword, or her ability to wield it.

Chapter Thirteen

Not even the memory of the prior night's visions deterred Jess from seeking out Rayne this day, though the worry about Cass's capture by the Vikings did interject itself in her thoughts throughout the day. But so did the recollections of Rayne's smile and the unexplained warmth and comfort Jess experienced whenever she stood in Rayne's company. Baron mentioned Rayne kept away from Jess during the week because Jess was overly busy with the dig, which was true. She was busy, but Jess thought part of the reason Rayne kept her distance was also the result of Rayne's irrational past conclusions about educators sneaking up on her once again.

As soon as their day of excavation concluded, Jess freshened up, put on her favorite form-fitting jeans and a sleeveless, purple, knit top and moseyed over to Eagles Landing. She'd slung a thin, white, cotton sweater over her arm to wear for later, but the air had chilled during her time in the trailer, and she put it on midway during her walk.

As Jess opened the heavy, wooden door to step into the pub, Rayne stood on the other side about to walk out. Both remained motionless and momentarily speechless.

"Hey," Rayne finally said. "Wow, you look great."

Jess smiled. "Thank you. I'd say the same for you."

"Thanks, though I doubt I'm anything to chat about, after a full day on my feet in a smoky pub. What brings you by? Come for dinner?"

"Yes and no. A little birdie hinted that some people have noticed I've been working too much, and in reflection, I discovered the birdie is right."

Before Rayne could answer, a couple stood outside the door. "Excuse us," the young man said.

"Sorry." Jess was about to step farther into the pub when Rayne motioned her toward the door. "Let's step outside a minute. It'll be easier to talk."

As Jess exited, she felt the warmth from Rayne's hand on the lower part of her back. A flash of heat rose up through her chest and throat. She took a deep breath, not quite grasping why her body reacted so to Rayne's touch.

"Thanks," Rayne said. "I didn't want to get sucked into another conversation. I just wanted to get home and relax. It's been a busy week."

Jess felt a pang of disappointment course through her as she intuited Rayne may not want company on a Sunday night. What was she thinking? Rayne lived a life without Jess in it before they met. She engaged with other friends and family and pursued other interests. Jess should have called first and arranged to meet Rayne, not ambushed her at the pub.

As if Rayne picked up on her mood shift, she added, "But it's great to see you, Jess. Did you want to talk to me, or am I holding you up from dinner?"

Embarrassment replaced disappointment and settled in Jess's cheeks. "My main purpose tonight was to see you. I know I sort of ignored you this past week, but I also noted you've not made an effort to see me either. I thought I'd find out what was up with that."

"You did, did you?"

"Yes." Jess motioned her hand toward her head and along her body and then glanced at the Eagles Landing sign. "Thus, the reason for my presence."

Rayne's expression changed from neutral to what Jess surmised as confidently smug within seconds. "In that case," Rayne said, "I have an idea. How about dinner at my place? I'll cook. In truth, I've already prepped most of the food, and I made more than enough. I planned on bringing part of the leftovers to my grandmother tomorrow. One less day she has to cook after getting out of hospital and a way for me to make sure she eats."

"Jeez, I'm sorry, Rayne. What happened to her?"

"Long—"

"Story. I know. Maybe you can tell me about it on the way to your place?"

The right side of Rayne's lip and cheek raised in unison, apparently as a result of her amusement to the indirect dinner acceptance response. "Sounds like a plan."

****

After she greeted George, Jess paused and took in the natural-brick-clad house, Rayne's home. A four-foot by four-foot foyer with a slate floor and brass chandelier above opened into an expansive living room. Light-grey, ceramic-stone planks, made to resemble wooden floors, extended in a left-to-right pattern from the living room into the kitchen. From where she stood, Jess saw white kitchen cabinets, stainless steel appliances, and a center island with two wooden stools.

As they moved into the living room, Jess immediately noticed a circular Viking shield, picture frames filled with pictures of knights and castles and old English landscapes, and a metal shield and facemask that would have been worn by said knights over a thousand years ago. Only after the shock of the wall hangings subsided, did she notice a grey sofa, with orange and teal pillows, positioned against one wall. Matching armchairs in front of and to the left and right of the sofa, as well as a rectangular glass table, with a rectangular base the texture and color of the ceramic floor, also came into sight. A modern, geographically patterned area rug of black, yellow, and orange completed the living room. A flat-screen television hung opposite the sofa. Jess faced Rayne but didn't know what to say.

"I told you I took an interest in medieval art," Rayne said.

"And artifacts," Jess added. She placed her hand over her chest. "Rayne, your house is incredible. It's nothing like I imagined it."

"You imagined what my house might look like?" Rayne said with a smirk.

"Of course, why wouldn't I? I'm curious by nature."

"Mmm-hmm, I see."

Jess rolled her eyes. "Whatever. Are any of the items on the wall originals?"

"Yes. They all are. Acquired over many years, and some handed down through generations. That colorful Viking shield to the right of the bookshelf's my favorite. This one's obviously been restored with a leather covering, but it has original wooden parts underneath."

"It's beyond amazing," Jess said.

"Yeah, I love it. I'm sure you're hungry, and I know I am. If we're going to eat anytime soon, I should cook. And if I don't feed George soon, he's not going to be a happy camper. Can I offer you something to drink while you wait on dinner?"

"A glass of red wine would be great, if you have it. If not, beer is fine, or water for that matter." Jess followed Rayne into the kitchen, George on her heels.

"A woman who's easy to please, I like that."

"I wouldn't jump to any conclusions too soon, if I were you."

****

Conversation before and during dinner flowed free and easily, somewhat to Jess's surprise. She wasn't much of a talker and didn't think Rayne would open up, but she had. Jess found they shared several interests in common such as hiking, a love of dogs, chocolate, reading, and good food.

"Rayne, this dish is beyond excellent. What is it?"

"It's a Norwegian dish my grandmother calls Kjøttkaker. She adds cut up onion to the meat and a secret mix of spices, then rolls them into balls before frying them, but I like to flatten them out first. The brown gravy is the same as hers, but she also makes the meal with creamed cabbage and whole potatoes, while I prefer the red cabbage and mashed potatoes."

"I love it, and I think I'd like the red cabbage and mashed potatoes better, too. I appreciate you cooking. It was very thoughtful."

"I enjoy cooking and I'm pleased you agreed to come by."

"I'm glad I did, too. I call dishwashing duty, though. No arguments," Jess said.

After they'd eaten rice pudding for dessert, of which George partook, Jess slid her sweater off her shoulders and draped it over the arm of the sofa.

Rayne entered the living room and stopped.

Jess sat and patted her stomach. "I'm so stuffed right now I think I'm going to pop."

Rayne laughed, in what appeared to Jess as a nervous laugh, and she noticed the heat of Rayne's eyes on her. "You okay?"

Rayne blinked as if caught dreaming and continued into the living room. "What? No. I mean yes, brilliant." She tapped her stomach. "Other than I may have overeaten as well." She continued toward the armchair next to the sofa where Jess sat and fell into the cushions. She adjusted her position several times before finding the right spot. "You probably don't want to talk shop, but how's the dig going? I heard you found a body."

Jess watched in amusement as Rayne rushed through her words. Did Rayne take in a deep breath when she glanced over at her, or did she imagine it? She decided she must have imagined it and quickly refocused. "Two bodies actually, and I think there are more. One was Bishop Leon II of Mettlenbury. I matched his necklace to a painting in one of the history books I brought with me. The other body is a Viking and also male." Jess watched Rayne's muscles relax as she listened. "What surprised me, besides the unexpected preserved condition of the skeletal structure, was the bishop was buried in a Viking settlement. The inscription in the stone rune said 'friend.' I don't think St. Albans will be pleased with that discovery."

"Why not? I'd think they'd be ecstatic with the find. I think it's awesome. And isn't the bishop who they hoped to find from the start?"

"He is. And you'd think they would be, but besides wanting to find the body of the bishop and claim that victory as their own, I think they also wanted to prove he'd been captured, robbed, and held against his will by the Vikings. After all, such a story would support what most history books would have us all believe—Vikings pillaged the Catholic churches and monasteries and killed indiscriminately. In some cases, that rang true, but from my understanding, this wasn't always so. Bishop Leon wore his necklace as well as a gold ring when we unearthed him. No one stole from him. And honestly, what the Catholics did to spread Christianity wasn't holy either."

Rayne nodded. "Right. Holy wars? Please. So you haven't told them yet?"

"No. I know I have to, but I thought the longer I wait, the better. I don't want them to pull the funding."

"You think they'd stoop so low?"

"I wouldn't put it past them."

"Let's hope they won't. Did you know St. Alban, whom your uni is named after, was the first British saint?" Rayne said.

"I did not know that. Thank you for schooling me."

"Schooling you? Hardly. I didn't know, either, but I looked it up."

"Did you? And why did you do that?"

"Touché. All right, you win. I only mentioned it because I thought St. Alban being British was ironic. Next topic."

"Unfortunately, as much as I'd like to continue our chat, it's getting late. I should go."

Rayne glanced at her wristwatch. "It is late, which is why George and I will accompany you to your trailer."

"I appreciate the offer, but it's not necessary."

"No, we absolutely will walk with you, won't we, George?"

At the sound of the word "walk," George sprang up and ran to the foyer. He circled twice and stared at Jess and Rayne.

"Guess he answered your question," Jess said.

＊＊＊＊

"I confess I'm glad the two of you are escorting me. It's darker out here than I thought it would be," Jess said.

"Nighttime is dark."

"True, but since I've been here, I'm usually in by nine o'clock, if not sooner."

"And you're unfamiliar with the area, which doesn't help," Rayne said as they neared the front of the trailer. "Hold off. Bloody hell."

"What? What's the matter?" Jess asked. She stopped next to Rayne.

Rayne's tone must have startled George. His hair stood up on his back, and he gave a guttural growl.

"It's okay, boy. Sit," Rayne said. She faced Jess. "Did you leave the door to the trailer open by any chance?"

"No, of course I didn't." Jess caught sight of the slightly ajar door. "Oh no," she said and strode off toward the steps.

Rayne's fingers wrapped around Jess's bicep and yanked her in reverse. "What are you doing?" she whispered, as she loosened her initial grip. "You can't go in there. What if someone's inside? We're staying out here, and I'm calling the constabulary."

"The constabulary?"

"Police, yes. The Gloucestershire Constabulary."

After the call, Rayne eyed Jess. "They're on their way. You're probably right that there's no one in there now, but it's better to be safe." Rayne petted George on the head, rubbed her hands together, and pivoted from one foot to the other as they stood in silence for several minutes. "This is my fault. This place was never really safe enough for you to stay here. I should have known better."

A puzzled expression crossed Jess's face. "What are you talking about? The trailer serves fine as a temporary residence. I've been on excavations and lived in tents, for heaven's sake. It's no big deal."

"No big deal until now. What if you were inside when the person or people broke in? I should have—" Before Rayne could finish what she wanted to say, the police arrived.

Jess and Rayne watched in silence as the car pulled up to the site. A six-foot-three, thin, cleanly shaven officer stepped out of the vehicle, leaving the car running and headlights on. The white car sported the prominent lettering of POLICE in blue on front of the hood and on the lower side door, from what Jess saw, and the doors were painted blue and yellow in color. The young man approached, but before he could speak, Rayne extended her hand. "PC Strongwell, thank you for coming."

The officer shook her hand. "Ms. Kvale, good to see you again," he said. He faced Jess and nodded. "Ma'am."

"Hello, Officer," Jess said. "I'm Jessica Madison."

"Ms. Madison. What's the problem here?"

While Rayne took the lead and explained them arriving to the opened door, Jess sorted through her memory banks as to why Rayne's last name rang a bell. And then it hit her.

They waited outside until Police Constable Strongwell completed his search and waved them in. "Wait here, George," Rayne said.

"I assume this is your trailer, Ms. Madison?" PC Strongwell asked.

"It is. I'm renting it."

"From whom?"

"I don't know. The university, St. Albans in Connecticut, where I teach made the arrangements. Joel Fisher brought the trailer to the site. The university hired him. He's a local handyman-driver of sorts." Jess watched PC Strongwell take notes.

"I know him. I'll talk with him tomorrow," PC Strongwell said. "I'd like you to take a look around the trailer and see if you notice anything stolen. What I can tell you is someone was definitely in here. A few items are scattered about, as you can see, but in your office, or bedroom, the lock on a metal box in the cabinet next to the mini fridge was drilled through. There's nothing inside but a handful of papers."

"Drilled through?" Jess said.

"Yes, with a power drill. There are metal shavings on the floor underneath the lock."

"Jesus. It's like they knew about the safe. I'll take a thorough look around, as you suggested, but I can already tell you what they took." Jess stepped into the office, crouched on her knees, and checked the safe to confirm her fears. Then she stood, lifted a book from the shelf, and leafed through the pages. She turned the book to face the constable and held it out in front of him. He and Rayne eyed the open pages at the same time.

"They stole the bishop's necklace and ring?" Rayne asked.

"Yes. You're welcome to take a picture from the book, Officer. A few days ago, we uncovered the body of Bishop

Leon II of Mettlenbury, estimated to have passed somewhere around the end of the last millennium, or the start of the 11th century, A.D. 1000. Both the silver necklace and ring contained rubies, which are valuable on their own accord, but to a collector of medieval artifacts, the value is unimaginable. These pieces of history don't belong in criminal hands. They belong in a museum."

"I understand. I'll take a photo, thank you, and dust for fingerprints. After, I'll rope off the trailer and will return in the morning. It looks to me like the thief or thieves wanted to give the impression someone broke in, but they may have had a key."

"Why do you say that?" Jess asked.

"The bottom pane of the window panel in the door was broken, but it was broken from the inside out. There are no glass shards on the floor inside."

Jess confirmed the officer's observation but said nothing.

"I suggest you don't stay here this evening," PC Strongwell added.

"She'll stay with me," Rayne said.

Jess flashed Rayne a defiant scowl. "No. I absolutely will not. I can stay in the trailer. It's fine. Whoever broke in got what they came for. I doubt they'll be back tonight."

"You don't know that," Rayne said.

"No. But I know you don't want me living with you, Ms. Kvale. Anna Kvale's daughter, am I right?"

"Granddaughter. I can explain."

"I'm not sure you can."

Rayne motioned Jess to the side, away from PC Strongwell. "I told you before your living in the trailer was my fault. I was about to tell you why when PC Strongwell arrived."

"Go on."

"My grandmother suffered a stroke the day before you arrived. I wasn't aware she'd rented a room to you."

"Until Joel told you so," Jess said.

"Correct. But, honestly, at the time, I didn't know you at all. Baron said I should've given you the room above the bar, but I said no."

"Baron was right. He is the better catch. At least one of

you was looking out for me," Jess said, as she grabbed her elbow for comfort.

Rayne appeared momentarily puzzled, as if she searched for meaning to what Jess had let slip.

Realizing she'd ignored the issue of Rayne's grandmother being ill, she said, "I'm sorry about your grandmother. Is she okay?"

"Thank you. She will be. Look, I didn't think a room above a noisy establishment such as our own was a good idea. I didn't know at the time you couldn't find other accommodations. No one told me. Joel simply said you found a place to stay, and later, when I saw the trailer, I figured the accommodations must be fine, or you'd not have agreed to stay."

"The trailer was fine and still is fine," Jess said.

"The bloody hell it is. Please stay with George and me. We both want you to." Rayne directed Jess to the front door, her hand resting on the crux of Jess's back. "See," she added as they looked out the window.

George's tail wagged vigorously. A happy George, coupled with the heat of Rayne's hand on her, and the memory of that same tender gesture when they'd gone out to dinner, was too much, but she didn't let on. "He's happy to see you, not me," Jess said.

"Now we both know that's pure rubbish."

Jess's voice softened. "I don't want you to feel bad about not renting me a room and certainly not about what happened today. It's not your fault. My accommodations were not your responsibility, and I'd probably have done the same as you at the time and been cautious. I even told Joel I didn't expect anyone to go out of their way for someone they didn't know."

"It's sorted then. Pack whatever you need, and let's go."

"I don't recall agreeing to go with you, but considering my circumstances, I believe I will accept. Thank you. I'll text the team with a brief heads-up and let them know not to come tomorrow. I don't think they'll mind a day off."

"Not bloody likely."

****

As tired as Jess felt, she couldn't immediately fall asleep. George decided to lie at the foot of her bed, which made her smile. She wondered if Rayne was asleep already. She must have been exhausted as well, having worked all day and then having had to deal with all her issues that night. They'd sipped a cup of tea before bed and talked for an hour. Rayne assured Jess the mess would eventually get straightened out and not to worry, but she did worry. How couldn't she? She hadn't told the university of her findings yet, and now the theft hung over her. If it ended up in the papers and someone got wind of it in the States, a high likelihood existed that would be the end of her work in England.

Jess tried to pry her mind off her troubles, but instead, thought about Cass's troubles. When she tried to clear her mind and will herself to think of happier thoughts, like those of her friend Ellie and what she was doing, she was unable to. She descended into thoughts of Cassethea, and the woozy feeling that became all too familiar now overtook her on the cusp of sleep. Her thoughts clouded. Fogginess filled her mind as she drifted farther and farther back in time.

Chapter Fourteen

Cass sat uncomfortably for hours, alone, hands tied behind her back and feet bound. She leaned against the rough trunk of a towering thirty-five-meter English oak, under its hundreds of branches of round lobed leaves, as darkness and the cooler evening encroached. Visions of empty spider orb eyes flashed before her, and a chill ran up her spine. Several times she contemplated whether she should have allowed herself to be taken by the Vikings or if she should have let Gray intervene or fought Koll when they were alone. He'd walked her to the secluded spot under the tree and bound her. She still carried her dagger and had an opportunity to strike at him, but to what end? She guessed he kept her from the others because he didn't want Tove, the woman who seemed to yield some power in the group, to find out about her. She wasn't sure how she'd be kept in the dark if Cass was supposed to row for him, but she'd worry about those details when the time came. For now, she hoped she'd get close enough to the Vikings' camp to perhaps see her mother and sister. Regardless, for tonight she wasn't afraid. Gray hid nearby. He provided all the comfort she needed, and the majestic oak provided a roof above her head.

Hours passed before footsteps broke the eerie forest silence. "I brought you dinner. Have to make sure you keep up your strength for tomorrow," Koll said and laughed, as if there were humor in his words. Rather than hand her the bowl, he set the bowl on the ground. "Lean toward me."

Cass hesitated at first but ultimately did as she was told. She kept her eyes focused on his every action, ready to call for Gray's help should she need him. Koll reached behind her, his body odor penetrating her nostrils, and unfastened her hands. Instant relief coursed through her wrists and shoulders as she shifted her arms in front of her and rubbed her reddened, sore wrists. The over-tightened hemp rope cut into them with no mercy. In places, they'd bled.

Koll shoved the soup in front of her. "Fresh deer. Eat. And hurry. I can't be away from the others for long. We wouldn't want someone from the other group finding you prematurely, would we?"

Cass hid her disdain and took the stew. She held the bowl to her mouth and breathed in the aroma of fresh sage before she placed the bowl against her lips and tilted the steaming goodness into her mouth. Energy the food provided coursed through her body. As much as she wanted to defy Koll, sickened by what he and his fellow Vikings had done to her village and to Gollyn, for her safety, she held the vile words in and focused on the meal. The tender meat fell apart in her mouth, and she ate heartily. However, the more she ate, the more pressure it caused on an already overfilled bladder. She needed relief in the worst way, but didn't want to jeopardize her disguise either. When she finished eating, she watched Koll pick up the rope.

"Wait. I need to relieve myself."

"Then get up, turn around, and be done with it."

"That's not exactly what I meant."

"Fine," he said in a tone of annoyance before he knelt and untied her feet. "Don't think about running though, and stay where I can see a better part of you."

Cass exchanged a wordless glance with her captor, signaling acquiescence to his demands. She pulled her legs under her, stood, and stretched out her stiffened spine. She strode a fair distance through the woods until she heard Koll yell, and she stopped. She lowered her trousers behind a shrub and squatted over the ground, nearly weeping in relief as the pressure on her bladder subsided. She hadn't even bothered to scan the undergrowth for snakes or other creatures, her need was so great.

Once again able to think more clearly, she realized she'd have to make the same request in the morning. Would Koll think her request odd? Would he grow suspicious? She needed a plan. She'd say the food unsettled her stomach. She didn't think Koll would deny her request under those circumstances, or accompany her to find out if she were lying. Satisfied she now possessed a plan, she returned to the majestic oak in the woods.

****

In the morning, after having been granted another private bathroom break, Cass shortly thereafter found herself on the deck of a Viking longboat, six oarsmen on each side. Ahead of the boat she stood on, traveled another similar-sized boat. The boats were pointed at both ends and wider in the middle. They were made of overlapping wooden planks held together with iron rivets. Nerves on edge this morning after not having slept much, Cass was filled with trepidation regarding the trip they were about to make. In the interim between capture and this moment, she'd gained no insight into where they were going. She'd said good-bye to Gray the night before, knowing only the next day's journey for her would be by sea. After Koll left her, she figured he'd not return until the morning, and so she'd called Gray to her and spent the night cuddled next to him, safe and snug. She'd miss him, she knew. And as she stood aboard the foreign vessel awaiting further instruction, her heart already ached.

Her thoughts were interrupted by a shove between her shoulder blades. Koll directed her to his usual rowing seat, while other Vikings glanced in her direction and then ignored her. Koll stood with shoulders back, clearly proud of himself, but Cass didn't think the other Viking men shared in his glee. The oar proved heavier to move than she thought, and she wondered how many hours she'd be able to row and not collapse from the strain. She was a quarter the size of these men, but Koll didn't seem to care. Face to the sun, he pulled what appeared to be a dried piece of meat from a satchel he'd tied to his belt and chewed off a healthy piece. He placed the remainder of the dried jerky in the pouch. Every so often, he'd scoop water from the boat bottom with a wooden bowl and throw the contents over the side. Otherwise, he did nothing.

Within three hours, Cass's shoulders, back, arms, and ribs felt the intense burn of her unfamiliar situation. Fatigue set in, but she would not complain. She couldn't let the men think her weak or inferior, though clearly in stature she was. She'd need every advantage later, when she rescued her family. Blisters formed on the sides of her thumbs and hands. When they burst, the pain was intense; the constant rowing no help.

The knowledge of Koll's line of sight focused on her more often than not caused Cass more distress than the pain in her hands and upper body. She struggled to hide the discomfort and strain her body endured. She'd never worked this hard. She thought about her prior grumblings in the field on those rare occasions where she was called upon to weed or harvest. She wished she were in the fields now. But the farm no longer existed, nor did the house or Gollyn. A life of uncertainty became normal now. In every direction she looked, water surrounded them. No land was visible. How much longer would they be at sea? She prayed for strong winds to catch the sails, but none came. No wind, no rest. Instead, the fire-red sails lay limp.

"Looks like your time of leisure has come to an end, Koll," one of the men, who sat on the side of the boat opposite Cass, said.

Cass glanced at the man, estimating him to be a few winters younger than Koll, but his equal in stature.

"What are you talking about, Orm?" Koll said before recognition hit. The lead ship had slowed, its oars drawn in.

Cass didn't know if she should consider this turn of events favorable or not, but the fact they stopped moving for at least a few minutes was gift enough.

"What should I do with him now? Throw him overboard?" Koll asked, his stare fixed on Cass.

"You should've thought about that yesterday when I told you to leave the kid be. Tove won't be happy, but you need to tell her the truth. That's the best chance for mercy you'll have with her."

"I'm not afraid of Tove."

"Maybe you should be," Orm said.

Cass didn't understand why they argued. Clearly, none of the men suffered regret or grief over killing her brother, six winters her younger, or destroying their village. Why should they argue over her now? Granted, she was relieved there existed disagreement on whether to throw her overboard or not, but the discussion itself made no sense under the circumstances. In the event consensus did not veer her way, she tensed her muscles in anticipation of grabbing her dagger and identifying the points of entry where she'd exact her pain, and on whom she'd exact it first.

As they drifted toward the lead Viking longboat, they were pulled alongside by the other boat's oarsmen. Cass's focus shifted to a woman on the other boat, dressed in men's fighting gear, walking toward them. Her braided hair shone blonde. She wore a silver band across her forehead, an emerald the size of an acorn mounted in the center. A similar band of silver wrapped around her right bicep like a snake. At the ends, the band curled, and she wore a wide leather bracelet on her wrist. A matching leather band with intricate carving bound her white tunic around the waist, and held a gleaming sword. The tunic draped above her knees, partway over grey leggings, and leather straps crisscrossed up long legs from her boots. A red cloak covered her shoulders, secured by a round, miniature silver pin shaped like a shield. Her muscular arms, tanned from the sun, remained visible.

Cass felt a familiar desire to touch the woman's arms before realization reminded her of who she was and what she'd been a part of. The woman, whom she assumed was Tove, contemplated her. Blue eyes pierced Cass with questioning scrutiny, the intensity of which Cass had never before experienced, not even with Julia. She desperately wanted to break their connection, but couldn't pull her gaze away.

All other eyes within the boat, except for Cass's, were focused on Koll.

"Explain yourself, Koll. I don't recall a new member of our group dining with us last night. Where did she come from?"

Cass's heart sank. She knew. Cass locked eyes with Koll, whose head snapped around in an instant.

Koll's eyes narrowed. He faced Tove. "She?"

"Yes, she. Has the sun rotted your eyes?"

As the crew laughed, Tove waved a hand and quieted them. "You and I will talk later, Koll. In the meantime, bring the girl to me and all the possessions she had on her when you found her. I stopped our boats because both Ulf and Rune fell sick. Since you appear fresh and up to the task, Koll, you can substitute as oarsman for one of them." Tove glanced at the other men, each one individually. Seemingly satisfied, she strode to the helm of her boat.

Koll's face pulsed red in anger. "Grab your sword. I'm not carrying that hunk of metal for you," he barked at Cass. "Or better yet, do yourself a favor and throw it overboard."

Cass stepped back as he moved toward her, thinking he would take her sword, but instead he picked up Cass's bag. Then he reached out and grabbed her arm tight at the bicep. He leaned in toward her neck and took an exaggerated deep breath.

Cass didn't understand what his action meant, but unease crept up her spine.

"This isn't over between us," he whispered into her ear.

Cass jerked away, putting a sliver of distance between them, before he grabbed her again and dragged her roughly behind him.

"Watch it, Koll," one of the men said.

Koll shot an ice-cold stare at the man but said nothing as he changed boats, Cass in tow.

****

Cass surmised they reached their final destination a few hours later when they'd maneuvered through the rocky shoreline of an isolated island. Although hate of the Vikings still coursed throughout her body, the emotion was softened by the hope of finally seeing her mother and Emma, who she hoped were being kept on the island. With the destruction to their village as Saewyn described, there must have been other Vikings living in this group who'd perhaps traveled ahead. If she'd not allowed herself to be caught, she never would have found the island or had a means to get there.

The uncertainty of what lay ahead still unnerved Cass, as did the cold stares from Koll. It was apparent she'd need to keep an eye on him, since she was certain he'd keep a tight watch on her. The security she'd felt the night before, whether real or imagined, no longer existed. She no longer had Gray by her side; the dagger she wore remained her only weapon. Tove carried her sword and bow and arrows. It was clear to Cass that Tove was angry with Koll for hiding Cass and her belongings from her. And why wouldn't she be mad? To the conqueror go the spoils, Cass thought, disgusted. At least Tove hadn't asked her to row once they'd switched boats, she'd grant her that. Tove only asked if she would clear water from the boat, which she did with no thought regarding the request one way or the other.

The island spawned several rocky slopes, but once the land leveled out, it didn't look much different than the green, grassy pastures, rolling hills, and scattered forests of Mercia, though the shrubbery stood shorter. Also, the trees nearer the coastline leaned in the direction of the constant wind that pummeled the island, a cooler wind than what Cass had grown accustomed to.

Farther inland, the group split up, with Koll and half the men walking east, and Tove and the others northwest. Cass breathed a sigh of relief at the sight of Koll's departure. She noticed Tove glanced in her direction as she did so, before she gazed once again straight ahead. Fifteen minutes later, Cass's eyes widened. They came upon a twenty-foot, grey, wooden structure with a curved roof and bowed out walls constructed of tree trunks. With the roof covered in grass and moss, it was as if the building rose up from the ground around it.

A brick chimney stuck out from the center of the grassy roof mound. Cass saw no windows in the structure and only one opening in the center of the longer side of the building. Around the outskirts of the structure, felled oak trees and an ash tree lay, along with cut planks and boats either under repair or under construction. To the right side of the house stood another roofed structure also longer in width than breadth, but half the size of the house they currently walked toward.

Animal pens with hens and goats and pigs were erected nearby, and Cass spotted what appeared to be a garden in the distance on the other side of the smaller house. With each step they took closer to the main structure, Cass's heartbeat quickened, in part due to not knowing what awaited her inside, and in part due to hoping to see her mother and Emma again.

Without warning, Tove stopped and extended her hand in front of Cass, effectively stopping her movement, as she directed the others to continue on without them. Once they'd gone, Tove said, "First, I apologize on Koll's behalf that you now find yourself in our midst. Koll should know better. We will not harm you. We'll decide how we move forward tomorrow. In the meantime, what's your name? I'd like to know how to introduce you, before we go inside and you meet the others."

"Introduce me as what, your slave? I'm sorry if I don't believe you won't harm me, but I think if you were standing where I am now, you'd think the same way. Where are my mother and sister? Will I be allowed to see them?"

Confusion evident on Tove's face, she said, "I don't know what you're talking about."

Cass clenched her fists. "You don't know what I'm talking about? Your people ravaged my village, burned our houses, killed and injured many of our fathers and brothers, and took our mothers and daughters. I only allowed myself to be captured to bring them back."

Tove studied Cass. "Although I admire your vigor, your anger is directed at the wrong person, or shall I say people. I'm sorry Koll stepped out of line, and I'm not quite sure what to do with you in the current state you find yourself, but believe me when I say we had nothing to do with the destruction of your village or the taking or killing of your people. I am sorry for your pain and loss. We'll talk more later, but for now, please tell me your name. I'm Tove."

"I know. My name is Cassethea," Cass said with a touch of venom.

"And where are you from, Cassethea?"

"Mercia."

Tove nodded. "Thank you." She extended her hand to the direction of the door. "Please."

As soon as they entered the building, Cass glanced from one corner of the structure to the other but saw no familiar faces. Was what Tove told her the truth? Did she have nothing to do with the capture of her family members? Tove seemed truly distraught by Koll's actions. But she was their leader, and a Viking, and therefore couldn't be trusted, Cass reminded herself. She'd overheard many of her father's conversations with visitors about the raiding and looting ways of the Viking intruders into England and King Ethelred II's ineptitude in stopping them, or any of the other kings, for that matter. But thoughts of her father only brought more anger and disgust. At this point, she didn't know who to believe.

"Everyone," Tove said, "I'd like you to meet Cassethea from Mercia. Cassethea is to be treated as a guest in our house. She was wrongly captured by Koll during our hunting expedition."

Cass ignored the onlookers and the rumblings between them and instead focused on her surroundings. The inside of the rectangular house didn't look much different than their own, though it was longer and wider and the floor was dug down about a foot along the entire center and hay covered the hardened dirt. Wooden posts held up wood beams that ran across the center and from one side to the other. The kitchen was the central room. A raised center platform served as a table, and the platforms on each side were used for sitting, and likely for storage and sleeping as well. The ends of the room were partitioned off. Cass couldn't see behind the partitions.

Cass turned her attention to the inhabitants of the house next. The family unit consisted of six men, four women, and three children, but Cass saw no older family members. Orm, who'd clashed with Koll, was one of the men. Two of the children ran toward her and wrapped themselves around her legs, before their mothers could grab them away and apologize. But being introduced and meeting Tove's family, who seemed friendly, only confused Cass more. Where were her mother and Emma?

Dinner passed as a solemn event. Though Tove made attempts to interact and bring the family into the discussion, the fact Cass would not eat didn't go unnoticed. She also didn't share in drink that was passed around in an intricately carved and inscribed horn. Due to its pointed end, the horn was not set down during the meal. As hungry as she was, the ache of loss spreading in her heart prevented her from eating.

****

After dinner, Tove directed Cass to the sectioned off room on the far left side of the longhouse which turned out to be Tove's bedroom. In the corner, Cass spotted the sack her mother had given her the night her father had thrown her out, her bow and arrow, and her sword. Tove motioned for Cass to sit on the bed while she poured water from a container into a bowl.

"You can sleep in here tonight. I'll sleep on the floor. On the other end of the house is a washroom and also storage room. Feel free to walk about. You'll find strips of smoked meat in the storage room, if you find yourself hungry later."

"I won't," Cass said, "but thank you."

Tove merely nodded.

"You trust me to be alone in your house...with your family, with my sword resting a few feet away?"

"Yes."

"Why? You know nothing about me."

Tove placed a cloth into the bowl of water and wrung it out. "That may be true, but I've attained a sense about your being, and I'm rarely wrong about these things. Besides, if you wanted to hurt someone, you had ample opportunity to have done so already with that dagger strapped to your ankle."

Cass reached to her ankle to ensure the dagger was still there. "How did you—"

"I'm also very observant, unlike Koll."

Cass sensed the truth in those words. She flashed to her earlier encounter with Tove on the boat. How quickly Tove had assessed her as a girl, and how it felt as though Tove was reaching into her soul for more.

"Enough talk for today." Tove reached toward her. "Give me your hands."

Cass looked away. "I'm fine. I don't need any help." Cass may not have located her mother or Emma, but that didn't mean they hadn't been taken, or that they weren't kept in another location, or that Tove and her people weren't responsible for the death of her brother, or that they didn't know where her mother and Emma were.

Tove pulled a three-legged stool from the corner and set it in front of Cassethea. "I know you are angry with me, but I swear on my parents' graves that neither I, nor my family or any of my people, had anything to do with the horror you described. I understand it may take time for you to heal and to see the truth in what I'm saying, but please, until then, try to withhold judgment. Let me do what little I can to help you." Tove stared directly into Cass's eyes. "Cassethea, please look at me."

Cass lifted her eyes into the penetrating blue warmth she saw before her. Tove appeared sincere, but how could she be sure? How could she trust? Cass breathed deep. She extended her blistered hands and flesh-torn wrists with reluctance.

Tove grimaced at what she saw, before she took Cass's hands into her own. She gently wiped away the grime and crusted rivulets of blood. Then she rubbed in a cool salve and wrapped Cass's hands in the softest cloth Cass had ever felt against her skin. "Sleep now. We'll talk more in the morning," Tove said.

Cass nodded. When Tove left the room, she undressed, leaving on her tunic, and crawled under the bearskin bedcover.

Chapter Fifteen

When Cass awoke, she hoped she'd awoken from a bad dream, but seeing the unfamiliar surroundings, she knew her current situation wasn't a dream. Her life dramatically changed the night her father disowned her, and it continued to morph since. All she could do now was take each day as it came and move forward as best as humanly possible. As she sat up and swiveled on the bed, about to stand, her feet brushed over the top of Tove's stomach. Tove lay on the ground next to the bed.

"Morning," Tove said as she rubbed her eyes, inched away from Cass's feet, and sat upright, one hand propped behind her. "I hope you don't mind I slept in here, but I thought it safer...for you. I don't trust Koll."

Cass nodded and glanced at her covered hands.

"How do you feel?" Tove asked as she stood. She wore only a white linen tunic.

Cass's eyes caught the round fullness of Tove's breasts under the tunic, and her breath hitched before she forced her gaze elsewhere. She flexed her hands into fists and released. "My hands are still sore, but not as bad as yesterday."

"Keep the bandages on. We'll take a look at them again tonight. I think you should stay here until we know they've healed properly. Do you agree?"

"Do I have a choice?"

"You will always have a choice."

****

Two weeks passed since Cass's abduction, during which time her hands and wrists healed. Tove allowed Cass to search the island to satisfy herself that her mother and Emma were not held captive. Tove accompanied her when searching the longhouse Koll inhabited with his family, but otherwise, Tove left her on her own. In her gut, Cass came to the realization early on that Tove had told the truth, but she still needed to prove it to herself by eliminating viable hiding places. Tove being truthful hadn't eased the burden Cass carried or the drive to find her mother and Emma. Those factors intensified with each passing day. If Tove and her band of Vikings didn't take her mother and Emma, then who did? At that moment, Cass felt very much like a helpless child, not like a girl maturing into a strong woman.

Cass decided she'd speak with Tove about her future plans, but she didn't see Tove upon waking or notice her in the kitchen. Only Rune's wife, Thyra, was visible as she cleared breakfast bowls from the table. Rune was one of Tove's four brothers.

"You slept hours past sunrise this morning," Thyra said. "You must have been tired." She stood as if waiting for a response but received only slight head movement from Cass in acknowledgment. "Are you hungry? How about a bowl of porridge while it's still warm?"

"Thank you. Porridge sounds wonderful. Do you happen to know where Tove is?" Cass asked.

"She said she didn't want to wake you, but I should tell you she went hunting." Thyra set the bowl in front of Cass.

"I wish she had woken me. I would've enjoyed going with her." A part of Cass wished Tove had asked her along to take her mind off her troubles. The distraction could have been healing, and hunting again would have been fun. Cass shrugged off her disappointment. "Maybe I'll go gather mushrooms and see if I can catch a few fish for dinner."

"I like your plan," Thyra said with a wink. "The thought of fish pan-fried with mushrooms is already making my mouth water."

Although she'd spent only a couple of weeks in Tove's house, everyone treated Cass in a kind and friendly manner. Thyra was no exception. If she were able to catch them fish for dinner, then in her mind she could, in a small way, repay the family for their hospitality and for never having judged her, which was not something she could take credit for not doing to them. She thought bringing food to the table was the least she could do before she moved on. The moving on part was the part she needed to speak with Tove about. After eating, visiting the washroom, and dressing, Cass grabbed her bow and arrows and stepped toward the door.

Thyra took stock of Cass, her head slightly tilted. "Fishing with a bow and arrow? I've not seen this technique before."

"It can be done," Cass said.

"I'm sure. But in the event you encounter problems, take this, and also a basket for those mushrooms." Thyra handed Cass a metal-tipped, wooden spear for fishing and a hand-woven basket.

"Thank you." Cass had never fished with a spear before. An attempt at spear fishing would be a new adventure. She touched the bow slung over her shoulder, more confident with its use, and content to have a backup in case the spear proved fruitless.

"Do you care for company?" Thyra offered.

"I'm sure you're plenty busy, but thank you anyway. I need some alone time to sort out my future, and hunting or fishing helps me clear my mind."

****

Within a couple of hours, Cass had collected a basket full of fragrant mushrooms and she changed course toward the stream. The water ran swift and colder than she thought. The sun had been strong that day, and the coolness of the water tempted her, reminding her of careless swims with Julia. When she closed her eyes at night, and she thought of Julia and the kisses they shared, it was as if no time had passed; the heat of those moments freshly rekindled. But then equally as quickly, she'd be reminded that Julia did not really want her, she wanted Prince Richard, a man she'd met only once. Why was life so unfair?

Cass pushed the unhealthy thoughts into the recesses of her mind and focused on what remained of the day ahead. She glanced around to make sure no one was near before she undressed. As she dipped into the cool wetness, the heat from her body escaped. The water caressed her skin like a lover she'd yet to experience. She relished the softness of it and closed her eyes, enjoying the feeling. Once fully refreshed, she stood and moved to the side of the stream, only to notice her clothes were nowhere in sight. Panic pulsed in her veins. Her line of sight darted from left to right and back again, an unease settling in the pit of her stomach. And then she saw him.

Koll sauntered from behind a tree, Cass's clothes hanging from the tip of his sword. "Looking for these?"

Cass sank into the water and covered her chest. "This isn't funny, Koll. Hand me my clothes."

He laughed heartily. "Why don't you come to me and take them?"

"You know why."

"Yes, I do. I told you this wasn't over, didn't I? You made a fool out of me in front of Tove and the others."

Cass's teeth clattered. She knew she couldn't stay in the water much longer and not suffer because of it. Numbness encroached on her toes and hands. "I did nothing wrong. If you had left me alone, none of that would have happened and neither of us would be here now."

"Yes, and what a shame that would be now, depriving myself of the fun I know I'm going to have with you. Pity I didn't know who you were sooner. I replay over and over in my mind how differently that first night would have gone." Koll licked his lips slowly and moved toward the stream. He tossed Cass's clothes off the end of his sword and stuck the tip into the ground.

Patience seeped from him. "If you're not coming out, then you'll force me to come in and get you, and believe me, you don't want me to do that."

"I don't know what you want, but I'd think twice before you take one more step, Koll. Tove wouldn't approve of what you're doing," Cass said, her breathing labored.

"Tove...Tove...Tove. Yes, I'm certain she wouldn't approve, and for more reasons than you probably realize, but she's not here right now is she? You and I are. I'm going to ask nice one more time for you to come out. If not, I'm coming in. Either way, I'm taking what I came here for. I've waited for this day long enough."

Cass's mind raced furiously in search of an escape plan, but an empty void greeted her. Her thoughts seemed frozen in ice. All she could think of was to run, but before she could move, Koll stepped into the water.

In two large strides, he was on her. Cass screamed as he seized hair at the top of her scalp. Her body crashed against rocks, and her knees scraped along the jagged bottom as he dragged her toward the edge of the stream. He tugged her viciously toward him and pushed her fully to the ground.

Cass screamed again as he grabbed her ankle and pulled her away from the water. She reached for tufts of grass to slow her progress, but she was unable to grasp a firm hold, her numb hands practically useless. She cringed, knowing he ogled her nakedness, powerless to do anything about it. He dragged her across the ground, writhing. When he stopped, he rolled her over and straddled her.

When he leaned his weight over her, Cass punched him in the side of his face with as much strength as she could muster, but he merely slapped her harder and laughed. He gathered her hands and held them above her head with one hand. With his free hand, he roughly grabbed at her chest and squeezed her breast. Tears rolled down her cheeks. "Get off of me!" she yelled, but Koll persisted.

"I think not. You're softer than I'd imagined you'd be, and feistier, too. This will indeed be a welcome pleasure." He released her hands and lowered his trousers. Cass moved her aching arms from above her head and covered her chest. She closed her eyes. If only Gray were with her. Rather than face the present, she let her mind wander in desperation. She mind-connected with an eagle. She called to it.

As Koll kicked her legs apart, the eagle swooped over him. He ducked and swatted after it, watching as it circled again. "What the hell?" he yelled. He grabbed his sword and held it above him. As the eagle approached a second time, Cass glimpsed her dagger lying on the ground, hidden behind a large stone. She stretched her fingers out as far as the tendons allowed and pulled the dagger toward her. Continuing to struggle from under his weight, she loosened the dagger from its sheath and clasped it tightly in her hand. The events that followed happened almost simultaneously with speed.

As the eagle swooped once more, Cass jabbed the dagger deep into Koll's thigh. He yelled out in pain and cursed furiously but didn't move off her. His eyes flashed with glances between her and the eagle, as if deciding who to deal with first. He yanked her hand from the dagger, and she grimaced in pain and yelled out from the pressure when he placed it under his knee. He picked up his sword a second time and raised it at the approaching eagle. But before he raised his arm fully, a familiar and distinct sound sliced through the air.

Koll's body jerked forward. His eyes went wide, and his sword arm swayed in the air. The sword dropped by Cass's side. The eagle continued its downward descent, claws spread open. His talons scratched Koll's face and eyes in one quick motion. Cass released their connection, and the eagle lifted higher and flew away.

Koll fell sideways off of Cass. She rolled him off of her the rest of the way and scrambled along the ground toward her clothes. She clutched them in front of her as she shook violently, more embarrassed at her nakedness than conscious of her pain. As she was about to dress, Tove approached and their eyes met. Tove bent down to help Cass up and embraced her in the safety and comfort of her arms. When Cass's nerves calmed and she allowed herself to look over at Koll once more, she saw blood-soaked clothes and an arrow protruding from his upper back.

****

Cass lay in the darkness, hoping sleep would claim her, but it would not. "Tove? Are you awake?"

"Yes, Cassethea. What is it?" Tove whispered from the floor.

"Today...by the stream...how did you know I was there?"

"Thyra told me you'd left in search of mushrooms and to secure fish for dinner. I wasn't tired, having returned from the hunt earlier than I expected to, so I decided I'd search you out and see if you had any luck fishing. Thyra said you looked puzzled when she handed you the fishing spear."

Cass chuckled, surprised she'd be able to feel humor so quickly, but being around Tove allowed her to decompress. "Yes, I imagine I did. I'd not spear-fished before." Cass fell momentarily silent, realizing she'd not gotten the chance to fish at all. The air felt suddenly thick. "Thank you again for today. I don't know what I'd have done if...if you weren't there. The darkness in his eyes...I can still see it as if he were standing in front of me now."

"Shhh, it's okay. It's over now, and he never got what he wanted, thank the gods. Though I'm not certain you needed me. You seemed to have done a good job on him yourself. The eagle, swooping down from the sky...I've never seen anything like that before. I'm guessing you have, though, haven't you?"

"Yes." The silence that followed sucked the air from the room. "I've always possessed certain abilities I realized early on were different from what most people experience. I never talk about them, though."

"I can understand that."

"About three weeks ago, it was revealed to me in my dreams—memories of stories my mother told me in my sleep—of why I have the abilities I do," Cass said.

"And why do you, if you don't mind me asking?"

"I am supposedly star born."

"I understand," Tove said in a faint whisper.

"You do? How? I don't understand it myself."

"In different ways, but also through stories told to us as children."

"Tove?"

"Mmm?"

"Would you sit here on the bed with me?" Cass heard Tove breathe deep, as if deciding whether or not to comply. When she heard Tove stand, she sat up and lifted the covers for Tove. The bed moved, and the softness of Tove's leg touched against her own. Her breath caught. "Thank you," Cass managed to say in a mix of emotion. "What does star born mean? Do you know?"

"Yes. Every hundred years or so, it is said four children are born, exactly one year to the day apart. Each is entrusted with one of four major powers, given to them through one of their parents and one of their ancestors in the skies. The powers are of water, fire, earth, and air, in that order. Often, the child never knows it possesses this power, and sometimes it comes to the child only out of necessity. Your star born power must be earth. It explains what happened with the eagle, your fearlessness, and the determination I saw in you that first day we met."

"I'm not sure how fearless I am."

"Believe me, you are."

"My father called me a witch," Cass said, her voice shaking.

"No. You're no witch," Tove said. In a softer voice, she added, "You are special."

Silence spread throughout. "Tove?"

"Mmm?"

"Do you mind holding me tonight? I'd rather not be alone."

A deep inhale and exhale of breath followed. "Yes, Cassethea...I can hold you tonight. You are safe with me. And tomorrow, I'd like to tell you something."

"Can't you tell me tonight?"

"No. You need your rest tonight. I'm tired as well."

"I have something to tell you tomorrow, too," Cass said, before her breathing slowed and the horror of the day, along with Koll's dark, soulless eyes, faded from her thoughts.

Chapter Sixteen

They sat next to each other on a felled ash tree after eating breakfast together in silence. They looked upon the grass and fields of Tove's home and listened to the pigs grunt in their enclosure. The hens chased each other from one end of their enclosure to another. Pungent smells of mixed variations of manure were another pleasant reminder of normalcy.

"The hens are noisy," Cass said.

"Maybe they sense a fox nearby. It's good we're sitting out here."

After an awkward silence, Cass asked, "What is it you wanted to tell me?"

"I've known since day one the whereabouts of your mother and sister weigh heavily on your mind. I didn't want to say anything to you about them until you were certain yourself that we had nothing to do with their capture. After you spent those couple of weeks searching, and after having spent enough time around us, I'm confident you've reached an inner certainty," Tove said.

"I have, and I'm sorry I doubted you."

"Don't be sorry. I'd have reacted the same way. What I wanted you to know was, for years we've heard stories that a King Andron, from your country, north of Mercia and the River Trent, disguises his soldiers in Viking clothing—Vikings his men killed—to rob and steal and pillage the land and people around him while facing no retribution."

"I've heard of him," Cass said, "and rumors that he enslaves people, including those from outside his kingdom's span of control, but nothing has ever been proven. And I know nothing of them disguising themselves as Vikings."

"He's not been caught because he's clever, Cassethea, not because he's innocent. It remains wholly possible he's the one who raided your village and took your people."

"My neighbor, Saewyn, who survived the attack, said she was one-hundred-percent certain the raiders were Vikings, and that they traveled west toward the Severn River—"

"What if the raiders were indeed King Andron's men disguised as Vikings, and what if they purposely traveled west so watchful eyes would see them? Then, once out of sight, what if they veered northeast in the opposite direction? The deception makes perfect sense," Tove said.

"Yes. It would give them time to escape without being followed," Cass conceded.

"Since the day you told me what happened, it's the only possibility I could think of. We were hunting where you thought those raiders would be, but we didn't see or hear anyone. If there were another Viking party in the area, I'm certain we'd have known about it."

Cass considered Tove's words. "If there's the slightest sliver of hope that's where my mother and Emma might be, then I need to go there. Will you return me to my home?"

"You are one person, Cassethea. What do you think you can possibly accomplish against a clever king with his army?"

"You're right. I am only one person. But as one person, no one would suspect me. And I have the power of extra sets of eyes and ears I can tap into when needed." Cass's excitement grew, and she paced in front of Tove.

"Not so fast. How many days were you on the road before my men caught you?"

Cass hesitated. "One day."

"One day. One day is exactly my point. You are not ready to take on such a task. What would be the point in letting you go simply to get yourself killed before you could help anyone?" Tove asked.

"I am ready. I have to be. My family needs me."

Tove's expression changed. Cass detected hesitation and sadness behind her eyes. "I'm telling you I'm ready. I have to go. I can't sit here and do nothing. It's not who I am."

Tove stood and faced Cassethea. "I'll make a deal with you. When you can beat me in a swordfight, I'll let you go. Before then, you stay and learn to fight and protect yourself. I sense greatness in you, Cassethea, but you can't rush it. You need to let it grow. I know it's not what you want to hear, but doing otherwise would be certain death to you and a lifetime of enslavement and misery for your mother and sister."

"I'm ready now. Let me get my sword," Cass said with certainty.

"You are not ready."

"I am. I can prove it."

"Only if you agree we have a deal on the terms I've stipulated," Tove said.

"I don't like what you propose, but what you say also makes perfect sense, so yes, we have a deal. But I'm telling you, my stay will be short-lived."

"For you, I wish that were true," Tove said.

****

The eventual duel lasted fifteen minutes, and in the end, Tove emerged victorious. She leaned on the pommel of her sword with one hand and extended the other to Cassethea, who sat, hands on bent knees, downtrodden, breathing heavily.

"Don't looked so surprised, Cassethea. I'm sure I have a couple of winters worth of experience over you, and I'm taller and stronger, but strength can be built and proper sword-wielding skills can be taught. The fire you have in your heart cannot be taught, and it's not something anyone can take from you, nor will the fire fade. Honestly, I was surprised you lasted as long as you did against me."

Cass's gaze lifted upward to meet Tove's. She absorbed the sincerity in them and reached for Tove's hand. Tove's words weren't spoken in mockery. "Perhaps there's much I still need to learn."

Tove grinned at her sparring partner. "Indeed. Is there also something you haven't told me regarding your sword?"

Cass didn't change her expression.

Tove said, "I carried the beast from the boat, if you remember. I placed it in my sleeping quarters, but it took most of my strength to do so. It isn't possible you could have wielded it today for as long as you did."

"Is that why you chose my having to beat you in a sword fight as the condition of my release?" Cass asked, with a glint of humor.

"There may be merit in what you say. However, be that as it may, I'm more interested in whether there are other powers you possess that I'm not aware of. Are there?"

"Not that I know of. I believe the power rests in the sword. I met a knight of King Alfred III's, a Sir William, by chance on a hilltop near my home where I often took our sheep to graze. He battled with another man there who tried to steal this sword from him. Sir William ultimately gave it to me." Cass used the sword to help her onto her feet. Once upright, she slowly unwrapped the animal skin from around the hilt, exposing the encased jewels. "He told me not to tell anyone about it, but I want you to know its origin. I don't want to hide anything from you or lie to you, Tove. Not anymore." Cass swallowed hard as the brilliance in Tove's eyes shone upon her.

"I appreciate your honesty more than you know. The sword is touched by magic?"

"Yes. Sir William said it was to be wielded by a star born destined to fight evil and free the oppressed—a warrior. Of course I argued with him. I told him he must be mistaken and pointed out all the reasons he had to be wrong about my being this warrior, but he insisted he was right. He said only the chosen one could lift and wield the sword."

"I can vouch for him there. There exists no way I could have fought and won today using your sword." Tove stopped. "I'm sorry I interrupted. Please go on."

"He said he searched two years for the rightful owner, but with no luck. He said he always thought he was looking for a man. It never occurred to him the warrior might be a woman. When I picked up the sword, and he saw how easy it was for me to lift it, his skin color paled at first, and then flushed crimson. Seeing his reaction, part of me still wouldn't believe him, but shortly after he left, many things in my life started to change, sadly not for the better. But it was through these series of events that my mother's words came to me in my dreams. Words she whispered to me many nights as I slept of me being star born. And now that you explained what star born means, all of the craziness is beginning to make sense."

Tove caressed the side of Cassethea's face. She moved her hands along the sides of Cassethea's arms, as if studying them or admiring them, or perhaps both. Cass was uncertain. But the heat that spread through her from Tove's touch was certain and all consuming. Her heart raced and her breathing deepened. Face flushed, she let Tove roam unhindered as Tove focused attention on Cass's right arm.

"Right here," Tove said, as she slid her thumbs across Cass's forearm. "You see these eight brown sun marks? They belong to those of The White Bear, healer and champion of all animals. The markings are arranged in the same pattern of stars in the night sky. These stars rest not far from those of The Eagle, who has the power to bring rain and lightning. I'll show them to you one night when the clouds aren't covering them."

"I look forward to it. I wonder now if my friend Julia might not have been star born too and carried the mark of The Eagle. There were so many hot days we spent together, but when I sat next to her, the air felt somewhat cooler, as though a light mist surrounded us. Whenever I'd mention to her we needed rain, that evening, it would rain. And she seemed drawn to the water, always wanting to swim in the stream..." Cass didn't elaborate. Her mind drifted to one moment when they undressed and swam in proximity, touching and laughing, and Cass recalled the heat between her legs scorched her even in the cold waters. As her memory faded, she noticed a shift in Tove's demeanor.

"You cared deeply for this Julia? Cared for her more than as a friend?"

Cass was surprised by Tove's apparent understanding of her deeper feelings before she shook her head. "She is to wed a man this midsummer, and she looks forward to it. We were just good friends."

"I see."

"Yes. It doesn't matter anyway. I don't want to talk anymore. Will you train me to fight as well as you fight?" Cass asked, though the hint of the sadness she'd seen in Tove seemed to linger on and she didn't understand why.

"I will, but we won't train with our swords yet. It's too dangerous. We'll use sticks at first so we can focus on technique, and eventually, we'll return to the sword."

The sticks they chose were thick and cut to the exact length of their swords. Cass remembered the many times her brothers sparred and the few in which they allowed her to join them. She was eager to prove herself to Tove after her first defeat, but Tove struck first, catching Cassethea on the arm, then across the belly.

"Keep your sword centered when you're contemplating where to strike your opponent. Provide yourself protection at all times. Watch the position of your opponent's feet, the width of their stance, and the subtleties in how they shift their weight or flex their muscle. Anticipate their next move before they do," Tove said, as their sticks struck together again, and again, and again.

Cass found it difficult to keep her eyes on Tove and listen and absorb her words at the same time, but she was determined to learn all she could and master what she learned.

"Good. Keep your feet shoulder width apart for more balance and flex your knees. Straighten your back. Shift your weight slightly toward me and lead with your sword hand."

Cass did as she was told and felt the increased jolt with her next strike.

"Good. Now work on evading my blows by ducking, twisting your torso, and stepping back. And when you sense an opening from your opponent, lunge forward and strike without hesitation."

Cass recognized the opening when Tove provided it, but she hesitated.

"No, not exactly," Tove said. "Try again. Yes, much better."

The remainder of the morning went on much the same way, with Cass not letting up, sweat pearling on her skin, until in response to one of Cass's lunges, Tove ducked low and leaned far backward, supporting her arched body on one hand. In an instantaneous motion, she swiped across Cass's feet with her legs, toppling Cass to the ground.

"That's it for today," Tove said.

"You cheated," Cass commented with zest and a pout as she lifted her aching body.

"There's no such thing as cheating when you're fighting an opponent who plans to kill you. They will do anything...and use anything they can, to their advantage. Trust me on that tidbit of knowledge. Now, come on and let's eat. I'm starving. Tomorrow's another day. Save part of me for then," Tove said, her lips partly turned up.

****

"I saw the two of you sparring today, and although I can't tell who won, I have to say you both look worse for the wear," Toke said before he tore a piece of wild duck from the bone.

"Funny, brother." Tove swallowed a mouthful of food. "Perhaps tomorrow you'd like to test your skills on me then, would you?"

"Not a chance. I'll leave the two of you at it," he said, giving his brothers Orm and Valken a mischievous grin. "Besides, I wouldn't want to take advantage of you after the stout effort you expended today."

Cass watched the playful banter and was warmed by their affectionate display.

"Enough now, you bunch of heathens," Thyra interjected. "Stop picking on your sister. Not that I have a better topic, but we have to discuss Koll's burial. Estrid learned Koll's burial will be tomorrow. I think we need to go together as a family, regardless of what happened. Everyone knows his fate was just, but our families still need each other. Our survival depends on it."

Tove spoke first. "Agreed, and as much as I don't want to go, because he does not deserve it, I will."

Cass sensed Tove's eyes on her. "I agree with Tove. You should all go. I can watch the kids for Rune and Thyra, and Orm and Estrid, while you're gone, if you want, unless it's your custom they attend as well."

"Thank you, Cassethea. The children don't need to be with us. We accept your offer," Estrid said.

Toke handed Cassethea the horn full of bjorr. "Tove told

us her thoughts on where your mother and sister might be, and we agreed she could be right. Is that why the two of you were sparring? Are you planning on going after them?"

Cass took a swig of the sweet, fruit wine nectar and passed it to Tove. "Yes, I am, when your sister thinks I'm ready, more or less." Cass knew the date of her departure would depend on when she'd be able to beat Tove in a sword fight, but she didn't want to reveal those details to the rest of Tove's family. From the corner of her eye, she caught a glimpse of Tove's lips turn upward.

"Good luck," Rune said. Then he and the rest of the group laughed.

Stories of each family member's day followed the laughter, as did storytelling of what Cass first thought must be tall tales for the kids. But then, based on her own encounter weeks ago with the monster spider in the woods, she wondered if they were tall tales at all and paid closer attention.

****

Cass followed Tove, surprised when they entered the forest. "Why aren't we practicing our sword fighting today?" she asked in dismay. She wanted to train as fast and as hard as she could. Each day that passed, she envisioned the suffering her family was going through.

"Correction. Practicing your sword fighting. I thought I'd mix it up and teach you how to build a boat today." Tove handed Cassethea a thick blade with a wooden handle on each end.

"Tove, I'm sorry, but I don't have time to spare building boats. You know this."

"What I know is, you need to have faith in me building your strength and your skills. We talked about this. Believe me that I will not consciously waste one minute of your time. I know what consumes your mind every day. I want to help you. I will help you. But you need to trust me."

"I'm sorry. Of course I trust you."

"Good." Tove picked up an instrument similar to the one she'd given Cass. They walked closer to the trunk of a felled ash. "We're going to scrape the bark from this tree. The bark rots the wood quicker if left on, so it has to be removed. I'll show you how to do this, and then you'll give it a try."

Tove held eye contact with her a moment longer than customary, and Cass swallowed hard. Tove extended her arms and set the blade of the instrument, which she held tight on both sides by the wooden handles, onto the bark and pulled back in one smooth, continuous motion. As she pulled, parts of the tree bark loosened. She continued the process over and over, but instead of keeping an eye on Tove's techniques, Cass's eyes focused on the rippling, taut muscles in Tove's well-defined arms, and the sweat forming on them, causing them to glisten in the light. Never had she seen muscles as well-defined on a woman, and the sight was surprisingly enjoyable to watch.

"You think you can do this?" Tove asked, one eyebrow raised.

Cass snapped out of the mesmerizing daze she'd found herself drawn into. "What? I'm sorry. Yes, I can do it. I'll get started now."

"Great. I'll work with you. Start on the far end of the tree, and I'll continue from the middle here."

If Cass thought rowing had been hard work, scraping bark off a twenty-meter ash tree was worse. But she quickly realized why Tove asked her to do this task and understood why Tove's body was so fit. As she drew off strips of bark, she wondered how hard Tove's stomach muscles were, as hers strained from the effort and the angle at which she had to work over the tree trunk.

After stripping the tree bark off the top and sides of the tree, they broke for a quick lunch and Tove explained how to saw off the first layer of wood. Tove stood on one side of the tree holding one handle of a saw, and Cass stood on the other. Cass felt Tove's power with each thrust of the saw and watched her focused determination. The smell of fresh-cut wood permeated the air and Cass's nostrils. The work was grueling and backbreaking at the same time. Cass ached for a dinner break. By the time evening rolled in, they were only halfway through their first cut along the length of the tree.

"Good work today, Cassethea. You can leave the blade

where it is. We'll continue tomorrow. For now, let's go eat," Tove said.

Cass tossed off the leather mitts Tove had given her and stretched her back. "You'll get no arguments from me. Food and sleep are what I need most. I don't know how you do this by yourself. You have my newly acquired admiration, that's for sure."

****

On the evening of the fifth consecutive day of work cutting boards out of the tree trunk, Cass was thoroughly exhausted. Her muscles were strained, yet at the same time, she felt invigorated by the work and sweat. She found herself looking forward to getting up each day and working with Tove, even though the task was arduous. She'd not experienced such satisfaction of accomplishment before, and she liked it. But this evening, Tove promised to show her the stars of The White Bear, and she was excited to see them.

Dinner was exceptional. Estrid grilled fresh salmon seasoned with ground mustard seed, along with parsnips from the garden, which were eaten with vigor. They drank mead and talked and laughed, like many nights before. And as much as Cass enjoyed dinnertime, it reminded her of the family she no longer had.

Cass followed Tove out of the house after dinner. They lay on the ground next to each other and stared up at the brilliant night sky, a soft breeze blowing across their bodies. "Ohhh, stretching out like this feels so good on my back," Cass said.

Tove laughed. "It does, doesn't it? And it's such a beautiful night."

Cass felt the effect of the mead relax her. "It is beautiful," she said into the quiet. They'd watched the deepening red hues of the day fade into the pitch darkness of night. After several more moments of silence, she spoke again. "Tove?"

"Mmm?"

"I want you to know I so enjoy dinners with your family. Dinner around the table with them is so different from what

I've been used to."

"Didn't your family eat together?"

Cass touched her toes together. "We did, but we were never at ease. There was always tension. My father did most of the talking, and more often than not, it was like an interrogation when it came to us kids. Maybe everyone didn't feel that way, but I did. Gollyn probably did, too."

"Gollyn is your brother?" Tove asked.

Cass thought about her last discussion with Gollyn and the odd connection they had, neither of them being her dad's favorites. "Gollyn was my brother. He was killed during the raid, stabbed through the stomach. He was only nine winters."

"I'm so sorry, Cassethea," Tove said in a soothing voice as she reached out and stroked Cass's arm.

"Thank you. I have two other brothers, Sedwick at twelve winters and Alfred, the oldest, at sixteen winters. They both went to fight in King Herrwald's army, I've been told."

"It's honorable of them."

"Yes. It's all they ever wanted to do. Alfred would have gone soon anyway, had the raid not happened. Sedwick is still young, but under the circumstances, he didn't have much choice. I'm proud of them, though. It's surprising they came from my father's seed. It's my mother they take after. We all do, really. Emma, the youngest does, too. She's sweet and innocent."

"I know you miss them. Think of this though. It's very likely, no matter how far away they are, they're looking at the same stars you and I are looking at now," Tove said.

A calm silence settled between them, as tears ran from Cass's eyes. "It's nice to think that's true."

Tove said, "Did you want me to show you the stars that outline the shape of The White Bear, or would you rather we do it another night?"

"I'd like you to show me now, and would you show me The Eagle, too?"

Tove didn't answer right away, but then Cass heard a quiet, "Of course."

As Tove pointed to the constellations, and by the light given off by the glow of the half moon, she matched the

marks on Cass's arm with the stars in the sky. The intimacy
of Tove's touch sent welcome shivers through Cass. And the
connection she now saw between the marks on her arm and
the stars in the sky silenced her for some time.

"Tove?" Cass said.

"Mmm?"

"What happened to your parents?" Cass turned to see
Tove staring straight into the stars, seeming to collect her
thoughts.

"We lived farther north than where you live, farther north
than where we live now, across the North Sea. The land was
similar to our home here but much vaster and much colder in
the winter. One night, around mid-summer, the Danes
invaded our homes and took what meager possessions we
owned. My parents were killed as were my aunts and uncles
and most of their children. I'd say half of our village
survived, including my brothers and myself, but the rest of
the village didn't come to our aid. They had their own mouths
to feed. They couldn't take us on as well. Before his death,
my father built longboats. I used to watch him and work with
him. That's where I learned the craft. Most of our boats were
destroyed or taken by the Danes. Boatbuilding turned out to
be what kept my brothers and me alive. We were provided
food and shelter for our labor. I was several years younger
than you are and became the head of our household. Once
we'd built several ships, there was no longer a need for us in
the village and our food supply was cut off. Hungry and
without shelter, we took our own boats and went on raids, my
brothers and I, to survive. We never killed unless we had to in
self defense, and we only took what we needed to survive and
to trade. We raided only until we found a new safe place to
call home and start over. On one of our excursions, Rune met
Thyra and later Orm met Estrid. As you know, Toke and
Valken remain single, as do I. Our life is much better now,
and we don't steal, though we do hunt on other lands for
food. I remember clearly, though, those first nights after the
raid, where we had nothing to eat, and every door I knocked
on turned us away. I can't blame them. That is the way. The
weak must make way for the strong. From the time we were
children, we were told stories of how grandparents honored

their children by leaving the household, once they felt they'd become a burden, and headed for the cliffs. Children born deformed are left in the cold to die. It is nature's way."

"Tove, those stories are horrible. That's a terrible way to live. It's cruel." Cass turned her head toward Tove, but Tove didn't look at her.

"Is it? I think it's crueler to let them suffer mentally and physically, than to let the will of the gods prevail. It's the way it's always been. It's also because of our history that I was able to accept what happened to us. At the same time, the Danes forced us into a situation we didn't want to be in. Yet, we managed to survive. It made me who I am. Your fight to survive will make you who you are."

"Thank you for sharing that part of your life. I'm sure it wasn't easy to retell your story."

"I was happy to share it with you, but it's you I should be thanking," Tove said, the moonlight glistening in her eyes.

"Hardly." Cass perched up on an elbow, reached over and brushed a loose strand of hair from Tove's face. Then she quickly cleared her throat and sat up. "I think we better go inside."

Tove said nothing but nodded in concurrence.

****

Weeks morphed into months of boat building and vigorous training that Cass looked forward to every day. Sword-fighting training, interspersed with boat building and hunting, filled her days. She finally learned to spear fish. In between the work, they often took breaks swimming in the sea, one trying to outdo the other. Cass even learned to climb the side of a cliff. And often after dinner, the family would play games to see who could jump the longest or who could pick up the largest boulder. During those contests, it was clear that Rune and Orm were trying to impress their wives, and Cass once thought Tove might be trying to impress her, but then she shook off the thought.

And in those months, Cass's upper body became well defined and strong, as did her stomach and her legs. She resembled nothing of the girl who was taken months before.

She was quick and agile and alert, and she had Tove to thank for all of it.

Cass enjoyed spending time with Tove, probably more than she should have. She and Tove became inseparably close. Cass continued to share Tove's bed with her, enjoying each other's warmth and closeness, though they never touched in any way other than friends would. Part of her wanted to know what it felt like to kiss Tove and feel her skin against her own, but another part knew she'd have to leave eventually. So, for the most part, she put such thoughts of Tove out of her mind. No good would come of it anyway. Julia was proof of that. Still, even as only friends, Cass was unsure how she'd bring herself to leave one day, but leave she knew she must, and soon. The pull was always present on her, and as autumn turned to winter, more so. And even though she'd not yet beaten Tove in a sword fight, she knew the day was close, which meant leaving was as well. Cass sensed Tove knew it, too.

After the winter, and after the snows thawed, the inevitable happened. Cass defeated Tove in a sword fight like none other. Cass finally found a weak moment and lunged forward without hesitation as Tove had taught her, tapping Tove on the chest with the point of her blade. The moment was bittersweet. Cass thought she'd be exhilarated by the victory, but Tove's sinking expression matched an odd pain Cass felt in her heart. When their eyes met, understanding transpired that no words could replace.

Tove extended her hand. "Congratulations, Cassethea. Well done. I've known you were ready for some time now, but you have proven yourself today. Let's celebrate with everyone as we should. Rune, Orm, Toke, and Valken will be proud of you as well. I know you've sparred with them on days I was away. After all, we must live for the future and not in the past."

Tears fell from Cass's eyes. She said nothing, at first, but stepped forward and embraced Tove. She held her for a long moment before letting go. "You're right. I have to take care of my past, though, or I'll never live in peace. Visions of my mother and Emma and the conditions they may be living under haunt many of my dreams. But thanks to you and your family, I believe in myself now more than I ever have."

Tove gave a final squeeze and backed away from Cassethea. "You will always be family, Cassethea. Please remember that."

Chapter Seventeen

Jess awoke with tears streaming from her eyes. Her first thought centered on why Cassethea had to be born into such a difficult life. Her dreamtime into the past kept extending into longer and longer intervals, which also drained her energy more, and today, she'd not woken up in the trailer, she'd woken in the spare bedroom of Rayne's house. Momentarily disoriented, the memory of the trailer break-in flooded her mind, as did Rayne's protectiveness and kindness offering to take her in. She felt lucky to know such a good person. As her eyes focused and her brain kicked into gear, her body called out for coffee.

With Rayne not yet awake, Jess quietly started a pot of coffee and headed into the shower. Then she dressed, poured herself a cup of coffee, and walked out onto the back patio. George slipped past to do his morning business.

The early morning air held its usual chill, and Jess wrapped her hands lightly around the mug. What was she going to do about the break-in, or about their discovery of the bishop, and the facts surrounding him that pointed away from him having been robbed and held captive by Vikings? How would she break the news to the chancellor? She'd have to tell him, right? Should she call Ellie? As Jess tossed conflicting thoughts back and forth through her mind, she grinned as George lay on a raised mound on the property, where the sun shone on him. The yard was mostly secluded with trees all around. Only one part of the backyard was sunny and open. Rayne's house and property were certainly nicer than her apartment, regardless of the apartment's more modern styling. "Playing king of the mountain, are you, George? I'm going in. Are you coming?"

George merely lifted his head, stared in Jess's direction, and whined before resting his head between his paws and relaxing in the sun.

"All right, suit yourself," she said and walked inside.

A few steps in, she heard the shower running. For a brief second, she envisioned what Rayne's body looked like under the spray of water, with her head leaned back and water cascading over her taut muscles and hardened nipples. As the sound of the water ended, Jess shook her head. "What the hell is wrong with me? Focus. Make breakfast. Yes, make breakfast. Good idea, Jessica."

She rummaged with vigor through the cabinets and refrigerator as if on a mission, a mission whose goal was to concentrate on anything besides Rayne's naked body. And what better than food to distract one's thoughts? Jess located the bread, butter, eggs, and milk, and went to work. With the bread in the toaster, she heard George bark at the door. "Of course, now you want to come in," she mumbled under her breath on her way to the door.

When Rayne entered the kitchen, Jess stood next to the round, wooden table with four chairs, George curled up underneath it. She glanced up as she set a fork next to Rayne's plate. A stack of sliced and buttered toast sat at the center of the table. "Hungry, I hope?"

"How did you guess?" Rayne said, as her line of sight shifted to George. "Looks like I'm not the only one either."

"Yeah, I'm sure he's hungry. I didn't know what you feed him though, so I did my best to convince him to wait for you. Also...I may have dropped a few pieces of toast his way."

Rayne's expression changed to one of amusement. She ambled toward the lower cabinet door to the right of the kitchen sink and pulled out a container of dry dog food. George lifted his head, sprung up, and pranced next to his food and water bowls. As soon as Rayne emptied two, half-cup-size scoops of food into his food bowl, George dug in and chomped away, on occasion glancing up at Jess and Rayne.

"That should hold him over. You know, you didn't need to make breakfast. Half the time I just eat a bowl of cereal," Rayne said.

Jess thought about her layout in the trailer these past

weeks. "Same here, except on weekends. Then I usually make myself a decent breakfast."

"I noticed you filled George's water bowl with fresh water, too, so thanks for that." Rayne poured herself a cup of coffee and sat at the table.

Jess walked over from the stove with a pan of eggs in one hand and a spatula in the other. "Not a problem. I'm glad you didn't mind me starting breakfast, although I have to admit I felt awkward going through your cabinets." Jess scooped out two eggs and placed them on the plate in front of Rayne. "I may have been a little nervous this morning, too, and often I cook when I'm nervous. As for your eggs, I guessed sunny side up."

"Perfect. And as far as I'm concerned, you can rummage through my cupboards anytime. No need to feel awkward. Besides, I'd be daft if I complained about you cooking for me, wouldn't I?"

Jess laughed. "I suppose so."

After Jess plated her own eggs and sat, Rayne continued the conversation. "What were you nervous about?"

"Hmm? Oh...well, maybe not so much nervous as...never mind. I'm not sure what I'm saying." Jess felt her cheeks redden.

"Right. Well then, how'd you sleep?"

"It took awhile to relax and get thoughts from last night out of my head, but once I did, I slept like a bear. Waking up was another story and took more doing. How about you?"

Rayne shifted in her seat, grabbed a slice of toast, and dunked it in the egg yolk. At the same time, George lapped up copious amounts of water and retreated under the table by Jess's feet. "It took me awhile, too."

"Sorry about that. I'm sure all the commotion didn't help. Thanks again for letting me stay with you. I do appreciate it."

"I'm pleased you did. I should've offered sooner. Clearly..." Rayne gestured in George's direction.

"He is a nudge, this one."

"You have no idea. He's lucky he's cute. So for today, what are your plans? Will you be okay alone? I was planning on working at the pub until seven or so, unless you needed help with the constabulary."

"I'll be fine. I appreciate the offer, but I need to handle this on my own. Besides, I have to call the chancellor, too, before he hears the news of the theft from someone else. Bad news travels fast. You'd be surprised how much backstabbing goes on behind the scenes in higher education; people jockey for your position or talk crap because they don't like you."

"Can't see why anyone wouldn't like you."

Rayne's words warmed Jess, but she wasn't about to let on she was flattered. "Right, says the woman who wouldn't give me the time of day the first time she met me, because I was a teacher."

"That's a bit harsh, wouldn't you say? Besides, my own scientific research proved me right."

"Is that so? Are you sure the jury's not still out on that one?" The corner of Rayne's mouth curled upward before she stood and carried her dishes to the sink.

"I think you know the answer to your question, Ms. Madison," Rayne said as she turned and held Jess's gaze.

Jess's heart hammered in her chest. Why does this woman affect me so every time she looks at me? Damn her. Did she have a sixth sense? Suddenly Jess felt naked. Could Rayne possibly know Jess was falling for her? Falling for her? What in the heck? "Perhaps. I suppose time will tell." Jess picked up her plate and coffee mug, trying to hold her hands steady and break eye contact with Rayne. "Would it be okay if I texted the students to stop by Eagles Landing today for lunch? I don't know how long the police are planning on keeping the place roped off, and it would save you or Baron the trip of having to deliver to the site where we're not supposed to be today anyway."

"Of course. Good idea. You'll be with them?"

"Most likely, yes."

"Brilliant."

****

The front door closed, and Rayne walked into the kitchen holding an Eagles Landing catering bag, George at her heels. "I hope you didn't eat dinner yet. Phillip made a cauliflower cheese casserole and beetroot salad. I know that doesn't sound fancy, but believe me, it's fantastic," Rayne said.

"You have impeccable timing. I was about to throw a frozen pizza in the oven, but the cauliflower and cheese sounds much better...and healthier. It'll be nice to be able to have dinner together for a change. I've been here three days already, and I think I've seen you only once, with our schedules and all."

"I know. I think you're right." Rayne took the containers out of the bag and placed them on the counter while Jess grabbed two plates. "The last time I saw you was on Monday when you ate lunch at the pub with your students. They're a lively bunch, aren't they?"

"I haven't actually spent much time away from the site with them, but yes, they can be. Marco's a bit of a playboy. He's good-looking and knows it, too. It's a shame. Not his handsomeness, but the fact he acts like he's God's gift to women, because I think Shelly, my other graduate student, is particularly fond of him. He's also a computer nerd, believe it or not. Justin and Mike are more into sports from what I overhear of their conversations. Susan likes to stir the pot. She's very intuitive."

"Is that right? She gave me that vibe the first day I met her. I noticed she was studying you quite intently."

"Yes, she does that now and again, when lightning strikes her."

"I'm not sure what that means," Rayne said, "but I think it may be best if I don't find out. Do you want to eat in the living room? My back's killing me today. We got a liquor delivery at the pub, and I think I may have pulled something hauling it in from the lorry."

"The living room's fine with me. Where was Baron when the delivery arrived?"

"He helped, but still."

"After dinner, you should put some heat on your back or take a hot bath," Jess said. "You know, to relax your muscles."

"Good idea. I'll go get the heating pad now."

When Rayne returned, Jess carried their food into the living room while Rayne opened the wine and filled their glasses. Jess sat on the sofa, her eyes momentarily drawn to the restored Viking shield and other artifacts in the room before they refocused on Rayne, who sat about two feet apart from Jess.

As soon as she sat, Rayne stood up again. "You mind giving me a hand with this?" She leaned forward, her hands on one end of the rectangular table. "It's a bit heavy to lift alone. I want to move it closer to the sofa."

"Is moving the table a good idea, considering the condition of your back?"

"It's fine. It's not that heavy really, just more awkward."

Careful not to rock the wineglasses while moving the table, Jess once again found herself admiring the muscular definition in Rayne's arms, purely in a platonic manner, of course.

"Have you heard any news from the constabulary about the burglary?" Rayne asked, after she placed a spoonful of casserole in her mouth.

Jess had already scooped up a spoonful, causing her taste buds to dance. "Mmm, oh, my God, this casserole is unbelievable. Please be sure to compliment Phillip for me." Jess moaned once more before answering Rayne's question. "And no, I've not heard any news yet on the burglary front."

Rayne held her spoon motionless on the way to her mouth at the sound of Jess's first moan and seemed doubly flustered when she moaned a second time, as she returned the still fully laden spoon to her plate. She nodded and her gaze dropped quickly from Jess to her plate.

Jess stared at Rayne and then smiled a knowing smile. "PC Strongwell spoke with Joel Fisher and his wife, but he thinks Joel had nothing to do with the theft, other than perhaps blab too much about what we were uncovering. He says he thinks he did so only for conversational purposes. He appears to find what we're doing fascinating. His wife confirmed he'd been home all last Sunday night. PC Strongwell also mentioned he spoke to Morey, the construction company owner. He said there might be something there, but he wouldn't say what exactly."

"Typical. Honestly, I don't see who else it would be if they think whoever stole the jewelry opened the door with a key and made it look like a burglary later," Rayne said.

"I agree, but apparently they think there's more to it."

"There always is, isn't there?"

"There can be." After a prolonged silence, Jess said, "Rayne, do you mind if I ask you a personal question?"

"Of course not." Rayne sat back and relaxed into the sofa.

"When you told me you and Baron had taken over the pub from your father, you said running the place wasn't what you always wanted to do. What did you want to do?"

"I went to uni to study to become a psychologist and have my own practice. I wanted to help people who had issues they couldn't deal with on their own."

Rayne inhaled deeply. Jess kept quiet, knowing more was to come.

Rayne glanced into Jess's eyes as if searching for reassurance. Jess nodded, and Rayne continued. "Growing up, I had a best friend in school. She lived one town over from us, but we managed to get together on the weekends and we saw each other in school all the time. She wasn't athletic and not what most would consider pretty, so she got picked on a lot. Her lack of friends might even be what drew me to her in the beginning. I didn't think it fair for people to tease her, so I sort of became her protector in a way. She was a good person with a good heart. She loved animals and poetry and art, which is odd for a kid her age. Anyway, we became fast friends and taught each other about things neither one of us probably would have given a toss about otherwise. Her family moved away when I turned thirteen. We kept in touch, but talking on the phone or writing wasn't the same as spending time together. In her letters, I sensed her becoming emotionally distant. I tried to help her, but I couldn't get through to her. A year later, I got word she'd killed herself— the result of bullying at her new school. It gutted me."

Jess placed her hand on Rayne's leg. "I'm so sorry."

Rayne seemed to pull her thoughts into the present and focus on Jess. "Thank you. It's been many years, though, so I'm better about it. Sometimes I feel guilty for agreeing to take over the pub with my brother. I think about what I could have done with my education versus what I'm doing now."

"I get why you'd feel that way, but if your parents' business had gone under, you'd have felt guilty, too. And if you don't mind my saying so, I've seen you interact with your customers and the regulars at the bar. Whatever it is you say to them makes a difference. They're happier around you."

"That's only the effect of the alcohol on them."

"No, it's more than that. You treat the regulars like family, and I think some of them need a sense of connection in their lives. There's something special about the ease with which you talk to them and comfort them. I've seen it. It's inspiring to watch, frankly."

Rayne stared at Jess for a moment. "I'd not thought about the effect of my presence in the pub before. I do try to make everyone happy. So does Baron. And I don't do that because happy people buy more drinks. I care about them all."

"I believe you do. All but foreign teachers," Jess said.

"Right...all but feisty foreign teachers. I have to say, though, it sounds like you've been watching me pretty closely, with all this insight into me you seem to have acquired. Why might that be?"

"That explanation, Ms. Kvale, is better left for another day. I think it's time for me to get some much-needed sleep."

"Good luck with that."

Chapter Eighteen

Returned to England's western shore by Tove and her brothers, Cass stood on the water's edge, a stabbing pain in her heart. She and Tove walked along the shoreline out of earshot of the others, who waited by the boat after they'd said their good-byes.

"Are you sure you don't want me to come with you?" Tove asked in a strained tone.

"I'd love for you to come with me, but we both know you're needed by your own family. Plus, if I'm lucky, perhaps my family's been found by King Herrwald's army by now. I'll need to check with Saewyn before I travel anywhere." Cass tapped the side of her backpack. "Thank you for the map to King Andron's kingdom and for everything you've done for me, Tove. I don't know how I'll ever be able to repay you."

"You can stay alive. Will I ever see you again, Cassethea of Mercia?"

Cass reached for Tove's hand. She soaked in the love emanating from those brilliant blue eyes as the stabbing pain intensified in her heart. "I hope so, my friend, I hope so." And then, for reasons unknown, Cass's eyes fell to Tove's lips. She moved closer to Tove, and as Tove lowered her head, Cass kissed her on the lips, softly and with all the emotion she possessed in that moment.

When their lips parted, Tove appeared dazed. After a few moments of silence, she said, "I better go. Take care of yourself, Cassethea, and may Gaia watch over you."

And with those words, Tove turned on a heel and strode to the longboat and her brothers awaiting her. Cass's hand rose in the air in good-bye, knowing Tove wouldn't turn around. Cass was surprised by the ache in her heart. Her breathing was tight, and her legs weak. The realization of what Tove meant to her was still unclear, yet at the same time, seeming to find the light. A part of her wanted to follow Tove, but she knew that path was impossible. She had to find out what happened to her mother and Emma, if she wasn't already too late. Cass shook off the negative thought and refocused. With each step toward Mercia and Saewyn's sister's house, Cass gained strength from the earth beneath her feet.

****

The visit with Saewyn ended bittersweet. The reminder of a life she'd once had, and the comfort and security that life had provided, clashed with the reality of a future that would continue to be much different. Arielwund and Emma hadn't been found by King Herrwald's army. The army searched only a few days before the kingdom came under attack by Arabs from the east, and so the army redirected the search to protect the kingdom and those who remained. No news existed regarding the whereabouts of the king's daughter, Julianta. Cass honestly believed it couldn't have been true that Julia had been taken, and if she had been taken, she thought for certain the king wouldn't have stopped looking for her. Yet Saewyn's brother pointed out that if the king didn't also have a son, or if his son had been taken rather than his daughter, the search would likely still be on. The reality of Saewyn's brother's statements was difficult for Cass to accept. She couldn't believe the king would ever stop searching for his daughter until she was found, but the fact that all the female villagers and children taken remained missing, along with Julia, with no search ongoing, was proof this was indeed the case.

The thought sickened Cass, the same as it had sickened her the day her father threw her out of her own home. She couldn't understand why she'd meant so little to him, she or her brother, or why Julia meant so little to her father. With those thoughts, she marched toward the remnants of her burnt-out home, toward the garden. In front of the makeshift grave she'd erected for Gollyn, she said a few words and a prayer for the success of the trip she was about to undertake.

Then she pulled out the map Tove had given her and began her travels northeast.

****

The first week of her trek was arduous and beyond lonely, but Cass found food plentiful and built fires at night for protection and comfort. The weeks that followed were more difficult. Cass experienced more days of rain than sun, unable to start fires for warmth. Food grew from scarce to nonexistent. Cass couldn't understand the shift happening. Her mind, too, remained silent with regard to connecting with other animals; it was as if the animals had disappeared. The handful of fruits and mushrooms she found along the way weren't enough to sustain her. Her use of energy was high from walking all day. Lightheadedness often became an issue, and she found decisions more difficult to make.

In the beginning of her journey, she kept up with her upper-body training, the way Tove had taught her. Each night, after setting up camp, she found and lifted a ten- to twenty-pound rock, hoisted it over her head, gently lowered it, and repeated the process multiple times until her arms ached. She wanted to remain physically strong, knowing she'd need every asset at her disposal when the time came to free her family and Julia. But as the days passed and the food opportunities grew scarce, she lost the strength to train at night. She lost considerable weight, and with the weight loss, her progress slowed and her thoughts often drifted. Focus became a commodity more and more difficult to find.

Cass wished Gray was back in her life. He would keep her mind sharp and her body warm at night and, possibly, keep her fed. This night she slept with blistered feet from the seemingly constant dampness, after having now walked half the total distance she'd hoped to. When sleep took her, she drifted into dreams of stories told to her by her mother of her ancestors, of AEthelflaed, eldest daughter of Alfred the Great. She envisioned AEthelflaed fighting off Norman and Viking raiders. But then her thoughts would inevitably float back to Tove and the friendship they shared and then to Julia and their friendship. But Gray wasn't in her life and didn't appear en route, and Cass once again spent a fitful and chilled night alone.

The next day, uncertain how she'd rise and continue on, Cass convinced herself the weather would break and that food would once again become abundant. And so she did rise and push forward, legs strained as if they dragged a heavy chain around her ankles. Her mind wandered often and played tricks on her. All the while, she sought out other animals with her mind, including Gray, with no connection made.

As darkness drew near another night, Cass thought she saw a hut-like structure ahead in the woods, the woods that had provided at least a wisp of protection from the relentless rain. Her heartbeat quickened as she smelled smoke from the chimney, yet at the same time, her senses fired signals of caution. As she waited behind a tree, she saw a woman wearing a dark cloak and wool cap step from the entrance and round the corner.

Cass glanced into the structure from where she stood and saw no one else inside. When the woman returned with an armful of cut wood, Cass thought she saw her glance in her direction before going inside and closing the door. Cass decided if she didn't seek help now, she may not last through the night, and this home appeared safe enough. Mind set, she slogged onward toward the structure and knocked on the door with what failing strength remained.

Cass gasped when the woman opened the door. She embodied a strikingly similar appearance to Julia. She was perhaps a couple of winters older, more mature, but had the same flowing golden hair and green eyes as Julia. Cass thought she heard the woman say, "Come in, I was expecting you," but then she thought her mind was probably playing tricks on her again. Next, she remembered drinking a tepid, fruity liquid and being put to bed, but she remembered nothing else of that evening before she awoke the next morning.

****

A ray of sunshine shone through a hole in the roof's thatching, onto Cass's face, waking her. She sat up, her head foggy but not to the extent of hiding her embarrassment. She woke with no clothes on. She held the linen blanket above her chest and, lifting her head, searched her surroundings. In the center of the small, arched-roof structure she saw a circular stone oven. In front of the oven, a few feet from the hearth, sat a rocking chair. Herbs of many sorts hung from thin crossbeams of branches from the ceiling.

Two wooden bowls, two cups, and two spoons had been placed across from one another on a wooden table located perhaps three feet from the rocking chair. Next to the table, resting on the dirt floor sat two large, wooden chests, pushed against the opposite wall. Cass's dagger lay on top of one of the chests, and her sword, in its sheath, stood leaned against the other chest, as did her bag and bow and arrows. To the right of those chests, closer to the fire, a wide bench rested against the wall with rolled blankets on top. Cass's clothes, however, were nowhere to be found. She sat up as the front door creaked open. She drew the blanket more tightly to her, trying to wrap part of it around her back.

In the opening stood Julia's double, holding a bundle of wood in her arms and Cass's clothes on top of the wood. She paused and smiled at Cass before kicking the door shut behind her. Without a sound, she placed Cass's clothes over the back of the rocking chair with one hand and then dropped the wood on the floor next to the fire. She pulled off her cap, tossed her long, blonde hair back and forth, and took off her jacket.

"Good morning, stranger. I'm encouraged you're finally awake," she said, as she hung her coat and hat on pegs in the wall next to the door. Then she returned to stand next to the fire. "I was beginning to think you'd never wake up to eat, and by the sight of you, eat you must."

The flood of memory Cass had, of having knocked on this woman's door the night before in the rain, came back to her at the sight of the woman's body, hair, and eyes. "Who are you? You look oddly familiar to someone I know."

"I do? What a strange coincidence," the woman said, her laugh forced. "My name is Haddontek, but you can call me Haddie."

"Haddontek sounds like a man's name."

"It does, doesn't it? Let's say my parents cultivated an odd sense of humor and leave it at that, shall we? Though you're one to talk, dressing like a boy, when clearly you are a young woman."

Cass felt her cheeks blush. "Why are my clothes by the fire?"

Haddie took two steps backward toward the hearth. "They're drying. You couldn't stay in them. You were soaked, and both you and your clothes smelled badly. When the rain let up, I carried your clothes to the creek to wash them. I hope you don't mind. I don't believe there was a better option."

Cass couldn't seem to focus well, but the thought of a stranger undressing her, even a beautiful woman that reminded her of Julia, produced a sense of unease. She wanted to be grateful for the woman's hospitality, but somehow, she couldn't.

"Why don't you get up, and I'll pour us a bowl of mash."

Cass raised her eyebrows as she glanced at her hands clenching the blanket. "Like this?"

Again, Haddie smiled. She walked over to the wooden chest against the wall opposite Cass and extracted another blanket, along with a sash to tie it with. As she walked closer to Cass, Cass felt drawn to her. "Here, put this on for now. Your clothes shouldn't take long to dry."

"Thank you." Cass took the blanket and wrapped it over her shoulders as Haddie walked to the center of the room. Then she stood. She glanced down at herself and cringed as she saw her thin frame. At that moment, she realized how close to death she may have actually come. As she tucked the blanket tight around her, she added, "Thank you for taking me in last night."

A laugh echoed in the tight enclosure. "Last night? You've been asleep for three days."

"Three days? That can't be."

"Oh, it very much can be so, which is why I'm thinking you must be starving right now." Haddie scooped out a second overflowing ladle of mash and placed it in Cass's bowl. Then she filled her own bowl and sat, eyes focused on Cass. "By the way, you haven't told me your name yet."

Cass had already stuffed two mouthfuls of mash in her mouth before her eyes lifted and she stared into the pools of green, momentarily distracted. She swallowed and wiped her mouth with the back of her hand. "Sorry. My name is Cassethea, but you can call me Cass."

"All right, Cass it is then. I think you and I will become fast friends, Cass."

"Although I appreciate beyond words your having taken me in, I'm afraid a friendship is not likely to happen. I can't stay long. My family is in trouble and they need me," Cass managed to say between spoonfuls.

"We'll see," Haddie said. "Time will tell. Now drink up. The elixir has healing qualities that will help you get on your feet quicker."

Cass wanted nothing more than to get back to her prior self in strength and mental clarity, so she nodded and drank.

****

The days were passing and Cass's body was gaining mass and strength once more, but not much else was registering with her. Her days were spent gathering stones and branches and moss that Haddie used to expand her hut and repair the roof. Cass also carried water to the hut and hunted. The animals that were previously absent were now plentiful, and the rainy days that plagued her trip were gone. Rain happened only at night.

In return for Cass's labor, Haddie cooked for her. Each night they ate together and talked, but Cass couldn't remember what they talked about, only that they had talked. And in the evenings, Cass was so tired she went to sleep not long after their meal was consumed. She couldn't remember much except that her dreams held the underpinnings of darkeness and despair. Some nights she thought she heard the rocker creak as she imagined Haddie rocking back and forth in it, but the thought never lasted long enough for her to discern if the sound was real or not. Cass's days and nights went on like this, day after day, night after night.

But on this one night, Cass's dreams were not of darkness and despair, but of goodness and hope. She saw

Julia's soft face cupped in her hands. She leaned in to kiss her, and as their lips lightly touched, Cass's breathing quickened and the vision of Julia shifted to that of Tove. Cass smiled into welcoming eyes of blue and kissed Tove gently at first, gladdened that Tove returned the kiss with equal intensity. Warmth filled her chest and chased away the darkness.

The next morning, Haddie appeared on edge and distant to Cass. She told Cass she needed to make a trip into town to buy provisions and asked Cass to continue on with her work on the hut while she was away. There were other days during Cass's time with Haddie where Haddie also left for a day or two and returned, telling Cass stories of disease and dying when she returned. Cass didn't know the people Haddie spoke about, yet somewhere deep inside, she sensed she should feel empathy for them and for their loss, but she didn't. The grim stories seemed not to bother Haddie either, so Cass shrugged off the odd sensation.

She remembered after dinner one night asking Haddie why such a beautiful woman as herself lived alone, and what had become of her parents. Haddie merely responded that her mother died of fever and that her father left shortly thereafter. She told Cass she enjoyed living alone, for the most part. And before Haddie walked out the door for this trip, she stared long into Cass's eyes, her brows wrinkled, as if puzzled. Cass didn't speak or ask Haddie what troubled her. She merely turned and walked out the door in front of Haddie. Haddie went in one direction, and Cass headed in the other to search for more stones for the expanded hut, her face expressionless, just as she had every other time she and Haddie temporarily parted.

By midday, Cass had made five trips back and forth between the hut and the spot along the stream she'd carried most of the rocks from before she realized she'd not eaten breakfast. When she entered the hut on her sixth trip, a bowl of mash and drink sat on the table in what had become her spot. Cass scooped the food back into the black pot that hung on a bar inside the brick stove and set her drink on the counter. She wasn't in the mood for the fruity elixir this day, and last she checked, her body had returned to its toned and muscular self, so she didn't feel she needed it. Instead, she ripped off a chunk of bread and cut off a section of cheese and carried the food back with her as she headed toward the stream.

During the walk, she began to sense random thoughts trickle into her mind and hear more sounds, sounds she'd not heard in what seemed like months. Her dreams from the prior night made their presence felt as well. When Cass reached the stream, she placed her lunch on a rock, leaned in, and cupped a few handfuls of water. After drinking the water, she sat and ate and quietly listened to the water ripple over the rocks. When was the last time she'd relaxed to listen to the water? When was the last time she'd asked herself that question?

As Cass chewed on the fresh bread, she stared into the water. Thoughts of Tove kissing her flashed through her mind, and she felt a longing to see her. Then flashes of Julia's face and Tove's face intertwined with Haddie's face and interrupted her thoughts that were capped off with a glimpse of a wrinkled old woman with green eyes.

Cass dropped what remained of her bread and gasped. She rubbed her hands over her face. What's going on? Am I going mad? She sat motionless. For how long she sat, she didn't know. A howl in the distance distracted her. Was it in the distance, or was it closer? She glanced as if in slow motion around her, not quite taking in all her surroundings but somehow absorbing more than she recently had.

Sensing possible danger, Cass stood and grabbed two stones, the size of which filled her palms, and strode toward the hut on the same worn path she'd trudged days on end. Every now and then, she thought she spotted a flicker of an animal pass next to her but ignored what she thought she saw, convinced her mind was playing tricks on her. Perhaps she needed to lie down. Maybe the heat was affecting her. All the way to the hut, she stopped and turned numerous times, as if a ghost was following her, but no one was there. She felt something rub against her leg but held tight to the rocks she carried and kept moving, eyes focused forward.

When she reached the hut, she dropped the rocks and opened the door. She walked in, sat on the bed, turned, lay down, and closed her eyes. The howling in the distance didn't go away, and she wondered for a brief moment before falling into sleep, if she'd closed the hut door. She was too tired to check, but somehow she thought she had. Oddly, the howling didn't frighten her as she thought it would; it merely lulled her to sleep.

Chapter Nineteen

Cass woke to licks on her face and a grey wolf hovering over her. As soon as she opened her eyes, the wolf stepped back. Cass sat up. "I know you, don't I?" Cass said.

The wolf howled and ran toward the open door, then back to her, then to the open door once again.

"Whoa, hang on there a minute. What's the matter with you, and how did you get in here?" Cass asked as she tried desperately to shake the cobwebs from her thoughts. Then her mind connected for a brief second with the wolf. At first, her ability to connect with the wolf surprised her, but she tried again and connected a few seconds longer and then a few more seconds. Suddenly, she yelled "Gray!" and ran over to him and hugged him. "How long have you been here? Wait. Where am I?" Cass glanced around the room as if seeing it for the first time. Pieces of her memory and of the night she found herself outside the door in the rain flashed back to her. She sat and petted Gray. "Something is very wrong, Gray," she said, as her stomach growled. "Let me get us something to eat while I try to figure this out."

Cass stood and walked toward the oven. She opened one pot which had mash in it and the other that contained a meat stew. Although it was morning, the stew called to her. She filled her bowl and Gray's and ate without speaking. Cass wracked her brain for answers but found none. She filled their bowls a second time and then poured herself a cup of the elixir, needing to calm her nerves. She set the cup on the table next to her soup and finished her second bowl. As she reached for the cup, Gray growled deep.

Cass sensed fear for the first time in Gray's presence. "What are you doing? What's the matter with you?" Cass watched as Gray kept his teeth bared. As she released the cup, he seemed to relax. "That's better. For a minute there, you scared me." Then Cass picked up the cup and put it to her lips.

Like a shot of lightning, Gray sprang up on her and knocked her and the cup to the floor, teeth visible once again.

But before Cass could get up, she watched in horror as the elixir, which had spread all over the dirt floor, pulled itself together into one mass and moved back inside the toppled-over cup. Cass pushed herself from lying on her side to sitting on her bottom, and like an upside-down spider, scurried quickly away from the liquid, Gray by her side backing up as well. "What the...did you see that? Gray, did you see that?" Cass glanced at Gray and then realized what had happened. He'd sensed what she couldn't. He'd saved her life. She looked into his eyes. "You knew, didn't you? Thank you, my friend. I don't know how you found me, or where I am, but I think we better get out of here and quickly."

Cass searched the hut for any information that might help her piece together the confusing puzzle of what had happened to her and who the woman was that took her in. She rummaged through the unlocked wooden chest and pulled out a black tunic with a hood and a gold sash. The tunic was long and broad, much too long for someone Haddie's size. Perhaps it once belonged to Haddie's father? She uncovered talismans and other stone bowls of odd shapes and sizes. A chill ran through her when she reached deeper and pulled out a dagger. The dagger had ornate carvings etched in the handle, but they were of skulls and faces depicting anguish. The handle felt hot in her palm. A dark energy seemed to penetrate the room. She tossed the dagger into the chest and quickly shut the lid. "Let's go, Gray. We need to get as far away from here as we can, and fast."

The farther Cass and Gray traveled from the hut, the clearer Cass's thinking, and the lighter the tightness in her chest. However, a thin thread of energy still tugged on her, trying to draw her back, but she continued to move forward. She shuddered to think what would have happened to her had she not experienced a brief moment of clarity, and had Gray not come along when he did. She'd heard of dark forces before, but she didn't believe in them, probably because she'd never encountered them. All her life, her thoughts were good and honest, focused on helping other people and animals and being a good daughter. Her thoughts had been pure...well, relatively pure before she met Julia. Now, she didn't know what to think. What thoughts were hers, and which ones weren't? What desires were real, and which ones weren't? What did Haddie want with her? And how much time had she lost in Haddie's grasp when she should have been searching for her family and for Julia?

****

The farther Cass and Gray traveled from Haddie's homestead, the better Cass felt. Whatever thread chained her to that place had torn its last fiber, and when it did, Cass sensed the hold on her release instantly. She was sure Gray sensed it also. Cass was thankful for Gray's presence. The two friends walked together, mostly in silence, though Cass sometimes shared her inner thoughts with Gray. Cass hunted for their dinner in the late afternoons, which they always shared, and Gray brought them food in the morning, after a night spent hunting. And for most of the night, except when Gray hunted, they slept together peacefully by the fire and kept each other warm.

But as each day passed, the nights filled with more and more dreams—or perhaps memories—of Cass's evenings spent with Haddie. The memories came only in brief flashes. The images were scattered and never long enough for her to discern meaning from them, but they brought with them a sense of unease. She recalled flashes of the golden-haired Haddie up at night, standing in front of the fire of the brick oven, the glow from the flames lighting her soft facial features. She mumbled and waved a smoldering bundle of dried herbs in her hands, but Cass recalled no feelings connected to that memory. If what she thought she saw was even a memory. Other times, she'd see the same scene of Haddie standing before the fire, but Haddie would switch from a beautiful woman to a wrinkled old woman, and her amiable, smiling face would turn to a steely-eyed one. It was always at those moments Cass would wake, and a sense of unease would return, making it difficult to return to sleep, when rest was what she desperately needed after tiring days of walking and watching out for danger.

On this morning, Cass awoke to Gray's howl. A fat rabbit lay next to the fire, and Cass smiled. She grabbed her dagger, skinned the rabbit, and cut off the hind legs. She tossed the remainder of the carcass to Gray. "Thank you, Gray," she said, and placed another log on the fire, while Gray ripped into his breakfast. "Do you know, watching you eat makes me almost lose my appetite?"

Gray lifted his head only for a moment before finishing off the rabbit, bones and all.

Cass ran a stick through the rabbit legs and held them over the fire. "Yeah, didn't think you'd care."

After breakfast, Cass checked her map. She mind-connected with a falcon flying overhead and compared the layout in front of them to the markers on the map Tove made for her. She wondered how Tove was feeling. Did Tove think about her at all? Did Tove have deeper feelings for her, or was she simply another person that passed through Tove's life? She hoped she had deeper feelings, feelings like those Cass had dreamed about. She touched the deerskin map and ran her hand slowly across its surface. She pictured Tove's brilliant blue eyes, seductive smile, and soft lips, and breathed deep. Then she rolled up the map. "All right, Gray. Let's get moving. We've got a way to go yet." She pushed herself to her feet.

Not much excitement filled the morning quiet, other than them searching for a way around a wide bog, which would not have been passable had they attempted going straight through. However, in the afternoon, Cass heard agitated voices talking up ahead. She signaled to Gray to be quiet, and she crouched lower to the ground. She made her way toward the commotion, but stayed behind tree trunks and ground cover as best she could. She spotted a man and woman in peasant attire sitting in the front of a horse-drawn carriage, trying to keep their horse steady, pleading with a man on a horse off to the side of the road, also dressed as a peasant, but armed with a sword. A second man, already off of his horse, strode to the back of the wagon, which was made of interwoven sticks and branches about a foot or two high on the sides and open in the back. The man spat on the ground and rubbed his unkempt beard. "Huh? Well, what have we here now?" Cass heard him say. He approached the wagon with the same cockiness in his walk and right of entitlement as Koll displayed those many months before.

A visibly nervous young girl in a woolen dress sat off the back of the wagon, legs dangling over the edge, feet bare and dirty. She sat next to a basket, bundles of vegetables, and sacks of grain.

"Oh, I think I'm going to enjoy this," the bearded man said. He stood next to the rear of the wagon and grabbed the girl's arm with one hand, yanked her closer, and squeezed her breast with the other hand. The girl cried out.

Cass cringed at the sight. Her hands trembled as flashbacks of her encounter with Koll raced through her mind. "It's not you, it's not you. Pull yourself together. This girl needs you," Cass whispered to herself, but her hands wouldn't still.

The girl's parents pleaded with the men to stop and be on their way. The mother screamed they had nothing of value, but the stout man on the horse with a bulging belly said he begged to differ. When the father handed the wife the reins from their horse and jumped off the front of the wagon, the burly man got off his horse and drew his sword. "I wouldn't do anything stupid if I were you," he said. Simultaneously, his partner in the back of the wagon tried to kiss the girl. Up to this point, she'd managed to evade his mouth, but soon he'd have her. Chills ran up Cass's arms. The trembling in her hands subsided somewhat, and as risky as she knew it was to reveal her presence, she couldn't stand by and do nothing. She wouldn't be able to live with herself if she did. "Stay close by me, Gray, but don't attack until I say."

Cass jumped out from the behind the tree and onto the dirt road, Gray by her side as they moved purposefully forward. In her deepest, loudest voice she said, "I think the two of you need to move on and leave these good people alone."

Cass noticed their initial lines of sight shot directly to Gray, which kept them from responding for a second, but then the burly man standing next to his horse laughed. "Is that so? And who are you to tell us what to do?"

"I'm someone who knows right from wrong, and what the two of you are doing, or are about to do, is wrong," Cass said.

"And I suppose you and your wild dog are going to stop us? Don't be ridiculous, lad," he said and spat on the ground.

As the man was about to pull out his sword, the father lunged, but was slapped forcibly on the side of the head, causing him to fall to the ground. The towering man repeatedly kicked the father as his wife looked on and screamed.

Cass closed the distance between them when the man grabbed for his sword. She heard the girl scream again as the other skeletal man pushed her down and jumped on the wagon, ignoring Cass and Gray as if they were no threat. Cass's pulse quickened and her heart throbbed. "Gray, attack!" she yelled.

Gray bared his teeth, ran, and jumped onto the wagon, wrapping his jaw around the man's arm. At the same time, Cass drew her sword. She confronted the other man as he was about to thrust his sword into the father's chest. "Do it and it's the last thing you will ever see," Cass warned.

The man spun on her. Cass noticed his unshaven face, torn tunic, and narrow, hollow eyes. "Come on, you scraggly runt. Come and get yourself killed," he yelled then stepped forward and swiped his sword in front of Cass. She blocked the strike, and the next, and the next, until realization set into the man's eyes that his opponent was more than he appeared. All the while, the other bony, lanky figure of a man struggled with Gray.

"Leave now and I'll let you both live," Cass said.

"Oh, we're not going anywhere, and neither are you. I'll bury your body myself, next to these 'good people' once I'm done with them," he said and lunged at Cass. The man was two times bigger and stronger than Cass, but she was quicker. She spun around several times, blocking blows in front of her and behind, and then faced forward to inflict her own strike on his arm. The man's face contorted, and he raised his sword again, but instead of striking down on Cass, he kicked her hard in the knee. She collapsed and heard the man laugh. She turned her head to look at Gray.

The other man, bleeding badly, managed to throw Gray off himself and up against the side of a tree. He jumped off the wagon and approached Gray, holding a dagger in his hand. Gray was barely moving. Cass knew she didn't have much time. Her gaze returned to her opponent, who stood holding the hilt of his sword over his head, both hands high in the air, about to thrust the blade into her heart. When Cass saw his muscles constrict for their final blow, in the last second, she rolled to one side. The blade pierced the ground where she'd lain. Cass seized the moment. She sprung up and sliced her blade through the man's side. His eyes opened wide. Blood seeped from the gaping cut, and he dropped his sword and fell to his knees. Before he hit the ground face down, Cass grabbed her dagger from its sheath and sent it flying into the other man's skull. That man's dagger dropped from his hand, and he fell like a stiff board to the ground.

Cass ran to Gray. "Are you all right, Gray?" His clouded eyes turned clear, and he stood on all fours. "Great job, Gray. You did real well." She patted him on the head. Next, she ran to check on the girl and the family.

The mother wrapped one arm around her husband and comforted her daughter in a hug with the other. The daughter shook and remained visibly distraught. "Thank you, young man," the woman said. "How can we repay you?"

"There's no need. We were happy to help," Cass said.

"We live in Tamshire, Jorgen and Braenna, and our daughter, Sienna. If you ever need anything, please ask for us. We'd welcome the chance to repay our gratitude," Jorgen said, squeezing his wife and child once more. He reached into the wagon and grabbed a bushel of carrots and beets. "Please take these at least. We don't have much, but I'd be grateful if you accepted this gift."

Cass reached out for the carrots and beets. "Thank you. You better get on your way, and I think we'll do the same." Cass watched as Sienna sat back in the wagon and kept her eyesight on Cass the entire time. As they pulled away, a small smile peeked from the girl's less-frightened face. Cass read her lips as she mouthed the words "Thank you," and Cass responded, "You're welcome." And with that, Cass placed her hand on top of Gray's head. "I say we go slowly the rest of the way today, and I'll catch us a nice dinner tonight. We'll turn in early. I think we both need the rest."

Before they continued on their way, Cass approached the dead bodies. She stripped the weapons from both men and relieved the horses of their reins, leaving the light saddles on them to which she attached the one man's sword and the other's dagger. Each rider carried a sack of coins on them as well, which she took and placed in her backpack. She kept their blankets, planning to use them as ground cover for her and Gray. She dragged both men off the road, into the bushes. Cass wasn't happy to have killed the men, but she was unable to reason with them and she knew it was either her life and the family's, or their lives. She chose life for her, Gray, and the family. Coming to terms with her decision, she started walking. When she did, the horses followed, in the same effortless way her sheep had followed her back in Mercia.

Chapter Twenty

Cass stepped short and slow to ensure Gray could keep up with her. They wouldn't make much ground today, after the run-in with the men and Gray's injury, not to mention her own slightly swollen knee, but moving forward felt better than sitting still. She also didn't know if the two men traveled alone or with other people, so she decided it was best to put some distance between them and the bodies. After a couple of hours walking, they came upon a stream. The horses drank heartily, as did Gray and Cass. "Let's follow the stream a little farther, Gray, and then we'll call it a day."

As the sun lowered in the sky, Cass spotted an opening in the hillside. "I think this is it for the day. You don't look like you're going to make it much farther, my friend, and I'm not sure I will either." She inspected the shallow cave. She didn't notice any recent animal droppings or food scraps or bones that suggested they were intruding on another animal's den. "Stay here with the horses. I'll gather some wood and make a fire," she said to Gray, who had simultaneously lain down and dropped to his side, head resting on the ground. Cass chuckled. "Well, that was an easier command than I thought it would be."

When she returned, Cass had amassed enough wood to start a fire and keep them warm for the night. Once the fire was well underway, she grabbed her bow and arrow, and headed for the stream. As she stood at the water's edge, images of Tove ran through her mind: Tove's smile and her warm hand on her shoulder, on one of the days she'd taught her to spear fish. Although in time, Cass had managed to catch a fish or two spear fishing, she'd always fared better with her bow and arrow. She'd had more years of practice doing so, and now with her stomach empty and grumbling, she opted for the method that would ensure greater success.

And while she waited to spot a fish, she couldn't help but retrace the lines of Tove's face in her mind and recall the softness of her lips.

Realizing in short order that drifting off to thoughts of Tove would not bode well with catching dinner, she refocused and soon caught a hearty meal for herself and Gray. The two partners spent the evening by the fire, Cass cooking and both feasting. As the flames died down, Cass draped their newly found blankets on the ground, upon which she lay curled around the fire, keeping an eye focused on the cave opening. Gray snuggled beside her. Soon, they drifted off to sleep.

Throughout the latter part of the night and early morning, Cass tossed and turned. Her body felt as though consumed by fire. Broken images of Haddie drifted past her in disturbing ways. Haddie as she stood by the fire. The black cape from the trunk, its hood draped over a darkened face, yellow eyes glowing beneath the hood. A wrinkled and angry face, visible by the rays of light cast upon it by the flickering fire. Haddie's chants drifting through the air. Cass's sword, gleaming as it lay on the stone in front of the fire. Haddie's hands rising in the air as the sword lifted as if of its own accord before falling, the metallic clank loud and harsh. The same scene repeated, over and over. Each time the sword fell, Cass's body jerked from one side to the other. Haddie's frustration grew, and the tone of her chants increased in volume, until yellow eyes turned to black and the chanting stopped. "Curse this damned sword. I will have you yet," were the last words Cass heard.

She woke drenched in sweat. She wiped the droplets from her face with shaking hands. Gray had moved a slight distance from her and lifted his head when she awoke. "I'm all right, Gray," she said, as she physically touched her body to reassure herself she was awake. "I dozed into a bad dream, that's all," she added, not certain her words held true. The sight of Haddie appeared so real. When she lived with Haddie, had Haddie been up at night while Cass slept and Cass hadn't heard her? How could that be so? How could Haddie have hidden that part of her, and what was she trying to do with her sword? The thought of Haddie being a witch and having kept Cass against her will, to use her to expand her home, and all the days lost, angered Cass, but she knew it to be true. In recent dreams now, she'd twice seen Haddie as a witch, not as the beautiful blonde woman who rescued her and happened to look so much like Julia. Would Cass ever be able to put her lost time with Haddie out of her mind? She didn't have the answer, but she also hadn't gained the luxury of time to worry about it. She had family to save, and Julia to save. Any other thoughts would have to stay in a lesser compartment in her mind until everyone was free.

That morning and the following two days, it rained heavily, so Cass decided it best they remain in the shelter of the cave until the rain stopped or at least slowed. The extra time also gave Gray a chance to heal and her knee as well. Unfortunately, there wasn't much to do but sleep, hunt, and eat, but considering Cass continued suffering from fitful sleep, the extra rest during the day was welcome.

On the evening of the third day, the rain subsided, and the following morning, the sun once again peeked over the horizon. Cass and Gray ate breakfast. They and the horses drank from the stream before heading away from their guaranteed water supply and what had been an abundant food source. With Gray running much better, Cass mounted the one brown horse that had a white, almost cross-like patch between his eyes. The horse provided welcome relief to her knee, and they were able to cover a much-greater distance during the day. However, the chafing to her legs and ache in her thighs let her know at the end of the day that she'd have to break into horseback riding much more slowly.

Day after day, they walked and rode, hunted and ate, slept and ate again, and avoided people as best they could. During that time, Cass continued to practice her swordsmanship and all the exercises Tove had taught her. She focused each day, more and more honed into the task that lay ahead. After their dinners, Gray mostly watched Cass practice her skills, and later in the evenings, Cass would wake to find Gray gone. Each morning though, he'd return, usually with a rabbit or other small animal for them for breakfast, but the last two mornings, he returned later each time.

On this morning though, three days after they'd crossed the River Trent into King Andron's territory, Cass awoke alone. When she searched for Gray, she initially didn't see him but then up on a hillside, she saw him standing next to another, smaller wolf. Had he found a mate? She thought he had. She mind-connected with him and could sense his happiness. She was happy for him, too, though she knew this was his good-bye and she'd not see him again. She thanked him once more for his friendship and companionship and for helping bring her to the place she needed to be. She thanked him for saving her life, because without him, she was certain she'd still be under Haddie's spell. She wished him a good life and a long life, as tears streamed down her face. Then she waved one last time to him, and he and his mate were gone.

Chapter Twenty-One

Jess woke with a tear in her eye. These visions into Cassethea's life were becoming no less sad. It seemed that every time she awoke, sadness hung over her. She wished for an easier life for Cassethea, for her to find her mother and Emma, and save Julia. She wasn't sure if she wanted to see Cass with Julia again, or with Tove. Her heart seemed to be pulling for Tove.

As she walked the short distance from Rayne's house toward the dig site, Jess recalled their dinner conversation from the night before. That night was the first time Rayne opened up to her emotionally, telling her about her best friend taking her own life, and as a result, her going to the university to study psychology, and then her giving up her own dreams to help her family run the pub. Jess couldn't remember ever meeting such an honest and good person. She felt lucky to know Rayne. Those feelings, along with the alcohol they consumed, must have invaded her thoughts that evening when she had lain in bed, because instead of sleeping, she thought about a naked Rayne taking the muscle-relaxing bath she'd suggested to help with her back pain. Jess decided she should have kept her helpful thoughts to herself.

When Jess reached the site, she saw Shelly and Justin in one of the lined-off dig squares and Susan a few squares farther away. "Morning," Jess said to Shelly and Justin, as they greeted her in return. "Are Marco and Mike in the trailer?"

"Mike's inside, but Marco's not here yet," Justin reported.

Jess caught the glimpse of disappointment on Shelly's face, although Jess knew she tried to hide it. "This is the third time he's been late in the last week and a half. If either of you see him before I do, please ask him to come see me."

"Will do," they replied in unison.

Jess breathed deep. She liked Marco, but this dig was part of his graduate studies, and the school was paying for him to be present. She would not tolerate him disrespecting her or the institution, or more importantly, their findings and the importance of them, by continually showing up late. The sooner she'd speak with him, the better. She made her way over toward Susan.

"Morning. Marco late again?" Susan asked.

"Morning. He is, but I'm guessing after I talk to him, this will be his last late day," Jess said.

"I wouldn't count on it. I saw him with the same local girl a couple of nights in a row now. They were drinking pretty heavily. And, well...you know what I'm saying."

"I do, but trust me. He'll be on time from now on. I don't care how he spends his evenings, unless it interferes with the work we're doing here. I'm flexible, but enough is enough."

"Yeah, plus, poor Shelly," Susan said.

"You know she likes him?"

"It's hard not to. She doesn't hide her feelings well. Of course, he's blind to her."

"Yes, unfortunately, that appears the case. I think she'd be good for him." Jess walked to an adjourning lined-off dig sector, knelt, and unrolled her kit of most frequently used tools. She extracted her diamond-shaped pointing trowel and retrieved a dustpan from inside the white plastic bucket behind her. She methodically scraped clear the area she'd left off with the day before. She interrupted her work once that morning to talk with Marco, and after several more hours of scraping, which uncovered what appeared to be pieces of a food-storage container, stood and stretched. She carried her filled bucket to the area where Marco stood shaking a rectangular sieve screen used to separate artifacts and ecofacts from the otherwise useless sediment. Though Marco usually worked in the trailer on computer cataloging and site reconstruction, Jess had remanded him to a task today she knew he'd not enjoy, but she did so to remind him repeated tardiness wouldn't be accepted.

"How's it going so far?" Jess asked, her tone friendly.

"Not too bad. Nothing earth shaking to report, though. I see you brought me another present." Marco eyed Jess's bucket.

"I did."

"Listen, I want you to know I'm not upset you put me at this station today. In fact, I know I deserved it. I'll be on time from now on, I promise. It's just—"

"No. There shouldn't be a 'just,' and I don't need or want to hear more. You already apologized earlier. You and I are fine, as long as you take this excavation as seriously as I do and respect it for the unique opportunity that it holds."

"You know I do and will," Marco said, looking into Jess's eyes.

"I believe you. After lunch, you can get back to your regular work." Jess glanced at her watch. Another hour and lunch would be delivered, hopefully by Rayne. Even though Jess saw Rayne in the mornings and evenings now, she felt like she couldn't see enough of her. It was both an unfamiliar and welcome situation at the same time.

Three quarters of an hour later, Jess heard Susan swear.

"Holy crap, Jess. Take a look at what I found," Susan said.

Jess stood, brushed the dirt off her knees, and stomped over next to Susan.

"I used the dental pick and brush to carefully remove this item. The deeper and deeper I dug, I realized I may not have simply found a fragment, but a completely intact piece, and look, I was right. When I lifted it all the way out, nothing was damaged." Susan held up an intricately carved and inscribed drinking horn.

Jess gingerly took the horn from Susan. Her breath caught. Not only was it unusual to find a completely intact and undamaged drinking horn, the inscriptions were what made her heart race. She recognized the horn and the pattern of the inscriptions. It was the horn Cass drank from many nights during her dinners with Tove on the island. Dazed and in a whisper Jess said, "I don't remember seeing Cassethea's name on here before," without realizing she'd spoken aloud.

Susan glanced at Jess with a mix of excitement and puzzlement. "You've seen this in a drawing somewhere before?"

Jess stood frozen, unable to answer at first. When Susan's question finally registered, she said, "What?"

"You just said you didn't remember seeing Cassethea's name on the horn before. You must have seen it depicted somewhere then." Still receiving no answer, Susan added, "Hello, earth to Professor Madison."

Jess remained stunned. She turned the object in her hand and carefully fingered each rune letter. When the sarcastic words "Professor Madison" sunk in, Jess lifted her gaze to Susan. "There are several names on this cup. One is Cassethea. From the names that surround it, I believe she could be Cassethea of Mercia."

"No shit! Really?"

Jess smiled for the first time as the fog around her cleared. "Watch your mouth, Susan."

"Sorry, boss. Are you serious right now, though? Wasn't Cassethea a myth or legend? I thought she wasn't real."

"Yes, well, you and the majority of other scientists in the world are of the same mind," Jess said.

"But not you." Susan had an intrigued expression on her face.

"No, not me. I haven't told many people what my belief was. The few I did tell chastised me and told me not to waste my time chasing after a tall tale. Of course, those same people were men, so no surprise there. The chancellor was one of them."

"Well, you're right about him. I'm sorry. I love our school, but that man is a chauvinist pig. Who cares what he thinks?"

"Yeah, well, I don't, except for the fact he'll likely see this discovery as strike three," Jess whispered, lowering the drinking horn.

"What do you mean by 'strike three'?"

Before Jess could answer, she noticed Marco heading to the far side of the dig site, Justin and Mike running down the trailer steps, and Shelly standing and dusting herself off.

Lunch had arrived, and Rayne was the person delivering it. Lunch delivery had saved her from having to answer two questions she wasn't sure she could. The one Susan had asked earlier, in response to words that unknowingly slipped from her mouth, and the "strike three" question. Hopefully Susan would forget about both questions by the time lunch was over. Younger people tended to have short attention spans. Jess thanked the Internet for that.

As Jess watched Rayne unpack from a distance, her lips turned upward and her heartbeat quickened. What the heck was wrong with her? She was acting like a schoolgirl with a crush. A crush? Was it a crush? She certainly found Rayne to be kind and beautiful and sexy and oh so hot. Sexy and hot? Oh so hot? Seriously? Pull it together. She's a friend, nothing more. Yet, as she neared the table and her eyes met Rayne's, she took in Rayne's devilish smile and knew there was more between them, much more. Part of her wanted Rayne and wanted her deeply. She couldn't keep her thoughts off her. She wondered if Rayne felt the seemingly unstoppable pull, too.

****

Later that afternoon, Jess marched off into an open field next to the dig site, far enough away for no one to overhear her conversation. She needed to call her friend El. She couldn't stop mulling over the fact that the drinking horn they found at this dig site had Cassethea's name on it, and more importantly, Tove's name next to it. The puzzle pieces were starting to fit together. Was the horn proof Cassethea existed and that her dreams were in fact more than dreams as El had suggested? And was she having the dreams because they found the home where Cassethea had lived and likely had been buried? Could this really be happening?

The excitement was too much to bear, as was her struggle with whether or not she should tell the chancellor. They were so close. If she was honest with him and he decided to pull funding, everything she worked for might be lost. How would she bear it? But honesty was always the best policy, wasn't it? And what about Rayne; was she honest with Rayne? Not only about her growing feelings, but with the dreams she was experiencing and her hidden reason for having wanted this dig in the first place.

The phone rang three times before El picked up. "Hello? Jess?"

"El, thank God you're home." Jess paced back and forth.

"Are you okay? What's the matter? You sound stressed."

"I'm fine, or at least I think I am. I don't think I'm going crazy anymore, so that's a plus."

"Why's that? Did the dreams, or visions, stop?"

"No. In fact, I have them every night now and they're lasting longer and longer. El, this woman's life was so difficult and yet amazing at the same time. The dreams are visions into her life. I know it now. You were right. They're too real to be anything else, and on top of it, I think I found proof of her existence today, which is also why I'm calling you." Jess let her line of sight drift toward the dig site to see if anyone was watching her, but it didn't appear as if anyone was.

"No shit! For real?" El said.

Jess laughed. "Although Rayne has a bit of a trash mouth like you, I do miss the way you swear."

"Glad I could be of service. Especially given the fact that swearing comes so naturally to me."

"No kidding."

"Look, Jess. Stop stalling and give me the lowdown. And after you've done that, you can fill me in on the trailer theft. I heard you were okay, so I didn't call. I wanted to see how long it would take you to call me. Not bad, Ms. Madison, not bad."

"Great. Bad news really does travel fast. The trailer theft is part of the problem. The trailer was broken into while I was having dinner at Rayne's house. And I know you're dying to interrupt me right now, but don't you dare," Jess said, hearing a "Hmph" at the other end of the line. "We had found the Bishop of Mettlenbury's body a few days earlier. He was still wearing his jeweled ring and cross. I suppose word got out somehow, and when Rayne walked me home that night, the trailer door was ajar. The ring and cross were stolen. So, of course I had to call the chancellor. Not only was he not happy the bishop was found in a Viking settlement with the letters spelling 'friend' on a rune stone above the bishop's grave, but the theft infuriated him on top of that. Two strikes against me, he said. One more and the excavation would be over."

"As if you have any control over history. That man is

such a pompous ass. And yes, I will circle back to Rayne. Continue, please."

"Today, one of my undergrads found an inscribed drinking horn at the site, fully intact and undamaged. It was the same horn I saw during one of my visions. This part is long, and I'll fill you in later about the details of Cassethea's life at this time, but the short of it is that her father banned her from her home, thinking her a witch—which she wasn't. Days later, her home was raided by what was thought to be Vikings. Her mother and sister were taken, and her youngest brother was killed. She set off to find these Vikings, but another group of Vikings found her instead. This Viking group's leader was a woman called Tove. As we know, a woman leader was highly unusual back then. At any rate, Cass is taken by a member of the group, and long story short, although she initially thinks they took her family and killed her brother, they didn't. She grows close with Tove. I saw visions of their life together for a while and the meals they ate. The drinking horn discovered today, here, was the same drinking horn I saw in my dreams, I'm sure of it. But on this one, Cassethea's name was etched. And it was etched next to the Viking leader Tove's name. The other names etched below and next to each other descending by age are Tove's brothers and their wives."

"Which means..."

"Yes, which suggests Cassethea and Tove were a couple. She was gay, as I suspected from my dreams. Which is great, except as it relates to the chancellor."

"If you tell him, you think this excavation is over?"

"Yes. But eventually, or sooner, he'll find out anyway. I don't know what to do," Jess said.

"And what about Rayne? What did she say when you told her? Unless I'm missing something here, you two sound like you're pretty close, no?" El asked.

"Yes and no. Second problem is, I didn't tell her...yet. Not about my self-imposed life's obsession of proving Cassethea is not simply a myth and not about finding the drinking horn. And the thing is, I like her...a lot. I like her probably more than I should or maybe not more than I should, but you know what I mean. After the trailer was broken into, she offered for me to stay with her in her home, which I now am. She's been wonderful to me. Too good, really. But how do you explain to someone that you're experiencing visions into another woman's life, a woman who lived over a thousand years ago, and not have that person think you're completely crazy?"

"I see your dilemma."

"Don't be a smartass."

"Who's swearing now?"

"Knock it off, Compton. I'm serious here. What am I going to do?"

"You're going to do the only thing you know you can do. Tell the chancellor the truth. And explain your life to your girlfriend."

"She's not my girlfriend. We've not kissed."

"But you want to, don't you? I can hear it in your voice. You're already a lost cause. You don't know it yet," El said.

There was a long pause. "It could be that I do know it. I can't stop thinking about her, and I'm pretty sure she feels the same about me. I've even had impure thoughts about her."

"Ohhh, excellent. Now we're finally getting somewhere."

"El!"

"What? Seriously, tell her what's going on. Honesty often brings people together. And if your revelation scares her away, then so be it. She's not the one for you. But if it doesn't, then who knows? Sky's the limit, as they say."

"You're right, as always. Thank you my friend. I better get back to the site. Before I go, how are you doing? How are things with you and Gayle?"

"I'm doing well, and we're both doing smashing, thank you for asking. I'll try and call you one day next week, and we'll catch up. Sound good?"

"Sounds great. Thanks again, El. I don't know what I'd do without you."

"Darn right you don't. Now go dig up some more wicked history."

Chapter Twenty-Two

The emptiness Cass felt as soon as Gray disappeared over the hillside with his mate was similar to the ache she'd first experienced when Julia told her she planned to marry Prince Richard of Normandy, and then again when Tove had returned her to the shores of her home at the start of her journey to find her mother, Emma, and Julia. Of the three heartaches, the one with Tove had, surprisingly to Cass, been the most painful, but the ache of not seeing Gray was only slightly less so. She still had possession of the horses, but the connection with them wasn't the same. She'd saved Gray's life, and in return, he'd saved hers, twice. Their bond was strong and unbreakable.

With Gray gone, Cass rode the remainder of the way to King Andron's castle, easily covering three times the distance on horseback she otherwise would have on foot. She chose to ride the brown horse with the white, cross-like patch on his forehead. They were a good match; the horse followed her directions with ease.

Her first night of sleep without Gray to cuddle up to was restless, and even with the fire, she felt chilled. In the afternoon of the second day, as the sun neared the horizon, she reached King Andron's castle. She walked the horses to the edge of the woodland and stood in awe of what her eyes took in. Built of stone, the castle sat perched atop a cliff, below which waves from the North Sea crashed against the cliff's rock. The castle was twice the size of King Herrwald's, bigger in both breadth and height. Two towering, dark-wooden doors protected the entrance, and six towers jutted up from already high walls surrounding it.

Cass suddenly felt very small. Her throat constricted. How was she going to manage the rescue on her own? The answer revealed itself quicker than Cass anticipated. She needed to know about her opponent and study him. Study the workings of the castle and then find a way in.

She slunk deeper into the forest but still within view of the castle. She mind-connected with an eagle above to get a closer view of the courtyard inside the walls and of the many guards wandering the interior. That night, she slept without a fire and was grateful for the warmth from the extra blankets she'd carried with her. The following morning, as the sun pierced through the lingering mist, she studied the castle some more. When the sun moved past its highest point, Cass couldn't believe what she saw. But what she did see strengthened her resolve and convinced her that Tove had been right. She'd located the place she was destined to be.

A band of what appeared to be Viking men entered the forest not far from where Cass knelt hidden. They led a group of six women and three female children. All were gagged and bound to one another with their hands tied behind their backs. Once they were inside the forest, the men took off their helmets, and by doing so, also removed braided, golden hairpieces. They held their helmets under one arm as the man in front reached toward the ground, cleared debris away, and lifted a wooden door with a circular iron latch at the top. One by one, the men and their prisoners disappeared beneath the ground.

Cass's heart beat quickly. Is this how King Andron hid his bad deeds from his people? If he had a tunnel dug from here to somewhere in the castle, the feat was a significant undertaking, one she was certain wasn't carried out by his people but probably by prisoners he'd enslaved. As the last man was about to disappear below the earth's surface, one of Cass's horses stepped to the side and snapped a fallen branch. The man's head swung first to one side and then to the other. He waited, holding the wooden door above his head for what felt like the longest minute in Cass's life, and then he was gone, the door no longer visible.

Cass breathed deep. She wiped sweat droplets off of her forehead and upper lip with the back of her hand. She faced the horses. "That was much too close. You almost blew it, you two. Next time, you better not move an inch," she chided, as four innocent, wide, brown eyes locked with hers.

Cass had learned of a possible way in. She now needed to watch for patterns and then exploit them.

****

Cass was violently yanked to her feet in the dark by rough hands, the chill of the night air hitting her awakening body at the same time steely eyes bore into hers. The stench of stale ale and urine penetrated her nostrils.

"Didn't think I'd seen you, did you, lad? Seen more here today than you bargained for, did you?" The man shook Cass and slapped the side of her cheek. "Answer me!"

The sting was immediate. Cass tried to get hold of her situation. She couldn't see much in the blackness, but when she glanced to both sides, she saw another soldier with him. Escape didn't appear to be a viable option. "I don't know what you're talking about. I didn't see anything," she said.

"Liar!"

The second slap landed harder than the first, and Cass tasted blood in her mouth. She spit the metallic-tasting liquid out. "I'm telling the truth. I was just passing through."

"Why would a lone traveler need two horses? Aye? Passing through, my arse. Do you know what the penalty for lying is, or worse, spying?" When Cass didn't respond, he said, "No? Well, you're about to find out."

With those words, Cass was jerked forward. The soldier's hand dug firmly into her right bicep, followed by another hand grasping her left bicep. She struggled admirably to shake free, but to no avail. The soldiers were bigger and more muscular. They led her and the horses out of the forest and toward the castle, as if she wasn't struggling at all. Once they passed through the gates, one soldier released her and led the horses in one direction, while the soldier who'd slapped her continued to walk with her in another direction. The soldier forced Cass down a flight of stairs and into a long, narrow hallway, one lit by an occasional torch on the wall. Cass counted three turns before they came to a stop in front of another thick, wooden door guarded by a soldier.

"Open up," the soldier holding Cass commanded.

Behind the opening, Cass walked onto a platform and

then down an L-shaped set of stone stairs into a cavernous, rank pit. Built into the circular space along the walls were holding cells filled with male prisoners. Cass gagged involuntarily and nearly vomited at the stench but was pushed mercilessly forward. As the entrance to her cell creaked open, and she was shoved to the floor inside, her hand grazed the cold and damp surface. She quickly returned to her feet.

"A few days in here should take the kick out of you. Then you'll be put to work. Welcome to King Andron's dungeon." The man laughed as he walked away.

Cass took in her cell, which was relatively large, but mostly barren. A wooden bench stood against the rear stone wall, and a wooden bucket was set on the ground not far from the bench. A tattered blanket covered the bench, but Cass could imagine what the blanket smelled and felt like, and she gagged again. The sides and front of the cell were made of metal bars.

She turned to the man in the cell to her right, but he sat on his bench, eyes staring at the ground. His tunic and trousers were torn and filthy and hung like rags from his bony body. A rat scurried through the cell from one end to the other. Cass sensed the man felt her looking at him, but he wouldn't look her way.

"Eyes forward!" one of the guards yelled. "Since you're new here, you're given one warning. After that, you will be lashed. If you disobey a second time, food will be withheld from you. My suggestion is you rest until dinner. From the size of you, you're going to need all the energy you can get."

Cass couldn't believe she'd made it so far only to end up imprisoned. However, she wasn't about to give up. She was strong. She was smart. She had resources she could summon if needed. How they could help her at this moment, she didn't know. But now, more than ever, she was certain her family and Julia were in this castle. She needed to stay alive long enough, and as healthy and ready as she could be, to rescue them when the moment presented itself. However, at this moment, to appease the guard, she did as she was instructed and walked toward the wooden bench. She picked up the blanket and brought it near her nose, but as expected, nearly vomited at the stench of it and tossed it to the floor. She lay on her back on the hard surface and closed her eyes. However, she didn't sleep. She would need to be alert at all times, and in the meantime, would hope and pray for a miracle.

Dinner proved less than stellar, but edible. Cass ate everything, determined to keep up her strength for whatever lay ahead. When the guard stationed in the center of the room was relieved, and the other guard took over, Cass waited until that guard sat in the chair and dozed, his back to Cass. While he slept, she took lunging steps from one side of the cell to the other and back again until her thighs ached. After lunges, she did push-ups, trying to ignore the dirt, cold, and grime under her palms.

At night, she mind-connected with a rat, which cuddled against Cass's belly. Cass lay on her side facing the wall. Although the rat was small, he gave off a tiny bit of body heat, which helped in the dank surroundings. Eventually, the rat came on his own accord, with Cass not needing to reach out to him.

Each morning, after breakfast, the guards gathered the prisoners, extracted them from their cells, and chained them to one another. At night, before dinner was served, the prisoners returned, sweaty, drained, and clearly exhausted. Cass wondered where they'd been taken. Part of her thought it couldn't be worse than being stuck underground, that they at least saw daylight, for they were all well tanned. But the other part of her didn't want to find out where they went. Yes, she was strong, but she was young, and no matter how fit she was, she was no match for a full-grown man. Cass tossed all negative thoughts from her mind and focused instead on what she could control: eating, sleeping, exercising, and...always watching.

****

Cass didn't need to wonder much longer where the prisoners were taken during the day. On the fourth morning, the guards opened her cell with the rest of the prisoners' cells and latched her to her neighboring cellmates. Still no one looked at one another, and all eyes remained downcast.

Cass managed to catch glimpses of her surroundings, though. Once out of the dungeon, she counted the steps from one turn to another until they reached the far side of the castle and were led outdoors. The brightness of the sun nearly blinded her. At first, she couldn't keep her eyes fully open, but eventually she re-adjusted to the light. As they neared a smaller gate along the castle wall, she smelled horses and heard their neighing. After they marched through the gate, they were led along the cliff's edge, likely a path chosen by Andron's men to lessen the chance of escape. Cass didn't care; she was elated to be outside. The fresh air was invigorating. It gave her hope. But hope could be dangerous as well. Hope gone unsatisfied for too long could quickly lead to despair. Hope—however powerful—had to be kept in check.

A fifteen-minute walk from the castle revealed their stopping place: another circular pit in the ground, which appeared to be completely dug out of rock. Cass soon confirmed it was, because their day was spent swinging pick axes into the walls, loosening rocks, and hauling rock away. Luckily, before she started, she saw the men grab strips of cloth and wrap their hands with them, which is exactly what she did. Had she not, she was certain her hands would have been badly blistered by the end of the day.

The morning temperatures remained pleasant, but the sun beating on rock seemed to heat the inside of the quarry unusually quickly. Many of the men discarded their tunics after lunchtime, which worried Cass greatly. She wasn't a man. She couldn't take her tunic off. Would she be questioned about not doing so? She prayed not.

The work was extremely grueling, but the guards who watched over them weren't mean. They were given as much water as they wanted, and food at lunchtime was plentiful. Talking wasn't accepted, though, and neither was looking directly at the guards. Cass hoped her identity would remain hidden, as long as she could keep up with the work, and she also hoped the days wouldn't get any hotter than they already were.

Day after day, the routine remained the same. They would eat breakfast, get taken to the quarry, work, eat lunch, work some more, get escorted back to the castle, eat, sleep, and repeat. After five days of arduous work, Cass gave up on the lunges and push-ups. She was too tired to do anything but sleep. Days morphed into weeks, and weeks into a month.

But one morning began differently than the rest. One of the prisoners woke coughing and grabbing his stomach. Soon after, he vomited. The guard called in a healer, and the prisoner was given a thick, dark mixture of liquid to drink. Afterward, he was chained up to the rest of them and they were led to the quarry the same as always. It may have been due to the earlier delay, that on the way out of the castle, a woman rider with long, black hair galloped alongside the prisoner line, trying to beat them to the back gate. As the rider passed, Cass caught a glimpse of the woman. She wore a bright-blue dress and leather boots. For a second, their eyes met. After she passed, the woman immediately slowed her horse to a trot. When the prisoner line and Cass caught up to the horse and rider again, Cass caught the woman's eyes once more and this time held her gaze for a moment. Grey eyes speckled with yellow bore into her. Cass felt exposed but not in a good way. The woman's eyes were piercing and not sympathetic in the least. Emotionless was the word she was looking for. Yes, the woman expressed no emotion. Once their visual connection was broken by Cass glancing away, the rider kicked the horse into another gallop and sped past the group and out the gate until Cass could no longer see her.

In the last five minutes of their hike from the castle to the quarry, Cass felt the day's heat on her neck. She realized the day would be a scorcher. And within a few hours, the heat in the quarry spiked to the point Cass felt lightheaded and nauseous. She kept up with water intake, but the heat radiating from the rock was intense. When she asked for water only a short time after having drunk some, the guard yelled at her.

"What's wrong with you, lad? Why are you still wearing that damned woolen tunic? Look around. Only you are too stupid to make yourself more comfortable. If you took your tunic off, maybe you wouldn't need as many water breaks."

Cass looked from right to left and back again, seeing the guard was right. The situation she'd feared for weeks had finally presented itself. She was the only prisoner fully clothed. "I'm fine. My skin burns easily in the sun," Cass said.

"Hell yeah, it does. Because you never let it see the light of day," the guard said.

"I'm fine," Cass persisted.

"Don't be stupid. Take it off. You don't have some hideous scar or disease to hide, do you?" the guard said as he stepped closer.

Cass took a step back. "Of course I don't. As I said, I burn easily."

A second guard walked over, a wicked grimace on his face. "Let us be the judge of how quickly you burn, shall we? I'm finding the day as boring as watching sheep graze out here. I think I'd enjoy something else to focus on. How about you, Eriwyn?"

Cass was near frantic. No, not again, she thought, and held back the rising bile in her throat. She stepped back even farther, but as she did, the second guard grabbed her and ripped the tunic over her head and threw it to the ground. Cass stood in the beaming sun, breasts exposed, her identity as a woman revealed. Fear coursed through her as the eyes of both the guards darkened.

"Why has everyone stopped working? Get back to work the lazy lot of you!" Eriwyn yelled, his eyes focused on Cass's hardened nipples.

"Holy hell! Your skin burns easily, my arse!" the second guard, who'd stripped her of her tunic, yelled. "All this time you've fooled us, but we're not fooled anymore. This boring day has suddenly become very interesting." He grabbed his manhood. "You are mine now," he said, stepping toward her.

"Wait, Holthric, someone's coming," Eriwyn said.

"What are you talking about? No one visits this desolate hole in the ground," Holthric said, but he stared at the moving cloud of dust as it approached.

Cass saw the dust cloud, as well, and heard the pounding of horses' hooves. When they stopped, the dust cloud enveloped both her and the two guards.

"What's going on here?" an icy voice yelled.

Both men turned to face the woman on the horse.

"Nothing is going on, Princess," Holthric said. "We have everything under control. One of the prisoners stepped out of line and was about to be disciplined. You should not be out here. Why have you come?"

As the dust settled, the woman in the blue dress scanned Cass's body from top to bottom. Cass thought she perhaps lingered on her breasts too long. Then she turned her attention to the guards. "You will not tell me where I should or should not be."

"Yes, Princess," the men said in unison as they bowed slightly at the waist.

The rider steadied the horse, which appeared impatient at standing in one spot.

"Also, do you think me stupid? Do you think I cannot see the prisoner behind you is a woman? Give her clothing back," the princess said. "And you," she said as she pointed to Eriwyn, "take this prisoner to the castle immediately. If you or anyone else puts one finger on her before you hear from me again, I will have you skinned alive. She is to stay in her cell until you hear from me or from one of my soldiers. Is that clear?"

Eriwyn bowed once more. "Yes, Princess. I will do as you say."

As Cass pulled the torn tunic over her head, she made eye contact with the woman, but again, sensed only a cold emptiness in return. Regardless, the woman spared her the immediate fate of what might have happened, and for that she was grateful. She held her hands in front of her as instructed. Eriwyn tied her hands tight and walked her from the quarry.

The princess stayed behind them until they were several minutes into their route back to the castle. Then she kicked her horse and galloped ahead of them until she was out of sight. When Cass returned to the castle, she was thrown in her cell once again. She received no lunch, but the eyes of the guards were constantly on her. She felt them even as she sat on the wooden bench, eyes drooped downward.

Tense hours passed. Cass wondered what was going to happen to her next, but nothing happened that day. The work crew returned, and they were fed, but no plate was placed under the bars of Cass's cell that evening. In the morning, breakfast was served to the other prisoners but not to her. She grew thirsty but knew better than to ask for water. Lunch passed with the guards eating, but no sign of anyone coming to get her, as the princess had indicated. At this point, she didn't know what was worse, waiting on an unknown fate, or starving to death.

But she didn't have to ponder the options too long. Shortly before the work crew returned on the second day of confinement, a well-dressed soldier entered the dungeon and asked the guard to release her on Princess Dallia's orders. When the guard unlocked her cell and yanked her from it, Cass smelled his disgusting, foul breath as he smirked inches from her face.

The princess's soldier didn't grab her arm when she was remitted to his custody, but instead, pointed for her to walk in front of him, which she did. From behind, he directed her where to go. They walked far in the castle, many a passerby eying her as if she were a rat under their feet. At a large central hall, she was instructed to go upward to a second floor. There she was directed into a large sitting room and then into a similar-sized room with a porcelain tub. In the room, two women stood.

"Thank you, soldier. Please stand guard outside the door," the older woman said before she closed the door and turned to Cass. "My name is Geraline. I am one of Princess Dallia's servants. My assistant is called Salleen. The princess has asked we bathe you before you have dinner with her. And what is your name?"

Cass had never been bathed by another person before, except possibly her mother when she was younger, but she had no memory of this, and she didn't feel comfortable undressing in front of two strangers. "My name is Cassethea, but please, I can bathe myself."

"No, that will not be possible. We were given instructions, and we must carry them out. We have no choice in this matter. Please understand," Geraline said.

Sensing her sincerity and not seeing another option, Cass nodded in agreement and undressed as told.

Chapter Twenty-Three

When Cass entered the spacious room adjoining the bathroom, she saw Princess Dallia standing next to a rectangular, wooden table in the middle of the room. The elegantly carved table was set for two but could fit eight. The princess wore an elegant, yellow, embroidered robe with slippers that appeared to be constructed of the same material. The walls of the room were lined with bookshelves interspersed with landscape paintings and paintings of the princess and likely the king and queen. Cass saw more comfortable chairs to sit in than the number of people she knew. On the stone floor were laid intricately designed carpets, and the room had its own fireplace. There were no guards inside the room, though Cass was certain they were close.

"Come here and sit across from me," Princess Dallia said as she waved Cass in her direction and then sat at one end of the table.

What the princess would want with Cassethea, she had no idea, but she had no option other than to listen to her. Cass walked toward the table. Whatever material the navy-blue trousers and white tunic she was provided were made of didn't scratch as her brother's clothes did. They felt soft against her skin. Cass didn't know clothing such as she now wore existed. And her skin smelled fresh, like pine, the same as her bath water. When Cass sat, the princess studied her.

"Are you hungry?" Dallia said.

Cass was beyond both thirsty and hungry, but she didn't want to appear desperate. "Yes, I could eat."

Geraline and Salleen were summoned and entered the room. They filled both silver goblets with drink and her plate with crisply grilled pheasant; steamed, leafy green vegetables; and round, grilled potatoes. The smell of the pheasant made her stomach growl. She surmised this must be how Julia had eaten every day in her father's castle, but with that thought, a part of her appetite disappeared.

When Geraline and Salleen finished plating, Dallia waved her hand and they exited the room. "You know you don't need to keep your eyes lowered to Geraline and Salleen, or to me for that matter, Cassethea," Dallia said.

At the sound of her name, Cass froze, wondering how Princess Dallia would have known her name, but then she realized Geraline would have told her. "I didn't realize I was doing so. It must have become habit," Cass said before ripping off another bite of pheasant and chewing with vigor. Sensing Dallia's eyes on her, she forced her own glance upward and confirmed her suspicions. She owed the woman more than rude manners. "Thank you for what you did for me yesterday, and for the bath, the use of these clothes, and this food."

"The clothes are yours to keep, regardless," Dallia responded, her tone revealing nothing further.

Cass mulled on the word "regardless." Regardless of what? If Dallia wasn't going to say anything, Cass would have to ask. She couldn't stand the tension of not knowing why the princess rescued her. "I hope I'm not being rude, but what is it you want from me, exactly?"

"I think you're not blind to the fact that I find your body highly evocative. You dress and cut your hair as if you were a young man, and your body is taut and muscular like a man's, yet you are female. Oh, so very female. And I, as it were, am partial to female company."

"You have two female servants," Cass replied. "And you likely have female friends as well. Why me?"

"Yes, I have all of those things and much, much more. But I don't believe you understand what it is I'm trying to convey to you. I prefer the company of women in my bed. Men are crude, insolent, vulgar, and unkempt idiots for the most part. They are hairy and rough to the touch. But women—women are soft, and strong, and fierce all at the same time. Their energy is endless. They move me in ways men do not. I believe that part you may already be aware of yourself, am I right?"

Cass glanced away for a moment, Dallia's words spinning in her head. "I don't understand. It's not possible—women together. It's against the rulings of the church."

"Believe me, it is very possible and not at all unusual. It's simply not spoken of or condoned. However, in my position, my father allows me any indulgences I please. I'm his only offspring, so he likes to keep me happy. And there is something about you that physically draws me to you. I want you to be my paramour, to be available to pleasure me, whenever I ask it of you." Dallia laid a barren pheasant bone on her plate.

Cass hoped the confusion wasn't written all over her face, but she didn't exactly know what the princess was asking. She knew in part what was being asked of her, because she had kissed Julia and also Tove and had wanted to do more with both. What that more was, she didn't know, but her body had desired it. To learn that she not only had these feelings, but other women had them as well, was empowering. At the same time, Dallia wanted her as no more than a slave, if she understood her correctly.

The thought made her uneasy. How was Dallia any different than the guards in the quarry, or Koll? A shiver ran through her. She had no feelings for Dallia. She would need to have feelings to kiss someone. Kissing Dallia would be wrong. And what would happen to her when Dallia tired of her? Would she be sent back to the dungeon? Cass felt the blood drain from her. "I...I can't do what you ask," she finally said.

"Why not? I'll show you exactly what you need to do. You need not worry about those finer points. Or do you deny me because someone else holds your fancy? Another woman?"

Cass's eyes opened wider, but she said nothing.

"Don't seem so surprised. I sense the desire in you." Dallia took another drink from her goblet.

"That's not totally it," Cass said.

"What then?" Dallia's tone sounded aggravated.

"I can't tell you."

"Oh, I think you better tell me. In fact, I'd say your life depended on you telling me. Since I know nothing about you, and I've told you quite a bit about me, why don't you start with why it is you ended up in my father's prison in the first place? Or is that what you can't tell me?"

"I did nothing wrong."

"Someone who does nothing wrong is not someone who would be imprisoned. Did you steal from us? Are you a thief?"

"No."

"What then? I warn you, Cassethea, my patience grows thin. Though I may want something from you and would be very unhappy if I did not get what I wanted, I won't wait forever for you to speak the truth."

"I was passing through this kingdom to retrieve what was already mine. I stole nothing."

"Continue."

"My mother, sister, and best friend were taken from our homeland, many moons since. It was suggested to me in my wanderings that they were wrongly captured and imprisoned in your father's castle," Cass said.

"Those words alone could land you in the dungeon. And what then if those suggestions were true and you found them here? What would you do?" Dallia twisted a strand of her hair around her index finger.

"I would rescue them and take them home."

Dallia laughed. "What a lofty goal to think you could achieve such an undertaking with no help. Part of me admires the veracity in you, but part of me thinks you are also naïve and foolish to believe you could pull off such a task on your own, assuming anything you said is true."

"I haven't lied. And I will not rest until I find them."

After a couple of minutes of silence, Dallia said, "I see. Then maybe I can help you in that regard. I know everything that goes on in this castle, or almost everything. My father doesn't think so, but that's only because his ego gets in his way sometimes, and he thinks he's smarter than me. I use his misguided thoughts to my benefit. What are your mother, sister, and friend's names?"

Cass tried to read Dallia, but she couldn't. Was she truly going to help her, or was she setting a trap? Would she know about her family if they'd been captured, and if so, would she let them go if she did? As a woman, would she sympathize with their plight? Or would she let them go only if Cass did as Dallia asked of her? Could she even do what Dallia asked, in her soul? She thought not. There was no way to know what was in Dallia's heart or how she would react. Yet Cass needed to do what she could to find out if her family and Julia were in fact captives and were still alive. The possibility of being reunited after so much time rose stronger within her than her fears. Cass took a deep breath. "My mother's name is Arielwund, my sister is called Emma. Emma is seven winters now. My friend's name is Julianta."

Dallia remained silent at first. She intertwined her fingers and tapped her index fingers together as if in deep thought. Her gaze drifted upward as if she were searching memories from another place, and then she nodded her head. "Yes, I remember them," she said solemnly. "I'm afraid I don't want to tell you what I have to tell you next."

Cass felt the air escape her lungs and the burning amber within flicker violently as if it were about to be extinguished. Her heart ached as her breathing slowed. "Tell me, please. I need to know," she managed to say in a whisper.

"First, know that they weren't kept in the dungeons and weren't tasked with hard labor, as you were. They were, however, kept as slaves. I believe in the kitchens. About three moons after they arrived, they tried to escape. I don't know what they were thinking, but apparently you are all made of the same stubborn cloth and false beliefs. They were unsuccessful in their escape. All three were killed. I'm sorry."

Cass couldn't wrap her head around the fact that all her travels, all her training, all she'd been through with Koll and Haddontek, and the toil in the castle was for nothing. She'd never had the chance to save her family and Julia after all. All the work, all the worry, wasted. They were gone, and she'd failed them. She struggled to catch her breath. Tears streamed down the sides of her cheeks, and the amber within her flickered to extinction. The flame that drove her relentlessly went out. Her life no longer had meaning. As the life-force within was replaced with an unending hollowness, Cass said, "Teach me what you want me to know."

Dallia didn't hesitate. She took Cassethea's hand and led her into her bedroom. Mounted above the bed were Cass's sword and dagger, in an "X" pattern. The animal skins had been removed from the handles, and the gems glistened in the glow of the lit sconce on the wall.

"Where did you get those?" Cass asked. Not that she cared anymore, but she thought it especially cruel to place them above the bed. Obviously, a calculated move on Dallia's part to reinforce who was in control, in case there was any doubt. But Cass had no doubt.

"You know where I got them. My father gifted them to me after I enquired about your belongings yesterday. The sword is useless. I had to have two soldiers bring it here yesterday, it was that heavy. But the dagger—the dagger could still be used, and quite effectively, I'd imagine. I trust you won't touch it. I don't want to remind you that if you hurt me, your suffering at the hands and loins of the guards would be far greater than any suffering you could imagine upon yourself."

The words didn't penetrate. Cass merely said, "I wouldn't hurt you."

"Excellent." Dallia undid her gown and let a hint of her nakedness into Cass's view. Then she slowly removed the tunic from Cass's torso, her eyes lingering on the muscle and small but firm and supple breasts that lay beneath the fabric. "Watch and learn from me this time, but don't touch me. What I do to you, you will in return do to me when I ask it of you."

"I understand," Cass said.

After Dallia's lesson and Cass's first attempt to pleasure the princess, Cass dressed and was escorted to what was now to be her bedroom. As Cass walked into the foreign room toward the bed, the steel lock on the door clicked behind her. The living space was tiny but sufficient. Along the stone wall opposite the door was a narrow window with vertical bars across the opening. Cass hardly realized the bars were there and didn't care that they were. She remained a prisoner, and a slave of a different sort. So be it. What difference did it make? All her tireless efforts and high hopes got her nowhere.

She neared the window and glanced out to the rocky cliff-side and sea below. For a moment, she allowed herself to think back to her climbing lessons with Tove, but sensing a stabbing pain in her chest, she quickly blocked Tove from her mind. She didn't deserve Tove. She didn't deserve life. But she'd not take her own life either. That she'd leave up to Gaia. In the meantime, no more struggles. She'd do what Dallia asked of her for as long as she asked. And when Dallia was through with her, she hoped her end would be merciful and swift. That much, at least, she thought Dallia would owe her.

Chapter Twenty-Four

Cass awoke to the clank of the door lock. A middle-aged soldier with dark eyebrows and thick, curly, black hair carried a plate filled with bread, eggs, and a slice of cheese, along with a mug of mead. He set them on a waist-high, wooden dresser by the door, the musculature in his arms visible. Cass thought of Tove's arms for a second until the plate touched the dresser's surface and redirected her thoughts. Cass hadn't noticed the dresser the night before. But then, she hadn't noticed much. She was surprised, though, that Dallia had made her leave the bed.

"When you're done eating and are fully dressed, knock on the door. The princess wishes to see you after you've eaten," the soldier said.

"Thank you. I will do as you ask," Cass replied, her voice monotone, even to her own ears.

She waited until the door was closed but didn't hear a click. She didn't hear footsteps leave either. Cass rolled out of bed and slipped on her trousers, tucking in her white tunic. Next to the dresser stood a square, wooden stand with a bowl of water on it. Next to the bowl sat soap and rectangular squares of cloth, neither of which she'd noticed the night before either.

She bent forward and cupped her hands, allowing the cold water to refresh her face. She wet one of the cloth squares, lathered it in soap, and washed her face. The softness of the material surprised her. She ran it over her neck and forearms before rinsing it out in the bowl, wiped off any lingering soap residue, and used another cloth to dry herself. She ran her hands through her boyish hair several times as she allowed her arms to air dry. Hungry, she lifted the plate of food off the dresser and sat on the corner of the bed. She ate and drank everything, though it had no taste to her.

Strange, she thought. She left the plate and goblet on the bed, stood, and strode toward the door. She breathed deep and knocked. The soldier opened the door and escorted her to Princess Dallia's quarters.

Cass wasn't entirely sure how to act in front of the princess, considering she spent the night before satisfying Dallia's needs only to be dismissed like a servant. She slightly bowed her head. "Princess," she said.

"Ahh, Cassethea." Princess Dallia's gaze unabashedly scanned Cass's body. "You are a soothing sight to my eyes. How did you sleep last night?"

"Fine, thank you." Cass recognized the lust in the princess's eyes and wasn't sure how she felt about knowing her desire.

"I slept better than I have in years, thanks to you," Princess Dallia said, a wicked grin forming on the right side of her face. "I think our arrangement will work out fine, don't you?"

Cass held no thoughts about the subject or her predicament one way or the other. "Yes, I believe so."

"Good, that's what I was hoping to hear. Come to me, Cassethea," the princess commanded, motioning with her index finger for Cass to move closer.

When Cass approached and stood a foot from her, Princess Dallia pulled Cass's tunic from her trousers. She ran her hands over the fabric and over Cass's breasts. "You feel so good," the princess whispered. "Your body is exquisite." Princess Dallia dropped her hand into Cass's and pulled her backward. "Now take me to my bed and thrill me."

****

After Cass and the princess spent a vigorous morning in the bedroom, Geraline and Salleen brought steaming bowls of stew into the room. Cass noticed sideways glances of interest mixed with scrutiny cast in her direction, until Princess Dallia waved the servants off.

"I'm taking my horse out for a ride this afternoon, but I'll be back tonight. I'll call on you then," the princess said.

"Can I ride with you? There's not much to do in my

room, alone. I'd like to feel the sun on my face and the power of the horse between my legs," Cassethea said.

Princess Dallia laughed. "Yes, I'm sure you'd love to have access to a horse, but I fear that would be the last I would see of you, my handsome Cassethea."

"Why do you say such a thing? No, I have nowhere to go. I would stay by you."

"As nice as your promise sounds, I'm no one's fool. You will stay here. But, I agree you will need to exercise your legs, so I will have a guard accompany you around the upper quarters of the castle. It's the best I can do for now," the princess said before sipping from her goblet.

"Thank you. A walk would be appreciated."

"Very well, I will see you later. Guard!" The princess waited for the guard to enter. "Take Cassethea to her room. In an hour or so, I want you to escort her around the upper level of the castle, wherever she wants to go. She is to be treated as one of my valued servants. Is that clear?"

"Yes, my princess," the guard said. The man was the same soldier with curly, dark hair that had walked Cassethea to the princess's room earlier that morning.

****

Close to two hours after Cassethea left the princess and was escorted to her room, the soldier returned. Cass first heard his footsteps and then the clank of the lock and a knock on the door. "Enter," she said.

"Are you ready to walk the castle?" the soldier asked.

"Yes, thank you. May I lead?"

"You may."

And with those words, Cass felt the first bit of freedom granted her in the months she'd now spent at the castle. The hallways and corridors in the castle were wide and vast, providing plenty of exercise room. The parts of the walk she valued the most were those around the courtyard opening and those along the far side of the castle where she could see and hear the sea splash against the rocks. There, she would stand at times, and unbeknownst to the guard, mind-connect with a passing bird. She'd see the world once more from above, even if she experienced no actual joy with it. Her gift gave her a false sense of freedom, which was both welcome and unwelcome at the same time.

Cass spent week after week in much the same pattern. Princess Dallia called upon Cass in the mornings and evenings, and Cass spent the afternoons walking the castle. Her guard, who now called her Cassethea, and whom she called Seffan, seemed to relax in her presence more and more each day. "I don't know why Princess Dallia continues to believe I need accompaniment during my walks," Cass said, as she stood overlooking the courtyard. "It's not as if I'm going anywhere, or have anywhere to go, for that matter."

Seffan glanced around him as if to ensure no one would overhear him. "I have to agree, Cassethea, though I don't mind accompanying you. It's either this or training with the troops, and walking with you is easier than training with them."

"What is it you do when training?"

"They have us run long expanses back and forth, fight hand to hand, practice sword fighting, those sort of things, but they do it until you darn well can hardly lift an arm or move a leg. At least, that's how I feel when we're done."

Cass said, "I'd almost welcome a sword fight. My mind feels as numb as my body. I used to practice swordplay with my brothers when I lived at home. We used sticks, of course, but it worked out fine. My father didn't approve of my taking part, but then there wasn't much he did approve of when it came to me. You can hone your skills well with sticks. My skills have advanced more significantly since then, though." Cass let her mind drift to the many lessons with Tove and allowed the memory of Tove's sparkling blue eyes to penetrate her hardened core. "The more I think about it, I'd say I have some fierce skills. Better than most."

Seffan laughed. "Is that right? Better than a trained soldier in King Andron's army?" he asked in a taunting manner.

"I'd wager better, yes," Cass said, with a half smile. The smile was the first bit of emotion she'd felt since learning of the deaths of her mother, sister, and Julia.

"In that case, I shall find us a training area and see how

accomplished you really are with a sword. But you can't tell Princess Dallia. She'll have my head."

"Not to worry. Princess Dallia and I don't speak much." Cass's words were a reminder to her of how low she'd sunken. "I think I'll start back for my room now. I'm suddenly tired."

"Lead on, but remember. Tomorrow we spar."

****

And spar they did, day after day, week after week. Seffan had located a cavernous room at the far side of the upper floor that the king once used for training, up until the time the king found solace in food of greater value to him than staying fit. At least that's what Seffan surmised and told Cass. Regardless of the reasons, they now had a spacious room to themselves, away from prying eyes, and perfect for swordplay. Unfortunately for Seffan, and likely much to his surprise, Cass won more matches than she lost. But the two not only sparred with sticks, they also ran sprints from one end of the room to the other and back, and engaged in other similar contests, contests that were constant reminders of Cass's time spent with Tove. Each day with Seffan provided Cass with an increased sense of independence and a reminder of the days when she thought herself invincible enough to conquer anything. The reminders of her time with Tove also made each return to her locked room at the end of the day a greater and greater contrast to that prior life.

On the third week of her afternoon walks, Cass glanced into the courtyard and caught sight of a young woman with long blonde hair who walked with Julia's gait. In that brief moment, a flash of heat coursed through her and she allowed herself to imagine Julia lived, before the sickening truth sank in and the hope drained from her veins. Julia was dead. Cass chided herself for allowing childlike wishes to cloud her reality, yet a part of her wondered if Julia might in fact be alive. Could the possibility exist? And if the possibility existed and Julia wasn't dead, perhaps her mother and Emma lived as well. Could Princess Dallia have lied to her? For what purpose?

Allowing foolish thoughts and hopes into her mind wasn't helpful to maneuvering through her days and more distracting during her beckoned encounters with the princess, Cass couldn't stop them from happening. She looked forward to her walks more and more and stopped longer by the courtyard in hopes of seeing the woman who reminded her of Julia.

As she trained longer and harder with Seffan, a renewed energy found its way into her limbs and lungs with each breath. Yet at the end of each afternoon, she'd return to her room without any sighting of the young woman, a fact which should have led to the realization she'd perhaps created the image in her mind. An image unreal like the deception Haddie perpetrated. But the thin thread of hope she already wove prevented her from drawing that conclusion. Instead, she decided confinement to the second story impeded her from uncovering the truth, whatever it may be. For the first time in weeks, she wanted again. She wanted the freedom to roam the castle and beyond. She wanted to ask passersby her own questions and confirm or rebuke what the princess had told her. However, a problem existed. Princess Dallia would never allow her such freedoms.

But Cass soon discovered she didn't need Princess Dallia's approval. What she needed was an unprecedented opportunity, one she miraculously received. After lunch on this miraculous day, Seffan didn't stop by her room at his usual time to accompany her on her walk. The entire afternoon passed without Seffan. And as her door unlocked and opened before dinnertime, without a knock, Seffan wasn't standing before her. A younger guard, holding a plate of food and a goblet of wine, stood before her.

"Princess Dallia extends her apologies for not being able to dine with you this evening," the guard said as he scanned the room, apparently searching for a place to set the food. "She's entertaining a visitor."

Cass walked toward him and took the plate and goblet. "Thank you for letting me know about the princess. Could you tell me if Seffan is ill? He normally comes after lunch to escort me on a walk, but I've been confined in here all day."

"Seffan left the castle to attend to a personal matter. I

believe he'll be back tomorrow," the guard said, before he turned to exit.

"In that case, after I've eaten, am I to understand you'll accompany me on my walk? My daily exercise is per the princess's orders," Cass said. Sensing his hesitation, she added, "You don't need to walk far with me. I'm sure you're already aware I'm confined to the second floor. Seffan walks with me to the main staircase and waits for me there until I return. Since the staircase is the only way down, short of climbing, there isn't much to worry about, is there?"

"No, I suppose there isn't."

"I'll knock on the door to let you know when I'm ready to go then." Cass sat on the corner of the bed with her food.

****

Cass could hardly believe the young guard let her continue past the staircase, while he stood in wait at the top of the stairs. When she passed the first turn in the hallway, she glanced behind her and watched him sit. She relaxed somewhat, but not knowing whether he'd change his mind or not and follow after her, she moved quickly toward the courtyard opening. There, on a corner and partly out of sight from below, she leaned over and scanned the rock wall from where she stood to the ground below. There appeared to be enough protruding stones she could use as foot and hand holds that she might be able to scale down the wall. Unlike the cliffs she practiced climbing with Tove, these stones were dry, not wet and slippery. They provided a fair chance of a successful descent. She was going to do this. She would seize the opportunity provided her. She might not be given another.

Cass leaned farther over the top of the wall. She grasped the wall from both sides, slid on top, and twisted her body and legs over the edge. There, she searched blindly with her feet for a resting point and eventually found one and then another. Her white-knuckled fingers strained to hold onto the sections of stone above her head. She descended slowly and deliberately, in less time than she'd estimated.

After inhaling a deep breath of relief when she reached the bottom, she rubbed her hands together and brushed off her trousers. The question was...where to now? What had she been thinking? Risking discovery to find a woman she'd only seen from behind, who she thought walked like Julia? This was turning into a stupid idea. This person could be anywhere or nowhere. Most likely she was a projection of who Cass wanted her to be. Cass decided she couldn't stand around idle. She already climbed down the wall and now could not risk being seen from above if the guard suddenly decided to follow after her.

To Cass's right, merchants stood by their carts selling bread and cheese, vegetables, bowls and baskets, jewelry, and other assorted items, though some were already packing up their belongings for the day. Cass turned right and made her way along the line of them. As she did, she glanced at her surroundings, but she saw no one who looked like Julia.

After passing the row of merchants, Cass turned a corner and walked faster, knowing her time away from the guard was limited. She walked through a row of meager residences, which were built within the outer reaches of the courtyard but within the castle walls, although they were clearly not part of the main castle structure where the king and his family lived.

With dusk fast approaching, Cass didn't have much more time, but she continued through the maze of narrow alleyways until she caught sight of a young woman handing an older, hunched, and emaciated woman a loaf of bread. Cass's heart nearly stopped. The younger woman who'd caught Cass's attention continued on and walked around another corner. Cass recognized the walk and followed, sensing the searing eyes of the older woman upon her. Before the young woman reached the inner castle walls, Cass called out in a raised whisper, "Julia?"

The woman spun on her heels and faced Cass, clearly startled and afraid. She stood as if frozen in place. When it appeared as though recognition set in, the basket the woman carried dropped from her arms. "Oh, my God, Cassethea, is that you?"

Cass ran toward the woman and grabbed her by the arms. She stared into those unmistakable green eyes. "Gaia," Cass said. "It is you! I thought you were dead. I've not stopped searching for you from the moment I found out what happened to you, but Princess Dallia told me you were dead." Tears streamed down Cass's cheeks.

"Shhsh, I'm very much alive." Julia wiped the tears aside with her thumb. She ran her fingers through Cass's boyish hair and scanned her body from top to bottom. "Look at you. Your hair. Those clothes you're wearing. Where did you get those impressive clothes?"

Cass noticed for the first time that Julia wore a servant's dress similar to one Geraline wore. "It's a longer story than probably either of us has time for, but Princess Dallia gave them to me. It's not exactly what you think, but it may be partly what you think. At any rate, I came to rescue you, my mother, and Emma. Julia, are my mother and Emma alive as well? The princess told me they were dead. Please tell me they live."

Julia still appeared as if in shock and did not answer immediately. "Yes, yes, they're alive."

Cass dropped to her knees. "They're alive? Truly? Please don't jest with me. I can't take losing them a third time. It would kill me."

"It's true. They live. They both work in the kitchens. I see them sometimes." Julia's eyes lowered. "I'm the servant of the queen's brother, so I have freer rein than others. Many have it much worse than I do."

"The queen's brother? Princess Dallia must have known you were all alive then. She said you tried to escape."

"Any attempt at escape would be foolish. I knew that. I never tried to escape."

"As servant to the queen's brother...is that why you're out here, in the streets?"

"Yes. He actually gives me a small allowance to spend on myself. Cass, my God, I really can't believe it's you."

"It is me. How are mother and Emma?"

"As far as I know, their health is good, although Arielwund lost much weight. How do you know the princess?"

"How I know the princess is a long story. I do know her but not in a friendly way. I'm also not free, but I will find a way to free us, now that I know you're all alive, of that you can be sure. I've not come all this way to lose now."

"Are you alone, or did others come for us? I wonder every night where my father is, and why he's not come for us."

"I came alone. I can't speak about your father, but there was talk of Arabs invading, after Andron's men left, the men everyone was fooled into thinking were Vikings. He's not coming, but perhaps I can get you all freed. I can reason with the princess. If she won't let me go, maybe I can convince her to at least let the three of you go."

"No, Cass. We couldn't leave without you."

"If I can arrange it, you would need to go. I'll figure a way to escape later if I must, but at least my mind would finally rest, knowing you'd all be safe."

Julia barely let Cass finish before she kissed her on the lips. Julia's eyes shot open, and she held her hand in front of her mouth. "I'm so sorry, Cass. I forgot about your feelings for me. I didn't mean to—I mean I'm so happy to see you— please don't be upset."

Cass stood shocked for a moment, but she didn't feel desire toward Julia as she had in the past. "Not to worry. I've grown up since we were innocent kids on the hill. In some ways, I wish I hadn't, but in other ways I'm glad I did. I have to go now before—"

"There she is! Seize her!" the guard Cass had left at the top of the stairs yelled.

"Julia! Go, before they see you. Go now," Cass pleaded.

Moments later, the soldiers descended upon her.

Chapter Twenty-Five

"I'm thrilled our schedules lined up, and we can finally eat a quiet dinner together again," Rayne said. She sat at the edge of one of the sofa cushions in the living room and leaned forward to cut into the steak she'd grilled.

The corner of Jess's lips turned upward. "Oh, you are?"

"Of course. Why wouldn't I be? I enjoy your company, and I think you enjoy mine."

"I enjoy your company a great deal."

"Then why haven't you said more than two words to me until now? What's wrong? You're not your usually feisty self. Ever since I brought lunch by the other day, you've acted distant and somehow off."

Jess lifted her gaze. "Feisty, hmm?"

Rayne nodded. "Yes, feisty. One of the many qualities I like about you, I might add, though you cleverly avoided answering my question."

Jess blushed and now felt worse than she had the last couple of days for having kept Rayne in the dark. She withheld the truth from Rayne about Cassethea because she didn't want Rayne to think her crazy and lose her, but at the same time, her conscience wreaked havoc on her inner peace, or in this case, lack thereof. Jess breathed deep and studied Rayne's expression. What shone back was nothing short of pure concern. What else had she expected? Rayne was a unique and caring person to the core. She deserved the truth. Even El agreed with Jess on this issue, and how often did the two of them agree on anything? Jess found Rayne's eyes and held her stare. "I've not been feeling all too feisty lately. Although I haven't lied to you about there being nothing wrong with me when you asked, I haven't been totally honest either."

Concern crossed Rayne's expression. "Go on, please."

"Remember the night I found George and brought him to the restaurant?"

"You mean the night George found you and brought you to the restaurant?"

Jess smiled. She loved the fact Rayne tried to make her happy and lighten the mood whenever she sensed Jess was in a tight spot. "Yes, my apologies. Anyway, you and I talked about my work and about the excavation that evening. I told you about my hope of finding Bishop Leon II's remains, which is in line with the school's goals. But I added I was also secretly following my gut and hoping to discover truth in what was otherwise currently myth."

"Yeah, I remember those cryptic words, though I don't recall you saying 'secretly' at the time. You did say if you disclosed your reasoning to the university, you were certain the excavation wouldn't have seen the light of day. I was curious what you meant, and still am, but at the time I didn't think I had the right to ask. I hardly knew you."

"I figured as much and appreciated you didn't, but if you let me, I'd like to tell you about it. I don't want any secrets between us, and my life's starting to feel like one big secret. I only ask you to keep an open mind," Jess said.

"Of course, I'm a liberal. Seriously though, I hope you know you can tell me anything, Jess."

What Rayne said was true, but telling her the truth still wasn't going to be easy. "The real reason I wanted this project wasn't to find Bishop Leon, although that's how I framed it to the board. I wanted to find proof of Cassethea of Mercia's existence. Cassethea was born before her time, really. Scant stories buried among tens of thousands of pages of history suggest she was a warrior who rescued enslaved women and children. She carried a sword too heavy for a man to yield, yet used it effortlessly in her battles. She's depicted as a myth, and if mentioned in history classes anywhere, is spoken of as such. I don't know why, but once I learned about her, I've been obsessed with proving she was real. What little I uncovered in my research before making this trip hinted at the possibility she might be buried at this site."

Jess glanced at Rayne to gauge her expression and contemplate her next words. The easier part of the story to impart was behind her. But rather than judge her, Rayne showed intent interest. Jess gained confidence from Rayne's demeanor and continued. "When you brought us lunch the other day, Susan had moments before uncovered a Viking drinking horn. The horn was fully intact. Cassethea's name was etched into the horn, next to the female Viking leader's name, Tove. The horn contained names of Tove's brothers and their wives etched below and next to each other, descending by age from the widest part of the horn to the narrowest.

"I know who those people are, not because I saw it written anywhere else in the literature. I've seen the horn, minus Cassethea's name, in visions I've experienced about Cassethea and her life. The visions came to me the first night after we broke ground on this dig site. First, I thought they were fanciful dreams, something I created in my sleep, but the details were so real. It was like I was transported back in time and allowed to see what Cassethea saw through her own eyes, and what she felt. It scared me, really. I thought I lost my mind. I spoke with El about it. I think I told you about her."

"You did."

"She believed I was given a gift. She said visions can be the extension of someone's soul. She mentioned reincarnation, transcendence, immortality of the soul—the continuation of a person's existence through time and space. She said the Egyptians believed the spirit, the body's life force, its immortal soul or Ka, lived forever."

"Meaning El and you now believe Cassethea's soul has reached out to you in these dreams, or visions?"

"Yes."

Rayne sat quietly for a moment, appearing to let Jess's revelations sink in. Breaking the crush of silence, she finally said, "Bloody hell. It's no wonder you've been so quiet lately. I can't imagine what it must be like to be you right now. What you say—it's truly amazing."

Jess exhaled and sunk into the back of the sofa. "So you don't think I'm crazy?"

"What? No, of course I don't. But I understand why you've kept this information to yourself until now. I can't tell you how much it means to me for you to trust me with this, Jess. I promise I won't disclose what you told me to anyone. The whole thing is fantastic. I...would you mind telling me more about her?"

"I'd love to. She's not had an easy life..." Jess told Cass's story through the evening and into the early morning hours, ending with the last scary bit of information she'd learned of when the guards seized Cass.

****

Jess awoke on the sofa with Rayne's arm wrapped around her middle and Rayne cradled behind her. She didn't remember falling asleep, but she couldn't recall such a peaceful sleep in years. Although Jess coveted the closeness and security of being enveloped by Rayne, she gently lifted Rayne's arm from her midsection and slowly slid off the sofa. Careful not to step on George, she gently replaced Rayne's arm onto the sofa. She stared down at Rayne's peaceful face, wanting desperately to kiss her lips. As the heat within her rose, she shook her head and whispered to herself, "Get a grip, Madison," before she slunk away toward a hot, no, make it cold, shower. After her shower, she entered the kitchen and made breakfast. George sat on the floor behind Jess while she stood in front of the counter. Moments later, she heard the now familiar voice that managed to warm her insides.

"You're an angel. I smell coffee." Rayne entered the kitchen after taking her own shower. "And good morning to you, George, you traitor."

"Hey, you, be nice to George. And if you think coffee's the bee's knees, I scrambled eggs and toasted bread, too." A weight had been lifted off Jess's shoulders from the night before.

"Picking up a bit of the local Brit lingo, I see. I'm impressed. May I?" Rayne reached for a plate.

"Please." Jess took the other plate and followed Rayne to the kitchen table, George on her heels.

As soon as Rayne sat at the table across from Jess, she looked Jess in the eyes, and Jess felt the familiar pull between them.

"Thank you for sharing your story with me last night, Jess. It's truly amazing. You now have me worried about what happened to that young woman. If you find out more, will you please tell me?"

"Yes, of course. She's on my mind often during the day, today even more so."

"That's understandable. This excavation must have turned into more than you ever imagined it would be."

"Yes, it's become more than I imagined, and in more ways than one," Jess said.

"But something's still bothering you?"

"Yes."

"When you mentioned Cassethea's name was inscribed on the drinking horn next to Tove's, this signified they were together, correct?" Rayne asked.

"Yes, the placement strongly suggests they were coupled in the equivalent of what we consider marriage today."

"Personally, I find the discovery remarkable. But once your chancellor finds out, you think this means the end of the excavation?"

"I do, and yet I think I still need to tell him. I'd welcome your opinion. I've tossed it around in my head for days, but so far have only come to the conclusion that telling the truth is best."

"I agree. The truth is always the best option."

****

Jess stormed into Eagles Landing at the end of her day, searching for Rayne, but she spotted Baron behind the bar.

"Hey, stranger, are you looking for Rayne?" Baron asked.

"Hey, Baron, yeah, I am. It's good to see you. Is she in the kitchen?"

"She is. Go on back there. I'm sure she'll be glad to see you, but beware. George the beggar is with her."

Jess smiled and let a sliver of her anger and frustrations go. "Thanks for the warning. I'll prepare myself." As Jess stepped into the kitchen behind the bar, George let out an abbreviated bark and sprang toward her. He bumped into her legs and sent her wobbling several feet in reverse. "Whoa, you crazy mutt." She regained her footing and scratched his head.

"I recall mentioning to you that George is no mutt," Rayne said as she shifted her attention to Jess.

"Yes, I distinctly remember being told that by an overly protective parent. George doesn't mind being called a mutt though."

"Is that right?"

"Absolutely...my intuition tells me so," Jess said.

"And there's no arguing with women's intuition."

"Exactly. What do you think brought him by the pub today without first stopping by the site to visit us this morning?" Jess asked.

Rayne stepped closer. "Food—what else would drag him from his new best friends? Are you hungry, too?"

"No, I'm not hungry. Aggravated, maybe, and disappointed, but not hungry. Actually, I'm sorry to bother you at work. I'll go. This interruption could have waited."

"I don't see your coming here as an interruption, and if you could've waited, I'm sure you would've. What's troubling you?"

"I called the chancellor this morning. It turns out honesty isn't the best policy. It's over. He's put a stop to the excavation. He didn't say no right away. He said he'd call me back after discussing it with the rest of the board. In the end, he blamed his decision on the board of trustees, but I know he wanted the same outcome. I haven't told my students yet. I didn't know how to approach them," Jess said, her hands trembling.

"Tosser." Rayne moved close and took Jess's hands in her own. "Easy. It will all be okay. Maybe you shouldn't tell them it's over yet."

"Why not? I may as well rip the bandage off now."

"No. I've given some thought to the possibility of this outcome and came up with an idea that might work."

"You have?"

"Yes, I have. I think you need to go public."

"Go public?"

"Get your situation out on the Internet. Create a blog or

web page with pictures of the site, some background, historical facts, pictures of you and your students, some of the artifacts you've already found, and the fact that funding has been pulled from you. Ask the public for donations, or charge a fee for visitors to see the site and the artifacts you've uncovered. I mean, you're bound to draw interest. You're sitting on the discovery of a long-lost bishop. Vikings are involved, and the possibility exists of discovering a mythical person from over a thousand years ago who happens to be gay. And if that weren't enough, add to it the intrigue of a theft. What's not to love?"

"The chancellor wouldn't like it."

"All the more reason you should do it. That wanker wants to twist history to fit his beliefs at the cost of science. Do you know what the truth could mean to young girls, to girls and women uncertain of their own sexuality? To have proof homosexuality existed over a thousand years ago between two incredibly strong and independent women? How could you leave now and not find out if you were right?"

Jess stared into Rayne's eyes and then at their entwined hands. "You're right. How could I leave now?"

****

The next day, Jess explained to her graduate and undergraduate student coworkers what Susan's discovery of the drinking horn meant. She told them about her discussion with the chancellor and the ultimate decision by the board of trustees to end their funding. To soften the blow, she explained she'd called UK Berkeley and reached mutual agreement that their previously scheduled presentation at the university would remain intact. Her team who'd become like family, agreed they needed to continue on, funding or no funding. Jess mentioned Rayne's suggestion about creating a blog or web page, which ignited lightning-fast interest. Marco offered to create the website. Justin offered up pictures for it, and Shelly offered to add the historical background.

The students pooled their skills, and once the website was up and running, small but plentiful donations flooded in.

Word spread more quickly than Jess imagined. Even El e-mailed Jess before she could tell her what they'd done. Jess had trouble keeping up with reading all the positive messages while still working at the site.

Several days later, while Jess was on her knees clearing a section of ground, a shadow crossed into her line of sight. Jess turned and shielded her eyes.

"Hello, excuse me, but are you Professor Madison?" a young woman with straight, long, dark hair said.

Jess let go of her trowel and slowly stood. "I am, and you are?"

The woman extended her hand, and Jess shook it. "I'm Maria Cortez, third-year university student of archaeology from the next town over and want-to-be volunteer with your excavation crew, if you'll have me."

"I don't understand," Jess said.

"I saw your website. I think what you're doing here is great, and I want to help. And I'm free the rest of the summer. I spoke with my professor, and he and my university agreed to extend one credit for the work I'd do here. And I'm not the only one who wants to help. Other classmates from last semester are equally eager," Maria said. "Please say yes. Chances like these don't present themselves every day."

Jess stood speechless. When her voice returned, she said, "Yes, yes, yes. We'd very much welcome the help from you and your classmates. Thank you. I didn't realize there'd be so much interest, but I'm beyond thankful for it. You'll need to bring your own tools."

"Not a problem. Do you think after a week or so, we might get our pictures on the website, too?" Maria asked.

Jess laughed. "Of course. Justin will be happy to oblige."

"Awesome. We'll see you tomorrow morning then," Maria said.

****

From the next day on, with the additional help, the excavation moved along at an amazing pace. Computer reconstruction of the site, available for the public to view, took shape, as did the recovery of more bodies. Much to

Jess's disappointment, however, none of the bodies they'd uncovered were Cassethea.

During these days, Jess also noticed an increased frequency of glances exchanged between Maria and Susan. Jess always thought a gay gene resided in Susan but wasn't completely sure. Perhaps Maria's sexuality was part of why she was drawn to their cause in the first place. Whatever the reason, Jess was happy to have so much help. The subtle signs of Susan and Maria's affection reminded her of how much she missed Rayne. They'd both been so busy in the past week, with her at the site entertaining their new visitors, and Rayne at the bar feeding them. Jess decided she'd find a way soon to remedy the growingly untenable situation.

Chapter Twenty-Six

Princess Dallia paced to and fro as Cass stood in the room, having been forcibly pushed before the princess by the soldiers who dragged her back from her short-lived excursion.

"Did you really think my guard was stupid enough to trust you?" Princess Dallia asked, in a harsh tone.

"He's young, and new, so yes, I thought I could trick him."

"That was a most foolish move. Haven't I provided you with everything you need: shelter, food, companionship?"

"Companionship? Is that what you call my service to you? And what about honesty? What about providing me with the truth?"

"The truth? What are you talking about?"

"I may have snuck away for a short while, but I wasn't planning on going anywhere. I saw a familiar figure in the courtyard the other day from the balcony. She walked like my best friend, Julia. For days, the possibility of her being alive gnawed at me. I had to discover the truth."

"And so you disobeyed my orders?"

"Yes, I had to. You wouldn't have let me go on my own if I told you what I saw," Cass said, hatred penetrating her eyes.

"You're right, I wouldn't have. But that gives you no right to go against my wishes."

"Why did you lie to me?" Cass asked.

"What are you talking about? I didn't lie to you. And you are in no position to demand anything from me."

"I suppose it was foolish of me to think that after all the ways I've pleasured you, you might see me as more than simply an object you own."

"Yes, exceptionally foolish."

"Regardless, the person I saw from the balcony was indeed my friend Julia. She told me my mother and Emma live as well, yet you cruelly told me to my face they were dead. You sucked the life from me that day. Doesn't that bother you in the slightest?"

"Sparing you the knowledge of their existence, when I knew you'd never see them again anyway, didn't seem cruel to me. I did you a favor. And in doing so, I also managed to gain what I wanted," Princess Dallia said.

"I don't see your charity the same way as you do. However, I'm willing to forgive you and continue our arrangement if you agree to let them go, unharmed."

Princess Dallia laughed wickedly. "You are willing? You think you have a choice? I hate to disappoint you, Cassethea. In addition to you being my servant, these people you're willing to risk your life for are my father's acquisitions, not mine. I have no say in their release or capture. You, however, were given to me by my father, and therefore, I have every right to determine what happens to you. Do I need to remind you of the lustful loins that await you in the dungeon, should I decide to send you back there? Surely, remaining as my companion is a far better option, no?"

The frustration and hatred brewing in Cassethea didn't allow her to think strategically. "No, I don't think I could touch you anymore, knowing you lied to me and knowing you wouldn't even speak with your father or attempt to help me in any way. You have the power to release my friend and family but simply choose not to."

The princess's eyes narrowed. She didn't speak at first. "Your answer is most unfortunate, both for you and for me, but also for your special friend Julia. I know who she is. She's my uncle's servant, but soon she'll be mine. You see, you will attempt to have your way with me, and I will scream out, calling you a witch. My guards will take you to my father, who will undoubtedly make an example of you in the courtyard and burn you at the stake. And while you scream out, your precious Julia will scream out as well, in my bed, in ecstasy. She will scream not only at the same moment you scream, but every night thereafter, as I take continued pleasure in her body, a body that will never be yours. You were a fool to reject me, Cassethea, and you underestimated me. It's a shame you'll have to die for such foolishness, but so be it." Princess Dallia ripped the sleeve of her dress and the opening of her dress around her throat. "Witch! Guards, guards!"

Before Cassethea could tear her eyes from the wicked grin on Princess Dallia's face, hands grasped her tightly around the arms. She kicked and squirmed, but to no avail.

"Take her to my father. Tell him she is a witch! Tell him she tried to take advantage of me. She will burn at the stake!" the princess yelled, as Geraline and Salleen also ran into the room.

As Geraline wrapped her arms around Princess Dallia in comfort, her eyes met Cassethea's in sadness and knowing, but all Cassethea remembered was the pleasure behind the princess's eyes when she yelled for the guards.

****

Cass woke as the sun hit her face. Badly bruised and beaten, she'd been kicked unconscious the night before in the king's chambers by his guards. She now found herself tied to a wooden stake in the middle of the courtyard. She glanced at her feet, which were bound as well, only a foot or two above a bonfire-sized pile of wood at the base of the stake.

People stood outside their balconies, staring down at her, and others gathered in the courtyard, keeping distance between themselves and her, as if truly believing she were a witch and might curse them if they got too close. For the second time in her life, the vile word of "witch" was used against her, and now, it was going to be her demise. Her blood boiled when she recalled the smugness of Princess Dallia's glare the day before. The thought of her hands on Julia's body made her sick to her stomach. Julia wasn't like Cass. The princess would break her, of that she was certain. And what would happen to her mother and Emma? Would they then remain slaves until they died? Would they have to watch her be burned before their eyes? Cass thought for a brief moment that perhaps Princess Dallia had been right. Perhaps not knowing the truth would have been better for

Cassethea and Julia and her family. But with her next breath, she knew she shouldn't think that way.

As the morning progressed, sneers and accusations were hurled in her direction; people obviously were more comfortable speaking freely when hidden in a crowd than when standing alone. Droves of peasants streamed in through the open castle gate, ready for the day's entertainment.

Cass's chin touched her chest as her head hung low. What could she do? She was innocent of any crime, and so were Julia and her family. How could people revel so in another's pain? They didn't know anything about her. It dawned on Jess that perhaps their ignorance was part of the problem. They didn't know her. She decided before she'd be put to death, she'd make sure they knew something more than they knew now.

Shortly before noon, Cass saw the king, the queen, and their entourage seat themselves before the people. Princess Dallia wasn't among them. Cass wondered if she'd in fact taken Julia to her bed. She cringed at the thought, as the desperateness of her situation unfolded.

The king waved his hand toward the guards at the castle's entrance and watched as they pulled the heavy doors shut behind them. Then he stood and addressed his audience. "Wonderful people of my kingdom, welcome! Today we burn the soul of Cassethea of Mercia, woman dressed as a man, acting as a man."

The crowd gasped.

"Yes, I speak the truth. She disguised herself as a man and tried to beguile my daughter, your princess! She is a witch and is evil. She must die!"

Cheers rang out all around Cassethea, the sound deafening. Soldiers holding torches approached from both sides and stood awaiting further orders. Cass tried to clear her mind, she felt the wind pick up and watched as the flames on the torches flickered wildly at the ends of their wooden handles.

"What do you say on your behalf?" the king bellowed.

Cass gathered all the strength and confidence she could muster. She pictured Tove's face and her smile and recalled Tove's belief in her, and with her last breath, knew she needed to set the record straight. "I am no witch. You people are being fooled by your king!"

Loud roars and jeers erupted. Cass felt the impact of stones hurled at her, but she continued. "Your king steals women and children from other kingdoms and lands and brings them here as his slaves! His men dress as Vikings to hide this fact from his people and others! In the woods beyond the castle, he has built a hidden passage into the dungeons of this castle, to bring these people in without your knowledge! I've seen this with my own eyes."

"Liar!"

"Liar!"

"Burn her. Burn the witch!"

With those words, the winds continued to pick up speed, and dark clouds moved in. Cass found it increasingly difficult to speak over the crowd and the swirling wind. "I have not lied! These are innocent children and women he has taken and will continue to take. My mother, Arielwund, and my sister, Emma, are among those taken, and my friend Julianta, King Herrwald's daughter."

A collective gasp filled the air and provided Cass with hope. "I came to your kingdom to save them. Princess Dallia lied. I did nothing to her!"

"Liar!"

"What if she tells the truth?"

"Kill her!"

"Spare her!"

"Silence!" the king hollered, as the clouds churned in the blackened skies above. "We have heard enough lies and tall tales from the witch of Mercia. The weather worsens by the minute. We have no more time for untruths. By the powers given to me as your king and ultimate ruler, I pronounce Cassethea of Mercia, by admission of her own words, a spy. She is also declared a liar and witch. She will be burned. My decision is final."

The words reeled in Cass's head, but she somehow cleared her thoughts. She needed help and fast and summoned those she hoped could be of help, wondering at the same time if Julia was in fact star born of the water and if she caused the skies to blacken and the winds to roar. Cass reached out to her animal friends with her mind. The thought that perhaps Julia was trying to help warmed her heart. If she would die, at least someone was on her side, even when that someone was living through her own misery.

The king raised his hand in the air and held it steady, seemingly to add tension to the moment and exhibit his ultimate power. As his hand lowered, the wood beneath her caught fire. Most of the crowd cheered loudly, while others glanced to the skies, seemingly concerned by the worsening weather.

Beneath Cassethea, the flames grabbed quickly. She felt the heat rise. At the same time, she heard the shrill caws of hundreds and hundreds of blackbirds that came into view.

Cass stayed mind-focused as the birds swooped into the crowd and people screamed, "She is a witch! Protect yourselves." People scattered, but the castle gates remained closed. Rain poured from the sky.

Cass summoned her rat friend from the dungeon and other rats followed. Screams shot out everywhere. Half the rats climbed to the second story as the queen and others shrieked and scampered for safety.

"Open the gates!" people yelled.

"Let the rats out!"

"Let us out!" other yells followed.

The rains continued their downpour, sparing Cass as the flames couldn't take full hold under her. When the guards opened the gates, throngs of wolves charged from the woods and pounced on the guards. The mayhem was immense, and as everyone ran wildly in all directions, Cass's prison cell rat companion and two other rats managed to chew through Cass's ropes. She sprang from the pyre. As she landed on her feet, she felt the sting from blisters on the bottom of her feet. She bolted for the steps and continued up them, taking two at a time, not allowing the pain to slow her momentum.

A soldier at the top step yelled after her as she ran past. She stopped, turned, slid low, and kicked the soldier's feet out from under him. She grabbed his sword and continued along the hallway to the princess's chambers. As she rounded the corner, two guards confronted her, Seffan and another soldier.

"Cassethea, don't," Seffan pleaded.

"Get out of my way. I'll not kill the princess, but I need to get in there now. You know why. She has my friend." Cass raised her sword.

The soldier opposite Seffan advanced toward Cass and struck at her with his sword. They battled, but Seffan didn't step in to assist. The sword she'd stolen off the fallen soldier felt awkward to Cass, but she battled anyway. When the guard struck her arm and drew blood, she ended the battle abruptly with a blade sliced through his center. Immediately her eyes shot to Seffan. "I'm sorry. I didn't want to hurt anyone. Please stand aside."

Seffan lowered his sword. "I didn't think I'd see you again. I'm pleased to be wrong. Give me a flesh wound. Then do what you must. I'll not stand in your way, Cassethea. May God protect you."

"I understand. Thank you, my friend. This will not be easy for me," she said, before she placed a glancing swipe of the blade to his arm and kicked the sword he'd laid on the ground away from him. Swiftly, she barged through the door and ran into Princess Dallia's bedroom. Cass gasped.

Princess Dallia had indeed remained true to her word. Julia lay splayed naked on the bed, her hands bound above her head, as Princess Dallia stood inches from Julia about to mount the bed.

Cass felt Julia's embarrassment when their eyes met, but she pretended she'd barely seen her. Cassethea said in slow and deliberate terms, "Don't take one more step, Princess, or you will be dead."

Princess Dallia turned, her eyes filled with fire. "You!"

"Yes, me. Disappointed? You should be. Untie Julia now and give her back her clothes. Hurry up! If you make one wrong move, you will be dead before you have the chance to regret it."

Princess Dallia did as she was told. When Julia ran to Cass's side, Cass said to her, "Go gather my mother and Emma and any of the other women and children who were taken against their will and who want to go with you, and hurry. Take what food, weapons, and supplies you can grab, and head for the stables. Get everyone onto a horse. Leave three horses behind for me, and take the rest. If the soldiers come after us, I want them to be on foot."

"Which way will we go, once we exit the castle? How will I find you?" Julia said.

"Don't worry. The horses will lead you. I'll know where you will be because of them, now go! And be careful. The castle remains in disarray this moment but probably not for much longer."

"Thank you, Cass. Please hurry as well and be safe," Julia said.

"Go."

Cass took the rope from Princess Dallia. She tied the princess's hands behind her back and then to the bedpost. She took a scarf and covered the princess's mouth, tying it tight behind her head. "I should kill you, but I'm going to let you live. You saved my life once, and now I'm saving yours. Consider us even. However, if you ever come after me or any of us, I promise you I will kill you."

Princess Dallia struggled to free herself and mumbled into the scarf, clearly furious.

Cass said, "When you're given the opportunity, you should try to be a different ruler than your father was. You could actually be a decent person if you believe in yourself and don't simply take what you want. You know I didn't lie to you. You know in your heart your father is wrong. I hope you can turn a corner and do something positive with the rest of your life. The hope you can is why I'm letting you live." Cass jumped on the bed and tore her sword and dagger from the wall. She spotted the sheaths in the corner and grabbed those and her bag and ran out of the room, sword in hand.

Chapter Twenty-Seven

Cass acknowledged Seffan one last time before she ran down the hallway and into her old room. She opened the dresser drawer, stuffed two tunics and trousers in her bag, and laced a pair of leather foot-coverings over her injured feet. Then she tore off one sleeve of the tunic she wore and wrapped it around the cut in her bicep, tying it off by grabbing the opposite end with her teeth and pulling tight, the fabric underneath already stained bright red. Satisfied, she sprang from the room and raced down the hall. She ducked out of the way of one soldier, slashing his side, then continued full speed down the long and wide staircase and into the courtyard.

The clouds had broken up, and the sky turned lighter. The birds continued diving at the soldiers, who swiped wildly in the air and at the rats and wolves at their feet. Cass ran for the stables. As she ran, she mind-connected with Gray. When their eyes met, no words needed to be spoken. She conveyed her gratitude and called for him and his pack to return to their families, worried for their safety. She instructed the rats to do the same.

As she sprinted through the entrance to the stables and reached for a horse, she was knocked forward and to her hands and knees by a painful crack against her back. The air was forced from her lungs. Her sword left her hands and hit the dirt floor. The horses neighed and stomped in place. Cass turned her head, only to see familiar, filthy, dirty teeth and a vile grin on the man's face. Holthric, the quarry guard from whom Princess Dallia had saved her once, stood erect behind her, holding a shovel in his hands.

"We finally meet again, but this time, you won't get away from me. All those days you spent satisfying our deviant princess, when you could have been satisfying me," Holthric said.

Cass fought to regain her breath, the pain in her arm and throughout her body intense. Adrenaline coursed through her. She'd not come this far to be taken down by lesser than a rat now. "If I were you, I'd turn around and leave now, before you end up in two pieces on the floor next to me," Cass said.

Holthric roared with laughter. "Shut your mouth! You're in no position to threaten me. When I'm done with you, you'll wish you were the one who was dead." He set the shovel to the side.

As soon as he took one step in her direction, Cass mustered her remaining strength. She lunged for her sword, gripped it in her hand, rolled onto her back, and sprung onto her feet in one continuous motion. At the widened eyes of her onlooker, she cut him in two across his midsection. Without looking back, she reached for the nearest horse and darted out of the barn, taking the remaining two horses with her.

Cass nearly vomited as the recalled vision of Holthric, sliced in two by her own hand, registered in her mind, but the thought of what he would have done to her was equally repulsive. She fought the bile down. She wasn't a killer. She killed when forced, when no other viable option existed. This man, she convinced herself, didn't deserve a second more of her thoughts.

Forgiving herself, she exited the castle walls. Once free, a sensation of being watched struck her. She stopped the horse and stared into the woods. She saw no one, yet sensed a familiar presence. Cass's horse turned on his hind legs as she fought to keep him facing forward. Unexpectedly, her thoughts drifted to Tove and a familiar ache entered her chest. She lingered a moment longer then kicked the horse's side and continued onward, calling back the blackbirds and freeing them of her mental hold.

Cass rode north for an hour before she caught up to the mass of women who rode with Julia. As she passed each rider, she searched for her mother and Emma and spotted them at the front of the group with Julia. She guided her horse to the front of the pack and stopped. All the other horses stopped. She jumped down.

Arielwund lowered Emma and then dismounted.

"Cass!" Emma yelled.

"Emma! Mother!" Tears streamed from Cass's eyes. She knelt to catch Emma as she ran full speed into Cass's arms. "Look at you! You've grown so much!"

"So have you," Emma said.

Cass hugged her sister firmly and raised her in the air before she set her back on the ground. Next, she reached out and embraced her mother. She held her tight and whispered, "I'm so thankful you're alive. Thank you for all the bedtime stories I hadn't realized you told. They've come to me over these past months and have saved us both." When she let her go, she saw tears in her mother's eyes.

"You don't have to thank me. I wish I could have told you in another way, but I knew when the time was right your gifts would be revealed to you. They are something your father could never understand. I'm so thankful for you. I wasn't sure I'd ever see you again. Thank Gaia you survived." A look of concern sparked in Arielwund's eyes, and she reached for Cass's arm. "You're hurt. Let me take a look."

Cass withdrew her arm. "It's nothing. I'll live. Seeing you all safe is more healing than you can imagine."

Arielwund touched the sides of her daughter's face. "I still can't believe you found us. Look at you. You're so handsome. You've more muscle than Alfred when he left us."

"And I've needed every bit of it." Cass glanced at the group of about fifty women and children. "We better not rest yet. I want to make sure we're far away from the castle before we stop for the night." She turned to Julia. "Thank you for getting all these women to come with you."

"Although some were fearful of what would happen to them if they escaped and then were caught, convincing them to come with me wasn't a difficult task. Most were more than eager to leave. Many of them came from the kitchens, like your mother," Julia said, before her eyes lowered. "Cass, thank you for saving me from—"

Cass leaned over and kissed the side of Julia's face. "No worries, my friend. What's important is we're all safe now, and I'm planning on keeping it that way."

****

The next morning, Cass felt nauseous. Arielwund made her a healing tea for her stomach and an herbal poultice for her bicep and the bottoms of her feet, which seemed to work like magic.

As soon as her stomach settled, Cass stood before the group of expectant women. She raised her hands in the air. "We may have been taken against our wills, held in captivity, and made to bear more burden than any one person should bear, but now we are free. We are stronger and wiser than before. We are as one. And we will never let another control us again!"

When Cass paused, cheers rang out among the women. Some raised fists in defiance, and others simply looked on, the earlier fear in their eyes gone. Cass continued. "My name is Cassethea of Mercia. My mother, Arielwund, and sister, Emma, were taken from their homes by King Andron's soldiers. Our home and most of the homes in our town were burned. Many men and boys were killed. My brother Gollyn is dead." Cass paused as her eyes connected with her mother's for a brief moment of shared grief, before she refocused and pointed to Julia. "My friend Julianta, King Herrwald's daughter, was taken by these spineless thieves disguised as Vikings. Many of you have suffered the same fate. King Andron is not the only ruler selfishly enslaving people. Many are enslaved by relatives or other leaders. I plan to stop such behavior. I will rescue those woman and children. Not now, but soon, as we work to build our own army of fearless women."

More cheers rang out. "Today, we make plans regarding all of you, and of getting those of you who want to go home safely home so we can all heal and regroup." Cass continued the speech. She found out who lived north, south, and west of their current location, who planned to travel and fight with her, and who wanted to go home, either for a while or for good. The plan was they'd all stay together for a few days, until Cass could separate them into groups. She needed to discern what skills they had and choose leaders, so that when they eventually divided, each party of women would have the protection they needed and the ability to feed and care for one another until they were all safely home.

After their meal that evening, Julia sat near Cass close to the fire. "What are you thinking about?"

Cass poked a long stick into the flames. "I'm worried about staying in this spot too long, but I'm also worried that if we don't spend the time we need here, some of the women won't be able to defend themselves properly once we part."

"Yes, I understand. I'm concerned about you, Cass, and so is Arielwund."

"What is it that concerns you both?"

"We're worried about this army of women you have plans to form. Your intentions are noble, but you're a woman. How do you expect to fight against men who are built stronger than you? You know many of the women here won't join up with you, don't you? Maybe none will."

"Then I'll do what I can to help those in need until others do join me." Cass watched as Julia shook her head.

"You are stubborn, Cass, but in a good way. I pray if you do this, you'll be careful."

"I'll do my best."

"I know you freed us, and honestly I'm not sure how you managed it. Maybe you'll tell me one day, but do you really have the skills to teach these women what they'll need to know?"

"I believe I have. I was taught by a Viking leader over many months—a woman—strong, kind, and talented with a sword. Her lessons are the reason I've survived. I'm sure any knowledge I'm able to provide is better than none. The skills learned will be useful to them, whether we meet up again or not."

"This Viking woman sounds special. I hope one day I can meet her."

Cass studied Julia's expression, encouraged by the pure kindness she saw there. "I'd very much like to see her again as well. Gaia willing, perhaps we both will."

****

Three days later, after providing the intense training promised, Cass was confident enough competent women existed in each group to get the rest of the women and girls home. She also felt they had a better chance of thwarting King Andron's army, should the army decide to search for them, if they split up. She asked the women who planned to fight on with her in the near future, to stay fit and practice their skills until they reunited.

And so, they parted, agreeing, for those who were interested, to meet in the same location on the eve of the third full moon. One group continued north, one west, and Cass and her people, southwest toward Mercia. Cass's immediate goal was to lead her family to safety, deliver Princess Julianta to her mother and father, and return as many others to their families along the way as were possible, all without running into King Andron's men.

The days were long, and some nights they didn't find food, but they were free. No one complained. During the travel home, Cass allowed her thoughts to wander, and inevitably, they wandered back to Tove.

The more she thought about Tove, the more she stared into the stars. Each night before going to sleep, she searched for the stars of The Eagle in the part of the sky near her own stars of The White Bear. The Eagle, who has the power to bring rain and lightning, was the sign she thought Julia carried when Tove had first told her about the symbol's meaning. But since the day she escaped the castle walls, she believed the symbol belonged to Tove. How she'd not sensed Tove bore the sign of The Eagle, she didn't know. Perhaps because her mind was focused on those she needed to save. She wished she could tell Tove she'd been wrong, and she no longer thought Julia was star born or carried the sign of The Eagle. No, in her heart she recognized Tove as star born and Tove as the person who saved her in the castle. Each day, that knowledge fueled the desire within her to touch Tove and to feel her body next to hers. With the knowledge she'd acquired of the many aspects of her own body and the pleasures she could bring someone else, the desire to physically share this knowledge with Tove only intensified. Most nights now, her dreams were of Tove.

Chapter Twenty-Eight

Jess walked into the house before Rayne. She scanned the living room and kitchen for George before ambling toward the sliding glass door. She spotted George on his favorite raised spot in the middle of the yard.

When Jess opened the slider, he lifted his head and ran to her.

"Hey, buddy. Are you hungry?" Jess petted George on the head and ruffled his ears. "I missed you at the site. Actually, I missed your momma, too. Baron brought us lunch today. You'd have had a good time with us. It was busy. Lots of people came out. They must have taken a long weekend. You would've gotten lots of attention." Jess grabbed George's food bowl and walked to the cabinet.

"Missed me, huh?" Rayne said. She stood at the kitchen entrance, a confident smugness etched on her face.

"Sneak up on people much, do you?"

"Hello to you, too." Rayne crouched and petted George, her eyes seeming to study Jess with interested intensity. When she stood up, she placed an Eagles Landing bag on the counter. "I brought dinner."

"Great. I'm pretty beat tonight. We had a busy day."

"So I've heard."

"The food smells wonderful. Is there something in the bag I can add to George's dish? I don't think he's going to eat the dry food if he knows we're eating one of Chef Phillip's wonderful creations," Jess said.

Rayne opened the bag, reached inside, and placed the contents on the counter. "Actually, I made the meal for us today. For the main dish, we have a creamy, roasted artichoke and red pepper tagliatelle with baby spinach, asparagus, and cherry tomatoes, all sprinkled with chili flakes and parmesan. I also cooked and prepared a shredded duck salad with pickled ginger, bean shoots, cucumber, and watermelon, with a blended lime and hoisin sauce. And, yes, I brought a small container of shredded duck for George."

"You're very thoughtful. After such a tantalizing introduction, I can't wait to try your creation," Jess said, her cheeks warming.

While Jess fed George, Rayne opened a bottle of white wine. "I'm not a big white wine drinker, but this will pair better with our dinner."

"Agreed. How was business today?" Jess took a seat on the sofa next to Rayne. The few times they managed to eat dinner together, they preferred eating in the living room.

"It's been great. We've had so many more customers than normally. Tiring though, too," Rayne said, as she spun the tagliatelle around her fork.

Jess took her first bite of dinner. "Oh, God, Rayne. This dish is fantastic. You're a great cook."

"I'm gratified you like it."

"Like it? I can't describe to you in words right now how much I'm enjoying this."

"Then my plan is working," Rayne said in a mischievous tone. "How's the dig coming along? Any breakthroughs on the Cassethea front?"

"Sadly, no, but I experienced another vision last night."

"Will you share what you saw with me? To get an almost first-hand glimpse into that life and time is beyond fascinating."

Jess found Rayne's excitement endearing. She told Rayne what happened after Cass's capture and the harsh aftermath of Cass being beaten and tied to the stake in the courtyard. When she was about to explain how Cass freed herself and rescued Julia and her family, her cell phone rang.

"Hello. Yes, this is Jessica Madison. Oh, hello, PC Strongwell..." Jess glanced over at Rayne and raised an eyebrow. "Yes, I see...that is good news. Thank you for calling. Yes, I'll tell her. Have a good evening." Jess ended the call.

"PC Strongwell says hello?" Rayne said.

Jess's expression was one of happiness, but she also appeared conflicted. "Yes, they found the person who stole the jewels from the trailer."

"Was it Joel Fisher's boss, Morey?"

"No, but you're close. Morey's daughter apparently. PC Strongwell reached out to all the pawnshops and jewelry stores in the area. He asked the owners to call if they received an inquiry to buy the cross or ring from a customer. He provided the store owners with photos—the photos he'd taken from the picture in the book I showed him. Anyway, he said sooner or later, whoever stole the pieces would try to sell them, and they did, today."

"How did Morey's daughter find out about them?"

"Apparently she's the woman Marco, my graduate student, has been dating."

"I'll be damned. She took the keys from her father, strolled in and nicked the jewels, and in hindsight, decided to make it look like a break-in by shattering the window pane on the trailer door," Rayne concluded.

"Yes, you're exactly right. It shouldn't matter who the thief was, but I'm relieved in a way it was a woman and not a man."

"I understand. I'm sure I'd feel the same way. The break-in is still a violation of your sense of security, but the implications of what could have happened feel somehow less threatening."

"Either way, I suppose this means I should move back into the trailer..." Jess's voice trailed off at the end.

Rayne scanned Jess's face. "You don't have to go, and I think you know I'd rather you didn't. Do you want to leave?"

"No, I don't. I've enjoyed my time here with you and George. But you have a life, too, and it would be wrong for me to ask you to keep me on longer than necessary."

"Seriously? Keep you on? Asking you to stay with me is the best thing I've ever done. You must realize that by now." Rayne grabbed Jess's hand and rubbed her thumb across the back.

Jess couldn't think straight at that moment. Her body heated instantly at Rayne's touch. Living together, knowing she'd have to leave sooner or later, would make leaving that much more difficult. The smart answer would be to leave now, but Jess's resolve had long ago melted and she couldn't blame the wine. She reached for Rayne's other hand and held it tight. "I do realize." Her eyes lowered, and she considered Rayne's lips.

Rayne didn't hesitate. She leaned forward, barely brushed her lips against Jess's, then backed off and appeared to wait for Jess's response.

Jess inched closer to Rayne until their thighs touched. Her heart beat quickly, in rhythm with faster and shallower breaths. She leaned forward and placed her lips on Rayne's. She luxuriated in their softness. The jolt that coursed through her was so immediate and intense, she backed away to catch her breath. "Holy, good God. What is it about you, Kvale? Are you trying to kill me?"

Rayne's devilish lips grinned at Jess. "I believe you're the one who just kissed me."

"I did, but only after your lips taunted me. What did you expect?" Jess let go of Rayne's hands, and put more distance between her and Rayne on the sofa. "We can't go there. I want to go there, but we can't. I'm leaving in three weeks. Three weeks! As it is, I can't see how I'm going to walk away from you. Please. Don't you understand? If we do this, it will only hurt us both. Maybe I should move back into the trailer."

Rayne studied Jess. "I don't want you to move back, and if in your heart you don't want to either, then you shouldn't First and foremost, we're friends. Whatever happens, we'll deal with it, but I don't want more distance between us. If we only have three weeks, let's make the most of them. Come here."

Jess eyed Rayne skeptically until she took in her warm, reassuring smile. Rayne was right. Trying to ignore her or avoid her altogether was foolish. Jess moved closer. She allowed Rayne to encircle her in her arms. She rested her head on Rayne's chest and listened to her breathing. Heat coursed through Jess's body. What was she doing? Certainly staying with Rayne, considering their feelings for one another, was a bad idea, and acting on the thoughts running through her brain, even worse. Yet, she couldn't resist the pull. Her hand slid to Rayne's thigh. "I think I'm in trouble here," Jess said, her heart racing.

"I think I am, too," Rayne said.

****

Jess awoke as bands of sunshine streamed through the window and warmed her face. She savored the softness of Rayne's breasts pressed against her back and the warmth and security of Rayne's strong arm wrapped snug around her waist. She smiled when she recalled the intensity and insatiability of their lovemaking the night before. The responsiveness of Rayne's nipples as they hardened with only a light blow, and the moan she elicited from Rayne when she sucked her nipple and breast into her mouth while Rayne's fingers teased her to the brink of ecstasy and finally to ultimate release, was a memory she was sure she'd recall over and over and never tire of. And the discovery of Rayne's ancient, flattened-silver, sideways-triangular pendant that held the rune symbols for 'one,' seemingly the missing opposite match to her own pendant, surprised her. Rayne had spoken the truth all those weeks ago when she mentioned she had a similar necklace, and Jess had dismissed her comment. The discovery of the similar necklaces was so unusual that, for a second, she wondered about its significance. Yet more prominent in her mind at that moment were the salacious thoughts of her and Rayne making love together, causing her heart to pump faster once again.

For the first time in her life, she found herself with someone she couldn't get enough of. Jess gingerly rolled from Rayne's grasp and turned on her side. Her water-filled eyes of joy took in Rayne's handsome, angular face, smooth skin, and oh-so-soft and full lips.

Rayne shifted, as if sensing she were being watched. She stretched and grinned as she opened her eyes then brought her hand to the side of Jess's face. "Hey, you. You are the brightest light in my day."

Jessica ran her fingers along Rayne's cheek and inched closer to her in bed. "Now that's impressive, Kvale. With not a cup of coffee yet in you, and eyes barely open, you continue to flatter me. I return the compliment. You are the brightest light in my day as well."

"I'm honored." Rayne opened her eyes wider and then

scrunched her eyebrows together. "Hold on. What's the matter? Are you getting on okay? Have you been crying? Did I do something wrong last night? Are you having regrets?"

"No. You did everything right. I have no regrets. Those were happy tears. I was thinking about how we met, and the days that followed, and last night, and I can't believe I'm here with you, and that any of this is real."

Rayne's expression lightened, and a devilish appearance took over. "Oh, I can assure you this is real, but if you'd like me to refresh your memory, I'd be more than happy to do so. Resistance to my charm is futile. I think I've proven that over these past months."

"Hmph. You're pretty sure of yourself, aren't you? If anyone was resisting our getting together at first, it was you, Ms. I-don't-do-university-professors."

Rayne propped her head up on her elbow. "I object. I'm quite certain I never spoke those words."

"Maybe not exactly that way, but the gist was the same."

"I don't think—"

"You can't deny you were slow to warm."

"As were you, if I recall, Ms. Work-work-work-and-little-time-for-play. Not to mention your comment about us getting too close not being a good idea." Rayne raised her eyebrows. "And that's nothing compared to your erroneous impressions of me early on."

"You do know who you're talking to, right? You know your payback will be fierce, don't you?"

"It's possible that I do."

✳✳✳✳

After a memorable round of payback successfully distributed, Jess rolled to her side away from Rayne only to stare directly into George's deep, globe-like, chocolate-colored eyes.

With his head resting on the bed near Jess, he whined.

"Why is it you decided to come to me first instead of your mamma, hmm?" she whispered. Jess scratched the top of George's head as he remained transfixed where he was. "Okay, back up a little, buddy." Jess reached around George for the T-shirt she'd strewn over the nightstand the night before. She sat up, slid the soft, cotton shirt over her head, and stepped out of bed, careful not to disturb Rayne. She stretched as she ran her fingers through her shoulder-length, curly, brown hair, then searched for the remainder of her clothing. "Don't look at me like that. I'm moving as fast as I can. I'm hungry, too."

After George finished his business and she fed him breakfast, Jess let the heat of the water in the shower penetrate her muscles to relax the tension that crept into her mind. As wonderful as last night was, she knew she'd eventually pay a price. One more week, and they'd be wrapping up the dig, her last chance to find Cassethea. Then they'd summarize their notes, tie up loose ends, and prepare for their presentation at UK Berkeley. She shrugged off the worry. Rayne was right. They should enjoy what little time they had left together to the fullest extent.

Having convinced herself, at least for the day, Jess set the bar of soap on the shower caddy and finished rinsing off. She tousled dry her hair and dried off her slender, fit body before wiping down the mirror. She had to refocus on the dig and the day ahead and push other stray thoughts from her mind. As she rubbed in a vanilla-almond-scented body lotion, applied deodorant, and wrapped the bath towel around her, she did just that. Then she ran her fingers through her damp hair, the curls springing back to life. As she exited the bathroom, she nearly bumped into Rayne.

Rayne pulled Jess close and breathed her in, then lowered her head slightly and kissed Jess tenderly on the lips, allowing a moan to escape. When they parted, Rayne said, "You...in that towel...is so unfair right now."

Jess winked, her body coming to life once more and wanting Rayne with every fiber, but her stomach protested stronger for not yet having been fed, and it won out. "Ten minutes sooner, Kvale, and we wouldn't be having this conversation. If you hurry though, I might leave you some breakfast."

****

After a long day at the dig site, one of a remaining few, Jess was ready for a shower. As she neared Rayne's house on foot, she saw a narrow column of smoke rise above the one-story structure and headed straight for the backyard, the smell of charred steak becoming more intense with each step. As soon as she saw Rayne standing on the patio next to the grill, George jumped up and ran toward her. After petting George, she smiled at Rayne and kissed her on the cheek. "You're home early."

"On the contrary, you're home late," Rayne said. "You're lucky the salad took me awhile to make and that I decided we'd have baked potatoes with our steak, or you may have been eating a cold dinner."

"Do I still have a little time? I'd like to clean up before we eat."

"You do, but very little, unless you want your steak to turn into leather."

"Then I'm off." Jess winked and threw Rayne a kiss. Rayne never stopped amazing her and surprising her. Even though Jess knew Rayne had spent a long day on her feet at the pub, she still prepared dinner for Jess when she could just as easily have had her chef, Phillip, whip up something. "Don't miss me too much while I'm gone."

"Not possible."

Jess turned to see Rayne's stunning blue eyes linger on her long enough to send a jolt through her core. "You do not play fair."

"Fair wasn't my intention." Rayne broke eye contact and turned the meat over. A smoky sizzle erupted on the grill.

****

Halfway through dinner, Rayne placed her knife and fork on her plate, having eaten most of her steak and three quarters of her baked potato. She sipped the wine and leaned against the kitchen chair. "You've been quiet since your shower. How'd it go today? Do you think you'll be all wrapped up at the site this week like you planned and be ready to give your presentation in Waterbury on Friday?"

Jess had been quiet, but she hoped Rayne wouldn't

notice; however, she was troubled on a few ends. First, she was nervous about her upcoming presentation at the UK Berkeley University of History and Archaeology. Although a huge honor, she didn't enjoy speaking in front of so many peers. Also, the presentation signaled a definite end to the excavation, which in her mind was only half a success. She'd not found Cassethea of Mercia's body. Worse, Cass hadn't come to her in her dreams for several nights now, making Jess wonder why not. What if she'd lost the connection? And what about her job in Connecticut when she returned home? Would it still be there for her? Would she even want it if it were? Returning home once the fall semester was underway wouldn't bode well for finding a new job.

Jess finished chewing her last piece of steak and took a deep breath. "Excavation wrap-up went well today. I'm sorry I've been quiet. I've had a lot on my mind. And yes, the presentation is worrying me to a degree. I mean we're prepared and all. To a great extent, it'll follow the layout of the archeological report, giving the background on how we selected the site, what we hoped to find, and the history of the area. Then we'll expand into a more detailed description of the site. There'll be visual maps and pictures of the site at various stages, and I'll explain the obstacles we overcame, findings of the data we uncovered, and our ultimate interpretation of the results. We'll end with the computer layout of the final site reconstruction and the burial ground. It's somewhat concerning that we still have no explanation regarding the unusual preserved condition of the bishop's remains from the head taphonomist at the Oxford University Museum of Natural History, so I'm not sure how to address that in our presentation."

"I think if you lay out the facts as you know them to be, you'll be fine. Sometimes nature acts in a way that has no logical explanation. It simply is. Your findings are incredible. You'll be fine. I have faith in you."

"I appreciate the vote of confidence. I'm also worried that Cassethea won't return to my dreams. It's been a few days, which is unusual. And I'm not entirely sure where you and I go from here."

Rayne grabbed Jess's hand and stroked the top with her

thumb. "Maybe your mind hasn't been open to Cassethea. Could it be that you're overstressed, and maybe disappointed as well, with the excavation coming to a close? As for us, we can do whatever we want to do. My first suggestion to you would be for the time you have left, move your things from the spare bedroom into the master bedroom. I'm not planning on spending a minute without you, and I hope you feel the same."

Jess relaxed into Rayne's soothing, raspy voice, the corners of her mouth turning upward. She slid her hand from under Rayne's, pushed out her chair, and stood, causing George to lift his head as she walked toward Rayne. She clasped her hands on the sides of Rayne's cheeks, dropped her line of sight to Rayne's lips, and kissed her softly and with the deepest passion. When they finally parted, she said, "I feel exactly the same."

"I so want to whisk you into bed right now, but first I've got something I want to ask you." Rayne stood and pulled Jess with her. "Come with me. Let's sit in the living room for a bit."

Jess chuckled. "And what makes you so certain I'll go with you?"

"Your eyes tell me so."

"Do they? Then they should also be telling you that if you're not quick enough with your question, we may not make it off the sofa."

"As much as I like the sound of that, holding off on that action a few minutes might be worth your while."

"Then do your best, Kvale."

Rayne held Jess's hand as they walked toward the sofa and settled close together. Then she took Jess's other hand in hers as well and held it tight. "I know our lives have changed significantly over a very short period of time, and I know the way we feel about each other is real. I feel it every time you look at me and each time you touch me, but I also know it's fairly sudden and we've not had much time to absorb it all with work and everything."

"True. Go on."

"Now that the excavation is coming to a close, I thought the two of us might sneak away on a mini vacation. It would be a good distraction for you and my present to us. What do you say?"

Jess stroked the soft skin above Rayne's chest. "A distraction that involves a few days alone with you? How can I resist?"

"I was hoping you'd say that."

"Where would we go?"

"At Eagles Landing the other day, I heard one of our female customers, who isn't a local, talking to her friend about this great place she and her partner stayed at in Tamsfordshire. It sounded right up our alley. It's a remodeled castle that overlooks a vineyard. It's gay friendly and has a restaurant on the premises. The castle is called The Stanton House. And with a restaurant to boot if we don't feel like going out—"

"I can pretty much assure you we won't be going out often," Jess said in a sultry voice that appeared to have unraveled Rayne. "Wait, don't move." Jess stood and added two logs to the fire. When she returned to the sofa, she straddled Rayne, the heat between her legs unyielding. She kissed Rayne hard and lifted Rayne's cotton Henley over her head, feasting her eyes on the rapid rise and fall of Rayne's firm, plump breasts. The back of her fingers traveled along the side of Rayne's neck, down the center of her chest, and around hardened nipples. She pulled Rayne's sports bra off and, after doing so, was quickly relieved of her own blouse and lace bra.

She gently pushed Rayne flat onto the sofa as Rayne tried to take Jess's erect nipple into her mouth. "Oh, no you don't, Kvale. I'm taking control this time," she said before running her tongue around Rayne's areola and sucking in her nipple. Simultaneously she placed pressure on Rayne's core with her thigh. As Jess savored Rayne's body with her mouth and hands, her own wetness intensified. When Jess unbuttoned Rayne's jeans, Rayne bucked beneath her.

"Sweet Jesus, you are killing me," Rayne said as Jess's fingers undid Rayne's zipper and slid beneath Rayne's panty line. "I'm not going to make it much longer."

As Rayne's hands kneaded her backside, Jess stroked up and down Rayne's wetness, until she felt Rayne hold in her breath. She then moved rhythmically inside Rayne, taking her higher and higher until she shook beneath her with ultimate release. Jess slowly withdrew her fingers. She rested her head on Rayne's chest for only a few minutes before she slid her heated center on Rayne's leg, rousing Rayne once more.

Rayne's dark eyes engulfed Jess as Rayne turned and positioned Jess under her. She slid off Jess's pants completely, not taking her gaze from Jess's eyes. She gently, yet firmly, massaged Jess's breasts and strummed her nipple as she moved her leg against Jess's heat. "Oh, my God, you are so wet," Rayne said.

"You shouldn't be surprised. It's your body that got me this way." Jess ran her finger along the side of Rayne's chest. She lifted up under Rayne, wanting more. "Please, Rayne. Don't make me beg. I need your touch. I need you now."

As Jess's body welcomed Rayne's skilled hands, her mind separated from reality. Mere seconds passed before she cried out in sheer ecstasy.

Chapter Twenty-Nine

Jess marveled at the expanse of land the hotel sat on. As they motored up the long, cobblestone drive, she took in the neatly clipped, maze-like shrubbery, immaculately trimmed lawn, and tall, narrow trees lining their path, along with the centerpiece water feature. The castle itself stood at the top of a hill. Two stories tall with round towers at the corners, the stone walls were covered over half their surface in vines. The stonework was a lightly colored tan, like many of the houses in the Cotswolds, but made of larger pieces of stone.

Once Rayne parked, Jess said, "This place is fantastic. I can't wait to see what the inside looks like and the kind of view they must have from the second floor." She exited Rayne's car and gathered her luggage. The lavender scent from the flowers growing off the vines clinging to the castle walls filled Jess's lungs.

Rayne walked next to her. "I can't wait to see the inside either. I saw some pictures, which were stunning, but I'm sure in person the effect of seeing this historic place will be even greater. I'm glad we decided to come and that Baron was sweet enough to watch George. I kind of feel bad leaving him to take care of Eagles Landing without me, but I think with my cousin stepping in to help, he'll be fine."

"Your brother will be fine. I'm surprised you're worried. Between the two of us, I'm the worrier. Besides, I thought this trip was supposed to be a distraction."

"It is, and it will be. I promise to keep my focus on you, since you're my biggest distraction."

"Sweet talking will get you everywhere with me, Kvale," Jess said as Rayne held the oversized door to the hotel open and followed Jess inside.

"I like the sound of that."

"I thought you might." Jess immediately spotted the

check-in counter on the left and saw a small line. "Do you mind if I look around while you check us in?"

"Have at it. I thought you might not be able to wait to explore."

Jess's vision traveled around the wide open central entranceway. Massive chandeliers hung off long chains secured into the stone ceiling. Two wide stairways bowed out and met at a top balcony, underneath which modern elevators offered an alternative path to the upper floor. Beyond the check-in counter on the left appeared to be a dining area, with a larger similar room on the opposite side. In the central meeting area sat two sofas opposite one another and comfortable-looking chairs surrounded a fireplace. On one of the two, square, stone-covered columns in front of the central lounge area, Jess spotted a plaque and went over to read what it said.

The plaque gave the history of The Stanton House Hotel. The castle, built in the 10th century for King Herrwald of Mercia, remained with the king's ancestors until the mid 1800s, when it was purchased by a rich businessman who fortified the castle and rebuilt it as a residence. Jess's heart thumped wildly in her chest. She was standing in King Herrwald's castle, the home of Cass's best friend Julianta. Could this be for real? Goose bumps rose along her arms as she stood dumbfounded in front of the plaque.

She continued to read. The businessman planted a vineyard and established a well-known winery. It stayed in his family for several generations but then was sold, along with much of the vineyard. The winery, under new ownership, still exists, as does the other part of the vineyard. The residence was remodeled into the hotel. Hearing footsteps from behind, Jess turned to see Rayne brandishing a huge grin. "Did you know this used to be King Herrwald's castle?"

Rayne chuckled. "The look on your face is priceless right about now. I didn't know at first, but when I got online to research the place, I read about it. I couldn't believe it, although I don't know why I couldn't. England and much of Europe has so many castles refurbished into hotels, almost no one who lives here pays them much attention. Although I believe this 10th century castle might be the oldest. There are plenty from the 11th through 19th centuries though."

Jess reached for Rayne's hand. "You couldn't have found a better place. Thank you."

"You're welcome."

"I think I'd like to see our room now. What kind did you get us?"

"I booked our room, sight unseen, over the phone after talking to the owner. Although, according to her, this isn't the nicest or biggest room the castle has to offer, it is one that has more of the original structure intact to provide a greater historical feel of the castle than the other rooms have. I hope that's okay."

"Perfect. And the place is owned by a woman. Nice." Jess stepped closer to Rayne and kissed her tenderly on the lips. "Let's go find that room so I can spend the afternoon thanking you properly."

****

Jess stared at Rayne over candlelight that danced in Rayne's eyes as they held hands over the white tablecloth. They sat at the far end of one of several long, dining tables at the restaurant. The dark, wooden chairs were padded and intricately carved, with high seat backs. Patrons were seated in a family style setting, though one empty chair was left between each family or couple to provide some privacy.

The ambiance in the restaurant was so amazing, Jess almost didn't care how the dinner would taste. Numerous wall sconces lit the rustic room. Two huge fireplaces warmed the space both in heat and light. The sound of the logs as they popped, and the smell of wood burning, mixed with the scent of meat and fish searing in the kitchen, and caused Jess's stomach to grumble. Strings of tiny white lights around each stone archway and along the thick, central wooden beams that crossed overhead brought the room to life. Wine racks covered parts of one wall, and wine barrels standing near the walls served as resting places for green plants and various replicas of ancient artifacts. Among swords and face shields hung on walls were also pitchforks and thick, heavy oxen yokes.

The waiter took their wine and meal order shortly after they were seated. He returned with Jess's glass filled with a New Zealand Sauvignon Blanc and Rayne's an Argentinean Malbec.

Rayne lifted her glass. "Cheers to having found one another and this special place."

Jess gently touched the side of her glass to Rayne's. "Cheers. This is so romantic. Thank you again for suggesting this getaway."

"I think I was meant to overhear that customer talking about it. Seems like everything connected with you is somehow driven by fate," Rayne said before she sipped the wine.

"You could be right. How's the wine?"

"It's delicious. Fruity, but it also has a hint of cinnamon and pepper, and something else I can't quite place."

"Mine's very good also. I'm not a white wine drinker, but I thought it would pair better with the salmon." Jess paused for a moment, lost in Rayne's gaze. "I still can't believe we're sitting here right now, in what was once King Herrwald's castle. Can we take a walk on the grounds after dinner? I bet the outside looks incredible, lit up at night."

"I had the exact same idea. Of course we can."

"There's something I haven't told you," Jess said. "Not that I've been keeping it a secret for long, since it only happened last night, but I wanted to find the right time to tell you."

"Go on."

Jess sensed a look of concern on Rayne's face. "No, don't worry. It's nothing bad. In fact, it's good news, I think. I had a split-second vision of Cassethea last night."

"Jess, that's wonderful news."

"It is, except she appeared to be in distress. I sensed she wanted to reach me, but she was afraid at the same time."

"From what we know of her so far, an easy life doesn't seem to be in her cards, so I'm not surprised," Rayne said.

"No, it doesn't."

The waiter returned and placed their meals in front of them.

"Thank you," Rayne said. Then she directed her attention to Jess. "That looks great. Think I might have a taste?"

Jess eyed the colorful plate in front of her with pleased anticipation. Like artwork, the center held the grilled salmon covered in a citrus and beetroot puree, set on top of a parmesan spinach spaghetti squash with garlic. To the side rested a pile of parmesan mashed potatoes. Jess lowered her head and took in the scents. "You'll be hard-pressed to get me to share this meal."

"Is that right? Not a problem. That means I don't need to share mine."

"Does it now? Shows you still have a lot to learn about me, Kvale."

****

Jess said, "The after-dinner walk was both wonderful and much needed. I definitely ate too much and probably should've stayed away from that fresh, rosemary-infused bread they set on the table before the meal." She entered their room for the second time that day.

Earlier, after Rayne had checked them in, they'd taken the elevator to the second floor and found their room at the end of a long hallway. The hotel in some ways looked very much like any other, with carpeted floors, various colors on the walls, and modern lighting, but what differed between this hotel and others she'd been in were the high ceilings, arched doorways, and original castle stonework visible around each doorway and window. The windows in their room were set a couple of feet deep as well, all in stone, also arched, with wrought iron protecting the glass. The ambiance was a strange fusion of modern and ancient, but somehow it worked. The bathroom had modern fixtures with mirrors above the sinks and all the conveniences experienced in any hotel, yet the wall-sconce lighting, choice of color palette, and the exposed sections of wall with stone gave an undeniable historical feel. The bathroom off their bedroom even had a super-narrow, circular stairway down into the room, making Jess feel as though she were thrown back in time, if even for just a moment.

Rayne said, "I'll second your thought. I should've stayed away from the bread as well, although our walk helped. I love the way they lit the walkways and how the light cascaded onto the castle walls. It felt magical, even to me."

"It did."

Rayne glanced from Jess to the balcony and back again. She stepped toward the gas fireplace and flicked on the switch. Then she pulled out her phone, held it up, and moved around the room, as if searching for a signal.

"What are you doing? I thought we were disconnecting from the world for a few days?"

"We are. I just have to give someone a quick ring. Why don't you get ready for bed? I'll just be a minute. I'm going to ring them from out on the balcony. Maybe I'll get reception there."

Puzzled, Jess shrugged and did as Rayne suggested, not certain what could be so important that Rayne felt she needed to make that call. She also got the strange impression from Rayne that she wanted privacy. Then she shrugged the feeling off, thought she was acting paranoid, and proceeded to the bathroom.

Moments later, Jess felt cold air hit her body as Rayne stepped into the shower behind her. "That was a quick call." Jess ran her hands over her hair and face and half-turned to glance at Rayne's naked and muscular body. "I wasn't expecting you to join me so fast."

"Disappointed?"

"Hardly."

Rayne pressed her body against Jess's heated back. She reached forward and grabbed the soap from Jess's hands. She rolled it between her own hands, returned it to Jess, and whispered in her ear, "It's not like I have a girlfriend I was on the phone flirting with. It was all I could do to stay focused out there when all I could think about was the water dripping off your wet body in here."

"Is that so? That, Kvale, is exactly what I wanted to hear and what will get you in very, very big trouble." Jess started to turn around.

"Not so fast." Rayne held Jess in place as her soapy hands cascaded gently over Jess's chest, down her stomach, between her thighs, and over her buttocks.

Jess's breathing quickened, and her center pulsed with need as Rayne continued massaging her body. When she placed the bar of soap haphazardly in its resting place, Rayne's fingers stroked her center from behind. "Oh, dear God." Jess's left hand held her steady against the side wall. As the hot water continued to caress her nipples, she moved her pelvis against Rayne's fingers and spread her legs farther apart, begging Rayne to enter her. "Oh, my God, yes. Sweet heaven, don't stop," Jess cried out as her body moved against Rayne until she burst to release. Her legs nearly buckled beneath her, but Rayne held her up. Jess managed to slowly turn and face Rayne. She maneuvered Rayne into the direct line of the water spray and kissed her tenderly. When their lips finally parted, Jess said, "You cheated. Not that I'm complaining. But since I can barely stand right now, I'll get out of here and leave the shower to you. I need to lie down. But know that when you get to bed, you're not getting much rest tonight."

"In that case, you better hurry, because this will be one fast shower."

Jess was surprised how fast Rayne's shower truly was. Jess had dried off, tussle-dried her hair, and climbed into bed barely long enough to have warmed the sheets when Rayne's glistening body passed between the bed and the fireplace. Rayne climbed into the other side of the bed, and her presence heated Jess all over again. Although their afternoon lovemaking had been rushed and fierce and needy, Jess would make sure this night would be slow, gentle, and deliberate. Jess wanted to learn all the triggers that moved Rayne, and she had all night to do so.

When exhaustion overtook them in the wee hours of the morning, they snuggled, satiated, next to one other and soon fell asleep. Jess recalled the special moments of the day: gazing into the bright lit skies while holding Rayne's hand and kissing her under the stars. The same stars that shone over Cassethea and Tove over a thousand years ago. She felt more blessed than she thought she deserved to be. Moments before Jess drifted off, her visions blurred and flowed as if through a hazy funnel backward in time. There she saw Cass on horseback, strong and confident, leading Julia, Arielwund, and Emma home, while a band of soldiers rode swiftly toward them, swords drawn.

Chapter Thirty

"Halt!" the soldier in the lead yelled. "You trespass on the grounds of King Herrwald's kingdom. State your names and purpose! You are not expected by the king."

Cass stopped her horse, and the others followed. She recognized the soldiers' uniforms from when she'd watched King Herrwald's soldiers spar from far away on the hill, through eagle's eyes, secretly wishing she could be a soldier, too, and studying their movements in hopes of doing just that. The thought of the eagle brought Tove to the forefront of Cass's mind, and for a moment, her heart ached. She glanced at Emma, who sat in front of Arielwund on her horse, fear etched on her sister's face. Emma had already been through more than an average child of seven winters should have gone through. Cass needed to convey confidence for her at this time.

Cass straightened her back and shoulders. "My name is Cassethea. I live in Mercia, or shall I say lived there before our homes were destroyed by King Andron's soldiers dressed as Vikings, near a dozen moons ago. With me are my mother, Arielwund; my sister, Emma; and your Princess Julianta, who were all taken by King Andron. King Herrwald will want to see his daughter, I'm certain. We are tired and hungry and carry only kind thoughts of our king."

The lead soldier swung his horse around and conferred with two of the soldiers next to him, as he kept one eye focused on Cassethea.

Cass watched his facial expressions, understanding his doubt, as Julia wasn't dressed as a princess, but rather a servant, as were her mother and Emma. Moreover, they were dirty and unkempt from their long journey, having pressed forward relentlessly, afraid of being hunted and recaptured by King Andron's men before they could get everyone safely home. If she were the soldier who'd encountered them on the road and didn't know Julia, she'd have exhibited the same skepticism as he.

As the soldier's horse pranced backward a few steps and then forward, facing Cass, the soldier said, "We will escort you to the castle. If what you say is true, the king will surely recognize his daughter."

Cass nodded in agreement, and even though she knew they were in their own home territory and King Herrwald was a just king, she couldn't help but allow the feeling of powerlessness to sweep over her when the soldiers flanked them on all sides. Even the castle's stone walls, when they came into sight, sent a shiver down her spine. She had to remind herself the castle was merely a structure meant to protect the king and queen and Julia. The castle was not a prison. But no matter how hard she tried, her chest constricted tighter and tighter the closer they came, and her breathing became shallow. As if Julia sensed Cass's tension, Cass felt Julia's hand rest on her thigh.

"Don't worry. My father is a good man and will be thrilled to see me again. You saved my life, Cass. We all owe you a debt that can never be repaid."

Cass said nothing, but the warmth of Julia's touch and her gentle words helped relax her and reinstall her inner strength. Julia was right. She did rescue them. She had no reason to worry. She did the king a favor by returning his daughter to him.

****

With reluctance, Cass gave up her sword and dagger before meeting the king. Although she argued at first, reassurance from Julia and her mother caused her to acquiesce, even though she wasn't happy about it. Two soldiers held open large, heavy, wooden doors as they entered the castle and walked into a wide-open foyer. Guards stood on the opposite side of the doors and also at the base of the bowed-out, wide stairways that met at a top balcony, in the center of which hung Julia's family crescent. To the left appeared to be a dining area and to the right a large ballroom of sorts, and beyond that, another room into which they were ushered.

"Be seated. King Herrwald will be along soon," the soldier said.

Arielwund, Emma, and Julia sat on a sofa on one side of the room, and Cass sat in a soft, padded chair not far from them. In the center was a circular wooden table with ten chairs. Julia scooped Emma onto her lap, as if sensing Emma's uncertainty regarding their situation.

"This is my father's library," Julia said as she held onto Emma. "He has most of his important meetings in here. Sometimes I'd sneak to the door to see who was there and listen to them talk, even though they didn't know I was there and I wasn't supposed to be." Julia spoke in a mischievous sounding whisper and crinkled her face, which caused Emma to laugh. "Then, when they'd see me, I'd run from the guards, back up to my room. Even when I was bad, my father never scolded me for it. He's a kind man."

Just as Julia finished speaking, the doors opened. There stood King Herrwald and the queen, eyes wide open, as if in shock. "Julianta, by God it is you!" her father yelled.

Julia placed Emma on Arielwund's lap, sprang up, and ran to her parents. "Father! Mother! It's so good to be home. I missed you both so much." Julia spread her arms open wide and embraced the couple.

Tears ran down the queen's face as she hugged her daughter. "Thank you, God, thank you. Are you all right? Are you hurt? How did you get home?"

"She's fine, she's fine," the king said, taking a step back to study his daughter more closely. "I thought someone was playing a cruel trick on us when they told me you were here."

Julia loosened her grip from her mother. "Yes, well, I have so much to tell you both. If it weren't for Cassethea, I wouldn't be here right now, nor would her family." Julia glanced caringly at her friend. "Unfortunately, their home was destroyed with so many others during the raid, and for now, they have nowhere to go. I'd like them to stay with us for a while, if that's all right."

The king took several steps into the room. "Of course, of course they will stay! I am so sorry. I apologize. We were so happy to see our daughter, that we hadn't introduced ourselves. I'm King Herrwald," he said before turning toward his wife, "and this is my wife, Queen Winnifeld. Welcome."

Cass stood and bowed, as did her mother, who held Emma's hand. "Your Highnesses," Cass said. "It's a pleasure to meet you both. I am Cassethea, and this is my mother, Arielwund, and my sister, Emma."

Rather than shake her hand, Cass was astonished and left speechless when the king grabbed her into his huge arms and hugged her.

"Thank you so much for bringing my daughter back to us. I know I can never properly repay you, but I humbly ask you to let me try."

"I—" Cass began to say.

"Shush, no argument now. We'll talk once you're all settled in." The king faced Arielwund. "You must be so proud of your daughter. Thank you for having raised her as you did."

"Thank you, Your Highness. Yes, I am beyond proud of her, as I am of all my children."

"Father, Cass's brothers Alfred and Sedwick joined your army after the raid by King Andron's men."

"I see. Yes, of course, I remember." The king said to Arielwund, "And what of your husband? Where is he?"

Julia shook her head before Arielwund could answer.

"I'm so sorry. I didn't realize."

"It's fine," Arielwund said. "I believe in my heart that all things happen for a reason. Though circumstances put us in a difficult place, his ending was just."

"Perhaps that is true," the king said. "We can talk more. Tonight, though, we'll put all our difficult times behind us and we shall have a celebratory feast for your family's return and the return of my daughter."

****

Cassethea and Arielwund were each given separate quarters, and all were given clean clothes and hot water with which to bathe. Cass was more tired than hungry and was nervous about meeting other people at the feast, but she also hoped she might see Alfred and Sedwick again. Julia had been right. The king was a kind man. With vast gratitude, he offered for them to stay at the castle for as long as they wanted and gave them complete freedom in it.

After soaping up in the circular, wooden tub in the bathroom and scrubbing herself clean, Cass smiled when she saw the clothes provided for her. The king didn't have a dress brought for her, but instead, grey trousers and a white tunic, along with a colorful blue sash to tie around her waist. She wondered if Julia had spoken to him, or if he'd discerned her likes on his own. She toweled dry, ran her fingers through her short, brown hair to adjust the wisps that had grown longer in the front away from her eyes, and dressed. As she tied the laces of her leather sandal around her calf, she heard a knock on the door.

Cass straightened, then walked up the narrow, circular steps into her room and opened the door. "Alfred!" Cass reached out and pulled her brother into a tight embrace. "My God, it's so great to see you. You look well and so very handsome."

Alfred hugged her in return, holding her extra tight. "Cass, it's so good to see you again, and I could say the same of you. You've grown. Your hair is short, but it looks good on you. And there is substantially more mass to you." Alfred released his hold.

"Both were necessary. The hair served its purpose being short when it needed to be, but I think I'll let it grow out again. I have no further need to hide who I am and can certainly take care of myself now."

"So I can see and I've heard. Stories are buzzing about you, both good and bad, but mostly good. You'll need to tell me all about it. Come on, let's go to eat. Sedwick's getting mother and Emma, and we're to escort you to the dining hall. Thanks to you, I'll be eating well and in style tonight."

As they exited the room, Cass saw her mother and Emma, dressed in pretty dresses like Julia had worn, walking next to Sedwick.

"Cass, is that you?" Sedwick said in a near whisper.

"Of course it's me, brother. Who'd you think it was? Now get over here and give your sister a hug."

Sedwick glanced up at Arielwund, who nodded in reassurance, before he made his way toward Cassethea, Emma on his heels. Then he wrapped his arms around her, not as firmly as Alfred had, and let go, while Emma stood to the side of them both and had her small arms stretched toward each of them. "You appear well."

Cass noticed his hesitation and decided it likely had to do with the way they had parted, the night her father called her a witch. Sedwick should have known better, but he was younger than Alfred and always appeared to believe every word her father ever spoke. She'd been hurt by their silence back then, but she knew she had to forgive them if she wanted them in her life going forward. She bent over, picked up Emma, and kissed her on the cheek. "Yes, I'm well, all things considered. You look nice in your uniform."

"Thank you. I'm not old enough to fight yet, but I'm in training. Alfred keeps an eye on me."

"That's good. You should listen to him always," Cass said.

As if having sensed the awkward exchange between his brother and sister, Alfred broke the tension. "Come on, let us go before we get into trouble for being late to the meal. We'll have a lot of time to catch up during dinner."

"Yes, let us go," Arielwund said. "I'm hungry enough right now to eat the side of an ox."

With those words, Emma burst into laughter, as did everyone else.

Alfred said, "I am hungry as well and will eat the other half."

****

The long, thick, wooden table at the end of the room was laden with trays of pheasant and fish, trenchers with loaves of white bread and different cheeses, various bowls filled with olives and figs, and other assorted foods Cass had never seen before, as well as jugs filled with wine and ale. Eyes turned in their direction when they entered the room and seemed to linger longer on Cass than on anyone else. Their apparent judgmental assessment, likely due to her clothes and short hair, didn't upset her, though she noticed their glances appeared to fill her brothers with unease. When her gaze caught Julia's smiling and approving look, she returned the smile and sat where directed.

At the start of the meal, the king introduced Cass and her family and told some of the story of their capture, as much as Julia had conveyed to him by that point. The previously negatively assessing eyes watching Cass appeared to soften and almost admire her, making her uncomfortable for a different reason. She merely smiled and nodded between bites of food, but once the story was told, she settled in and talked with Alfred. "Did you hear how our father was killed?"

Alfred turned his gaze to the side and downward. "Yes, a fight in the tavern I'm told, over a spilled mug of ale, of all things."

"Why didn't he search for mother and Emma? Why didn't he bury Gollyn?"

"I hadn't heard about Gollyn until many days later," Alfred said. "There were so many of us and so much commotion. Besides the Viking raids, the Arabs invaded as well. And when I went back to where our house stood, I saw the grave for Gollyn."

"They weren't Vikings. They were King Andron's men in disguise."

"Does it really matter? They destroyed our homes and killed many. It could easily have been Vikings."

Cass caught Julia glancing in her direction with a smile of reassurance. "Perhaps, but it wasn't the Vikings. And yes, the truth does matter to me. The morning after the raid, which I had no idea had happened, I smelled smoke. I ran back to our home, or what little remained, devastated with what I found. I buried Gollyn. I don't understand how father could have left him, or mother and Emma. God help me for saying so, but he's lucky he died in the bar. I'm sorry. I know you looked up to him, as did Sedwick."

"Sedwick took father's loss harder than I did, in all honesty. When father was alive, and we were all together, I didn't sleep all nights right away, as I know you didn't, so I remember some of the arguments with mother and how he treated her. Sedwick though, he slept. And I think of Gollyn. Him leaving Gollyn is unforgivable in my mind." Alfred rolled up the sleeve of his tunic to reveal a cross marked on his upper arm near his bicep. "This cross is in memory of Gollyn."

Tears streamed from Cass's eyes. "Gollyn would have liked that. I've never seen markings like that before."

"Several of the soldiers have them. Some have incredible markings all over their arms. They believe it gives them power and makes the enemy fear them more. For me, it gives me peace."

Cass thought of Tove again and the ache she felt daily, missing her. She could use some peace as well. She let the thought simmer then shifted their conversation to brighter topics.

****

Julia hugged Cass one last time while Emma hugged Arielwund's leg as Emma and Arielwund looked on, the first to have said their good-byes.

"Are you sure you want to do this, Cass? You know how dangerous the land is out there, and it's not like you're going to avoid trouble. You'll be out seeking it." Julia let the tight grasp around her friend go.

Cass stood next to Starlight, the horse with the white patch on its forehead, that she'd had since after her capture by King Andron: Starlight, and the two horses Julia and her mother had ridden into the castle almost three months ago. She wore the white tunic, blue sash, and grey trousers the king had gifted her. She carried a leather trenchcoat, a change of clothes, a tent, modest food provisions, and medical supplies on the back of the spare horse closest to her. She also stashed half the money she'd gotten from the men she'd killed after escaping Haddie, into a bag, having given her mother the other half. With her sword slung across her back in its sheath and her dagger strapped in its sheath to her leg under the trousers, yes, she was ready.

"You know I need to do this. Emma and mother's house will be completed soon, and much of Mercia will be rebuilt as it was many moons before, thanks to your father. But there are women and children out there who are being wrongly taken advantage of, even as we stand here now, who can't help themselves. I'm drawn to helping them. Maybe the sword draws me to them. I don't know, but this isn't a choice for me."

"I understand and will pray for your safe return," Julia said.

Cass mounted Starlight and glanced one last time at her family and friends. "Say good-bye to Alfred and Sedwick for me as well. I'll be back, I promise. And best wishes to you, Julia, for your upcoming wedding. If I don't make it back in time, know that you have my warmest and deepest blessings."

Julia nodded, and as Arielwund waved, Cass waved back and kicked Starlight into a trot, then a canter, holding back tears that clouded her vision as she rode away, sitting high in the saddle, shoulders back.

Chapter Thirty-One

Not only was Sedra waiting for Cass on the eve of the third full moon since she and her rescued band of women had parted ways months before, but nearly half the women she'd rescued stood next to her as well, including Keatera. Sedra and Keatera were two of the three group leaders Cass had trained. Sedra had headed west during their departure, and Keatera north. Cass waved as she rode into the camp. After dismounting, she clasped forearms with the two leaders in welcome.

"It's wonderful to see you both," Cass said. Then she raised her voice. "It's wonderful to see you all!"

Cheers of a dozen or so women answered her, smiles upon their faces.

"Your hair grows longer, Cassethea. It looks good on you. No more disguises?" Sedra asked.

"No. I have nothing to hide any longer. I can protect myself well enough now."

"I have no doubt."

Cass glanced around the camp. The smell of cooking meat drew her gaze toward the fire in the center of the camp. Nearly equally spaced, simple V-shaped tents surrounded the fire, and the horses grazed nearby. She took in each woman, noting how fit they were and how eager they appeared. Cass was keen to lead them. "Do you have sentinels on watch?"

"Yes, of course. It's how you instructed us," Sedra said.

"And you've all trained? You appear to have," Cass said.

"Yes," Kaetera said. "And with each stroke of our swords, release of our arrows, or thrust of our daggers, we were fueled by the memory of our imprisonment and the joy of our release. I for one have been counting the days we would all be together again."

"It's like that for the lot of us," Sedra added. "We share

your vison, Cass. We'll talk more about it later. Go ahead and set up your tent and rest your horses before we eat. Let's celebrate tonight, as I'm sure tomorrow we'll start our planning."

"Yes, tomorrow we start planning," Cass said.

****

After breakfast, Cass, Sedra, Keatera, and the rest of the women, sat around the fire and spoke in great detail of their preparations for this day. They shared information they'd gathered in the months away from one another. After much discussion, deliberation, and debate, a decision was reached regarding their plan of attack and roughly how long they thought their upcoming journey would last, given the problems they already knew existed.

What they initially thought would last a year spent righting wrongs, extended into two long and often hard-fought years, traversing the southern edges of Northumbria along the River Trent, much of Mercia, and parts of East Anglia. Some days were long and nights cold, but they stuck together and grew closer as a unit.

In a village north of Gainsborough, near the River Trent, they rescued two children who were "sold" to a blacksmith in exchange for erasing their father's debt. Outside of Horncastle, they rescued a woman sold to her husband's brother, and two towns south of there, they found another woman undernourished and chained in a barn.

Across Mercia, over grassland, around marshes, over mountains, and through forests, the small army of women traveled fearlessly and rescued many. For each sacred soul they lost among their ranks, a woman rescued along the way would take her place and be trained by those who remained. Each battle bonded the women to one another. They were sisters. And because of their tenacity and successes, it wasn't long before Cassethea's name was whispered on many a peasant's lips and mumbled by many an angry slave owner or nobleman.

In what they agreed would be their last battle, unless a need once again arose, the band of women focused their closing effort on freeing dozens of children working on a nobleman's farm outside of Waltham. They set up camp ten kilometers away, in a wooded area adjacent to the outskirts of the farm. Cass surveilled the farm for two days through an eagle's eyes overhead. Her worst fears were realized when she saw children with undernourished bodies, pale faces, sunken in eyes, and filthy, ripped clothing, forced to work from early in the morning until late at night with little food and meager breaks.

She noted the number of guards on horseback, the expanse of fields each guard was responsible for, what times the owner left the farm and returned, and where the children were taken at night. The women sent one of their own into town to see what could be found out about the nobleman, or of other rumblings, but could find nothing. At night, they discussed what they had learned.

Holding a stick with a skewered, roasted pheasant wing at the end, Sedra pointed it toward the fire. "Clearly these children are being abused, but what doesn't make sense to me is where did they all come from? If they belong to the people around here, or to families in town, wouldn't they know they were missing? Wouldn't they have searched the homes and farms in the area looking for them?"

"Maybe they were sold, like so many are," one woman suggested.

"Makes sense," another said.

"Let's think about this for a minute," Cass said. "Sedra is right. Something's wrong with this scenario. Surely two dozen children wouldn't have been sold in the payment of debt, and I doubt at their young ages, any are thieves or worse. So from where did this nobleman acquire them?"

"Not only that," Kaetera said, "but will they even remember where they came from or how to get home? If we free them, will we be able to find their homes, and if not, what then? We'll all be going our separate ways once this is over."

"We can deliver those without homes to the nearest monastery," one of the women suggested.

Cass's eyes widened as their thoughts came together. "Yes, of course. What if the nobleman stole the children from the monastery? They'd be reluctant to let such news escape, considering all their wealth is accumulated from the donations of others, including the rich."

"It's possible I suppose. There is a monastery a day's ride to the east," one of the newest women said.

"I think it would be worth our time if I took a few riders with me and we inquired with the abbot to see if he knows anything, or has heard of anything."

"Your idea is sound, Cass, but what if, as you said, the abbot is fearful of relaying this information?" Sedra said.

"Then we make it clear to him what conditions the children are living under and see if he's willing to take them in when we rescue them, whether they originally came from the monastery or not." When Cass finished, she saw many heads nod in agreement, including Sedra's and Keatera's.

****

Upon Cass's return from the monastery, the women assembled around the fire. Cass recounted her discussion with the abbot and his initial reluctance to speak the truth, but then she spoke of the devastation evident in his eyes when he'd learned what had become of the children. According to the abbot, the children had amassed at the monastery over the years, some left to their care out of poverty and necessity, others gifted to them as their contribution to the church, and others simply showed up on their doorstep. The monastery taught many of these children to write, something most people didn't learn. The children assisted in transcribing old documents and helped with daily chores. Cass thought of Gollyn and his desire to live and learn in a monastery. Goose bumps ran along her arms at the recall. Had Gollyn's life gone differently, he could have been one of those children. The connection focused importance on what needed to be done.

After an awkward pause by Cass, Sedra broke the silence. "We should act tomorrow. One of the boys collapsed and died in the field yesterday. He fell, face down, into the dirt. He lay there for two hours before one of the men dragged him away and buried him. I couldn't stop crying."

Cass felt pain spike in her heart. Perhaps they should have acted sooner. Then again, if they had acted without proper planning, more innocents could have been killed. Cass understood they could still be, but she wanted to lessen the chances of failure.

One of the women spoke up. "The problem is, these guards are always so close to the children. We've talked about this before. How do we make sure they don't hurt them before we can get to them?"

Others nodded in agreement.

"I have a plan. This is what I think we should do," Cass said and then laid out her idea.

****

Cass rode up to the bearded, red-haired man on horseback who was stationed closest to the nobleman's house.

"Don't come any closer. What is it you want?" the man said.

"I'd like to speak to the owner of this farm."

"And who then might you be?"

"My name is Cassethea of Mercia." Cass noticed the recognition in the man's eyes and the shifting of his horse's hooves under him as he attempted to steady his mount. Cass smiled inwardly, knowing she could direct his horse to buck him off its back if she wanted.

"I don't think he'll want to talk to you."

"I'm certain he will. Tell him I have a generous proposition for him in exchange for his young workers."

The man hesitated for a few seconds. "Wait here."

Several minutes later, a man a few inches taller than Cass, with shoulder-length, jet-black hair, walked from the structure, flanked by two other broad-shouldered men. "You wish to speak with me?"

"I do."

"Then dismount your horse, so I can look you in the eyes. I like to be able to assess if I'm being lied to or not."

Cass lifted her right leg over the rear of her horse and jumped from his back. She stepped forward, in front of her horse, while the horse took several steps backward. She placed her left hand on the blue sash around her waist and kept her right hand free, ready to grab the sword from its sheath off her back should she need it. Then she looked him in the eye. "Better?"

The man grinned. "Yes, much better. What is it you offer?"

"I offer you and your men your lives in exchange for the children."

The man burst out in laughter. "Is that right? A woman, dressed as a man, comes to my house, offers me no money for my property, and expects me to comply with such whimsical wishes."

The two men guarding the nobleman stepped closer to Cass. She said, "You understood correctly. The children aren't your property. I spoke with the abbot of the monastery, a day's ride east of here, from which you stole these children. He wants them back, and I will take them to him. The only decision for you to make is do you want to hand them to me peacefully, or will you risk your life trying to keep them?"

"This is crazy talk. Kill her!" the nobleman yelled. Then he turned to the bearded, red-haired man. "And you. Get on that horse and warn the others. I doubt she came here alone."

The broad-shouldered, well muscled men approached Cass, swords drawn. Cass drew her sword at the same time she mind connected with the bearded man's horse. As soon as the man swung his right leg around and sat upon the horse's back, she directed the horse to run down along the field toward Keatera. Next, she defended a strike from the blade of the man's sword to her left as she kicked the other man in the stomach, dropping him to the ground. A second swipe from the man on the left's blade cut through her tunic and grazed the skin over her ribs, drawing blood.

She heard the children screaming and spun around. She sliced the man on the left through his midsection while his arm was raised above his head, sword in hand. In a continuous motion, she came face forward once again and sliced through the belly of the second man.

The nobleman stood as if in disbelief before he drew his own sword. "Amateurs!"

Cass stood with feet apart, sword held at the ready. "Stop this foolishness while you still can. No one else needs to die. Do what is right and just. Give up the children. They aren't your property to keep."

"What's right and just is for you and your band of strays to die. You've caused enough trouble for people like me." The nobleman sliced his sword in the air, as if flexing his muscles or trying to instill fear into Cass. "Wait and see how popular I will become when I'm the one who will have killed Cassethea of Mercia. My life will be even better than it is now, thanks to you."

"I'm sorry you think this way, but so be it."

The nobleman struck against Cass's sword first, but she wasted no time. Not long after their swordfight started, Cass finished it with a jab of her blade through the man's heart. She watched him fall to the ground, saddened that he'd not taken her offer, and that she had another death on her hands to bear. She pushed the thoughts from her mind, mounted Starlight, and rode toward Keatera.

Scanning the fields, she saw arrows fly from the trees on one side of the field and arrows fly from bushes and shrubs simultaneously from the other side. The men on horseback, several holding onto yelling and kicking children, first dropped the children, and then, riddled with arrows, fell from their horses.

Her army of women, Sedra among them, ran in to gather the children. Cass exhaled. Their plan had worked. The farthest the men ever were from the children, and the best chance the women had to save them, was when the children were in the fields working. With each fallen rider Cass passed, she noted the arrows protruded straight through their hearts. When she reached Keatera, she stopped and dismounted. "Well done. It's over. Did we sustain any losses on our side?"

"Not a one," Keatera said. "But I see you're bleeding."

"It's nothing. A surface wound at best."

"Right, a surface wound. Where have I heard those words before?"

****

The first few days after leaving her army of women, Cass found it difficult to adjust to being alone again. She was so proud of their accomplishments and of all the lives they saved or improved, and she missed her merry band of warriors terribly. Easing the pain was the knowledge she'd finally be able to rest again and see her family. In hindsight, the past two years felt like a whirlwind coming to a crashing end. What would she do now? She didn't really know what it was to relax and not worry every moment of every day.

As she contemplated her future, she walked over the top of a hill. On the other side, she saw three hunched, old women, dressed in soiled white cloaks, huddled over the rear wheel of their cart. As Cass neared, she noticed the cart was filled with intricately carved canes, stacks of clothing, many different shapes and sizes of wooden bowls and spoons, and many different types of dried herbs. The horse hitched to the front of the cart was exceptionally old from Cass's estimation, which had one benefit for the women: he'd not be stolen. Cass moved still closer.

"Excuse me, ladies, do you need any help?" The three women mumbled incoherently to one another under their breaths before they stood and turned toward Cass. Other than their thin, grey-and-white hair, their faces appeared fairly young and not at all unpleasant, which surprised Cass in a good way, since their hands were wrinkled and oddly bent and their shoulders hunched. Cass wasn't used to seeing such old people, as most didn't live past forty winters, unless they were lucky or possibly royalty. Perhaps they were healers.

"Thank you, young lady, we would welcome your assistance. Several travelers have passed us, but no one offered us help. Part of the problem is, we don't really know what's wrong. The wheel isn't cracked, yet the cart moves not."

"My name is Cassethea. I'm not skilled in this area, but let me see what I can do." Cass bent over the right rear wheel, and as the women said, couldn't find a problem. She walked to the other side of the cart and inspected the opposite wheel, noting it had a wooden rod in the center hole, held in place by a wedge through the middle of the rod, which appeared to expand the rod at the end wide enough that the wheel wouldn't fall off, but not so wide it wouldn't roll. Cass returned to the other wheel where not only was the wedge missing, but also the rod was partly snapped.

She said, "I located the problem, and I may be able to help you, but it may take awhile. You ladies should sit and relax. If I can't get this to work, I'll send someone out from the next village to help you."

While Cass worked on the cart, the women gathered wood and made a small fire. Cass glanced over once in a while to see what they were doing. They'd heated a kettle, and with a few ingredients from their cart, were cooking together and talking, but Cass couldn't hear what they were saying.

The hardest part of the task at hand for Cass was to remove the splintered rod, which was packed in tight. She managed to do that with brute force, and once the rod was out, she hunted for the proper thickness of branch from a hardwood tree. She found one and used her dagger to strip it clean and smooth. The next most difficult task was to fashion a similar-sized wedge and then be careful how far she hit it into the rod with a rock. If she split it, she'd have to start all over, which would mean a whole day lost. Before Cass finished, one of the old women walked toward her with a bowl.

"Would you like some tea? You've worked so hard."

Cass felt terrible that her immediate thoughts of the woman holding the tea went to Haddie and the elixir she made for her. She didn't know these women. How could she trust them? Likely, she shouldn't. "Thank you, but I—"

"You need not worry. I sense your unease, but I assure you, this tea is good for you. Come, sit with us for a moment and have tea with us. I'll drink this one and pour yours fresh if you like."

"All right, thank you. I am quite thirsty." As they walked, Cass asked the woman her name and found that the three women were sisters. During their conversation, she also learned they lived together and sold the goods from their cart on the road. Cass thought this a hard life, but perhaps, like she, they didn't want to be married and subject to the power of men over them. Perhaps their freedom was more important to them. Cass could relate.

When she stood next to the women's horse, before they were packed up and about to move on, she patted him on the neck and connected with him briefly. She felt bad that she hadn't trusted the women but blamed Haddie for having tainted her in that way. To make amends, and against their vehement objections, she purchased a beautiful bowl with a unique grain pattern for her mother and a wooden necklace of a bird on a wooden string for Emma. Cass waved good-bye and felt that wave of emptiness return.

With the delay, she estimated it would take another three days' ride to get home to her mother and Emma, assuming the weather cooperated. Maybe even a bit longer. She wanted to make sure she avoided crossing too near Haddie's place, for fear she'd reestablish control over her in some way. When that thread that held her to Haddie years ago had disconnected, she'd felt the release immediately. She never wanted to feel that tug on her consciousness again.

Cass shifted to better thoughts and pushed Haddie into the recesses of her mind. She couldn't wait to see Emma, her mother, and her brothers. Likely Julia would be in Normandy with her husband by now. Cass had missed the wedding. She hoped Julia understood. Would she see Julia again, or would she be in Normandy always? Would she see Tove again? Her heart ached at the thought she might not. She even found she missed Rune and Thyra and Orm and Estrid and the others.

Right then, she decided that after visiting with her family, she'd go to the last place she'd parted with Tove, to the spot on the beach where she kissed Tove good-bye before her journey began. She'd set up camp there if she had to. She'd wait for as long as it took. Eventually Tove would come back to hunt, if for nothing else, no? A spark of hope lit within her and warmed her insides. She now had something. She had a plan. And plans were what she was good at creating and executing.

Chapter Thirty-Two

When Rayne opened the front door to her house and Jess followed her inside, George came running. He jumped between Rayne and Jess before they could set their bags down, and as soon as they did, he demanded to be petted copiously, which he was.

Baron also approached and hugged them both. "Good to have you back. We missed you guys."

"We can see that," Rayne said.

"Hey, Baron, thanks. We missed you, too," Jess said.

"I hope you had a good time. You both look relaxed."

"We did, brother, thank you."

"I'm glad I could help. I'm going to get back to the pub, though. Cuz is there alone. We'll chat tomorrow," Baron said.

Jess caught his wink at Rayne and thought the gesture odd. But then, the siblings did have an unusual tit-for-tat relationship, so who knows what surprise he may have left her within the house.

"Thanks again, Baron."

"Anytime. Oh, and I left you guys some dinner, too."

"Handsome and smart," Rayne said before he walked out the door.

After they doled out more attention to George, Jess and Rayne relaxed onto the sofa. "Wow," Jess said, "what an incredible, but also tiring, few days. I'm not sure I'm ready to get back to reality."

"I feel the same way. How about having a glass of wine?"

"That sounds good. I don't want to unpack one item right now or think about much of anything." When Rayne returned with their glasses several minutes later, Jess added, "What took you so long? I could have stomped the grapes and poured the wine in the time it took you."

"Feisty, aren't we?" Rayne handed Jess a glass and touched it to her own. "Cheers to being open to possibilities."

"Open to possibilities? Never mind. I don't even want to know. Cheers to being open to possibilities, Kvale."

Rayne sipped her wine and waited until Jess took a sip of hers before she continued. "Good, I'm glad you agree, because I have a proposition for you, and all I ask is that you stay open to the possibility of what I'm about to propose."

Jess tried to read Rayne for insight into what she might say next, but she couldn't.

Rayne extended her hand. "Come with me."

Rayne led Jess up the hallway to the spare bedroom. Only, when Jess looked in, it wasn't a spare bedroom any longer. It was an office.

"What do you think? Do you like it? I asked Baron to call in a favor from a friend and build us this office. It's for you. I'd like you to stay, Jess. I don't want you to go back to Connecticut. I'd like you to stay in England with me. Since that night we first kissed, I've thought nonstop about you having to leave, and eventually, I devised a possible solution. You could take a sabbatical to write a detailed historical account of Cassethea's life. Or you could stay and teach at university. You may not be able to land anything this year, since the fall semester will start soon, but in the spring I'm sure you'd find something. You could substitute in the meantime, or do none of those things, but stay with me. What do you say?"

"I don't know what to say. When I think there's no way you can surprise me more than you already have, you do so anyway. Is this the call you made from the balcony, on our first night at the hotel?"

"Busted."

"You are unbelievable. So it's not this mini vacation that's making you ask me this, because vacations are always trouble-free and great. You felt this way for a while now?"

"I felt this way since the day you stood outside Eagles Landing's rear screen door and shortly afterward insulted me about not keeping a collar on George when you found out he was mine."

"So it's the straightforward women you like then, is it?"

"It's you, every aspect of you, that I've fallen in love with."

"In that case, the answer is heck yes."

****

"El, are you sure you don't mind doing this for me? I'll owe you big time."

"Of course, I don't mind. It's no big deal, Jess. I'll have Gayle help me. She's more of a fashion buff than I am anyway."

"That would be so great. You're the best. And thank Gayle for me, too. I can handle most of the move on this end over the computer, and I'm hopeful my landlord will cut me a break on ending the apartment lease early, but I could sure use more clothes right about now."

"Like I said, it's not a problem. We'll go there tonight and box up most of your clothes and have them sent over, though I hope Rayne knows what she's getting into. Did you tell her how many clothes and shoes you have?"

"I did not."

"Maybe you should and then call me back."

"Knock it off, smart-aleck. Although, maybe I will make sure she's okay with me moving some of my stuff in. I have a lot of books and research material in my office, too, that the university's going to pack," Jess said.

"I wouldn't trust those asses if I were you, especially not after the chancellor nixed your dig. Let me know what day they plan to be at your office, and I'll make sure to stop by. I bet Professor Heckman is already licking his chops at taking over your courses and probably your office."

"Yeah, honestly, leaving you and leaving him to my students, who thought they'd get me as their professor this semester, are two of my only regrets from staying here." Jess heard Ellie laugh heartily on the other end of the line.

"Won't they be unpleasantly surprised when they find out, and thank you for saying so about leaving me. I'm obviously missing you already as well. Hey, I better get going. I've got a lot to get done in only a little bit of time if

I'm going to help with this move."

Jess thought she heard El's voice crack a little. "Thanks again, El. We definitely have to all get together soon. I want to meet Gayle, and I definitely want you to meet Rayne. She's something else."

"She must be, to have caught you. Plus, this move is big, Jess, and so unlike you. I'm proud of you for going with your gut. And yes, I'd love for us to get together. I'm feeling a long-awaited vacation coming on sooner than later, so who knows. Take care of yourself."

"You take care as well, my friend."

Jess disconnected the call and crawled into bed next to Rayne, who'd already fallen asleep; she spooned Rayne and wrapped her arm around her waist. As contentment met drowsiness and sleep overtook her, her mind drifted. She saw Cassethea walking toward a patch of trees and suddenly felt her fear.

Chapter Thirty-Three

Cass walked next to Starlight, held her by the reins, and slowed her steps as she approached the tree line. A sense of unease swept over her. If it weren't for the much-needed water from the creek near the tree line, she wouldn't risk moving closer, but she had little choice. Starlight snorted and pranced as if agitated, as did her spare horse. She'd gifted the third horse to the monastery. "I know, fellas, I feel anxious, too. What I can't figure out is why."

As she was about to take another step, Starlight reared onto his hind legs. The other horse stepped in reverse. Cass spoke to Starlight gently and stroked the side of his neck to settle him, but she soon saw the reason for his distress. Fluorescent-green orbs the size of large beets moved through the shadows of the forest and out onto the well-lit meadow.

The sun struck the massive tip of a horn protruding from the head of the emerging creature, then the tip of its armored snout, and along the snout to the bright-green eyes. The sunlight moved beyond the eyes, where a hard shield fanned around the creature's head. The imposing figure stood on four scaley, thick-as-a-tree-trunk legs, at a height half as tall as her horse. It ambled slowly forward.

Cass tried to mind connect with the creature but was unable to. As it continued toward her, she understood why she couldn't. It appeared to be lizard-like, not a mammal. Just like with the spider, she was basically powerless in terms of using her star-born gifts. "We mean you no harm. We've come for water, and then we'll be on our way."

The massive lizard-like creature threw his head back and shrieked the most ear-piercing noise Cass had ever encountered. Starlight rose up again on his hind legs, along with the other horse, as Cass dropped to her knees, rested her arms on her thighs, and held her hands over her ears. She lifted her head to see the creature methodically approach, its sharp-toothed jaw open. She wanted to reach for her sword but couldn't; the shrill sound was unbearable. She forced herself to her feet. Warm liquid oozed between her hand and right ear, and she stumbled backward to put distance between herself and the lizard. "Stop! Enough!" Cass continued to stumble away with increasing difficulty, not sure how long she would last.

Her vision began to blur. The creature flung his head back, swung it violently in both directions, and stumbled. The piercing, high-pitched noise was replaced by a deeper cry of pain. An arrow flew through the air from the tree line into the back of the creature's neck, behind its armor shield. As the massive reptile spun around, Cass saw two arrows pierce his neck before he staggered and fell backward. Before she could draw her sword, a fourth arrow whizzed past and landed in his soft underbelly. The cries stopped. Cass wasn't certain if she was out of trouble yet or not, until she spotted the familiar and much-longed-for image of Tove running toward her. Was she seeing clearly? Was it truly Tove?

Still somewhat dizzy, Cass lurched slowly forward into Tove's extended arms. They stood, hugging, for several minutes, as joy engulfed and nearly overwhelmed Cass. "Gaia, it is you."

Tove separated from Cass and caressed her face. With her eyes focused on Cass's eyes, she said, "Yes, it's me. Are you all right?"

Cass saw the blood on her hand, likely from inside her ear, and nodded in disbelief. "I think so. What are you doing here? I've missed you beyond words."

Tove removed rounded, cork-like plugs from her ears. "I've missed you every day as well. Sometimes I wished I'd not let you go, but I knew you needed to."

"Yes, I did, but I never stopped thinking about you and wishing, in some ways, that I hadn't left."

Tove's gaze shifted to the eagle tattoo on Cass's arm.

She stroked Cass's arm gently near the markings she was born with of The White Bear. Tove's hand moved to the painting of the eagle on her arm. "What is this?"

Heat coursed through Cass at Tove's touch. "This was

my way of keeping you close to me while we were apart. It was a small way to give my soul peace and strength. I know it was you who brought the winds and rain to King Andron's castle the day I was to be burned. I sensed you near as I was escaping, but I was unable to locate you. It was you, wasn't it? You are star born of The Eagle with the power of water."

"Yes. I'm flattered that you endured this marking for me."

"I would do so much more for you. I should have sensed it earlier. There were times when we trained together that I wondered about the possibility, but I don't think my mind was clear enough then."

"I remember. Those were both cherished and difficult times, knowing I'd have to let you go, uncertain whether I'd ever see you again. Are you heading home for a while now? That's what I've heard."

Cass managed a smile, although her right ear still hurt and she felt dizzy. "I am, but I think I may need a couple days rest. I'd like to say I've never seen anything like that creature before, but sadly, I have. Would you mind walking me toward the shade? I need to sit. I'm not sure if my legs are weak from what I just experienced or from seeing you. My guess is both."

"Then I'm the lucky one, though I'm feeling somewhat lightheaded myself."

Cass crossed the creek with Tove, the cool water on her feet refreshing and the warmth of Tove's hand on her arm reassuring. The horses followed, stopping at the creek to drink. "You said you heard I was heading home. Were you looking for me?"

"I've tried to keep my distance from you, but at the same time, I wasn't able to let you go completely. I had to know you were safe. I know you probably don't want to hear me say that, but I can't lie to you. However, I was also out to hunt today." Tove grabbed the horn filled with salt from around her neck, its corked top missing. "I'd not expected to find a giant lizard-like creature though. This is certainly a first."

"I've not eaten lizard before."

Tove raised an eyebrow. "Care to try it?"

"We can't let good meat spoil," Cass said. "Give me a few minutes, and I'll help you with it. There's more meat there than we can eat and more than we can carry, but if you have salt to cure some, we can cure part of it and smoke part. The rest we can leave to the animals to finish off."

"We?"

"Yes, if you want for us to be a we."

"I've wanted that for a long time now. Long before we parted on the beach."

Cass touched the side of Tove's face, the heat within her rising as she listened to Tove's confession. She wanted to kiss her, to feel their lips touch, their tongues intertwine, yet an inner hesitancy held her back. "We have so much to discuss. This will give us a few days alone with which to do it."

****

During their days together while they prepared the meat and talked and slept next to one another under the stars, Cass and Tove began rebuilding the friendship they'd established on the island several years before. Each minute spent together drew them closer, as if they already had a bond between them that couldn't be broken.

When they were a day from Cass's home, near the cutoff on the trail that led to the beach where she and Tove had parted, Cass stopped. Her heart was heavy. "I don't want to let you go, but I know you'll need to get back to your fam—"

"Cassethea, no—"

"Don't. Let me finish. It's hard enough for me as it is. I'm sure your family misses you. Let's set a time, though, when we'll see each other again. I'll make certain to be here. After I visited my family I'd planned to come back here and wait for you anyway, for as long as it took."

"You...you did?"

"Of course I did, Tove. I'm in love with you. Isn't it obvious?"

Tears formed in Tove's eyes as she touched her hand to the side of Cass's face. "I love you, too." Tove lowered her head and touched her lips to Cass's.

The kiss, tender and gentle and curious at first, quickly became heated and searching, taking Cass's breath away. When they parted, she stared into Tove's blue eyes. "Go, before I ask you not to go."

"I've been trying to tell you. I'm not going."

"You're not?"

"No, but you'll have to wait another day so I can properly show you why."

"I think you will truly be the death of me."

Tove laughed and grabbed Cass's hand. "Come on. The quicker we travel, the quicker I can show you my surprise."

And the following day when they reached the Severn Estuary, not far from Cass's old home, Cass saw it: a Viking longhouse.

****

As the ivory horn filled with the fruity spirits of bjorr was passed around the table among loud chatter and laughter, Cass's heart felt as though it would explode. "I still can't believe we're all sitting here together again, and in Mercia of all places. I couldn't have been more shocked."

"Your expression was worth ten deer," Toke said.

"Twenty," Valken added.

"Stop that, you two." Thyra turned to Cass. "Don't listen to them, Cassethea. We're so glad to have you here with us again. Tove hasn't been the same without you, and I might add, she's been a bit of a bear." Her tone was pleasant, yet teasing.

"I'll vouch for that," Orm said.

"No ganging up on your loved one," Tove said.

Orm wagged a finger at her. "We may as well get our shots in while we can,"

Cass faced Tove. "I'm so thankful you are here and built this home, but what made you all come?"

"You were forefront on my mind, Cassethea, as the family can attest to. But we were also moving apart from Ulf, Bjorn, and the rest of Koll's family. Once he passed and they knew I was part of the reason, even though they knew the outcome was deserved, we all drifted apart. Food was becoming scarce as well, with us traveling to your mainland more and more often. We sat down together one night and talked it over. We decided unanimously that Mercia is where we needed to be."

"Well, I for one couldn't be happier," Cass said. She thought about how far she'd come. From sitting at the table in her childhood home, afraid of her father, often not free to speak her mind, the tension thick in the air, to the complete opposite of that. She was blessed. Though she missed her mother and Emma, she knew she'd visit them soon.

As the evening wore on and everyone prepared for bed, Cass felt awkward for the first time. Her line of sight caught Tove's. "Where shall I sleep?"

"You can stay with me if you like. We can just hold each other, if you're all right with that."

Cass wanted so much more with Tove, but she hadn't told her yet what happened with Princess Dallia. She'd not found the right time. Yet her desire to have Tove close was all consuming, and she thought she sensed the desire in Tove for her as well. How much longer could she deny her need? She had to tell Tove soon, and she would, if she could simply muster the courage. She knew she'd done nothing wrong, but the possibility of losing Tove when they'd just found each other again was unbearable.

Cass crawled into the bed first, shortly thereafter followed by Tove. Tove, being the head of the family, had her cloth-sectioned-off room at one end of the longhouse, the same as she had on the island. The heat from Tove's body next to hers wouldn't allow her to sleep. "Tove?"

"Mmm, what is it, Cassethea?"

"There's something I need to tell you. Something I hadn't mentioned before, but I need you to hear it."

"You know you can tell me anything. No words you say will make me change the way I feel about you."

Cass felt the bed shift as she assumed Tove turned toward her on her side.

"But know also that you don't need to tell me if you don't want to."

Cass faced Tove as well. "Thank you for saying so, but I need you to know...before...before we go any further."

Tove said nothing, but she stroked Cass's arm slowly and gently.

Cass told her story, which was difficult for her at first, but eased as she went on. "I think I agreed to her terms because I was broken inside. I thought I'd lost almost everything. All our training, all that I'd been through up until that point, my days spent away from you, all wasted. And the alternative I was offered? I'd rather have chosen death, but that option wasn't open to me."

"I'm sorry this person needed to assert her power over you in that way. It was in no way becoming of a lady, let alone a princess. You did what you needed to do at the time to stay alive. I would have done the same."

"You still want to be with me?"

"Of course I do. I told you that nothing you could say would change my mind. I know who you are. It's a tribute to you that you found your way through this, and although I'm sure the experience will linger with you in ways I'll not know, and for the rest of your life, you'll always have me by your side should you need me. Anything you ask of me, Cassethea, I'll do for you."

Tears of relief streamed down Cass's cheeks. "Had I known you'd be so supportive, I'd have told you sooner."

"I'm thankful you told me at all, and I understand why you waited. Love isn't something that can be taken. It has to be given freely."

"In that case, may I kiss you? I think if I don't, I'll lie awake the rest of the night."

"Yes, and may I return the favor?"

"You'd better."

Chapter Thirty-Four

Two weeks after Cass visited her mother and Emma in their newly reconstructed home and helped them tend their garden, she returned to the longhouse. When she walked inside, she found everyone sitting around the table, and at the far end sat a high member of the church. Cass scanned familiar faces to ensure no one had died. The member of the clergy wore a white tunic and a red, narrow strip of linen draped over his left shoulder, upon which was embroidered an ornate cross. He wore a silver cross around his neck with a ruby in the center and a matching ring on his right hand. The man's cheeks were round and rosy and matched his too-generous build.

Tove stood. "Cassethea, I'm glad you made it back in time to meet Bishop Leon II of Mettlenbury. He's traveling north to visit several of the churches in his parishes and stopped along the way for a visit."

Cass bowed slightly. "Your Grace." Then she turned to Tove. "You know one another?"

The bishop cleared his throat. "Please, allow me," he said to Tove before addressing Cass. "Several months ago, I was visiting one of our churches in Deerhurst. While there, a small group of Vikings stormed our doors. They were armed with axes and swords. They began to take goblets and crosses and other sacred artifacts. Unarmed, I and our priests could do nothing to stop them. Unfortunately, this is not an unusual occurrence. However, on this particular day, we were not to be robbed or our church plundered. Tove, Orm, and Valken stepped in. I owe them much. Possibly even my life."

"It's as though fate placed them near," Cass said.

"Either fate or a higher power," he said, then grinned. "And now imagine my surprise and delight when I find Cassethea of Mercia here as well, the same Cassethea that returned our children to us at the monastery not far from Deerhurst only some weeks ago, yes?"

"I and a group of friends happened to be in the area," Cass said.

The bishop laughed heartily. "Yes, yes, of course. And it's good that you were there."

"Is there trouble at the churches you're visiting, if I may ask?" Cass said.

The bishop breathed deep and leaned back. "For now, I ask you to keep what I say quiet, but yes, trouble spreads on several fronts. In many towns north of here, with numbers increasing with every passing of the moon, peasants and noblemen alike have taken ill. Besides the horror of the illness itself, farming and food production are on the decline and taxes are unable to be paid. The people instead pay money to a warlock who strolls into town, weeks after the illness's onset, to cure the town at a steep cost. This warlock, Haddontek, is thought to be assembling a mass of mercenaries with this money. Mercenaries he wants to use to take control of Mercia and Northumbria, thereby also controlling many of the shipping ports. The man is evil, dark. He's already begun pitting King Herrwald against his cousin King Alfred III through lies and deceit."

Cass caught Tove's concerned look, one that matched her own. "Wait, are you saying Haddontek is a man—a warlock? That can't be. I met this Haddontek, who went by the name of Haddie, though not of my free will as I later found out. She disguised herself as someone I knew at a time when I needed help, but when I escaped from her grasp, I saw images of her as a witch. This is why you must be mistaken."

"There's no mistake. Haddontek is a warlock. Warlocks possess evil magic. They bend the powers of nature and have the ability to bend reality. He can disguise himself in many layers and only let you see the layer he wants you to see. Only the pure of heart can fight his powers. Even a witch fighting him on her own could not defeat him. He is obsessed with the need to control. This is why I've come. The priests alone have been unsuccessful against him, and I believe it is he who brings the sickness then robs all of their money by healing them again, but only partly so."

Cass tossed his comments around in her head against her memory of what transpired with Haddie. The more she thought about it, the more the pieces fit together between what the bishop told her and what she thought to be true. She recalled the visions with Haddie at night by the fire with her sword. "I fear you're right. I also think he may be trying to pull me back, perhaps lured by the sword that Sir William from Northumbria, King Arthur III's knight, gifted to me. These past weeks, I've been fighting against this invisible thread he uses to control the mind. I broke the connection once. I don't want to be put in that state of mind again."

The bishop held his hand over his cross. "If what you say is true, then it is good I'm here. You have to continue to think positive and pure thoughts. All of you do. Our positive energy will weaken his powers. And his power is not unlimited. I will pray for you and for those he continues to injure. I need to confront him before he gains more power. I'm hopeful that my position in the clergy and connection to God will be enough to keep him at bay."

"I'll come with you," Cass said. "It's likely that as long as he lives, I may never have peace. I know of the despair you talk about that he spreads. It doesn't affect him at all. I think he relishes it."

Tove stood. "If you go, then I go as well. Together, we may have a better chance."

* * * *

Cass rolled on her side to face Tove. "This may be our last night alone, before we travel with Bishop Leon."

"Yes, I'm sure it will be. He said he'd return from his counsel with King Herrwald in the morning. Cassethea, I saw the disbelief in your eyes when he spoke of Haddontek. Do you think he was inappropriate with you in ways you may be unaware?"

"No, I'm sure he wasn't. After Dallia, looking back now, no, I would have known. Thank Gaia for that. No, I truly think he was obsessed with extracting the magic from my sword."

"Yet he wields magic of his own."

"Yes, but you heard the bishop about how power hungry he is. Maybe Haddontek knows more about the powers the sword has than I do."

"Perhaps he does."

"Thank you for offering to come with me. I worry though." Cass reached for Tove's hand. "I don't want to be the cause of anything bad happening to you."

"Believe me when I say that losing you would be the worst thing that could happen to me, so no worries, all right?"

"All right. Tove?"

"Mmm?"

"I need to feel you next to me tonight. I've wanted you for so long. My body aches for you."

"Are you certain?"

"Yes, with all that I am."

Tove moved closer, then Cass felt the touch of her hand on her face and her lips seek out hers. The explosion of desire that erupted through Cass with that kiss was beyond anything she experienced before. Her dreams of Tove on those many nights apart were finally coming true to life, and life was far exceeding her dreams.

****

The closer they got to Haddontek's domicile, the harder Cass had to fight to keep her mind clear. Soon they came upon him. He stood in the center of a meadow, in the black, hooded robe Cass had seen in the wooden chest in his hut. He was taller than she remembered, and he filled the robe fully. He was waiting for them, Cass was certain, making her all the more cautious with each step they took.

"Tove," Cass said, "please stay behind unless we need you. The less of a threat he feels he may need to fight against, perhaps the lower his guard will be."

"You should both stay behind," the bishop said.

"No," Cass said. "I'm going with you. He already knows I'm here. I've been blocking him as best I can for a while now."

"I'll do as you both ask." Tove melted from sight.

The ground softened as they trudged toward Haddontek, making the task of getting close enough to him slow and strenuous. Finally, when Cass saw his eyes of yellow, she stopped.

"I'm surprised to see you here, Cassethea, but ecstatic that you came, and with your sword, too. This was thoughtful of you. I guess you've finally put all the pieces of the puzzle that is me together?"

"I've put together most of them, with the bishop's help."

"Ah, yes, of course, with the bishop's help. So, Your Grace, you thought you'd come here and do what exactly? What your small army of priests couldn't do? And you brought Cassethea with you to help."

Haddontek laughed. "Neither of you is stronger than I am, not apart, and not together. This you shall soon learn. After all this time, Cassethea, I've discovered what I did wrong during those months you stayed with me. I thought by weakening your mind I could extract the magic in your sword. It is vast. It is much, much greater than you know. After you left, the thought occurred to me that perhaps I needed to kill you in order to release the power within. Being the patient man that I am, upon learning of your plans to rescue the innocent, I hoped you'd cause your own demise, but sadly I see I have to take matters into my own hands."

"You are an ill man, Haddontek. What you're doing to the people here is wrong," Cass said.

"She is right," the bishop said. "Your soul will burn for ages if you do not repent now."

"I can understand your righteousness, Bishop, even though it makes my skin crawl. But you, Cassethea, your words cut me. My mind is clear. You are the one who seems confused. I speak of ending your life, and you worry about people you don't even know. You should worry about your own life."

"I can take care of myself."

"Let's put that to the test, shall we?" Haddontek dropped his head back, lifted his arms in the air, and chanted as he slowly brought his head forward and made eye contact with Cass. His eyes turned from yellow to black, and his hands slowly lowered and came closer together, as if he were pressing an invisible force between them.

Cass heard the bishop praying and, from the corner of her eye, saw him hold out the cross on his chest. She felt an intense pressure squeezing her from the sides, making it difficult to breathe. Her right eardrum, having just recently healed, throbbed once again. Warm liquid leaked from her nose. Her arms were difficult to move. She was barely able to wipe the liquid away. It was blood. The bleeding intensified. Cass's vision began to blur.

"Stop this! Stop this! You must not do this! God will punish you!" The bishop stepped in front of Cass, partly shielding her.

"And I will punish you," Haddontek said.

Cass fell to her knees. Haddontek clapped his hands together, rubbed them swiftly, and stretched his arms out to his sides, shoulder height, palms up. He rotated his outstretched arms in small circles, drawing liquid up from the marsh. The quicker his arms rotated in circles, the more liquid rose and swirled around them. He thrust the swirling mass around and through the bishop, who wheezed for air as Haddontek continued to swirl the murky, acidic water around him. Haddontek's eyes opened wide and turned from black to yellow as he grasped his left arm, and she heard the familiar voices of three sisters begin a chant, the words of which she couldn't discern.

Haddontek stumbled backward and stepped away. "This isn't over, Cassethea."

Haddontek's blurry figure stumbled from view, and the arms of three women wearing soiled white cloaks reached for Cass before her vision darkened.

****

When Cass opened her eyes again, she felt weak, weaker than she'd ever felt before. She was lying on her back at a slight incline. She moved her hands from her chest to her side and felt thick branches. Near the rear of a horse next to her lay the bishop, also on an incline on a similar wooden structure. Her vision faded again, and when she opened her eyes a second time, Tove was kneeling at her side. Eventide had set in.

"Cassethea, you've lost a lot of blood. We need to get you assistance. The bishop barely lives as well. Those three women, they saved your life, but they said they can do no more for you or for the bishop."

"Haddontek," Cass said in a meager whisper.

"He's dead. I killed him."

Cass closed her eyes and whispered, "Tamshire."

"I don't understand. Can you say it again?"

"Take...Tamshire. Jorgen and Braenna."

****

Cass couldn't open her eyes, but she knew they had stopped. She heard strangers' voices overhead.

"Yes, yes, we do know hi—her. Bring her in, quickly, and the bishop, too," Jorgen said. "Oh, my God, what happened to them? This woman saved our lives about two winters ago. We thought she was a young lad. Her hair was short. She fought off two men who stopped us on the road. They would have...they would have...killed us and worse if not for her. Our daughter lives undamaged because of her."

Cass felt the warmth of a wet cloth cover her face and gentle hands move the cloth across her chin. She thought she heard Tove's voice, but silence took over once again.

****

Cass stepped from the longhouse and let the sun's rays envelop her. She walked toward Bishop Leon's grave, knelt, and placed her hand on the rune stone Tove had etched. "Thank you, my friend. You will never be far from my thoughts. Your sacrifice saved many and will continue to do so, I promise."

"Ready?" Tove said.

"You are relentless, so yes, I suppose I'm ready. Where are we going?"

"You know that's a surprise. Let's go."

"Tove, what are you doing? You have no idea how difficult it is to walk with your hand covering my eyes."

"I've been waiting for months for you to get better, and now that you are, you'll need to put up with me. I promise we don't have far to walk, the length of a field at most."

"Are we talking a peasant's field or a nobleman's field?"

When Tove's hand finally moved from over her eyes, Cass opened them. Before her was a small wooden house, a third the size of the longhouse, but similarly built. "Tove! I don't believe it. What did you do?"

"I decided we needed a place of our own. Not far from family, but enough that we have privacy. You tend to be vocal."

Cass slapped Tove on the arm and laughed. "You're not so quiet yourself, not that I'm complaining. Come here." Cass reached for Tove's hand, pulled her close, and kissed her. "I think I'd like to see the inside now, wouldn't you?"

Chapter Thirty-Five

Jess shot up straight in bed. "Oh, my God! It was under my nose the whole time."

Rayne shifted beside her partner. "What's going on? Why are you up? What are you talking about?"

Jess sprang out of bed and grabbed her nightshirt and a pair of shorts, just as George pranced into the room. "You knew, didn't you, George? You've been trying to tell us, and we've been too blind to see."

Rayne sat up. "Jess, what's going on? I've never seen you so riled up before, but you're not making any sense to me right now."

Jess absorbed Rayne's puzzled glare. "You're right, I'm sorry. Cassethea came to me in my dreams last night, Rayne. I know what happened to the bishop, and I think I know where Cassethea is buried."

"That's fantastic, Jess. Where?"

"On this property, the rise where George always lies in the sun."

"Are you certain?"

"I'm not positive, but I'm pretty sure. The placement and the shape make sense."

"Bloody hell. We need to find out then."

****

After taking care of George, showering, and eating breakfast, Rayne and Jess spent Saturday in the yard, digging on George's favorite spot, with George looking on, his tail thumping.

"You said you knew what happened to the bishop," Rayne said.

Jess had already told Rayne a good part of what she'd

learned in her dreams. "Marshland is acidic soil, which has the ability to break down mineral content at a quicker pace than soil which is alkaline. I know this is surreal, but I think Haddontek used his power to infuse the tissue pores and cells in the bishop's lungs with the minerals from this material, speeding up a process of perimineralization thousands or tens of thousands fold."

"Meaning he was trying to harden his lungs so he'd slowly die from a lack of oxygen?"

"Yes. And although scientifically, this doesn't seem possible, the bishop's remains indicate it very well could be true. And since I can't present these facts as I've learned them, it appears, scientifically, his current condition will have to remain an unknown mystery to be pondered for many future generations."

"So be it," Rayne said. "Hang on. I think I hit something hard."

"I did as well. Be careful here."

As they brushed away the soil, they uncovered what appeared to be not one grave, but two. They came upon two rune stones. The stone on the left held symbols that spelled "Tove," and under her name, the symbols for the word "one." On the rune stone to the right were the symbols for "Cassethea," and under her name, the symbols for the word "heart."

Jess and Rayne reached below their shirts at the same time and clutched the pendants at the ends of their necklaces. "This can't be for real," Jess said as she looked into Rayne's equally disbelieving eyes. "And yet with every fiber in my body, I sense it is real. It was one thing to contemplate our possible connection—"

"But it's another thing to contemplate our possible connection to theirs."

"Yes. Now what do we do?"

"Now you finish what you came here to do. The rest we'll try and figure out together later," Rayne said.

****

Exactly one week later, next to Cassethea's body, Jess,

with Rayne by her side, uncovered Cassethea's sword. Jess stood frozen in place, almost afraid to touch the sword.

"May I?" Rayne asked.

"Yes, please."

Rayne grabbed the pommel of the sword, first with one hand, then with two. She dragged it with much effort from the grave and hoisted it on its tip. "This sword is truly made of lead, but it's beautiful."

Even in its dirtied state, Jess recognized the sword immediately. To her, the jewels on the handle sparkled in all their glory, the same as she'd seen in her visions, the blade just as magnificent. As if in a daze, she stepped toward the sword and reached for the pommel. As Rayne relinquished her hold, Jess wrapped her hand around the pommel and lifted the sword skyward as if it were feather light. She stepped away from Rayne and sliced the sword through the air, feeling its incredible balance and power. Her eyes found Rayne's once again, and they held each other's stare.

"Jess, it isn't possible," Rayne said.

"I know, and yet, I'm able to lift it as if it weighed nothing at all."

Rayne stood silent for some time. "I know you want to prove to the world Cassethea is real, and her sword is a big part of that, but it's evident this sword must stay here, in this house. It belongs to you, Jess."

Jess nodded in agreement. "Yes, I think this is one part of Cassethea's story better left untold."

"All of this is so strange. How are you taking it all in?"

"Everything makes so much more sense to me now. My obsession with trying to prove Cassethea's existence. The life I chose to lead. All of it. And now it's odd, but I suddenly feel like I don't need to prove anything to anyone anymore. Not to my parents or my colleagues. It's like I'm free."

"I'm glad you feel that way. You stuck with your gut and heart all those years against the naysayers. And now you've proven Cassethea was no myth, that not all Vikings were bad, and that love between women existed even then. Your discoveries will give countless people new insights and understanding, and some, a role model in Cassethea that they can admire, see themselves in, and aspire to."

Jess's heart overflowed with love. She was so enamored with Rayne, and now she realized even more so why. "Kiss me, Kvale."

Rayne kissed Jess and was about to scoop her up in her arms, but she had to stop before she got her off the ground. "I think you best leave the sword here until tomorrow, or we won't be going anywhere fast."

Jess walked to the side of Cass's grave, placed the sword where she found it, and tossed several shovels full of dirt on top, just in case. Not likely anyone would be coming by, but Jess felt better that way. "Done," she said.

Without hesitation, Rayne scooped Jess up into her arms and carried her toward the house, George at their heels. "Do you believe me now when I said it seems like everything connected with you is somehow driven by fate?"

"Quite possibly I do." Jess sensed Rayne's joy as it intertwined with her own. She wrapped her arms around Rayne's neck and rested her head on her shoulder, unable to form words for the contentment spreading through her. She was eager to move forward with their life together and to begin writing about Cassethea's past.

In the night sky, The White Bear and The Eagle once again shone bright.

About the Author

Regina was born in Germany and obtained her U.S. citizenship at the age of nineteen. She grew up in New Jersey and currently lives in the mountainous suburbs of Northern New Jersey with her partner of twenty + years. Regina earned her Bachelors' degrees majoring in accounting and biology, with a minor in German. She's also a Certified Public Accountant and works for the Federal Government protecting the taxpayer's interests. She loves the outdoors and enjoys hiking, kayaking, reading, watching football, and trying out new vegetarian recipes.

Email: regina.hanel@verizon.net
Web site: www.rhanel.com

Books By Regina A. Hanel

Love Another Day

Plagued by nightmares and sleepless nights after a tragic loss, Park Ranger Samantha Takoda Tyler longs for a calm day at Grand Teton National Park in Wyoming. But when she's summoned to the chief ranger's office and introduced to Halie Walker, a photojournalist working for The Wild International, her day is anything but calm. When she's assigned to look after Halie, their meeting transforms into a quarrelsome exchange. Over time, the initial chill between the women warms. They grow closer as they spend time together and gain appreciation for each other's work.

But Sam's fear of loss coupled with rising jealousy over an old lover's interest in Halie grinds their budding relationship to a halt. Halie finds that anywhere near Sam is too painful a place to be, and Sam is unable to find the key to open the door to a past that she's purposely kept locked away.

With fires raging out West and in the Targhee National Forest, Sam works overtime, helping fill the staffing shortage. She misses Halie and wants to take a chance with her. Before she gets the opportunity to explain herself, Sam learns the helicopter Halie is on has crashed. Ahead of an oncoming storm, Sam races to the rescue. Can she save the woman she loves? Or will the past replay, closing Sam off from love forever?

Available on:

Amazon, Nook, Kobo, and Bella Books

White Dragon

The story of Halie Walker and Samantha Takoda Tyler continues a year after they first met in *Love Another Day*. Halie's efforts to reestablish a career while still recovering from previous injuries consume her time and focus, leaving Sam far from the center of her attention and their relationship under emotional strain. Adding to their troubles, someone unknown begins a campaign of attacks. Sam's horse Coco winds up missing, their home is vandalized, and worse. As anxiety builds, Halie's childhood friend, Ronni Summers, provides welcome support, but no one can figure out who is involved in the attacks.

Ronni's brief encounter with Cali Brooks taunts her dreams, but finding her potential soul mate again proves most difficult. As Thanksgiving approaches, a series of events bring Cali into Sam and Halie's life, and almost into Ronni's. New and old friends join together on Thanksgiving Day, but snowfall cuts the gathering short. What follows brings not only the White Dragon, but also revelation, love, and death; the question is: which is brought to whom?

Available on:

Amazon, Nook, Kobo, and Bella Books

A Deeper Blue

Sadness has a tendency to run deep, especially for Alexandra Jean Rey who spent most of her living years dealing with survivorship guilt. Raised by her grandmother, Alex allowed few people into her life. She lived one day to the next and often too close to the edge for comfort. But she was smart and strong, and found ways to manage each day as it came.

Her decision to leave her career as an animal behaviorist at Florida's H&M Aquarium, followed by the loss of her best friend Andre the same year, tested Alex's resilience. Andre's will left Alex with control of half of Island Water Adventures, a lifeline during a difficult time and the possibility of a new start. Yet life never comes in a neat package.

Alex learns she and Andre's partner Sean may lose Island Water Adventures in a will contest. She also discovers that the sound of one woman's laughter will set into motion a series of events that would impact her heart and life forever. Kailyn Montgomery is that woman.

Will Kailyn lead Alex to find a deeper blue, or will the past weigh too heavily on both their futures?

Available on:

Amazon, Nook, Kobo, and Bella Books

Bringing LGBTQAI+ Stories to Life

Visit us at our website: www.flashpointpublications.com